Get Home Free

By John Clellon Holmes

Go

The Horn

Nothing More to Declare

Get Home Free

John Clellon Holmes

THUNDER'S
MOUTH
PRESS
NEW YORK

Copyright 1964, 1988, by John Clellon Holmes
All rights reserved
Published in the United States by
THUNDER'S MOUTH PRESS,
93-99 Greene Street, New York, N.Y. 10012
Cover design by Juanita Gordon
Grateful acknowledgement is made to the
New York State Council on the Arts and
the National Endowment for the Arts
for financial assistance
with the publication of this work.

Library of Congress Cataloging-in-Publication Data
Holmes, John Clellon, 1926-
    Get home free : a novel / by John Clellon Holmes
        p.   cm.
    ISBN 0-938410-52-0 : $19.95.   ISBN 0-938410-53-9 (pbk.) : $8.95
    I. Title.
    PS3558.03594G4 1988
    813' .54—dc19   87-25367
                                                                 CIP

Manufactured in the United States of America
Distributed by Consortium Book Sales & Distribution, Inc.
213 E. 4th Street
St. Paul, Minnesota 55101
612-221-9035

**Dedicated
to December 15, 1960**

PREFACE

Some books are written out of the same mix of fear and bravado with which you leap from a burning building. *Get Home Free* was such a book—a novel that did not begin as a novel at all, but as two stand-alone novellas, only later to be tied together by the narrative account of a gone-bad love affair. Though the two major protagonists, Daniel Verger and May Delano, had been minor characters in my roman à clef, *GO* (1952), the new book was wholly a work of the imagination, its origins in two enigmatic images that had come to me out of nowhere, and remained on the edge of my attention—the first, of a reprobate old drunkard, sitting on a platform rocker on a Connecticut river-bluff, staring back into a lost past; and the second, of a black youth crooning blind blues out of the perpetual present of a Louisiana dawn. The body of the book involved nothing more than my search to discover how these two images related to each other, and why they had such a powerful hold over what was just then a badly shaken sense of self-confidence.

The first words were written one morning in early January of 1960 after the worst, and the longest, period of creative sterility that I had ever known. For eighteen months I had been writing every day, and for eighteen months I had been throwing that day's words away. There, in our drafty old house, in a small New England town, all but dead broke as the Eisenhower years drew to a close with a final yawn, I was as near to giving up being a writer as I had ever been. "I awoke this morning, thinking of Old Man Molineaux," I put down in a spiral notebook one morning, having no idea what was to come next, but following that sentence with another, and another, and nine months later finding I had completed two-thirds of a book—the "Old Man Molineaux" and "Hobbes and Little Orkie" sections, only to hit another, less formidable snag, and take over a year to finish the three New York interludes.

By late 1962 the manuscript was delivered to my agent, and it was finally published by E. P. Dutton in the spring of 1964. It received notices so mixed as to suggest that two different books were being discussed, sold poorly both here and in England, and has been out of print now for over twenty years. Despite this, some of my colleagues and some of my critics have persisted in considering it my best novel, and I'm inclined to agree with them, though my reasons are of the untrustworthy sort that makes a parent favor his most troubled child.

The ambivalence of mood out of which I wrote was evident from the start. The two novellas were to be in the first person, a point of view I had avoided in my work up until then because it made objectivity about the speaker's character so difficult. On top of that, though the first person voice in "Molineaux" was male, the voice in "Little Orkie" was to be female—a technical bear-trap into which the pride of far more accomplished writers than myself had led them to their comeuppance over the years. Beyond these hurdles, I would be operating on turf that was new to me, dealing, in Molineaux, with a sixty-year-old, alcoholic ex–river pilot in New England, and, in "Orkie," with a whole spectrum of characters, black and white, in a small city in the Deep South. I had nothing to go on but the mysterious and magnetic pull of my two source-images, an ability to extrapolate the pith of a life from a few vivifying details, and a state of mind both humbled and sympathetic.

The book that resulted is a dark, autumnal comedy, a good-bye book, a book about one of those periods of transition when what is ending and what is beginning are just about in equilibrium, one to the other. The post–World War Two era of my first two novels, GO and The Horn, is over, but the Vietnam War era of my nonfiction had yet to really begin. It is an ambiguous time—of affluence and lethargy, prosperity and conformity, false gaiety and deep unease. At the end of one life in New York, my characters try to go home again, Verger to the North, May to the South, hoping to stake out new ground in themselves on which to make new starts, and though the book ends with the suggestion that they have succeeded, there is no clear indication of what lies ahead for them.

Meanwhile there were the private pleasures that redeem the toil of novel-writing, if you have the luck—the pleasure of a prose style gradually simplifying in the sentence, hardening in imagery, and growing more exact as meanings surface through the words; the pleasure of "bits of business" summoning themselves up when needed; the pleasure of knowing that because one can write what one means in clear and precise language, one has a chance of discovering just what it is one is trying to say. All this can get a writer through the months of anxious mornings that accumulate into a novel.

In some ways, the book was ahead of its time, which may account for some of the confusion with which it was greeted. Old Will Molineaux's beery monologues, made up of equal parts of the workingman's mythification of the preautomated past and the countryman's Arcadiazation of the natural world, prefigure not a little the postindustrial, ecological thinking of the later 1960s. Though his rhetoric was meant to be comic, I made no effort to keep the Learish overtones out of it. Certainly the group of outcasts and renegades in the old Prenderman house in "Little Orkie" proceeded by some years the back-to-the-land urge that overcame so many of the young, who, a few years later, would take as gospel Timothy Leary's slogan, "Turn on, tune in, drop out." Even some of the schisms that would muddy the waters of the Civil Rights Movement by the end of the decade, like Black Power, mutter into life in the person of William Jesus Glover—aka Amil Ibn Sachib. Though places like Johnstone's Food House by the New Haven tracks and Fat's Wife's Place at the Rapides crossroads may no longer exist, in *Get Home Free* they still stand—the last eccentric outposts of the state of mind that is the real subject of the book.

Writing only to satisfy myself, I was justifying myself as well, though I didn't realize it at the time—justifying my feeling that the frontier spirit, the spirit of the Wild, which was the source of so much of what I loved most about America, was in its waning days at last, and that the polarization of America into its "better" and its "meaner" angels had proceeded on apace, and the country had become a haunted land—haunted North and South by a racial schizophrenia that exiled people like Old Man Molineaux and Paul Hobbes to the shadows of the black world of Ben and Little Orkie, as if seeking the ghost of that fraternity that has been America's continually postponed destiny all along. It was a land in which the idealisms, without which the heart of youth perishes, had been so degraded that Verger's tipsy keenings about America ("Don't nobody realize? *America* is Moby Dick—") echoed like so many burlesque funeral orations, and Orkie's survivor's blues seemed to mourn some lost innocence of the spirit, an innocence that could only be renewed in the flesh. Certainly for some of the most desperate people here sexual fulfillment has become something of a final sacrament, out of which a new faith might come—a conviction no more foolish than many others current at the time.

I found no villains in this autumnal America. The younger Molineaux aren't any happier or any less pathetic in their TV living rooms than the "Turtle" Cheneys and the Church Plouchets in their parishwide escapades. Love—unsatisfied, unrequited, unexpressed—hangs like leaf smoke in the air, and the book ends in a barroom where the illusory promise of sad bossa nova guitars muffles for a little while the roar of the wintry street outside.

This is a singularly romantic ending for a book whose dominant note is ironic, I suppose, and yet having reached that reconciliation with reality that comes to May as she feels the ants squiggle between her toes, that understanding that "need not be bitter simply because it is bleak," it seemed only fair to give my two young existentialists the chance to make one more brave vow in the possibility of human touch to redeem the kind of lives we lead, despite the philosophic odds against it. I wanted to think they had a chance for a provisional happiness, a temporary reprieve, knowing for a certainty they would have made one last try for it.

—John Clellon Holmes
October 1987
Old Saybrook, Connecticut

CONTENTS

"As the wild duck is more swift and beautiful than the tame, so is the wild—the mallard—thought, which 'mid falling dews wings its way above the fens."

H. D. *Thoreau*

"What is the knocking?
What is the knocking at the door in the night?
It is somebody wants to do us harm.

"No, no, it is the three strange angels.
Admit them, admit them."

D. H. *Lawrence*

NEW YORK: THE END

A dozen years ago, before the Fifties were as fat and foolish as they would eventually become, and people still believed the new decade was going to be a continuation of the wild postwar years, there was an autumn of bad parties in New York, most of which May and Verger attended. He was working for a public-opinion survey, and she was one girl in the two-girl office of a small-time talent-booker, and they were living together in Agatson's old loft in the West 20's, where May had remained after Agatson was accidentally killed under a subway train. She had gotten ownership because she was Agatson's last girl, even though the place was coveted by some people who were really hard up for a rental, and others who thought that a little of Agatson's destructive magic might linger in the unswept corners, along with the broken bottles, smashed 78's of Verdi, and old socks that were all that remained of his wild parties and his short life.

The same people came to the bad parties that had come to the good ones a year before, only the poets, who had argued about Pound with boozy combativeness then, were now conniving for instructorships in Midwestern universities, and last year's careless copy boys were this year's solemn rewrite men, and people

9

were having relationships instead of affairs. All the same girls came, their hemlines taken up, their necklines let down, just married or just divorced, their eyes a little more diamond-bright, their mouths a little less rose-tipped. The same people came, only more of them came in cabs, and wore ties, and had serious jobs, and drank seriously as a consequence. People brought total strangers, and the strangers phoned other strangers. There was less impulsive beer, and more calculated whiskey. The jazz was not played so loud, but everyone seemed to notice it more. It was a little harder for them to have fun, and when they did it tended to be ugly fun. People were surer of themselves, and less certain of everything else. There seemed to be more queers, and more brawls, and more talk. Two years before, they had been part of a postwar generation, veterans, a vanguard of something that never had a chance to materialize because Korea came along, making them obsolete; and Verger got in the habit of quoting bitter poetry to May as they brushed their teeth at four or five in the morning.

"You know how I explain it? . . . 'The pure products of America go crazy.' That's how," swishing water in his mouth and spitting it out. " 'The imagination strains after deer going by fields of goldenrod in the stifling heat of September. . . . Somehow it seems to destroy us,'" capping the toothpaste fatalistically. "Old William Carlos. *Years* ago. Don't think he didn't know why it happens. The end of a season like this. Everyone putting everyone else down, getting drunk and mean. Everyone going *home* that way. I tell you, New York's gotten pompous and phony. America's *old* all of a sudden," pausing to stare irritably at his tousled image in the glass as she lit a last cigarette. "Well, anyway, it's *true*," turning on her in his shorts to find her waiting impatiently for an Alka-Seltzer to dissolve. "But look at that. Even our stomachs've gone bad. Nerves, anxiety, what to wear tomorrow. Nobody's excited any more, nobody's disturbed. . . . And last year we were thinking about deer." He scowled with that tipsy gloom that is sometimes more comforting than sobriety.

"Here," she said wearily. "Will *you* get the light?"

"Used to be able to stay up all night, smoke packs and packs, drink anything in sight, talk for days," he muttered, choking off the glass in a gulp. "Ick! I should have had me a drink instead. . . . One more gaudy nightcap." He chuckled. "Well, damn it, I'm just gonna stay up anyway. You tell me why I should go to bed when—"

"Look, it's four in the morning, Danny. Do we *have* to argue? Couldn't we skip it till tomorrow?"

He pouted, curling his toes on the cold tile of the bathroom, waiting for the first soft, relieving belch. "How can we argue? You Southern belles never hear what a man *says* any more. Tennessee Williams's right about *that* much, you know."

"Well, who wants to listen to a lot of crappy poetry at four-thirty in the morning, for Christ's sake? And why do you always want to fight whenever you get drunk these days?"

"Must be someone left in America who wants to hear crappy poetry," he murmured just loud enough for her to hear. "But that's the point. There isn't *anyone* who wants to hear *anything*. Even all the girls you meet—"

"Now, of course, *that's* what you really mean," she shot back as she turned a warm hip away from him there in the bed. "Why don't you at least say what you mean?"

"I do. I say exactly what I mean. I ought to get the hell out of New York is what I'm saying," he repeated for the fourth time that week. "I ought to go back to Grafton, or just take off for Europe. . . . New York's not America, for Christ's sake."

"And what are you going to use for money, Mister Expatriate?"

"I'll get you to send home for a trunkful of Confederate. And besides, where the hell can you *go* these days? They hate Americans in Europe now."

"So what does *that* matter!" she exploded. "What do you care if they like you or not? . . . I swear that's the only thing that makes me ashamed of my own country—that we all understand it so little, and the secret's lost on us, and in growing up we came *down* so much. . . . The pure products of America *are* crazy, you fool! And Europe's just a self-conscious museum by comparison. Believe me."

"All right, so you've been and I haven't," he grouched out. "That doesn't prove anything."

"Well, why don't you stop complaining about America all the time? Really, it's so corny and—and, well, like some 'Greenwich Village Idiot.'"

His lips tightened. "Look, just save me any more pithy Streik-isms, will you!" Incensed that she should dare to quote Streik back at him. "Because he's exactly what I mean about America this year. He's just like my father used to be—charming, cynical, empty, absolutely absorbed in his own repulsive ego, and—"

"Oh, honestly, *why* do you always have to get so solemn and testy that way? He's just a guy, and he's fun, for God's sake! He's fun to be with. . . . Besides, maybe *you* should be a little more like your father, from what you tell me. I bet I'd have been intrigued with him."

"I guess *you* would. But don't kid yourself. He never loved my mother."

"But I'll bet she loved *him*. I'll just bet she *still* does."

The application of this to their relationship was not lost on Verger, despite his liquor, and all of a sudden he erupted: "Listen, just shut up to me about Tertius Streik, you hear? Do whatever you want to do, but don't try to justify it to me!" His mouth twisted into an ugly sneer. "Tertius Streik, indeed! I'll bet his name's really Horace or Wilbur."

"What do you mean by that? 'Do what you want to do.'"

"Oh, come on, *baby*. You think I don't know what you're up to? What do you think I am, a goddamn fool? . . . You want to sleep with him? All right, all right! But don't *lie* about it. I don't give a damn what you do, I have no strings on you, but I won't stand still for your ingrained Southern deceit!"

"I'm not lying. . . . Yes, I've seen him. Yes, I've bumped into him, but nothing's happened, and—"

"You actually expect me to believe that, don't you? You think I'll believe it because you think I can't afford *not* to," he snarled at her, though he knew she was telling the truth. "Well, listen, *babe*—listen, *buddy*"—both favorite expressions of Streik's. "I don't *have* to believe anything!"

"But you do. You have to believe I'm sleeping with him. Why? Why is that?"

"Horseshit. . . . And besides, do you actually think he'll satisfy you? Listen, he drinks too much, *baby*. All of you drink too much, and—"

"Stop it, Danny."

"—and he won't satisfy you. . . . You're frigid. *Admit* it. Go on, admit it. You can't love *anyone*. At least face it, for God's sake! You're a goddamn icebox."

The rage that brightened her eyes dimmed immediately with the tears it produced. "Don't you *dare* say that to me!"

"It's the truth. And if you think it's easy to live with you, you're—"

"Oh, you're really a *rotten* bastard, aren't you!" she cried out, sweeping the half-full glass off the bedside table. "Listen, *I'm* the one who has to live with it, so don't you dare say that to me ever again! I'm warning you!"

He sighed hopelessly, somewhat sorry he had said it, but suddenly wanting to miss the bad times ahead, and certain now that they would have to kill it before it would die. "Oh, all right, I didn't mean that. . . . Oh, come on, sweetheart, stop crying now. Didn't you hear me? I didn't mean it."

"I know. . . . It's just that I thought at least *you* would love me—"

"But I *do*. I do love you."

"I know, but—"

"And what in hell do you mean, at least *me*? Is that the way you think of me? Well, listen here, *buddy*—" And on and on, for lately they had reached that impasse in the emotions beyond which lies only the necessity to assign the blame, and Verger was trying to decide whether to go to Europe or not, and May had begun staying out later when walking Jefferson the dachshund, and getting raucous at parties, and seeing Streik on the sly. It was a period when Verger was telling himself that he put up with it because he needed a place to stay, and May was saying to almost anyone, "Oh, you know. It's when you become sort of buddies. Roommates. Just before you don't give a damn any more"; that time when each was trying to think of a way to tell the other that it was over between them, and both were preoccupied with the illusion (so necessary to the end of love) that it was the other who would be most hurt.

At four-thirty that afternoon, Verger was standing by the bed in wrinkled shorts and baggy skivvy shirt, studying May's sleeping face, turned into the wizened light, untroubled by dreams behind the eyes, unscarred by the emotions of the morning, maddeningly calm and very pretty. He had just come back from the bathroom where the reflection of his own ashen face, stricken in the talons of hangover, had seemed to him like someone else's face, a face he didn't like, the face of a haunted Laertes. He had slept wrong, and his cowlick stood up in back like a top knot; his lean cheeks were stubbled, faintly cadaverous, and the very idea of shaving made him groan; his grave grey eyes, wincing in the stark light of the unshaded bulb, were comically ringed with red; and he doused cold water over his face, as if he hoped it would wash away the ruins that he saw.

He got down another Alka-Seltzer, knowing it wouldn't help, gargled the sour lees of the night-before out of his mouth, and wandered back into the drafty rooms, suddenly disgusted by the dim, cheerless loft, by the heavy burlap curtains (left over from Agatson's tenure), the overflowing ceramic ashtrays where the hours and the nerves and the rebukes could all be tabulated simply by counting the butts, the unwashed plates with the remains of hasty and indifferent meals hardened on them, the half-empty bottle of Scotch, the whole glass and the broken one, the dusty phonograph records, the disorderly stacks of books, the heaps of clothes (his and hers) thrown down carelessly last night, and the night before, and the night before that. The whole place seemed cannily contrived by an avant-garde set designer to evoke, with nothing but inanimate objects, the hopelessness and waste of the past weeks. He wanted to yank down the drapes in a cloud of months-old dust, sweep all the litter into a dark corner, throw open the windows to that warehouse street of trucks and shipping offices, and let in the blank light of that overcast late-October afternoon to stun May's eyes awake.

But instead he stared down at her face, framed by a taffy-colored profusion of heavy locks on the pillowslip, last night's make-up half-worn away, lipstick cracked on the sensual mouth that pouted even when she slept, traces of mascara giving the crescents of her eyelids the emphatic, somber garishness of a sorrowing Spanish madonna, her nostrils flaring faintly with her regular breathing, the brown flesh of her wide shoulders smoother and darker than the sheet that had been pulled away from them when he got up.

He inspected her face, thinking with amazed rage: "Look at you. Sleeping! Just as sound asleep as if you'd been to a barbecue. . . . Is that all it means to you? Eh?" incensed, as always, by his inability to get their arguments into a perspective that would produce, in him, the indifference he fancied her to feel. "Well, go ahead, you bitch, sleep it off. . . . But *I* can't. I *won't*. . . . Not for any goddamn Southern whore—" breaking off at that idiotic word, exasperated by the moody reflex of puritanism that characterized his secret mind, and yet thinking crossly: "Well, what the hell else can you call it? Lying to me for weeks about Streik, lying to me for months about love. . . . But I'm through this time, one morning I'll look down, and I just won't give a good goddamn any longer," looking at her with a frown, already bored by the monologue, "And what does it *really* mean to me? Secretly, all words aside? . . . Nothing, not a single goddamn thing," taking bitter pleasure from that thought, for to abuse his spirit gave him the same feeling of contemporaneousness that abusing his body did—liquor and cynicism providing the illusion of hardheaded reality that people whose instincts are conventional, though their ideas are not, seem to need; thinking also, "Well, anyway I didn't tell her about the money—the letter's still in my coat, the check's safely deposited, I've got my escape-hatch—and no matter how much I wanted to get back at her, I wasn't fool enough to tell her about that," experiencing a private satisfaction in the deceit by which he had kept the letter a secret from May for a week, the letter which said in part: ". . . and so your Aunt Abby (you never knew her, she died in 1928, perhaps you remember Dad's stories—yes, she was *the* Abaca Verger, poor woman—though I never believed half of what they whispered later, she was always very thoughtful to me)—anyway, she left this bequest to you for when you turned 26—$1800 which, of course, was *more* then—and the particular age always puzzled me too, usually it's 21—but I have a notice today from the lawyers, informing me that it's out of the courts at last, and enclosing the enclosed check. . . ."

He frowned down at May, seeing no reason why he shouldn't just uncover her, pour a glass of water on her, tickle the soles of her feet with a mean snicker, put on loud records, slam doors—anything that would wake her, confused and unprepared, so that he could continue the argument, or start a new one, for he was clearer-headed (hung over or not) than she, even on the best of her mornings. He pulled the sheet away from her breasts on a whim, feeling a faint, aimless sexual urge, an urge that was more of an idea than an emotion, wanting to have things with her they had never had (knowing that was only the hangover, too), and at the same time wanting nothing with her ever again, for these days even the simplest, most mechanical embrace only served to remind him of the failure of intimacy between them.

He sat down on the bed, disconsolately covering her up again, unable to maintain the edge of his anger against the gas in his stomach and the throb in his head. His mouth tasted of the dead ends of too many cigarettes and too much emotion, and he automatically lit his first Chesterfield of the day, knowing it would sicken him, but stoical. He began coughing after the first acrid drag, and suddenly heard her voice of months ago, saying with a careless laugh:

"You smoke too much," snatching the cigarette away from him with a gay pout, to leave it moist and red on the end. "Just listen to that ghastly cough! . . . Daniel Verger, you sound positively tubercular—you sound Keatsian, you poor honey!" remembering the exact moment at the top of these very stairs, up which he had just struggled her suitcases and dress bags, because Agatson was too deep in his binge of that week to move her in with him, and so Verger had volunteered.

Sweating profusely in his Saturday corduroys, and unable to disguise how this had stung him (because by then she had become one more thing for which he envied Agatson), he blurted out: "Well, I—I am, I mean I was. But it isn't the cigarettes, damn it. I had a spot on my lung a year or so ago. . . ."

She had looked at him as if seeing his sandy hair, slightly stooped shoulders, and gravely spectacled face for the first time, her sparkling eyes suddenly quenched with an absolutely sincere solicitude. "Good Lord! Well, don't listen to me, honey. Promise you won't ever listen to what I say. I just talk and talk all the time because I can't stand silence. You promise me now, and forgive me for being an awful squelch, and lend me a dollar for the cab," and she rushed off to search for Agatson, in a plaid raincoat, and a tam, and too much lipstick, after giving him a fond little nibble on the cheek.

He leaned on his elbows, the smoke of the cigarette drifting up to water his eyes, remembering how pert and gushing and unreachable she had seemed to him in those days—hugging herself involuntarily to see Agatson walking on his hands and yelling obscenities at some party, violet eyes lit with a new emotion; giggling when Agatson touched her in some impersonal, outrageous way; alive to Agatson's dark and violent power, as everyone had been—the power of a man who cares about nothing, and so possesses the strength of disbelief in a cowardly time.

"Silence!" he thought crossly, looking down at her again. "You couldn't stay in *Paradise* for more than twelve hours without a radio." But just then she swallowed in her sleep, and the hint of a private, dreamy smile appeared fleetingly in one corner of her mouth, and he looked away to continue his pitiless train of thought, knowing well enough that she snapped on the radio the first thing on waking (in a gesture of one hand as automatic as the reach for the first cigarette with the other) because she had to obliterate the silence of time, which is so disturbing to the young and restless. He realized that he would probably always associate her with the steady buzz of trivial music and shallow voices drowning out the silences of contemporary history in her days. But he didn't want to think about it. It had taken him two weeks of living with her to realize that she never really listened to the radio, and he heard his own querulous voice as clearly as if a snatch of tape was being played back to him:

"Good God, sweetheart, how can you listen to that junk all the time? For Pete's sake, find something decent, can't you?"

"What? What do you mean? . . . Oh. Well, your trouble is that you can't concentrate. I was just wondering if I should wear this ridiculous old thing tonight. Do you think it's too whorish for all those fags? 'Cause I hate *not* being pawed almost as much as I hate the other," frowning over the dress, a cigarette drooping from her full lips, wearing nothing but his day-old shirt in which her breasts shivered, and looking like a pudgy little girl who is unaware of her failure to appear naughty.

"You're hopeless. Sometimes you're so Southern you're a parody."

"But what do you think? . . . You're not *helping* me here, honey, you're absolutely no help at all. . . . Because I can just as easily wear the lavender cotton," the lavender cotton that now hung off the back of the armchair a foot away, disembodied, badly wrinkled, near the top of the pile; and which he suddenly remembered she had been wearing two nights before when he had discovered her in the bar with Streik.

At that thought, he got up and went for a glass of water, having to use the last of Agatson's Harvard glasses because it was the only clean one left, and suddenly furious with himself for all the past weeks, for putting up with her infatuation with Streik, for ever having agreed to live with her in Agatson's loft—absolutely sure it all would have worked out differently had he insisted that they move into his cramped and ugly flat uptown. But he had never been able to imagine her there, and always thought of her in these bleak, untidy rooms, in which he had watched her new emotion gradually harden and erode and crack as her brief six weeks, amid the bottles and noise of Agatson's last days, clicked off toward his death.

The dirty corners were still thronged with squabbling, raucous ghosts (all the visiting hipsters, and fatalistic junkies, and mincing poets who had gathered around Agatson toward the end, like beady-eyed carrion circling a mortally wounded animal). The wild music, the drunken recitations, the bawled songs had left persistent echoes; and dented bottle caps, shards of opera records, and rubbery pieces of old orange peel from those days were still to be come upon in the depths of closets, or under the sagging couch. And among the voices that his hangover hallucinated there in the silence, as he looked around, was his own, endeavoring to reach May over the uproar of Agatson cavorting with a two-hundred-pound Negro girl, who had just taken off her blouse.

"You—you don't look so bad. . . . I mean, if you say he's been drinking for a *week* this time," though, of course, she looked awful, as if something had unaccountably loosened in her, as if she had been tagged around the eyes. She smoked with the deep, unconscious drags of someone no longer counting how many cigarettes he has had that day; one stocking was laddered, her lipstick had come off on the rims of innumerable glasses, the safety pin that secured the broken strap of her bra bulged through her dress, and she was muttering fiercely: "I'd throw her out, if it was me, if she was anyone else. But, no! Jesus, then I'd get it. But I can be more charming than he can. You watch me. You just watch me charm the pants off her. . . . Anyway, that's *one* thing they teach us down there," adding, when Verger failed to suppress a wry smile, "Well, Mister Funny, no one *asks* you all to just drop in, you know. And don't think I don't know why you hang around all the time. . . . God."

"All right," he replied angrily, starting to get up. "And what do you mean? I suppose you think I'm hung up on you, or something ridiculous like that?"

"Oh—*hell*, I didn't really mean you, honey. You know that. . . . Do I really look so terrible though?" one hand vaguely shaping the back of her hair.

It all came back to him: those hateful days of late summer rain drenching the misty blocks around the loft, when he dropped by on some pretext, unable to give his concern for her its proper name, or met her by accident on 8th Street; that time when she lost jobs, and got others, and hurried home, never knowing what she would find—a party, the d.t.'s, or an empty bed; those days building toward a disaster, during which he tried to give her money over stale coffee in empty cafeterias, saying: "Go on. Take it. What's the sense of starving? . . . And—well, you know how I feel about Agatson."

"Yes, damn you. I know how *all* of you feel about him. None of you know him at all."

"Well, listen," he remembered replying, piqued by the unreasonableness of this (for he had known Agatson for years), "*you* feel just like all his *girls,* too. You've got the idea you can save him."

But he didn't want to think about Agatson, and he didn't want to sit there and listen to May's even breathing either. It only reminded him that he could never sleep off the bad nights, the drinks, and the disputes; he was always beached in his dour thoughts and his throbbing head, and her very invulnerability, her stubborn gift for mending, infuriated him. He got up, and took two aspirins, and sprawled out on the couch, wondering why in hell he didn't just have a drink and be done with it. The sour last light of the day bathed the room in a bilious, undersea gloom. The muffled bangings and creakings of Saturday offices emptying two floors below reminded him that the building would be shut up for the weekend in half an hour, but for them; and suddenly he longed for the winter fences of New England, the dark twilight-woods on the edge of rocky fields, the crackle and hiss of sappy logs, a cold moon, the bare branches of old elms, the hand-sewn comforters of youth—everything he always associated with his mother, living alone in eastern Connecticut these past ten years exactly like the immemorial maiden ladies of the region, despite the grown son in New York and the husband with the new life in Washington. At the thought of whom, Verger thought: No. Better still, Europe. The asymmetry of quiet streets behind a cathedral, of fortified hill towns evoking simpler wars, of a palpable past. To rest. To be absorbed. To get happily lost in the useless beauties of any century but *this* one. For all of a sudden, his current life struck him as more beside-the-point than the most frivolous of Fragonards, and he was fed up with the rabbit warrens of New York, the harsh lights that never went off, the smoky rooms, the tired eyes, tireless voices, and insoluble problems. He'd had it; you had to be uncaring, unscrupulous, invulnerable to survive in it, and—

Invulnerable? All at once, the memory came back anyway, for the mind staggered by alcohol has no defenses, and she was huddled on this very couch in that strange, ingathered position, legs folded under, shoulders hunched in, her face pale and stricken and lipstickless where she had chewed her lower lip—that warm rainy night after Agatson's absurd death, when Verger, who had been his friend, climbed the murky stairwell to comfort May, who had been his girl—

"They're saying in the Village—they're saying you claim you were *married* to him. Four separate people told me that just this evening."

The electricity had been shut off a week before, and a warty stub of candle, wedged in a beer bottle and sitting on a pile of soggy magazines, made an island of light in which her hurt eyes flared suddenly. "I *was.* . . . Oh, I know what they're saying. But I was," the last traces of her Southern accent, blurred by several years in New York, giving her voice a stubborn whine.

"When?" he asked as tactfully as possible. "Because he didn't say anything to—"

"Last week."

He prolonged the lighting of two cigarettes, avoiding her petulant gaze. "Well, I *was*, Danny. We *were* married," she insisted pettishly, and then her chin quivered, and she began to sob all at once in soft, choking, helpless little gasps. "And, Christ, what do I care about *ceremonies* anyway, why should I have to produce some stupid *paper* like that?" tears running into the corners of her mouth. "We were married in—in *God's* eyes anyway! It's the same thing," letting herself *go* completely, as people do when they finally allow themselves to say all those old mawkish words they don't believe in for a minute, but which seem to express certain emotions for which they have not been prepared. Verger was slightly embarrassed. "And it isn't fair," she sobbed. "It just isn't *fair.* . . . Well, *is* it fair? . . . Because he was getting so much better. Really, we were having quiet nights, he was *talking*, and—" She sat there and blubbered openly, lips contorted around her sobs, and for the first time since he had come into the loft to find her, alone and already tipsy, he realized that her emotions were not quite real.

"Because I loved him, Danny. I really loved him, you know. I did. And if only everyone had stayed away, and not gotten him drunk all the time," echoing the classic aggrievement of all women who have ever tried to save a dedicated dissipate, and wiping at the fresh tears that brimmed her eyes at the thought. "And you don't know me, none of you really do, you don't know the way I am, you think I just feel things easily, simply, but— But why did it happen to me? I don't understand why it had to happen. . . . And, God, Danny, life *scares* me. . . . Because—well, I'd *counted* on it," the little-girl, dead-father terror in her large, moist eyes forever signaling to him the moment when their relationship changed, as it always does when one person bestows the secret of his weakness on another. She sniffled into her fist, feeling a little better, and then said: "It's just that everything always seems to work out the way I knew it would when I was thirteen. . . ." She shook her head, and there was nothing in her eyes suddenly, that nothing that is worse than the worst of somethings in our day. "Is there any more in the bottle, though? Because I ought to get drunk. I really ought to get drunk, I suppose."

He reached for her hand, which was hot and tear-wet and very small in his, and her emptied eyes looked at him, sad with trust.

"Look, I'll go down and get something," he said.

"All right," she answered, swallowing as she brushed her hair back from her streaked face. "I'll wait right here. Only hurry. 'Cause what would I have done if you hadn't come by? . . . And really—you're so sweet, honey. You always understood."

"Understood!" he thought caustically, for the word was hateful to him. "Did Agatson understand her? Does Streik? No, *I* do. *I'm* the one who understands. . . . And look at me." But if he had really understood, he would have brought her the bottle, and let her have another cry—the real one, the one that got to the bottom of her grief—and then gone away, and been done with it. He didn't want to remember how she had moved him; he didn't want to recall the stir of tenderness that had made him come by every night during the week that followed, or the fact that right now, even after last night, after Streik, after the hopelessness of love between them, he knew her too well to be indifferent to her life. There was no good in that, no help. "And what does it matter what we understand? My mother *understood* my father, and it was the most maddening thing about her. Christ, it infuriated *me* just as much as it did him. No," he went on windily. "We're all locked in our natures, and no under*standing*'s going to get us out. And no love either."

At which he belched involuntarily, crudely, taking vulgar pleasure in it, and then got up (he could never stay still for long when he was hung over), and went looking for his shoes. He sat on the bed again, careful not to vibrate the springs too much, because the prospect of having to cope with May when she awoke, of having to go on from the point they had reached when they gave it up, seemed an intolerable bore to him. "Love," he thought derisively. "Who cares about love? What can you do with it? . . . All I *really* loved was the way she undressed that first time. Everything else was probably just words," putting a foot into one of the shoes, and suddenly pausing to stare at it, remembering the sight of those particular shoes across the creaking floor, and the peculiar wan light of that first day, and the waiting; remembering his own foreknowledge, as he waited, that later he would remember it in every detail. Between the tying of one lace and the other, it came back to him in a flash, unmarred by the wiser hindsights that corrupt the past:

The stutter of a pneumatic drill, chalk-powdered men probing through the asphalt for one of the city's buried ganglia, old brickfronts stunned with noise in the waning sun, dust drifting through the bar of pale light that made a graphic oblong on the rugless floor, the brand-new shoes sitting side by side in that oblong, as if on display in a store window . . .

Precautioned, May returned matter-of-factly from the bathroom, her body a chiaroscuro in the street dust and cigarette smoke; the slopes of her breasts the color of milky coffee, the breasts themselves heavier, more drooping and wide-nippled than he had imagined them; the sheen of her curved shoulders glowing richly brown, the slight swell of her belly pale below the pinkish mark left by her panties' waistband; the dark soft place itself, at which he dared not look (as she sat up for one last drag on her cigarette) because of that something passive and banked in her averted eyes, which made her say: "I'm—I'm really too chubby these days. I mean, my thighs and everything. Do you mind, honey?" And then the palpable surprise of her smooth skin when she came down beside him with a tiny sigh, and gave her mouth up to that first hungry, open kiss that leads not up to the moment of assent, but beyond it to where the nakedness so intensifies the loneliness of the separate flesh that passion flares up its brief, unsettling denial.

The idiot chatter of the drill deprived them both of words, and Verger made love to her with a kind of harassed resolution (as if he wanted to get it over with) that gave his mouth, his hands, and the tensing of his flanks an urgency that was very close to the real thing. May helped a little, her eyes clenched tight as if to shut out a disturbing image, her lips moving in what he took to be little commands or urgings, and they hurried as if they were running fast, hand in hand, through danger. And then, shockingly, almost lewdly, the drill quit all at once, leaving a shameless silence in which their two gasping breaths, the suck and gurgle of wet flesh intertwined, the creaking of the old spring on which they labored together, her sharp, "Wait, wait"—all were as starkly audible as if they were overhearing some passionless coupling from another room. This pushed Verger over in a flash, and he sank down upon her with a down-flooding expiration of surprise and chagrin.

"Listen, I'm sorry. But that goddamn drill—"

"Shush," she said. "Don't be silly."

"Well, it kept distracting me."

"Give me a cigarette, will you, honey?" drawing a corner of the sheet over her loins like a napkin, and taking a deep renewing breath.

"But what about you?" he said, raising up on his elbow to reach the pack. "Are you all right? Because, you know, I've been scheming this for a week, and—"

"Of course I am, silly," she answered crisply. "But I'm famished, though. . . . Let's get up and have huge, gooey onion sandwiches, and then later—" And for a moment her eyes moved inquisitively over his body there in the dimness as she puffed. "You're much nicer without your clothes on, you know. Leaner. All white. You're more muscley, I mean."

He flushed, and on an impulse leaned over to touch one wide, still-stiffened nipple with his lips, feeling the mysterious life in it; and then, looking up, he saw there was an odd twitch in one corner of her mouth, her eyes were lidded as if from a wave of dizziness, and she was suddenly inert under his caresses. "Stop it now, honey," she scolded his hand. "No, really. You'll only get me all worked up again," pushing him away with fond sternness. "But I'm so glad we had it, Danny," vaguely mussing at his hair. "It's always so lovely afterward this way."

Her distracted little smile, the abrupt shift of her hips sliding a little farther under the sheet, her sudden attention to the cigarette that had gone out—something made him say: "Yes, but wait—did you come? You came, didn't you?"

"Oh, shut up, silly. Of course I did."

He sat up all at once, wanting a smoke himself, and she looked at him closely, strangely, as if stirred under her heart to see how absolutely complete and separate he was now that it was over. He frowned, and hesitated, and then said: "I—listen, it's foolish, but I think I love you," as if it was a difficult admission. "I think I did even when you were with Agatson."

"Do you, honey? I'm so glad. . . . And me too, I guess. . . . So," giving an odd little laugh, "I guess that's that, isn't it? . . . We'll have good times together, and help each other out."

"Anyway, I know you *didn't*," he said flatly, exhaling a long disappointed sigh. "You didn't come."

"Oh, stop it, Danny. Come here now."

"Well, *did* you or not? Because—"

"Oh, Christ, can't you leave it *alone!*" she flared back suddenly with a hopeless pout. "That goddamn idiotic question you men always ask! I hate it worst of all. I *hate* it! . . . Don't you realize how close I was? . . . I mean if you'd just leave it alone, if you'd wait—we could have tried again later. . . . But, no! . . . No, instead apologies, and sweet-nothings, and—and accusations! Just like you've put on your stupid glasses again. When I felt something really *tender*. . . . So that's how much *you* know."

"I know I'm sorry about it," he said wearily. "Don't you want me to at least be *sorry* about it? It isn't just casual to *me*."

"Well, don't you think *I'm* sorry too?" she yelled rashly. "But I don't want your concerns, and your apologies, and your—your goddamn owlish stares! I don't!" her face so abruptly purged of any expression that her next words seemed inevitable to him. "Oh, hell! Of course, I do. . . . I do, Danny. I really do. You believe me, don't you? I love you, and I *need* you, honey. . . ."

"Love and need," he thought, remembering that he had always felt unhappily superior to her because he had wanted to believe there was a difference between the two words. "Well, she was more honest than you were. At least admit it to *yourself*, you idiot, now that it doesn't matter any longer. At least learn something from this," pulling on his trousers with the impression that every dehydrated joint in his body was creaking so audibly that the sound might actually awaken May. And her words in the night when sleep wouldn't come, not three weeks ago, murmured softly in his brain—speculative words vying with the sound of traffic uptown that made the darkness poignant; the words of the separate nature, which can sometimes venture out so nakedly, so startlingly, in the warmth of a shared bed once the fever of the other nakedness falls:

"But why can't people *really* love people any more, honey? I never understood about that. Agatson, for instance—sometimes he used to whimper at night, cursing, begging, fast asleep. . . . And I mean the *old* way, the way we were all taught to expect."

"We none of us love our*selves*, so how can we love each other? We're all saying, 'I could love you, if you could only love me.' So we take opinion polls to find out what we feel. . . . I ought to know, shouldn't I? . . . And the world's colder as a result."

"But it seems to me it's *us* who are cold. . . . But maybe I didn't understand you. . . . But what's *wrong* with us, honey? What happened to everyone?"

"Good Lord, what can I say? It sounds so pompous. . . . But Hiroshima, Belsen, the foolishness at Torgau, all that—it reached here somehow, right here," suddenly irritated by his habit of abstraction, "But, Christ, how do *I* know! . . . Maybe it's that we know *what* we are—white, Protestant, middle class, oral neurotic— but not *who*. Do you see? . . . What we're looking for is not each other, but a glimpse of our own faces that will reassure us that we're not unlovable, after all. . . . So what chance does it have? Any more than a mirror facing a mirror could ever reflect either of the people holding them. . . . And everyone's so *tired*. I look at them, at everyone I know, and I wonder how they get through it."

"How do *you?*"

He stared at her, distracted by this. "Me? . . . I don't know. But that's different. . . . I mean, I wasn't talking about myself."

Her grave, violet eyes rested on his resolute mouth with melting warmth. "You know, sometimes you get a look on your face that makes me want to make you happy for the rest of your life. . . . Isn't that corny, isn't that silly?"

And because, by then, her failure had become his failure in his mind, he said half bitterly: "You think all I want is a substitute mother? God, I've had enough of *that* to last me a lifetime. So don't—"

"Oh, that's not what I meant. Really. . . . I meant I love you. I *do*."

"Well, I love you too."

At which she gave a short, unhappy laugh. "You're right. . . . What good is it?"

He looked for a shirt in the heap of her underwear on the chair, simply tossing her things onto the floor with a reckless disregard that pleased him because it was so unlike him. Her brassières, her white cotton pants, her single pair of lacy, frivolous $3.00 step-ins, her frilly garter belts and panty-girdles—how omnivorously he had concentrated on them once! What she had on under her clothes had been the giddiest of mysteries to him, and becoming a partner in the day-to-day intimacies of her life had assuaged that inmost feeling of estrangement which is at the bottom of our simpler urges toward one another. At least, for a while.

"Christ, what a humorless bastard you've always been!" he marveled, faintly enjoying the luxury of ridiculing himself now that he was different. "Why didn't you just take her, rape her, anything? Because this way, *no* one got anything out of it," amazed for a moment that she had taken up with him at all, and eventually even suggested that he move in with her when he had had to give up his summer sublet uptown.

"Well, you got used to them anyway," he murmured aloud, fingering the edge of scalloped froufrou on a garter belt. He got used to ducking under them, while shaving, as they dried on the improvised line over the sink; she no longer fled to the bathroom to prepare herself for love; he had a last cigarette while waiting, and put Jefferson into a closet, and what they shared of each other was shared against the background of muffled whimperings —until the mysteries of her female world, like all mysteries, evaporated into a collection of perfectly ordinary details.

Only the mystery of her failure—the flower that would not bud all the way, the rhythm that would not pitch high enough, the final profane thought she wouldn't think—remained lodged between them like a speck of soot in the eye of love. He looked over at her as she stirred in her sleep, to throw a bare, brown arm across her eyes, and thought of those lips pursed against his or turned away, the nails of that hand digging into his back as she gasped, "Not yet, honey, not yet!" which always seemed to freeze him for a moment (realizing they were on different levels of arousal) and then melted him too soon, so that the words he wanted to say, the words which involve the mind in the transactions of the body, all remained unsaid; his face above hers at the end, drowned against his will by an abrupt pleasure she struggled to experience; her eyes already anticipating his inability to prevent himself from asking how she had fared. He grew apprehensive and out of sorts over his desk during the smoky afternoons, and came home full of irritable resolve, and, holding back, labored mechanically until his heart thumped the taste of rust up into his mouth, and they were locked together in a desperate sweat of hopelessness, her teeth clenched on her own forefinger with her efforts. She lied to him, and he challenged her on the lies; his pleasure was sapped by the gloomy certainty that hers would never reach a culmination; and in the fights that followed, all the ugly, shaming words were said, so that he took to letting the lies pass unchallenged, and finally no longer even asked her, when it was done. She lay awake long afterward, listening to his even breathing, and sometimes touched him reproachfully, thinking he was asleep.

Finally, there was the rainy six-thirty when he let himself softly in the door, with a bottle of the Valpolicello she particularly favored, to hear the stark pant of indrawn breath, the quiver of the bedspring, and find her in the writhe and thrash of climax on the rumpled sheet, desperate mouth sucking on the pillow; nude, flung, diligent, all alone. . . . "But that way—I mean, that way I can *make* it. . . . How in the world do you think I get through it otherwise?" And he became as bitterly jealous as if he had discovered her in an infidelity, until tipsy and miserable they drew together, the night abruptly seeming too huge and inhospitable to be alone in, and later at least *shared* their separate pleasure. . . . But such sharings are a capitulation, an admission, a falling-short, and they were more alone after that, and stayed home less and less. . . . Nights, nights, and the parties that compressed them into a kaleidoscope of gaudy, harmless images. . . . Wild taxies, full of drunks, going somewhere no one would remember, to see somebody nobody knew, for a purpose never made clear, where a tableful of bottles waited, and there was loud music no one could hear, and hordes of people who were there for the same reasons.

Among them, eventually, Streik.

"Danny?" the spring creaking, an exhaled breath, the rustle of the sheet. "Oh, there you are," on which he turned to find her blinking herself awake, and raising up on one elbow. "Oooooh," she groaned, and lay back again.

"Hung over enough?" he said in a cruel, metallic tone.

"Yes," she mumbled, and then peeked at him uncertainly. "Is everything all right, though? How long have you been up?"

"An hour. . . . Oh, everything's just fine."

"Is there coffee?"

"I don't know. I don't want any," turning away, and going into the other room, unwilling to reassure her about anything; the sound of their ritual morning exchange infuriating him after the dead end of the night before, and the name stabbing through his aching head over and over again—Streik, Streik; the memory of those sardonic eyes mocking him as he kicked away a shard of the broken glass; the faintly curled upper lip (that gave Streik the look of a Tangier smuggler cashiered out of the Guards, or a titled racing driver pursuing his fatal smashup, or an orgy-master servicing people with money but no imagination) flashing before him so graphically that he slammed a cabinet door shut with a loud crash that made even him wince.

"Lord, are you *still* angry that way!" she said petulantly from the bedroom. "Well, at least hold off on any more corny New England inquisitions till I get some coffee down me. Do *that* much for me anyway."

She lay for a moment, waiting for her head and stomach to adjust themselves to the jangle of the radio and the taste of the cigarette. She needed coffee, silence, time, and wondered if she could get Verger to walk Jefferson, who came out from under the armchair at that moment and hopped up into the bed with her. "Little furry animals," she thought. "Much more comforting than big, hairless ones. . . . You don't carry anything awful over from the nights into the day, do you, Jeffy?" She snuggled the dog under her arm, cooing to him, "I'll take you out, darling. You just wait. . . . Were you a good boy?" knowing that Verger would refuse to do it with some remark like, "Let him use a corner for his mess—just like the rest of us," because he often tried to get back at her through the dog; and when she had rushed into the loft a month ago, to reach into her huge handbag and lift him out,

all shivers and black rolling eyes, exclaiming: "I couldn't resist . . .
only six dollars . . . and he peed all over my compact in the subway. I'm going to call him Jefferson, and get him a gold collar,"
all Verger had said was: "Jefferson *Davis?* Or *Thomas* Jefferson?"
exasperating her enough to snap back: "Oh, poof! Neither one.
. . . And don't you go and spoil it with all your anti-Southern bilge-
water either. . . . But look at him, honey! He's so tiny and darling,
I could fit him in my bra!"

"Has Jeffy been out?" she called to him willfully as she got up,
but there was no answer, and she knew he was pretending he
hadn't heard her. He was stretched on the couch, his nose in a
magazine, and she could tell from the puffiness around his eyes
and the set of his mouth how really bad he felt.

"Well, you could at least tell me whether he's been for his walk
or not, couldn't you?"

Verger looked up coldly, passing an unsteady hand over his
forehead. "No, he hasn't. He can use his box, can't he?"

She turned and went into the kitchen to make coffee, wanting
to provide no opening for further words until she was fully awake;
angry in advance when she thought of his coiled, ungiving mind
that always pounced on her when she was least prepared, remembering his droning voice, and covert peeks, when he said things
like: "But did you ever think that the Great Dissipates are really
the dedicated men of the modern age? They accept poverty, and
suffering, and humiliation in the name of an outlawed vision of
man's nature. I mean, excess is actually evidence of a *spiritual*
need. And you take Agatson, for instance. . . . You know what I
thought when I heard about it? I thought, 'World, receive your
victim—' "

"Nice fellow," she thought, drumming her fingers on the
countertop to hurry the coffee, "just scads of fun," starting to pour
a cup, only to spill on everything because the pot hadn't finished
dripping. "You'd think he'd at least make the stupid *coffee* when
he's the first one up," she seethed to herself, knowing that coffee
wasn't important to him, and that his hangovers were far worse

than hers. "But, no, he never thinks of me," remembering, for some reason, one bored ten o'clock, Verger's lips in a meditative purse over De Rougemont's *Love in the Western World* (which he was reading that fall) when she had gone up to him, naked for bed, lonesome and feeling tender, to stand in front of him, all of a sudden loving the funny way his hair grew over the fine curve of his head, murmuring, "Honey, I—I need a match," and when he gave her one without even looking up, pushing the book away with an embarrassed giggle, to which he only said distractedly: "But look, I'm reading, sweetheart. I mean—well, I'm in the middle of a *paragraph*."

She took her coffee and sat by the window, downing that first cup in steady little sips as if it was medicine, looking out at the cold twilight bleakly shrouding the chimney pots and rooftops, and recalling another window, late spring uptown, shabby pigeons and rusty TV antennas, and Verger fingering the smudged pages of a collection of Emerson's essays as he said: "But, you know, I'm no longer—I mean, it's all cleared up, you see—my chest, the lung. That is, I'm not—well, contagious or anything," so darkly earnest and self-conscious that she had felt warm toward him, though impatient.

"Well, I never thought you *were*, silly."

"But—" his introspective grey eyes peering at her as if he had decided to risk everything. "Well, people read Thomas Mann and all that, and—I mean, people always think—TB, germs, contagion. And it isn't true, you see, it's not."

She remembered wishing she had not come over on that restless urge to "get out" that the dreariness of Sunday in her world always roused in her. "Well, I don't think that way. What New England nonsense! And besides, I'd—"

Then he was standing over her, pale and indecisive with his cigarette, staring down into her eyes with a dark and hopeless resolve stiffening his lips. But when he awkwardly touched her shoulder, and sat down beside her all at once, inadvertently sitting on her skirt, and tried to kiss her with nervous, tight-mouthed clumsiness, she couldn't prevent herself from pushing him away with a piqued little frown. "Oh, don't let's get messy, honey. I don't feel that way right now—" just as if he was some love-struck teen-ager.

"All right. *All right*," he said. "I get the point. Christ, don't make such a big *thing* out of it! . . . I just thought, 'Why not?' . . . Isn't that what all of us say? Isn't that our explanation for everything? Well, why am *I* any different?" so that she spent another ten minutes trying to make it up to him, but didn't knock on his door again, not for a long time, even on the worst of Sundays, disliking herself for having hurt him.

"But anyway," she thought, "I didn't *mean* it. I didn't know what he was like then. And Agatson—" knowing unhappily that Verger had probably never meant to hurt her either, and had certainly comforted her more than Agatson ever had, and loved her more, too. Realizing this, she had an unpleasant sense of her own unreasonableness, the discontent that always rose up in her when she should have been most secure, the restless, unspecified yearning that always remained when her rawer anxieties were lulled.

"Well, I can't help the way I am," she concluded fretfully. "And, God, if he could just be some *fun* once in a while, instead of—" But that brought Streik to mind, and, satisfying herself that Verger was preoccupied for the moment, she let herself think of Streik as she looked out the window, remembering the first time she had ever seen him—at that hideous business cocktail party in the East 50's, when, from across the thickly carpeted floor on which stray girls sat in wide, blossoming skirts, she had noticed his lithe, hipless body and almond-skinned good looks, as he laughed into the face of their hostess's current lover—a fragile little customer's man in a Princeton tie, whose first name appeared to be Rogers. An indefinable combination of curiosity and contempt lurked behind Streik's crooked smiles, and made his black eyes gravitate to Rogers's nervous mouth, as if noting traces of canapé between his teeth—though, in fact, none had been served.

His gaze kept drifting away to check the new girls, as he said loudly: "Listen, buddy, when they start getting you to baby-sit their neurotic brats, you know they're sharpening up the old emasculator. Which in my vernacular means they're filing their goddamn teeth," reaching around behind himself to put out his cigarette, and inadvertently putting it out on the bare forearm of Clare, the hostess, whose five-year-old daughter had passed trays of cocktails an hour before.

Her screech had more to do with his remark than the burn, and she stood, white-lipped and vindictive, in front of Rogers, yelling drunkenly: "Throw that man out of here! Throw him out! Who invited him anyway? Did *you* invite him?"

Five new people arrived—two rewrite men who worked with Streik at Associated Press, and the three girls they had picked up in a bar across the street after he had alerted them to "get up here for the free booze." Everyone laughed louder, so that Clare's hysterical weeping from the bedroom wouldn't spoil their evening, and May found Streik nearby making himself a large drink.

"God, what a ballbreaker, eh?" he said with careless amusement. "Or do you know her?"

"I never saw her before in my life."

"Me neither. But someone ought to tell her we're running out of Scotch." His lidded gaze flicked down her dress with the sudden, disquieting warmth of the sun coming out from behind a cloud. "Say, who are you? Do I know you?"

"Not if you've *forgotten* that way," she answered coquettishly. "No, I'm just a helpless little thing who hasn't got herself anything to drink."

"Yes, but listen, *do* I?" giving her his fresh glass. "How drunk *am* I?"

May laughed teasingly, and touched Verger's arm. "Heavens, no. We don't know anyone, except—" looking around. "Well, the person who brought us must have gone home, I guess. . . . So now *you're* the only one we know."

"Say, I'm going to call you Flame Dawn," Streik said suddenly with a droll wink. "Don't you think she's Flame Dawn, buddy?

All that insane hair. She's one of the Wampus Baby Stars. . . . But, listen," interrupting himself. "Why don't we get out of here? I know a dirty party down in the Village—certified psychotics, a Calder you keep bumping into, marijuana—and this is," surveying the room scornfully, calculating the number of people against the amount of liquor, "this is *Westchester!*"

At which moment, a disheveled Clare wandered into the center of the carpet, vaguely waving the necklace Rogers had broken when he took her around the neck as a last drunken resort. Her mascara had run into garish streaks, like a clown's painted tears; her lipstick was smeared to one side by the clumsy and despairing kiss that had preceded the strangling, and she was yelling, "Somebody throw Rogers out of here! Throw him out, I tell you! I've got to be safe! I've got to be safe! Please, please," sinking down on the rug to pound her white little fists into the stain where a drink had been spilled.

"Think what her mother must have been like," Verger said disgustedly, "and then imagine what her kid'll be like in ten years. . . . Should we wait till she passes out?"

"Forget it, buddy," Streik said. "There's nothing but fags and bitches, fruits and nuts. And her kind throws up first. . . . So come on, come on."

Everyone headed for the door where the blonde-haired child was huddled among the coats, asking in a feverish little drone: "Do you know why she won't let me hug her? . . . Why *won't* she let me hug her? . . . My mommy won't even let me hug her. . . ."

"A thirty-five-year-old midget," Streik concluded. . . .

"What's so funny?" Verger asked in the middle of her reverie, and she realized that she must have laughed aloud at the very thought of Streik's cynical banter, which had excited her from the very first.

"Oh, nothing. I was just thinking how hung up we get—all moody and earnest and introspective. Look at us, sitting around here like lumps. . . . Let's go out and have a drink or something."

His mouth pursed into an unpleasant frown, as it disappeared behind the magazine. "Go ahead, if you want to. Call somebody up, and have them meet you. Call up your alcoholic friend, why don't you?"

"Oh, for Christ's *sake*, Danny . . . And you're a fine one to talk," she muttered, and then dropped it, because she hated that streak of cold jealousy that sometimes gave Verger's eyes a piercing, fanatical cast, and had always been a little afraid of it. "Why do men always have to get so unattractive when they're 'madly in love' that way?" she wondered irritably, remembering that cold jealousy erecting its perfectly logical delusion in a wasteland of smashed bricks at three in the morning; that taste for symbols (typical of impoverished times when objects once again become repositories of fathoms of meaning) making the three of them pause at an opening in a fence that was entirely fashioned out of the peeling old doors of torn-down buildings, to spy an eerie bricklot where a tenement had vanished to make room for the U.N., and climb the sawhorses to explore among the shards.

"Put it back together again, you silly bastards!" Streik yelled to the darkened windows on all sides. "Because, Christ, a guy can't tell the goddamn ruins of war from the goddamn ruins of peace!"

"Let's rebuild it on them!" she called out gleefully, teetering on her black suède high-heels among the rubble. "We'll come back every night and build walls, passages that lead nowhere, rooms only big enough," erupting in a secretive snicker, "for thirty-five-year-old midgets!"

Verger, fuming with drink, sat down and angrily started piling bricks in that desolation of chipped porcelain sinks, enameled banisters, jigsaw puzzle pieces that had slipped down behind a baseboard in 1928, cans, rags, moldy cigar butts, lath and tar-paper and plaster—all the eloquent rubbish that will remain when our cities come down. "What do you idiots care?" he muttered morosely. "People used to *live* here, you know! We might at least build 'em a monument or something. . . . And come *on*, May—it's happast *three!*"

"Well, what's so late about that, silly?"

"Hey, girl, your friend wants to build a *pissoir!*" Streik caroled savagely.

"Oh, he's very philosophical, poor baby," she explained tipsily. "Comes from reading questionnaires all day and big abstract books all night. . . . But let's dance in the funny ruins! I want to *dance!*"

Streik blew a burbling whistle into a piece of sink pipe, as her hands, white with dust, shaped the empty night around her into languorous, ghostly designs.

"I order you to come to your windows, you hopeless bastards!" Streik commanded, shaking his pipe at the web of washless lines. "Flame Dawn's doing her famous belly dance for the shahs and eunuchs! . . . Hey, there, buddy, get out your famous clavicle or something!"

"I assume you mean clavi*chord,*" Verger corrected petulantly, toppling the pile of bricks, "and, for the last time, my name's not *buddy* either!" he added in a fury. "Now come on, May! I'm *telling* you. . . . You've had enough to drink. Are you coming home with me or *not?*"

Out of the darkness, later, she heard her own musing ramble, as fragmented and baffling as the tireless flicker of the phantom neon on the ceiling, and the muffle of discordant horns four blocks away, and the idiot ticking of a cheap tin clock: ". . . love you all right, I guess . . . never have any *fun* any more though . . . kiss me a little just the same . . . and maybe have sours for our heads in the morning? if I'm a good girl? . . . don't know why we don't, but that's life they say . . . 'member saying 'that's life' when I was thirteen—that's life, that's life . . . never call me Babe like Agatson used to do, though, and tell me to shut up that way, never call me cute, funny names . . . Danny? You awake? . . . Kiss me, kiss me some."

"Shut up, you bitch."

And for what? Nothing had happened. It wasn't until later that Streik turned up at the same parties, and the three of them sometimes had dinner together, and she found herself bumping into him on the street while taking Jefferson for his walk. And by then Verger was sarcastic, distant, suspicious anyway; by then they were spatting about trifles, their fights were longer, louder, and more hopeless, and their reconciliations more mechanical, and less reassuring.

She lit a cigarette, staring down into that chilly street of identical stoops, mean doorways, and dented trash cans, thinking that winter was coming. She was always unhappier in the winter; even after four years in New York she was still not used to it. She caught colds regularly, and shivered on damp subway platforms, and her feet always seemed to be wet. She needed to be in the middle of something warm and absorbing when winter arrived, and her time with Verger was obviously coming to an end. There was very little left but all the unpleasantness that must be gone through before they could give it up, and the tears and despair that you owed any relationship that had been more than just casual. And afterward? Streik? She didn't know at that moment, and she was not even angry at being accused of lying when she was telling the truth. She looked down at the darkening doorways as the rain began to fall intermittently into the streets, hearing her own voice just two nights before, saying flirtatiously: "But you know the vision I have of life sometimes, Tersh? . . . A wintry street with warm doorways. Only the doors are never open, there's just a little bit of light glowing over the transoms. And somehow I never seem to get inside. . . . Isn't that just like corny old Tennessee Williams, though?"

It had sounded foolish once it was out, except that Streik's black, calculating eyes weren't listening anyway, but dwelt on her mouth in that intimate, impertinent way he had, as he said: "Well, the way to handle doors is to break 'em *down!* 'Cause you know what's behind them doors, baby? . . . Money, security, power, blondes, Palm Springs," suddenly taking her hand. "But come on, philosophy's for failures, like *these* specimens. . . . Just look at them," noting the throngs of people squeezed into the booths, or jammed four-deep at the bar of the Santa Maria on Bleecker

Street—every face turned away from the face to which it spoke, looking for another face, every mouth twitching with the anxious hope of an end to the nightly search, every eye mute with the hopeless anxiety of innumerable nights-before that had brought no rest. "God, is this a pigstye? a snake pit? a waxworks?" Streik exulted. "Look how *venereal* they all look! The goddamn air's *green* with plague! I love it, I love it!"

"You certainly don't sound like it, Mister Supercilious. . . . And, anyway, it makes me sad," for the bald ugliness of the place was what filled it to bursting every night—ugliness giving us a courage beauty never can, the courage of our secrets, of our flaws.

"You're *kidding*. This scum? A lot of nasty children showing each other their dirty underwear. This isn't *real*, baby. It's the Last Chance Saloon. From here, you either go fag, or goof, or junkie. . . . Or you make it midtown, and sing for your supper, and grow up." He ogled her roguishly, trying to keep his mind on the important thing, and tickling her palm to remind himself. "So let me take you out of it, baby. What do you say? And meanwhile, let's have us a coupla hundred drinks or so! Come on, come on!"

At which moment, they both noticed Verger, crowded into a corner of the bar, absorbed over his beer, and pretending he hadn't seen them. "Good Lord, what time is it anyway?" she exclaimed, squeezing Streik's hand as she pulled hers away.

But you had to talk to someone, you had to make time bearable, you couldn't survive with nothing but moody truths day after day. She couldn't, at least. People in their time owed something more to one another than just "love." But what? She didn't know exactly, and was suddenly swept with one of those black, causeless depressions that sometimes ooze up out of the modern soul, like poisonous miasmas.

"So what are we going to do?" Verger asked at that moment. "Have you had enough coffee now to talk about it? . . . And what the hell are you thinking about over there anyway?"

She looked at him from her gloom at the window, studying

the irritable frown he was trying to disguise, unable to articulate
the feeling of estrangement that occasionally fell like a veil between her mind and the world, isolating her—even from her
memories.

"Listen, are you all right though? . . . I *said* I was sorry about
last night, didn't I? . . . And at least *I'll* admit my part of it," he
added with a frown.

"No. No, really. I'm all right, it's just—"

The moment-to-moment unpleasantness of her life, the fact
that she cared about Verger but hadn't laughed with him for
weeks, the cautious diplomacy that was all that got either of
them through an evening together—all this came down on her in
a dismal wave at that moment, and then ebbed away, leaving
nothing but the fragments of a lonely and rebellious girlhood, like
so many treacherous pebbles, to wound her mind—her pettish,
pious mother, widowed after only a year, saying continually:
"Well, 'course your hair's just *impossible*, darlin'. But maybe with
a permanent your beaux won't notice so much" . . . the withering
August glare of Louisiana army towns in wartime . . . the empty
USO's where only the misfits came to listen to Tchaikovsky records . . . the boy friends who died inexplicably at the other end
of a telegram . . . the songs she'd danced to all night that seemed
to express better than anything ever would again the strange convulsions, the keen poignancies of that unsettled time . . . her
mother, catching her sneaking in under the chinaberry tree at
five-thirty one morning, and shrieking: "Don't you care what I
have to put up with! What they're always hinting at at my bridge
club!" . . . But, more particularly, the absolute conviction (which
had formed in her then) that she would never live to be old; plus
that eagerness for life which, in people of her age, in that time,
resulted from pessimism, rather than its opposite. And, finally,
her recurrent nightmare of those years: empty, whitewashed
garden chairs, doomed twilight in the universe—incongruous
images of safety poised on the edge of a yawning abyss, out of
which waves of anxiety swam up like malevolent crows.

"But, Christ, isn't it better that we *talk* about it? I mean, what's the use of letting it fester like this? It's got to come out sooner or later. . . . And it isn't *all* my fault, you know."

She sat at the window, weeping softly to herself, and wiping the tears away as they appeared.

"But, good grief, what *is* it! I mean, you might at least *tell* me. Is it fair to expect me to read your mind this way?"

But how could she tell him that it was as much the song on the radio, which he didn't even hear (the Porter, or the Weill, or the Arlen song—brief, and autumnal, and romantic), that had made her cry?

"God, May, stop crying that way. I didn't *mean* to hurt you. . . . But it's a *fact*, there are some *facts* here—and what the hell can I do about them if you won't even admit that they exist?"

She sniffled, and wiped her nose, feeling for him (against her will) in his very obtuseness, but not wanting to start everything up again. "Oh, I just hate the after*noons*, I guess. They're all like Sunday anyway, and—well, I just loathe any hour after twelve noon, I want the night to come so badly. I'll be all right now. . . . But *you* know what I mean. Isn't that why you like to have sex in the afternoon? It gets you through it," glancing at him to be sure he was accepting this. "And I don't know. Somehow we can get through the nights on our own."

"Yes, I know," he said, getting up. "And what's the good of talking, you're right about that. . . . What's so is so, and just a minute ago I was thinking, as I looked at you, that we should just shut up, and," his eyes filling with that stubborn, fatalistic glint of shy desire that she knew by heart, "well, just *fuck* or something, and the hell with it."

He stood there, indecisive and yet vaguely expectant, and the unwanted image of the way Streik would have done it made her say with a frown: "Not now, Danny, really. . . . I—I don't feel like it. I'm distracted."

"Oh," that distant light in his face dimming, his lips hardening around the rejection, as if she had purposely bruised the quick of a delicate emotion, and maimed it. "Oh, sure, it's all right with me! Don't give it a thought," he said with the curt bitterness of having to get back at her. "But I don't guess you could mind very much if I do what *you* do, could you?"

"Oh, Lord, Danny, why won't you be nice?" she exclaimed. "God, I'm so hideously *sick* of this! . . . I'm just not in the *mood*. Can't you understand that? . . . Why do you always make me feel like a—well, like a *ballbreaker?*"

"Because that's just what you are," he shot back as he got up. "Because it never occurs to you that my problem is just as real as yours—what's in *my* mind, what *I* need. And, frankly, I'm sick to *death* of understanding you."

The telephone shattered the silence half an hour later, to peal witlessly for a full five minutes as Verger swore at it—because it *had* to be someone liquored out of any idea of time, and his hangover had not improved any. "We might as well answer it," May said guardedly. "They'll only call back."

"Well, let them. I don't want to go anywhere after last night. God, haven't you had enough?"

The muffle of feet, pointless whoops, and high loosened laughter rose up the stairwell a little later, and Verger was certain it must be some of Agatson's old guests back from the ends of the earth, unaware the party was over; so that he locked the door, shushing May with a stern forefinger, to stand, barely drawing breath, during the insistent knockings.

"Look, if *you* want to go out," he said after they had gone away, "go ahead. It doesn't matter to me."

"Well, I don't know. Though a drink might make you feel—" just as a loud clatter commenced on the fire escape.

"Come on, hey! . . . Jack, Jack, Jack," caroled over the drenched backyards, and then Streik's face, rain-wet and flushed with drink, craned in through the curtains, singing out: "Yah, they're here all right, what'd I tell you? . . . What're you people—a coupla

Bohemian Commies or something? . . . Oh, Christ, maybe they were doing boy-girl . . . Were you in the middle of boy-girl?"

"Don't be idiotic." May laughed grudgingly, as she reached for a lipstick. "And come in from there before you fall off, you silly."

It all began again: the loft suddenly full of umbrellas, voices, puddles; a girl in a trench coat, carrying an LP record, who was introduced as Sally Spade; the two AP men, from the other party, in the middle of an incomprehensible argument about Lionel Atwill; a bearded waif in a huge maroon sweater, who was word-lessly drunk, and immediately locked himself in the bathroom; Streik shouting: "Come on, come on, we're all going out to have Jack Roses . . . hey, put on that fucking record . . . you got any liquor? . . . For God's sake, at least help Flame with the *ice*, Sal . . . drinks, drinks, drinks!" A thumping conga drum, five sput-tering bongos, and a reef of screaming brass lacerated Verger's aching head; and he got down the first sickening Scotch just to keep from blowing up. It all began again: Stan Kenton's "Jambo," packs of cigarettes carelessly torn open, the toilet flushing over and over again, a man wearing May's pink tam and insisting, "Greasy Thumb Gusick—Helmut Dantine—Joan *Crawford*, for pity's sake!"

"Do you want to? . . . If you don't want to just *say* so. . . . They're all going up to see someone off on the *Elizabeth*. . . . It might be *fun*. But listen, you don't have to come. I know how you're feeling."

"Sure. Sure. What the hell. Why not?" thinking over and over again as he looked into her guarded eyes: "Why not? Why not? We've nothing more to *say* to one another anyway."

A damp booth in Haverty's Bar down the block, Sally Spade buying "Danny Boy" while aloof, suspicious eyes frowned from under the greasy bills of truckers' caps, the table full of Jack Roses in sour-glasses, "Applejack and grenadine, baby . . . Harvest Moon Ball time . . . they'll make you howl in an hour. . . . But look at her, buddy, just take a gander at Flame!" Verger looking at May's hair, glistening with rain, just combed out, and May's eyes bright with an excitement disguised only from him, and May's moist red lips saying: "... 'cause gin makes me bitchy, and Scotch makes me cynical I guess, but rum always makes me feel kind of sexy," so that he downed drinks one on top of the other after the first couple spread their warm illusion through his belly, and Streik was calling out, "Cuba Libras! About ten Cuba Libras over here, barkeep! Ah'm lousy with the Yankee Dollah!"

A taxi splashing through wet neons, Verger (supposed to go in the other cab) having flung himself onto its floor at the last minute, woozy head down among May's ankles, and Streik's argyles, and Sally's pink knees—which he took to nibbling for some reason. "Hey, watch my stockings. Hey, that tickles." The gnashing gears of trucks, empty light on the loading platforms of West-Side warehouses, a snarl of cabs and steamer trunks beyond which the lights of awesome Jersey winked distantly in the downpour. The cavernous pier loomed above them, thronged and chilly, and the huge black presence of the ship, vibrating down in its bowels—a hive of gay lights, splashings, laughter, and muffled music—loomed over the pier into the sheets of rain that fell through New York's rust-colored false-night. Streik waved them up a gangplank, flashing his wallet at a guard, talking steadily; and then Verger was stumbling after the others through a maze of glaring corridors, stacked luggage, and shouldering people. "Twenty-five minutes, twenty-five minutes please," a metallic voice vied with the insistent bongs of the stewards, and Verger swerved to avoid a bawling child who had just thrown up in a basket of fruit, catching a glimpse of Streik's lean neck rounding a corner, only to become wedged in a crowd of raincoats and paper hats spilling out of a stateroom, beyond which he tried to shove his way, glancing in the door to find himself staring directly into the impervious, parchment-colored face of Somerset Maugham. He was swept out of the range of those cold, watery eyes by a sudden rush of shoulders and voices, "And, Andy, get us the *second* sitting!" only to discover that he had lost the others. "The bitch planned it this way," turning abruptly to come smack up against

Sally Spade, trench coat unbuttoned to reveal a black silk cocktail gown, "In here—where're you going?" that (blinking and amazed) he saw was really a slip. "Where'd they go? 'Cause she's got my cigarettes," letting her pull him into a stateroom that was jammed shoulder to shoulder, "Listen, who're we seeing off, though?" But she had turned away, still holding him by the arm, and was saying to someone, "Oh, we're friends of Adolph's. Did you ever see such a mob?" Verger, dizzy with the heat, let his head sink toward her dangling earring. "What the hell's going on anyway? Where's your dress? And who's Adolph?" Her gaze dwelt quizzically on his mouth. "Cool it. I don't know. But it'll get us a drink."

Paper cups of Irish whisky without ice, doleful foghorns far off, the aroma of shag tobacco, wet gabardine, new leather, a hoarse female voice saying over and over, "Cove. *Cove.* It's pronounced 'cove.' Where they have that horrible cathedral. *Cove.*" Verger swayed back against the metal bulkhead, studying the brass fittings on a closet door three feet away, until someone moved into his line of vision: a firm brown neck arching forward between the hands that held it, a familiar plaid raincoat vanishing as the two were pushed together by a shift in the crowd, the raised mouth and the lowered mouth meeting suddenly with a gay laugh. He stared blankly at May's full lips opened against Streik's, their tongues exploring, surprised to see how tranced and willing and pretty she was when she kissed. "The hell with it," he thought arduously. "Get in the closet. 'Least till the goddamn pilot's taken off. Never even tell her. Just evaporate, and be drinkin' wine next week, safely out of it."

Getting him out of the closet, after her "Why do you have to *be* this way!" had failed, necessitated Streik and a perfect stranger who happened to be nearby. Verger's pale lips were compressed into the stubborn, boyish pout she had seen there before. "But lis'en, it's a *British* ship, I tell you," he kept insisting, and then giggled, "Don't they give you your ration of grog even if you stow 'way?" and they actually had to unclasp his fist from around

the clothes bar. She helped him stumble down the cold length of
the pier shed, and he was distracted by baggage stickers. "Genova
—Napoli—Roma—Los *Angeles?* Ick! . . . But where the hell's
Wien? Where the knockwurst comes from. You see a Wien?"
pronouncing it "wine" with a snicker. Waiting in the street for
the others, among cab drivers and shouting porters, he sighed
heavily, trying to focus his eyes, though his glasses were streaming
with rain.

"Look, all right, I'll go home with you. How'd you ever *get* so
drunk?"

"I don't know," he mumbled, "jus' happened. . . . And I don't
want to go home. Want to escape to sober old Europe where they
got the knockwurst. Why'd you have to drag me back?"

"Oh, be sensible, for heaven's sake!" she snapped out, angry
with herself for feeling pique rather than pity. "Do we *have* to
do this to one another?"

"Don' know what you're talking about . . . and 'course we do,
I'm not *man* enough for you, did you forget? . . . And, anyway,
here comes your friend—"

Another cab, just the four of them this time, moving through a
forest of glistening umbrellas at the intersections, Streik holding
her hand from the jump seat, Times Square's eerie, tent-show
illumination flickering across Verger's blanked eyes and sullen
mouth. Piling out downtown, waiting while Streik paid, she
watched Verger crossing the street after Sally, and then felt a
firm, inquisitive hand on her shoulder, ". . . can't hold your liquor,
and handle your women, and bluff at poker, baby, a man's fair
goddamn game. . . ." Dark, echoing blocks somewhere near the
loft, ashcan lids stuttering with rain, a waft of jazz and voices
above her, shafts of wavering light from the opened windows of a
party; then just inside a smelly hallway, the clump of feet retreating up murky stairs ahead of her, she was turned around to
find Streik's mocking eyes calculating her, his hands exploring
her breasts impersonally, so that she heard herself saying, "This
little girl needs a whole lot of drinks first, but here—" reaching up

for him, thinking to get the kiss over, but then becoming involved in it by his tongue.

Thereafter, the crowded rooms of someone's studio, enormous ugly paintings detailing the labyrinth of the nervous system, a queer carrying a cardboard box of old piano rolls, a radio and a phonograph in discordant conflict, two scared Barnard girls pretending to be lesbians, a thief in a belted camel's-hair coat that bulged suggestively, and Verger, spied through an opening in the crowd, frowning over a quart bottle of beer as Sally Spade smoked his cigarette. "Oh, who wants to think about Korea?" someone nearby complained. "Where *is* Korea anyway?"

"Somewhere around Seattle, isn't it?" Streik yelled, handing her a glass, and licking his lips hungrily.

It all began again: her anger at Verger, the gnaw in her stomach because she felt no gnaw, the whisky that lulled it, Streik's attentive face proposing something, her intention to have a good time changing into the illusion that she was; flirting, then giddy, then laughing too loud toward Verger's blurred face half a room away, until she found herself alone for a moment by the door with an empty glass, and he stumbled past, and she plucked at his sleeve. "Get me a drink, will you? . . . And, God, whyn't you go home? You don't have to stay because of *me*, you know. An' you're a mess."

"Tha's your opinion. I jus' been talking to a dyke who doesn't think so. And I always make out great with iceboxes, don't you know that?" laughing pointlessly down into her face as he took her glass.

"Oh, Danny!" she cursed, swaying against him dizzily. "Won't you shut up! . . . Why does it have to be this way? Can't we at least leave *something* nice!"

Blinking and muddled, he took her by the shoulders. "But listen, wait a minute . . . we're buddies, and— Whoops, there I go *again!*" with a sad chuckle. "But listen, sweetheart, I," tears suddenly standing incongruously in the corners of his eyes, "What's the use, that's what I mean . . . oughta be grown-up about

it anyway. . . . And I can't take *some* things, you know . . . goddamn bug seems to have stuck me with the puritanical squareness
of the sick. Isn't it a scream? . . . So I ought to go home to Grafton,
and look at a tree—just forget Europe. . . . I'm only kidding myself
about Europe, like you said . . . 'cause you can't get there from
here. I mean, how do you expatriate yourself from your own
mind?" laughing, as if this was at once very funny and very profound. "And we're just two sick children, d'you know that? That
occurred to me. . . . But *anyway*, that's not the point—the point
is that I understand you, sweetheart, I'm stuck with that, too. And
I love you—all that—but," with a comic shrug. "But I'm just too
drunk to care about it, I guess."

"Well, so am *I*, for God's sake! So why do you have to—?"

"But wait a minute," shaking her, "that's not what I *meant*. I
meant what's the use going on arguing, and hurting one another,
when we could just—well," with an abrupt sigh of giving up.
"Look, wait a minute. . . . I'll get us a little drink," and he lurched
off into the crowd.

Streik turned up before he did, and was leaning over her, murmuring in her ear, when Verger came back with a single glass.
His bleary eyes dwelt for a moment on the two of them, Streik
staring him down, and then Verger began, "Listen, you two,"
breaking off to move May ahead of him out into the dim hallway,
"listen, come out here a minute." They stood together, the three
of them, in an odd and sobering moment of expectation, and
then Verger was saying, "She's pretty though, isn't she? . . . She's
really pretty, see. . . . But listen, she needs someone who'll tell
her what to do, an' look after her—"

"Oh, shut up, Danny," she started, baffled somewhere between
anger and amusement, his arm lying heavily across her shoulders.

"No, you shut up a minute, sweetheart. . . . Listen to me for
once, will you? . . . But look at her, she's all that brown, see, that
soft milky brown all over. . . . Here," and his hand was suddenly
undoing her dress down the front, fingers fussing at the buttons,
and opening it over her breasts. "See her. . . . She's that color all

over . . . she's—she's really *beautiful,* when you think about it," the sudden maudlin tears that he tried to laugh away dousing her flare of outrage. "Only don't leave her alone, she gets scared," eyes peering down at her with drunken gravity, "'cause she cries to songs, in the afternoons particularly. She knows the words to *all* the songs, see, and—well, that's the reason, I guess."

For a second, Streik couldn't seem to decide whether to say something, or merely pull Verger away, and meanwhile he stood there taking a peek at May's breasts, half naked out of her slip. Verger stared at her with a wan, disowning smile, murmuring, "It'll—it'll probably be all right anyway," and turned all of a sudden, and went off into the crowd.

"Jesus, your boy friend's a regular goof, baby. He oughta be—"

"Don't say anything, Tersh," buttoning her dress up furiously. "Please just don't *say* anything," not trusting herself to care any more, so that even later when the commotion began on the other side of the room (however much later it was), and she stared through the undulating smoke at Verger's flushed face, and heard his rasping voice that silenced some and roused laughter in others, she could find nothing to say or do.

". . . 'cause America's where *everyone* knows the words to the songs!" he was yelling in a harsh, staccato incantation. "America's a state of mind trying to become a point of view! It's a Comanche living in a ranch house!" yelling louder to be heard over the phonograph. "The degradation of America is epitomized by the James boys—Jesse and Henry! America's as sad and ludicrous as Tom Sawyer at thirty-five!" ignoring a burst of laughter. "Don't nobody realize? *America* is Moby Dick, and we're putting our five-dollar harpoon into the last priceless blubber on this earth! . . . Listen here, you guys," yelling into the gay faces that turned on him from the corners of the party. "It's where something's going to *end!* It's buffalo bones under the supermarkets! It's where the wound runs all the way to San Diego! One huge Brook Farm where nobody knows how to milk the cows any more!" He swung his glass in dangerous flourishes, spilling on a nearby girl, as someone let out a tipsy Bronx cheer. "But the *dogs* of America, you bastards! The whores sacrificed to Monopoly! The gym suits of Denver! W. C. Fields! The winds of Kansas mourning— I'll tell you what! The bad orgasms that make Topeka so grey! What Sam Houston did to his virgin bride we'll never know about! Coca-Cola insanities! The pious police! All the Sundays, everywhere!" laughing with such despairing rage that it ached all of a sudden in everyone who heard it. "Don't nobody realize that finally, and most profoundly, and—and most *hideously*, America's some stupid goddamn drunk standing up and yelling, 'America's where everybody knows the words to the songs!'" and he hurled his glass at the stark image of his own punished face in a mirror across the room.

Later, after someone put their elbow through a painting, and someone else burst into cursing tears in the uproar that followed; after she had fastened her eyes on Streik's lips, ceaselessly shaping words she couldn't understand, hoping that if she looked long enough sense would return; after the liquor ran out, and the stairways reverberated with people staggering off in search of more; after she had snatched woozy glances into the crowd that held on, failing to find Verger anywhere, and gotten angrier, and then indifferent; after finding herself inexplicably in Haverty's again, Streik still talking, ". . . bohemianism, liberalism, all that sour grapes—listen, *I* want dough, baby, bucks," his hand lying inert yet strangely insinuative up between her thighs; after she had leaned over to stop that flood of talk with her mouth, almost swooning when her eyes fluttered shut, only to have him peck her distractedly without breaking his sentence; after she stared at his lips that seemed to be saying: "Later, kiddo, it's only three-thirty, for Crissake!" and heard herself concluding: "I'll tell you something, though. We *do* drink too much"; after the empty streets, cold now and puddled, the rain having stopped at last, and the long difficult climb up the creaking stairs, Streik helping her, and then she helping Streik; after the clear thought that came to her on the last landing: "What are you doing anyway? You don't feel anything. . . . And he's off with that Sally Spade, and it's going to happen to us at last, and you don't feel anything about that either. . . . But maybe—maybe Tersh. And anyway, being alone . . ."; after she had dropped her key, and Streik had groped for it, only to drop it himself; after they had gotten the door open, and found one light burning dolefully that made her think: "Maybe he brought her here, he's just idiotic enough to have brought her here," and Streik's amused little glance told her that she had said this aloud; after watching him swaying over the whisky bottle, holding the piece of paper that had been propped against it, trying to make out whatever was written on it, and mumbling scornfully: "Bastard knew we'd make for the goddamn booze first. . . ."

After this, and the nausea that overtook her in dizzying waves, and the pulse she realized had been throbbing in her temple for an hour, she sat on the bed, still in her raincoat, holding the scribbled note (with the Old Grafton address on it, and the check for $300 attached), trying to understand the almost illegible words written there: "Every man for himself. No sense wishing it wasn't that way. You should of left me in the closet. Anyway, I lied to you about the money, so we're even. Which means quits, I guess. Remember I—well, whatever the word is." It was signed Dan Verger, with the Verger angrily crossed out.

She sat there numbly, and Jefferson came out from under the bed to nuzzle up into her lap. Streik had passed out into deep snores behind her on the sheets, and all at once she was too weary to cry, or be relieved, or even undress. "What'll I do," she tried to think, "what'll I do now?" But after a moment she lay down beside him, leaving it till tomorrow, forgetting to turn out the light.

OLD MAN MOLINEAUX
Verger · North · Day

I woke this morning, thinking of Old Man Molineaux—his yellowed long-johns and his fishing cap, his thundering belches and "Jesus-One-Eyed-Christs!" his canny little eyes under the unkempt brows. I woke into the warm surprise of having dreamt of him sitting in his platform rocker in the mellow, smoky warmth of that Indian Summer Sunday, brandishing the initial can of that morning's hangover, and staring out across the salt marshes, withered with October, toward the confluence of the River and the Sound, his scornful old mouth empty of curses and loquaciousness at last, looking at the watery horizon, not as a young man who sees it as a future he can still achieve, but as an old man realizing it is a past that he has missed.

For an instant in the dream, he was no longer the garrulous grouser of Connecticut River Valley barrooms, showing his discolored teeth in fiendish smiles; the comic staggerer down muddy back alleys, filling the frosty midnights with his angry songs; the maudlin stoic of horribly dehydrated dawns, beset by wife, children, police, and the entire "better element" of Old Grafton, or even merely the disreputable, sixty-year-old town drunk he actually was. For an instant, his small Molineaux-blue eyes were

53

empty of outrage or gaiety, and he was pathetic to me, staring
that way out toward a lost unknown, a relentlessly receding
dream. It was like the memory of that weaning-wrench that comes
when you first realize that your father is a harassed, flawed
human being, and not some kind of king. But then Old Man
Molineaux snorted in remonstrance to himself (just as he used
to), sniffing back his runny nose, and said something like: "Have
another can, goddamn it, if you say you can *drink!* Humph!
Drink! If you want to drink, Chief, you can't care! Not *this* goddamn year of the Republic!"

There was nothing specific in the dream that left me different
on waking from it than I had been when I went to sleep. It was
only the startling reality with which the unhindered mind can
sometimes evoke the past—the soggy afghan tacked to the back
of the rocker, the greasy length of fishline on which the rusty
can opener hung from the arm, the cans themselves sparkling at
the bottom of the galvanized tub like trapped carp—and the nagging poignance of loss that a dream leaves with you, like the
vague taste of last night's supper in the mouth. And now I am
filled with the sense of that time, a dozen years ago, when the
thing with May Delano ended for me in New York, and I went
home to Grafton for my first prolonged visit since the war, to
come to terms with a stalled life.

And dominating those three weeks of brief exile is the histri-
onic, beer-splashed, shambling, raucous figure of Old Man Molineaux himself, indomitable along highways in his Sunday search
for booze, capsizing with a giggling oath into shadbushes, com-
posing profane elegies to a perished life. I hear his rasping voice
from a back booth in Phil's saloon as I did that first rainy afternoon, when I got sick of prowling my mother's damp old house
under the damp old elms down Main Street looking for a book,
and succumbed to a New York habit and went looking for a bar
instead—in Grafton's case, the *only* bar. I hear him bellowing:
"And, goddammit, Ben, *now* the goddamn Democrats've cut down
that old horse chestnut this side the Fire House! Yes, they have! I

tried to take a leak on it last night sometime, and they took it away on me!"

I see him (as I turned around and saw him first): the sort of old codger that maroons himself safely in a bar on a drizzly New England afternoon, where he huddles at his ease in grimy corduroys mudded at the cuffs, and huge soaking work shoes that look like they are about to steam, the worn collar of his faded denim shirt almost as dirty as his neck, and the particular cap pulled down over the riotous brows so many times, in all weathers, that it has a specific indescribable shape unlike any other cap, and finally (incongruous and somehow woeful) the old tweed suit jacket wet-through and dried so often without being removed that its exact ownership could be ascertained from the shape alone, even years after it had been discarded. I see his seamed cheeks, red with drink under the white grizzle, his furious small eyes as pale and blue as a young man's eyes, his huge splotchy nose that I know at once is the ruin of a "family nose," the reeking smoke of a horrible cheap cigar wreathing across his face as he flourishes a large hand, so wrinkled and brown and arthritic that all the years (which drink has somehow kept from his eyes) seem indelibly recorded on it.

I see him, leaning forward toward his companion—a wizened little Negro with the lined, expressionless face of an ascetic, obviously a long-time recipient of Molineaux-confidences and Molineaux-opinions, for even during pauses he makes no reply, but only sips his beer frugally, and waits. He hasn't long to wait either, for after a fortifying gulp, Old Man Molineaux rears back, and cries: "Just chopped the goddamn tree down, and sliced it up like corn beef, and trucked it off to the dump! Wouldn't even saw it up for stovewood! Not them! Not on your life!" eyes widened with malevolent triumph. "Two hundred years old maybe, maybe more. Why, I can plainly recall when they hitched buggies to the con-sarn thing, and we always used to save them chestnuts in September to pelt peddlers with. You could get a horse to rear if you aimed for his withers," pause for a breathless chuckle.

"But, no! *Stove*wood? Who's got *stoves* any more? Who needs *wood?* They got these composition, realistic-looking brick logs, don't they? That they paid money for from Sears? That's what they got in their glass-brick fireplaces, don't they? And they got those red lights hidden back there, that flicker, and maybe even smoke a little, too—how in hell should *I* know!—don't they? So what do they want *trees* for? You get my point?" a further pause for this subtle exercise in logic to sink in, a pause suddenly broken by an unheralded belch that comes rumbling up the throat, and escapes from the unsuspecting mouth with a drawn-out "W-h-a-a-a-p!" after which Old Man Molineaux sighs, swallows, licks his lips, and comments: "Feels better coming up than it does going down. God-a-mighty, what a life!" I see the wink pucker Phil's florid cheek as I turn back to my glass, and when I leave a little later Old Man Molineaux's heaving snores are softly punctuating the dreary afternoon, like the sound of a flivver trying to make a hill, and Phil says: "He's a funny old bastard. His people were real fine folks once, but him— But ask your dad sometime, he—" breaking off at that, because my father has so utterly vanished out of Grafton's life that he might be dead for all Phil knows. Or I might hate the very mention of his name. Or feel unreasonably defensive about him in that town that his divorce and flight had mildly scandalized ten years ago.

But in my memory of those weeks, particularly as the dream evokes them, Old Man Molineaux is always in the foreground. I see Grafton's single street of stores through the prism of his curses. I remember the A&P, because circumventing the trashcans in the drab alley behind it was a nightly ordeal for him. Certain muddy roads that come up dead-end on the marsh, and are lined with run-down bungalows, each one seeming to have a tricycle tipped over in its yard, are forever memorialized to me, because here Old Man Molineaux paused in broad daylight to fumble at his fly, or there he came up short, staring with ferocious unbelief at a tree or house that was no longer there, and lectured, or ranted, or keened, depending on the contents of his belly. And of course Route One will never again simply lead out of Grafton in my mind, but will always be the setting for our odyssey to his son-in-law's marina on the river that last Sunday of all.

Actually, though, all this is hindsight, the editing of memory, for it was only gradually that he came to dominate Grafton in my eyes. For the first week, I was occupied with being a dutiful son. I managed not to get irritated by the sad little stratagems by which my mother hoped to make Grafton appealing to me again (the blueberry muffins, the knitted socks, the pointed avoidance of any questions about why I had come home), but neither did I tell her that I was seriously considering staying on, and by the second week I knew that it was impossible, and started to make halfhearted plans for Europe. I suppose I decided this primarily because I was bored, and the New York wounds were mending— the wounds of a bad love affair, and the whole sort of life out of which it had grown: the frantic postwar years when nothing seemed worth one's time but Third Avenue beers and Times Square bop, Harlem pot and Village sex; when the jangled rhythm of the war carried over into the fake peace, and we all wanted wild things, strange things, any extreme of spirit, and (all unknowing) prepared to put our hopes underground for the fatuous Fifties. All the night-long talk, and nerves, and drink, and exhaustion had burned me down till I was clear and minimal, and the thing with May, on which I had banked all that was left, seemed to have finished New York and that life for me when it fizzled out, and now it was clear that Grafton could never be anything more than a way station to somewhere else. So I was open, unjudging, marking time, and Old Man Molineaux easily came to seem the most substantial thing in that dreary town I had never liked, even as a not particularly rebellious boy.

Hearsay fleshed him out for me after that first time—my mother's cautious, "Yes, it's very sad about the Molineauxs. I feel so sympathetic toward his wife. She cleans for me once a week, you know. But like your father, he just never settled down, poor man"; the amused stories of a doctor to whom I went to get my passport shots; the laconic hints of storekeepers who had grown up there. My imagination, unoccupied just then after the rejection of New York, and having to tread water until my boat sailed for a Europe from which it had already extracted all it could, filled in whatever was missing; and half of what I know of him may not be actually so at all. But no matter.

For me, he will always inhabit the dank cheerlessness of those ugly valley barrooms when the cold afternoon rain unfocuses the sober street on the other side of the splashed glass. He stands weaving and blinking over countless tragic urinals at four p.m. when the day starts to wizen, and all boozers feel a lonely yearn for the comforting night to come. He vomits in the empty alleys in back of saloons in all the bitter red-brick factory towns of New England where I have ever been, and falls off his quota of stools into the crushed cigarette wrappers and ancient spittle, his outraged splutters rising in comic amazement from the floor. He is *one* (my particular one) among the others like himself, who are never more than five dollars away from outright destitution, and that last inevitable hangover that is somehow eluded by guile, and humiliation, and harmless thievery in cookie jars or under mattresses. And he is also, now, the drunken old reprobate with eyes narrowed in the bafflement of loss, sitting like a deposed king on his platform rocker, staring at the distant, exact place where the river meets the sea.

I learned facts, too, even some from him, though he wasn't partial to facts and treated them as prosaic obstacles to joy—rather on the order of Mrs. Molineaux. I learned that the stentorian voice was pitched to carry across stormy stretches of river and the shriek of bitter coastal gales roaring up the Sound, for he had once piloted as a living, some twenty years before, guiding coal barges and oil tankers through the treacherous channels at the mouth of the river. I learned that the river had quit *him* when, drunk one night, he adroitly piloted five barges so solidly aground on a shoal that one of them was still there, abandoned as a total loss, the haunt of winded gulls and a few brave lovers really

desperate for a place. I learned about his buried years thereafter
as a part-time switchman at the local depot, hiding his emptied
beer cans among the sooty weeds. And, most of all, I learned the
names and natures of his adversaries: the constables who often
brought him home, stale and garrulous with drink; and the prim
ladies with whom my mother drank Formosa Oolong (particularly a certain Mrs. Buckman, whose hair ribbons he had untied
in high school) who always averted their eyes and pursed their
lips on passing him; and the First Selectman of the town, who
patronized him with cigars; and the New Haven Railroad (from
which he got the monthly pension that ended up in Phil's register before ten days were out); and the Democrats, represented
by no-credit Gus Manzini in the liquor store; and finally, and
most galling to him, his two-hundred-pound wife, Bertha, from
whom he lived apart, and seventeen-year-old Billy, and nineteen-
year-old Wanda, and twenty-four-year-old Sally—all of whom
were in conspiracy to thwart and stifle and crush his "con-sarn
thirst for life"—his version of their efforts to get him to go to
Norwich State Hospital for the cure.

I see his mornings, as I came to imagine them while I lay in
bed with a cigarette, hearing my mother tiptoe up and down the
stairs, thinking I was still asleep. The camera-eye of imagination
roves down one of those very dead-end roads, puddled with
bright pieces of sky, to the slope-roofed, shingled bungalow at
the end, cellarless and humble under its elms, and the sagging
washlines, and the dilapidated chicken run, and the refrigerator
wheezing on the screened porch. And here comes Bertha, her
body gone to mammoth fat by childbearing and sweet milk chocolate, so that at forty-five she looks incalculably ageless in the way
of ignorant women, who remain stubbornly optimistic even in
their sorrows, and seem to progress from soft, girlish ripeness to
sloppy, ungirdled middle age with no period of prime woman-
hood between. I see her mail-order print dress, its garish flower
design faded across a massive bulwark of bosom, the plastic buttons separated by straining gaps, and a good two inches of

muslin slip showing below the back hem. Her calves bulge in the laddered stockings; the run-over tie shoes seem far too diminutive to bear her weight; she has no waist, very little neck, and two chins; and yet her face is somehow sweet, despite its plainness, the dark eyes hinting at simple expectations for this day. She hums busily to herself, and squints at the sky (clear and crisp with a touch of winter in it this morning), as if listening for the last birdsong, mutters something like, "No, won't rain, won't need the coat till later," undoubtedly thinking of her mile-long walk to that day's cleaning job (which I imagine is at *our* house), anticipating an uncomplicated half hour, and not thinking much beyond it.

Now she moves ponderously out of the yard, noting the puny flowerbeds, bordered by whitewashed stones, with a secretive, proprietary pleasure, and shifting the neatly folded shirt wrapped in last night's *Hartford Courant*, and the can of pork and beans and quarter loaf of unsliced bread, from one arm to the other so she can heft the gallon of kerosene in her stronger hand. I follow her, in my mind, up the muddy path that meanders through thickets of shadbushes as it ascends the rise beyond the house, and hear her deep gasps quicken as she goes on, slowing down some but not daring to pause, the gallon bottle swinging closer and closer to the ground. I watch her make the top (not a minute too soon), and lean against the giant old elm with the "No Trespass" sign nailed to its hoary trunk, and wait for her breath to slow, and see her take a quick inventory, as she does every morning, noting the one-room tarpapered shack with the stovepipe askew out of the roof, the woodpile strewn around a rusted hatchet flung down in a fury weeks ago, the old sea-green liniment bottles for Old Man Molineaux's "horrible sprung-back" (no new ones smashed, that's good), the stack of magazines rained into a pulp, the single collapsing high-top shoe pale green with lichen (frugality, whimsey, why one shoe? She never wonders), the galvanized washtub where red and yellow leaves float like Chinese paper flowers, the rotting Chevy car seat facing off the bluff toward the river marshes, and, finally, almost reverently, the platform rocker—its ripped afghan, its soggy pillow, its tied can opener at hand—standing as empty and crazy as the throne of a crackbrained king. No, nothing is amiss. If there are surprises, problems, difficulties, they are inside. She cocks her head, the faint black down on her upper lip dewy with exertion, and thinks her ritual thought, with the exact ritual twinge of alarm as every morning: "Perhaps he never got home at all. Perhaps he went looking for a boat. Perhaps he fell in the marsh. Or one of Billy's wild kid friends in one of them terrible cars they drive like madmen— Oh Lord!"

But, no. He is there, a sack of bones and paunch in the baggy long-johns on the bed inside, one lean foot of that shocking old-man whiteness protruding off the edge, the unraveling stub of a dead cigar still clamped between his teeth. He is there, as quiet and startling and awry as a corpse discovered in a remote farmhouse, that summons up dire visions of lonely, unwatched death in lonely, unchanged beds. Around him is all the litter, and chaos, and strew that womenless men find comforting: the ancient socks, the cans half full of mold, the bottle caps, the squashed roll of yellowing toilet paper, the rusty razor blades, the damp incongruous novels (circa 1908), the ashes, the disembodied chair rungs, the spoutless china teapot, the lonesome calendars and license plates and girlie photos tacked up around his bed. He groans softly in his sleep, he shifts his weight, he swallows without losing the cigar. He has the sad erection of an old man's dream.

His waking is arduous, and (as I imagine it, lying motionless in my proper Main Street bed) noisy with life's improprieties. "Oh, Lord! Good God Almighty, a man can't even get his goddamn sleep! . . . Un-g-r-u-u-h," clearing his parched throat with a horrible rattle, and touching his head (one vast, pulsing ache) as if to check its size. "Damn the Republic, I swear only *part* of me got back last night," pause to hack, mouth, and spit over the wall side of the bed. "But she don't care how you feel, not her. Lord Almighty, what a *head*. . . . Say, what time is it, Berth?"

looking over from his bed of pain. "Oh, no, not *beans* again! I knew it, I said so, I said it to Benny— Don't you care? . . . Well, I won't eat 'em, that's what. I'll go somewhere they'll feed me proper. I swear I'll *starve!* I mean it this time! . . . Oh-h-h, Lord!" Further groans as he staggers to his feet, only to discover once he is upright that the world is turning faster than it was last night. His long-johns hang in comic drape across his spavined chest, they are butt-sprung in the rear, and he scratches his crotch and says: "Pump me a bucket of water, will you, Berth?"

While she does this, he stands in a blinking shambles, curling his wrinkled old toes on the cold planks, the shameless bulge in his drawers poignant because he feels too horrible to even be aware of it. Bertha gasps at the pump and the pump (in need of priming) gasps back, and she bursts out before she can prevent herself: "Oh, Will, why don't you come down there again where I can look *after* you? This plunger's all rotted away! *Look* at that!" catching herself at the sound of her own irritation. "I could cook you up some nice eggs in the mornings, and—"

Old Man Molineaux has been eying the bucket of icy water, getting up his courage, but seeing the reflection of his ruined nose looking back at him, he recklessly plunges his whole head down into it, and almost immediately pulls it out again with the same aggrieved splutter of curses as every morning: "Oh, God! Oh, Lordy! Why do I live like this! No one cares what I have to go through! I tell you, it *drives* me down to Phil's, it does!"

"—and we'd save on the kerosene, too," Bertha goes on hesitantly, hopefully, "and you'd see, the children would—"

"Oh, *no* you don't!" Old Man Molineaux cries, dashing all hopes with a shrewd and sardonic squint in his rheumy eye. "You can't net me that easy, you and them ungrateful kids and Doc Menaker. You think 'cause I'm sick, and my goddamn back's gonna really go this winter (and it's real terrible these chilly nights, you don't know, just 'cause I don't mention it don't mean I ain't in horrible pain!), you think you can fool me, and get me back down there again, and then—wham!—run me off to the Old

Farm, and be done with me." Old Man Molineaux persisted in referring to the State Hospital as a "farm." "Well, not *this* goddamn
year of the Republic, no sir! There's things more important to a
man than having eggs, and jelly toast, and maybe even a sausage
or two—there's his ideas, his free spirit! Don't you realize that!
You can't snare a free spirit with your sausages, you idiot! You
think you can satisfy a thirst of the *soul* with a con-sarn cup of
coffee?" The allusion pleases him. "You always were a goddamn
fool, Bertha Kelly, you never could understand a Molineaux.
And that's the whole of it." He is fumbling around for a pair of
socks that match, and gets off his balance when he leans too far,
and overturns the bucket onto the clean shirt she has brought.

"Oh, Willy!"

Such trivial disasters with inanimate objects plague his mornings-after, and this one sends him into his initial fury of the day.
"That's what I mean, goddammit! That's an example! Making a
big to-do over a *dirty* shirt!" holding it up and shaking it at her
defiantly. "A man's *more* than a goddamn dirty *shirt*, you fool!"
throwing it away grandly, incensed by her dismay. "Kelly! Bertha
Kelly from Meriden! I don't care what you say, you'll always be
a goddamn *Democrat* Kelly, and you might as well accept it! You
might as well *live* with it, Bertha. Your kind's ruining this country, the Irish and the Italians—Gus Manzini, that's who! Just
nothing I can do about it! What do you expect me to *do?*" Now
he is struggling to get into his trousers, and having his difficulties.
"What can one single man do when his kids want to put him out
on a Farm, and his wife's always nagging him, and soon there
won't be any wild spot anywhere that he can go off to sober
himself up in the sun! I tell you I won't last out this winter, my
back'll finally go, or they'll cut my pension, or *some* con-sarn
thing. You wait and see. . . . *Then* you'll save on your kerosene
money, and have all day to worry about *dirty* shirts, and Mary
Buckman'll be around commiserating, the pious old bitch—as if
she never fiddled in an icehouse like anyone else! You wait and
see, it won't be long. No, sir!" And he turns toward her, rubbing

his wiry old beard in canny speculation, and adds with just the edge of a wheedle: "You got a dollar, Berth? Just till I get my check?"

With that, he would be off on his day, and she would not see him again until the next morning when some variation of the same scene would occur. That is, unless he had one of his "horrible nights," as (with sober chagrin) he dubbed those times when he raged home, maddened by some murky thought, some withering realization "of what my life's come down to," to stumble red-eyed into her living room, chased by fate, shouting and belching and weeping by turns, a wild and changeable weather in his soul. She knew this thwarted mood of his, and mostly tried to outwait it and get some coffee into him, but sometimes, if she was extra-weary from her mop and pail and dust-cloth days, she would exclaim tearily: "Oh, Will, go and get some sleep now, dear. You'll feel better, it's only your back. Now, don't do that, Willy," as he rashly swept the contents of an end table onto the floor. "Oh, look at that—your Aunt Martha's ironstone too—well, maybe I can mend it— No, now, Willy," as he smacked her in the face for no reason, tipping over a doilied chair. And then she would retreat, starting to whimper: "Now, Will, now don't do that, dear. No, Will, you'll hurt your—" smack, pause, his doomed old eyes expressionless, smack again. Then he would slump on the sofa, punished head on hand, and stare at her, sprawled and tear-stained on the floor (she cried from helplessness rather than pain, and from the image of herself on her knees at eighteen, removing his shoes the first time after their marriage). He would watch her trying to get up from amid the smashed crockery, great shivering masses of ungainly thigh revealed, and maybe murmur: "Lord-a-mighty, what'a my coming to, I'll go away and die, that's what—all I ever *wanted* was to get away—" And then he would stagger out the door, grumbling dolefully, and proceed up the hill, floundering into bushes, and whacking himself headlong into trees that had been "moved" since just that morning, his curses and lamentations fading after him, until (hoisting her sobbing weight up by the sofa arm) she figured he had safely made his sanctuary in one piece, and was probably pitched mouth-down among his mysterious old socks.

So, at least, she tearfully described her travails to my mother over mid-morning coffee. And so my mother passed them on to me, with such spare comments as: "People have their troubles, no one knows it better than I, but—well, your father, for instance, never *struck* me. No matter how I plagued him (and I'm sure I *must* have, as he said), he never forgot himself to that degree. . . . . But then Mr. Molineaux isn't himself, we mustn't forget that."

These "horrible nights" came upon Old Man Molineaux without warning. One time it would be the sight of Sally passing Phil's in the chilly, thronging twilights just before the stores closed, perhaps with a friend, another young mother; and from his place at the bar, he would see her lean, pretty face with the disapproving black eyes, the slender, haughty version of *his* nose, and the critical mouth always in the middle of a sentence (she talked continuously, she liked to talk, she was a Molineaux all right in *that*, at least), the face half-turned to peek into Phil's, her lips pursed with irritation at herself for even bothering, the eyes flaring a little with bitter triumph to discover him there after all, even though he was hiding behind his hand and watching her between his fingers. And in that split second, she would look right at him as if to say: "Oh, I see you all right! Where do you think I figured you'd be—at the *library?*" and she would look away, not even interrupting her conversation, with the renewed righteousness and indignation women always feel on passing a place tainted by men's weaknesses. And, though a moment before he had been saying confidentially to Ben: "Never let yourself get *anchored* by them, that's the thing," suddenly he would turn beerily woeful, and groan out: "They wouldn't put a pillow under your poor head if you was lying on the railroad tracks, your old back could be busted in three places, and all they'd say was: 'Can't you stand up straight!' They don't care what a man goes through—" At other times, one of his long, exaggerated harangues about the degradation of present-day Grafton would seem to evoke some image or some thought that would sober him, and he would trail off, and grow moodily irritated at the playful goading of the other drinkers, and perhaps mutter darkly: "Oh, well, you never mind— a fool's a fool, *I* know that—"

Once I was unwittingly the trigger, and Bertha's bruise the next morning rightfully belongs on my conscience. I had escaped to Phil's often enough by then to exchange nods with Old Man Molineaux. I had stayed long enough in the afternoons, and emptied enough glasses, for him to have found out from Phil that I was "Mrs. Verger's son, from down there on Main Street, out toward the Point. Up from New York, I heard," and this particular late afternoon there were only the two of us. I was bored, and thirsty, and angry with my mother for having vaguely hinted that perhaps winter-Europe would be bad for my lung, and angry with myself for being angry. The rain drummed comfortingly on the window, the radiator hissed and banged, and Phil was busy with inventory. Old Man Molineaux had reached the best point of his day, midway between the morning's agonies and the night's sodden oblivions. He felt talkative, and a little bored, and (most of all) securely solvent, having four dollars in his pocket, and his check due tomorrow. We got talking. Though he was older than my father (with whom I always felt like a glum schoolboy, even after I was twenty), booze is a leveler, and all real boozers have something in common that abolishes (for a moment at least) life's differences. I started buying him drinks, and let him go.

Having a new ear for his stories was as much a tonic for him as the full glass I kept under his nose, and his mocking tone gradually softened, the rasping voice grew warm in the steamy hush, and I was treated to a poetic evocation of the Grafton of his youth, the Grafton that was gone even before I was born there: a shifting montage of knickered boys whooping and ducking one another at the town pump (now a traffic rotary); and wild acrid 4th of Julys when Main Street lay under a haze of firecrackers, and maiden ladies pulled down their shades and had attacks of nerves; the windy night the river ferry (since replaced by a four-lane bridge) parted its cable with Teddy Roosevelt aboard; flattening pennies on the trolley tracks to New Haven (an all-day trip there and back in those days); the Hartford Night Boat trailing laughter and music down the vast dark hush of the river; the winking lanterns of shad-fishers seen from shell-littered beaches where the girls' mouths tasted of buttered corn roasted in seaweed; the winy smell of sawmills; new cider drying sticky on the chin; buggy harness and sweet horse dung; the historic fire that consumed the Fire House; fife parades chased through town by larking dogs; a pitchfork murder out on scary King Phillip's Road (now dense with prim tract-houses); the Great Elm Blight that killed all the trees; the scandal about the light-house keeper; the three-day blizzard when all the cows dried up; the auto cranks, and cracker tins as big as nail kegs, and birch beer in stoppered bottles; the parlor organs, and axle grease, and celluloid collars; the Old Leather Man—

"No one knew where he come from, see, but every spring there he was begging at the back doors. Talked French I think mostly, everything he wore was leather, even his queer old hat, and he had no socks at all, and slept somewheres up King Phillip's in a dry creek bed, and I always wanted to go off with him, see, and live that way—Lord Almighty, *wild* and who cares, new town tomorrow, trap a rabbit, get drunk in the woods, *need* nothing, you know? That always seemed the way a man should live. They got to locking me up whenever he come through. . . . God *damn!*"

His odd pale-blue eyes were suddenly clear and focused, he sucked a tooth ruminatively, and seemed almost shy for a moment.

"Well, I always wanted to get away anyway, see. This town was always too *small* for me, and there been Molineauxs here for two hundred years. Longer even than your folks. Oh sure— But, Lord Almighty, I run off the first time all the way up to New London in—good God, must have been nineteen-ought-eight—thought

I'd see what was doing, you know, maybe go for a deckhand, or join the Navy. But they hauled me back all right," he snorted derisively, "they always hauled me back," the sardonic cast hardening the eyes with lewd raillery, "but not before I got me a *taste!* You know? heh-heh-heh. . . . My old pa didn't get there quick enough to 'save me.' Why, goddamn, son, I had me almost ten dollars saved money in my pockets, and in them days you could buy *Turkish* fun for ten bucks—you know, pantie-loons, and jangly earrings, and *strange* notions—and get yourself so drunk before you went, you wouldn't a known *which* end was up!"

Followed a sniggering, comic story, in a heated whisper, that was not nearly as dirty as he thought, but in which I saw him, just over sixteen, in knickers and knee socks that wouldn't stay up; awed along the brine-tart harbor streets; solemnly nonchalant ordering schooners of beer in roaring saloons; eating a paper bag of oysters on a midnight pier; approaching the woman in the doorway (who looked like Mary Buckman's older sister, only pale with powder on her throat, lips thrillingly garish with mauve paint); arguing under the foggy street lamp down the block when she first noticed the knickers and sent the scornful echoes of her laughter reverberating back and forth between the shuttered buildings; utterly scared once the hateful knickers had been taken off in the room he remembered as exotically sordid despite the soiled camisole and the carnival kewpie; resolute on the brass bed rank with earlier guests; surprised at the crude explicitness of her instructions; shocked at one idea he got, only to be more shocked at her sudden shift of thighs to accommodate it; embarrassed by his underwear afterward; and finally humiliated on all fours before her thunder mug, heaving up all the beer, while she said a word he had never heard a female use before.

"I tell *you*," he said, back in his old form again, "them seawhores, you know—they get *wild* dealing with sailors all the time, who get these weird notions on watch, see—I mean, out *there*, who cares? . . . But they couldn't harness me after that. I was a wild one, a hell-raiser, I was dead drunk on apple brandy graduation night. *Always* in trouble, *all* the time, heh-heh. . . . Why, I couldn't wait to get growed enough to just *go*—Liverpool, Rio, Melbourne Australia I heard about. . . . Lord Almighty, the goddamn South *Seas*, son, why not? I mean, what'd I want to mope around a town like this for? Not *me!* Not this goddamn year of the Republic! . . . Oh, it's all right for some, I guess, if you haven't got a *thirst.* I'm not saying for anybody else. But not Will Molineaux, I'm bent different, and—"

And then, with the insensitivity of twenty-six, and with much too much beer fogging my head, I told him casually (perhaps complacently?) of my own sailing three weeks hence—$1500, severed ties, Europe for as long as it would last, a fresh life—I suppose I made it sound that simple, even though I was still assuring myself: "You can always cancel at the last minute. You don't have to think about it yet." He fell silent as I talked, and seemed drunker all of a sudden, and thirstier, and after a while he drifted away when Ben or someone else came in, and grew raucous, and then argumentative, and finally sat drinking through his money with a gloomy sneer. I wondered tipsily what I had said, and only later learned: I had touched his soured dream with my reality. For Old Man Molineaux had never gone.

Instead, he put it off, and waited too long, content to be a hell-raiser up and down the valley, an epic eater and singer and horser-around at church picnics, a reckless and adept handler of small boats in all weathers, a chronic odd-job man and fire-house lounger, who was always "shipping out next year." Any wild scheme was his meat. He was always to be found in October's icy duck blinds, tilting a jug at dawn; or swimming out through the lobster pots to the lightship on a dare; or inveigling the first french kisses out of ribboned girls who always married someone else; or around the keg of beer at his buddies' weddings, the first to scoff at their surrender of their freedom, and get hilariously drunk, and fall down—whomp!—before the thrilled eyes of bridesmaids; the last to stagger home, and take a steady job (denying it was that), and surrender his own freedom (denying that, too).

Instead of going, he had talked of going. "Christmas? Nope, by Christmas I'll be gone. Ought to be on a banana boat going through the Canal by then. Ought to have the *Pacific* under me by New Year's. You fellows shovel out my woodpile for me, will you?" But by that Christmas, exulting around a skaters' fire on frosty Quitman's Pond: "Just wait'll I get into this war! Yah, I'm going to enlist next month. And then you watch my smoke!" And by the next, mumbling beerily to a tug captain in a snow-blinded shack on the pier: "Yah, m'brother Rufe beat me out of it . . . then the con-sarn flu got him at Plattsburgh . . . an' *someone* had to hang around to milk Ma's cows! . . . But *now* I figure, see, get my pilot's license, jus' for experience, and then *next* year—" But by next year there were still ducks to wait for in the North Cove's misty blinds, and jugs to "take the frost off" while waiting, and improbable tales to tell when the belly warmed, and girls to spruce up for when he got home. There were still wheelhouses in which to drink his searing coffee out of a tin cup while picking out the nun-markers one by one in the murk of rainy river midnights in March; there were barge hands to pump who had been to Singapore, and river whores to bargain with in damp shacks in dying river towns, and river talk, and river lore. . . . That year, and the next year, and the next.

Until they said of him with a fond shake of head: "That Will Molineaux! Did you hear what he did last night? Drove Judge Retford's Reo almost off Greave's Point, right there at the lighthouse! Said he missed his turn!" A tolerant chuckle. "Suppose he's got to get it out of his system, though. Never got over Rufe's death, they say."

Until something soured in his thwarted heart—the steamy shipping offices, the rusty windlasses of migrant freighters, smoky sailings from Hoboken, hatch-top musings in the awesome emptiness of Atlantic dawns, red nights of flinging money down the dark maw of harbor-side Marseilles, Bremerhaven, mangoed Maracaibo, the purged return to the monastic fo'c'sle, all the lost ports and what was there—the wild, the cast-loose, the vagrant—all this diminishing, receding, finally out of reach.

Until he said to the wide-eyed, melon-breasted Irish girl from Meriden: "Oh, yes. Two years ago I almost went, and then Ma died, and—I don't know. There was the house, and they couldn't replace me till August. Still may do it though. . . . But, come on, haven't you always itched to kiss a sailor?" his rude fingers straying over her rolled stocking tops there in the front seat of his Model T up Mosestown Road by the old cemetery in the woods, his mouth swallowing her automatic "Don't, oh," his knee blocked by the obdurate gearshift from forcing hers apart, and so urging gruffly, "I got a blanket, though. Come on. Please," only, when he had her on the blanket there in the mossy dark, whimpering and aroused under the implacable eyes of unseen owls, to have her thigh touch something as she allowed it to be spread, something on which her fearful fingers picked out an inscription through the lichen, something that made her shriek and scramble up and away from him and it—a headstone weathered and awry, with a wingèd head carven crudely on it; and when he lurched after her, to find her in the car again, scared and superstitious, but in the *back* seat this time, he knew he had stirred her, and, fumbling with her combinations, knew as well that her warm, kneadable flesh was fertile just to the touch, ready for some ordained completion; and should have known that to expend himself into that sweet wetness was to sow forever, but was blinded by her body's absolute subservience to its natural function, and glimpsed the one and only time the purpose behind passion, the primitive mystery behind the groping act.

He could have gone away. This might have been the severing fact for someone else—the simple, frightened girl, working in the piano-action factory in Mosestown, who by the very look of her was destined to get inconveniently pregnant in just that way. Anyone else, tugging at their roots as he had done so long, would have thanked fate for the nudge, and fled. He gnashed with it for a week, and jobbers in shabby turnpike lunchrooms at unlikely four-corners heard his curses. Grafton sniffed collectively, and concluded: "A man of thirty-four! Passed out on the green across from the Congregational Church! Come first service Sunday morning, there he was—snoring! Really!" He railed, and listened coldly to her sobs, and made defiant plans alone on the beach, and even took her brutally in tears again one night, but in the end he married her, and that was that.

The happy months, the dreary years—crunching home in the iron, silent nights, his noble nose dangling a fanciful icicle, to the great warm mound of Bertha under the patchwork comforter, too sleepy to be agile when he slaked his brooded thirst on her, only shifting in heavy-limbed acquiescence, and shushing him because the kids drowsed seven feet away. Freezing up applejack in a barrel hidden in a thicket on the rise (before he built the shack), the clear tart liquor in the preserve jars, the liquor that was as golden as the autumn Sundays he and Ben, and sometimes others, sprawled in a special place out in the marsh, jawing and snoozing and drinking it, the Sundays Bertha said to neighbors: "This is Will's fishing day, this time of year," the secret place he sometimes went to alone to spy on birds, and mumble slurred moody things to them, and "pull his whistle" shamelessly in the sun. The moonless night he piled the barges up, spiked coffee sloshing down his shirt front when they hit, the yawing cables parting with a fatal crack, muffled "good goddamns" from somewhere forward, the wheelhouse lamps hanging crazily aslant as he stated: "Knew the con-sarn thing was *some*where's over on the lee side," enduring the harangue that ended with his suspension, in the pit of a hangover that would last three days. Chopping stovewood near sagging chicken wire on grey November days in the Thirties, sweating his suspenders black, thinking of the bottle he had hidden in a pile of ties near the switch. Teaching a bored Billy how to splice a line; righteously furious in Phil's the first time he saw fifteen-year-old Sally pass with a boy at ten o'clock; mawkishly cuddling chubby Wanda after a two-day binge, but cuddling Bertha less and less. Finally, building the tarpaper shack during a two-week layoff as "a sort of clubhouse, Berth, that's all," and taking to going off to it when the demons rose in him, and moving up there in a silly huff one night when Bertha wept: "I can't, I can't any more, I just *can't*—my old dad'd turn over in his grave, what I've put up with—" Until, having missed the sea, he took to seriously trying to drink it up, filling his belly with the potions of the Wild; able at last to see that, if he had never gone, it was out of some lack of rashness in himself, some part that held back from the ultimate casting-loose, a root in his nature that would not pull; but stubbornly unable to be reconciled to it. As on that afternoon I airily told him I was sailing in three weeks, even though I hadn't finally committed myself to it. Now, all these years later, I can see that my commitment probably began that very afternoon, and if I succeeded in the pulling-loose, it was not a little the result of his having failed.

• 2 •

I saw him a lot after that, though my recollection of it is confused. I suppose I actually spent most of my time moping around the house, reading family genealogies, boning up on my French, and writing long, hopeless letters to May, which I never mailed but reread over and over again, as if I was looking for a clue to something. I know my mother watched me smoking through supper, and afterward, when I got up to "take a walk," allowed herself to say no more than: "Of course, it's tiresome for you— I'm so dull these days—but do wear your coat, dear. I hate mothers who meddle, but—" And I know I loved her with the same inarticulate reserve with which she loved me, and yet was impatient with her because of it, and so hurried down the evening pavements to the comforting haze of Phil's where I could think of May with beery bittersweetness, which nerved me to think of Europe with the proper carefree anticipation, until eventually I wasn't thinking anything very clearly—at which point Old Man Molineaux always seemed to turn up down the bar. And so when I think of those weeks now I am almost always tagging along with him, perversely enjoying the spectacle we made—the dissolute old swamp-yankee toper, and the only son of a shabby-genteel Main Street family. I am tieless, and unpressed, and always a little high. I am listening to some fantastic monologue, and laughing a little too hard. We are standing side by side under the dripping pipes in Phil's bleak urinal, stoical (as all drinkers become) about the unflushed toilet and the infantile inscriptions, pissing into a common trough. But Old Man Molineaux is staring up and out the tiny window on the alley, where there is just a glimpse of stately clouds heaped high against the cold blue, and a long wavering vee of mallards migrating, and I hear his gruff murmur: ". . . safe in Jersey by sundown, see, somewheres in a woodsy lake only *they* know . . . ducking their heads in under, and squawking a little in the dark, you know—just to be sure they ain't drifted . . . squawk, squik-squik, squawk, that's how they sound. . . . I don't eat 'em any more—" And he shakes his old tool, spits, and says: "Might get us a six-pack for later, just to keep the frost off. You got any money?"

Or, properly tanked, we are bearding Manzini in his lair, it being Saturday night. Old Man Molineaux is feeling expansive, and pretends not to notice that it is almost seven o'clock, and time (that particular day) for the package store to close—an hour when all drunks are overcome with the shrewdest foresight.

"Goddammit, I tell you this town can't *afford* that new school," he is shouting good-naturedly to Ben. "I've considered it, I've looked into it. . . . They ain't even finished paying for the other one yet. Where they going to get the *money?* I'll tell you where they're going to get it—from *me*, from you, from every con-sarn one of us. *Taxes*, that's where they're going to get it! And them Democrats just raised the goddamn rate three mills a year ago, didn't they? I tell you, I'm gonna move away, I'm getting out—"

The Democrats (a minority in Grafton, who have yet to elect a First Selectman) nevertheless bring Gus Manzini to mind, and we set off to get a bottle of wine. The Liquor Store is right next to Phil's, their glass doors face one another in a triangular niche off the sidewalk, and so a man can get up his nonchalance with a beer before having to cross the fluorescent wasteland between Manzini's door and counter. Old Man Molineaux is imperious in his casual stagger, he stares provokingly into Manzini's tolerant, non-drinking eye, he refuses to acknowledge the humiliation of the small-town drunk, which is so much more complete than even the most abject city wino's, because the person who takes his sweaty, counted and re-counted coins, handing over in return the cheap bottle of oily, fortified California wine, not only knows *what* he is, but who, and why, and for how long. On top of this, there is the ritual exchange of perfunctory pleasantries about the weather, or, perhaps worse, the pointed avoidance of them in the simple and naked "Evening, Will. The pint or the half-pint?" to which Old Man Molineaux secretly longed to be able to reply with stately distaste: "I'll just have me the *fifth* of the Four Roses, Manzini, and throw in six cold Narragansetts just in case—and maybe a little sweet sherry for the women—" So far, however, pride had never vanquished prudence, even when his pension check was still inviolate in his pocket.

He stands, the greasy bill of his cap trailing a cobweb he has picked up fishing for his cigar under one of Phil's bar stools, and he is saying: "Nope, don't see a chance of it clearing till the wind swings around. Goddamn unlikely even then this time of year. . . . You know Dan Verger here? Young friend of mine up from New York. Going off to try them Frenchy wines, too. Eh, Chief?" I acknowledge Manzini's faint, meaningful smile with a curt nod, disliking his assumption that, of course, being my mother's son,

I disapprove of Old Man Molineaux, too. Or is he thinking of my father, and fancying he sees the same "irresponsible" look in my eye?

"Well, Chief, what'll it be? Let's see here," scanning the gins quizzically, passing on down the counter to the Scotches, still unable to make up his mind, and finally standing in an indecisive reverie before the ten-year-old brandy. "I just don't know," he says with ferocious seriousness. "Don't feel like messing with ice, and soda, and all *that*—that's for sure," peeking at me cannily through the cobweb, which he notices all of a sudden, and palms off his cap with a snort. "You people always talking about cleaning up the government, Gus. You ought to keep this place swept out, heh-heh-heh! . . . Well, what'd'ya say, Dan?" And, finally deciding that I'm not going to stand us to a bottle of whisky after all, he says: "Well, can't seem to make up my mind, might as well have the usual, I guess." But by the time the bottle of muscatel is off the shelf (where it is kept near the register to facilitate just such transactions), accorded a quick dusting by Manzini, mostly for my benefit, and wrapped up like a disreputable book in plain brown paper, Old Man Molineaux is engrossed among the champagnes, a wobbling comparison shopper, and I pay. "Well, Gus," he says grandly as we leave. "Don't lose faith in the country now, heh-heh-heh!"

Or later (was it the same evening?) we are passing through that area of floodlit exhaust where the Esso, Atlantic, and Mobil stations crowd together on either side of the highway, strings of little plastic pennants flapping in the breeze, gas pumps tinging out the gallons, and laconic, levied youths lounging around the cash register waiting to go into the Army—one of whom detaches himself, and approaches us in a slouch of insolent hips, side-burned, tight-crotched, and probably surreptitious even wiping windshields; hair pushed into a lacquered wave on his acned forehead, complacently greasy and unkempt—young Billy Molineaux, just seventeen. He has quit school in a flash on his sixteenth birthday, he comes home only to sleep, and the center of his world is under the hood of an automobile where there are none of the enigmas that plague him outside it.

He divines our condition in a single, expressionless glance, but does not lower the small portable radio from his ear (where it buzzes with shrunken saxophones) even as he mumbles: "They say one more time, Pa, like the other night, you know, an' they won't need you to agree—the Doc can just sign the papers—"

Old Man Molineaux makes no attempt to hide the suspicious-looking package, and his cigar assumes a jaunty, unscrupulous angle. "Well now, boy, what d'you mean? . . . What's that? 'One more time'?"

Billy is a veteran of these evasions, and only peeved because the other guys can see, but will not even comment over the sucking of their cigarettes. "I mean, like Sally come over in the morning and saw it, and made Ma tell," a frowning, slightly embarrassed peek at me, disheveled and swaying a little by then, as if all his father's troubles are the result of bad company (and later, indeed, I found out he was referring to the drunken aftermath, with Bertha, of the afternoon I told the Old Man I was off to Europe), "I mean, *I* don't care, I don't know nothin' about it, I just thought I'd tip you, that's all," a lonely eye following the stream of traffic, darting from car to car like a typewriter carriage.

"One more *time!*" Old Man Molineaux explodes in a fury. "I'll just be goddamned if I know what you're talkin' about! Jesus-One-Eyed-Christ, if I do! . . . And ain't Sal got anything to do at *home?* Ain't she got babies? Just like I say, these young fool girls today with their wash-o-mats, and bar-b-ques, and con-sarn *toasters*—and turn your goddamn *radio* off when you're talkin' to your old man! Can't you stand up *straight!*"

Billy is regretting his impulse (which he didn't understand anyway), for he pouts fatalistically, his Molineaux-blue eyes blank with failure to communicate, and I realize all of a sudden the subtle, maddening distance between a father and his son, those invisible walls the first burgeoning of masculine pride erects between the generations, over which (I see at last) the father hungers, no less baffled than the son. "Look, I told ya *I* don't care. You and Ma, Christ—though why do you beat her *up* that way? You know the way she is. And, like you're just gonna get yourself sent *away*, Pa—"

Old Man Molineaux blinks and splutters there in the cold, impersonal light of the intersection, longing for a drink to brace him. "I said turn your goddamn radio *off!* Don't tell *me* about your mother, I know your mother all right, don't you worry. Kids! Look at you! How're you gonna *make* anything of yourself? No education, hangin' around, thirty bucks a week—good God Almighty!"

Billy turns, the radio lowering in a slow arc, calm doomed eyes registering no hurt, his isolation redeemed as he knew it would be. "Okay, Pa, okay—*I* don't care—I mean, like," a disowning shrug, "okay, like *okay*." We are left there, tipsy beggars, an old man and a young fool, in the roar of a Studebaker, gunning to make the light. "Come on," I say, thinking I'm consoling him. "He just didn't know how to say what he meant, 'cause his friends were watching. . . . I'll stand us to a beer."

And later still (further in our cups) we were floundering across the marsh to Ben's house for some forgotten reason. Ahead, the unimpeded black river moves awesomely toward the imminent sea. Behind, the winter sun sinks like a cooling ingot into the birdless woods. The great night is gathering over us despite everything; Old Man Molineaux, hunched and indomitable ahead of me, defiantly bellows pilot songs from the last days of Connecticut River steamboating in a weirdly musical rasp: "Ho for Hartford, or we're gonna tie up late. . . . Peel the weather eye, boys, pick up o-l-l-l-d Bell Eight!" and I am a drunken spark of sentience on that unlikely marsh path, water in my shoes, thinking of the warm mittens of boyhood, and of my father's huge maroon turtleneck sweater moving ahead of me through leaf smoke on the Sunday-afternoon walks he and I took in October when I was nine, during which I always prayed that he would make no mention of the pointless squabble that had ruined the roast, and so spoil that hazy hour of suspension from life with a rebuke I would have to resent in my mother's name.

Then Old Man Molineaux has halted in a puddle, and I come up smack into him, and we are both suddenly sitting on wet rumps in the bitter reeds. "Goddammit, Chief, where's your legs! Where's your con-sarn swamp legs! They ain't got *legs* any more!" His seamed old face crazy and punished in the last death-red glow of the extinguished sun, as he teeters on one creaky knee, hands right down in the ageless, alluvial mud. "Lord Almighty, go get a piling crane," trying to get up, wheezing and snuffling with the cold; and then he tips over again, sprawling out full length, and a prolonged whapping belch rumbles up out of the waist-high grasses, followed by: "Ain't no one around but him though, 'n he don't mind—"

Then we have made the remote old marsh house with the worn linoleum, the enameled tin space-heater, the string of salvaged drawer pulls, the dismantled hand loom, and the stacks and stacks of musty, ancient books; and we stand dizzy amid the smells of grease, cabbage, kerosene, old people, damp dogs, and cat-mess in unswept corners; Old Man Molineaux tearing at the sealer of our bottle with bitten nails, Ben's small dark face deacon-like in steel-rimmed reading glasses, his narrow lap full of scrawny cats. A lean, yawning dog, as moth-eaten as an army blanket, licks our muddy shoes.

Waves of heat reel my head; I find myself sitting on the floor amidst the cats, dutifully taking my turn at the bottle when it passes, barely listening and hardly seeing—for how long I no longer recall. "Kids! Kids!" Old Man Molineaux is yelling, stripped down to his woeful underwear, but still rakishly sporting his cap. "Get me sent off to that con-sarn Old Farm yet. Just thank your goddamn stars you never had no mean kids, Ben—" Ben's impassive eyes do not express an opinion on this, though he is the last of his line, unbroken in descent from a bond-slave freed in Grafton (called Greave's Town then) in 1701, unbroken until

him. "That hospital's not so bad, Will. . . . Worse ways to pass
the winter. . . . I passed worse."

"Well, not *me!* Not this goddamn year of the Republic! . . . And
it's Sally, too, you know, who's behind it. She and Doc Menaker—
the thin nosy bitch! Oh, yes," winking and weaving. "Get the ol'
man penned, get the ol' fool out of sight up country," suddenly
bleary, "little Sal—remember Sal, Benny? Little thin legs on her,
no bigger'n neck of this goddamn bottle—I recall her crying to
her ma when they used to call her Stilty, some of them runty
Italian kids," suddenly maudlin, "I don't know. When kids get
mean like that, and want to *trap* you, *pen* you, *beach* you, and
they plow up the goddamn berry meadows, and saw down the
goddamn trees, and—" he sits down with a thump in a worn old
rocker, blinking and weary, "Lord Almighty, it's a *horrible* goddamn life! It's a guaranteed hell!"

Greasy light shivers in the almost empty bottle as I raise it, a
kitten's rough warm little tongue is diligent on my sweaty palm,
Ben's austere voice drones on quietly. "Well, you never would
settle, Will. You always put your head against it and pushed.
But no one can push it. Not these days. *You* can't push it. Not
any more."

The last of the wine is treacherous in my stomach, I find I am
staring witlessly at an ancient copy of Mather's *Wonders of the
Invisible World,* and I hear myself stammer out in the thick
solemnity of drink: "Here's where all the trouble started, 'cause
this lecherous old bastard made us all stop and *think,* and we quit
seeing things any more. . . ."

Later, staggering and slipping in the murmurous dark, an un-
accountable warm wind rushing through the huge night, staring
up at sharp stars, winter stars, Old Man Molineaux is retrieving
me from a marsh ditch, his crooked hand like a claw on my
splashed forearm, chuckling. "Lecherous old bastard, heh-heh-
heh . . . That's right! An old goddamn bastard that won't quit!
He's got it right, heh-heh-heh!"

And then it is morning, the morning that comes anyway no

matter what you have done to the night, that last Sunday morning, and the first thing I see is a disembodied foot, motionless in
the air, covered with neglected corns, and beyond it a ceiling's
reddish planking, every nail come through a full inch and
dummed back, and I feel as if I have been clouted in the head by
a bottle. Then I realize it has been only the *contents* of a bottle,
and I am lying on the floor by the bed in Old Man Molineaux's
shack with no idea how I have gotten there.

In the beginning, hangover can be as fragmented as drunkenness, and the next thing I remember is supporting myself by a
table edge, arduously trying to focus my eyes on a young couple
standing under the trees of May—the low-waisted dress, the
teetery shoes, the square, ugly pocketbook of the girl, her pretty
face shallow and flushed, one arm held at the elbow by the man
in the heavy box-suit and two-tone pointed shoes, his mouth
stiffened with self-importance, his thick hair combed down unnaturally, and his free hand lifted in a vaguely regal wave at the
camera. It is an old snapshot, browned and curling on the edges,
and someone left a wet glass on it a long time ago, and the water
stain frames the two honeymooning faces in a whitish aureole.

Then, I am outside in the mild morning that is odorous with the
dry musk of Indian Summer leaf fires on the breeze, squinting
against the glare of the sun on the water off across the marshes,
and staring down the fifteen-foot drop at the heap of glittering
cans and bottles in the reeds—a decade of them at least—that
forms a rusty, smashed monument to Old Man Molineaux's un-
slakable thirst.

I think, good God, what am I doing here? Am I really sailing
for Europe in less than two weeks? remembering equally bad
hangovers—but always endured in dim city lofts where last
night's radio has been left on, or in rainy riverside areaways with
my collar turned up, or under the crashing El on the way to a
Third Avenue saloon where everyone will be comrades in the
same agony. Here, the sour taste of cheap wine somehow seems
less damning; the russet morning is hazy with special memories

of boyhood that fill me with a sweetly maudlin illusion of perspective. I sit on the car seat with a first ghastly cigarette, wishing May were here, certain I could cut through all our difficulties
with a single word, but uncertain whether I would really want to
take the trouble, feeling solemnly, not unpleasantly old.

A terrible fusillade of coughs, broken at intervals by groans and
curses, interrupts me. "Oh, Lord . . . Good God Almighty . . .
Jesus-One-Eyed—" and a shattered Old Man Molineaux appears
in wrinkled bare feet, shirtless, eyes puffy, wisps of dirty grey
hair askew, an ugly red welt swelling under one bloodshot eye,
a moldy old high-top shoe clutched in one hand, of which he
seems to become aware for the first time on seeing me.

"Looks like I—u-n-ng-r-r-h-h—found the goddamn mate last
night, don't it?" staring at it with a puzzled blink, then casting
around for what to do with it, eyes lighting on the other one,
unmoved in weeks. "Oh, yeh . . . tripped on it comin' up, that's
right. Been looking for it sober for three months, and—" His face
is suddenly theatrical with a tragic thought: "Oh, Lord, then I
must a gone down there again after we got home," dropping the
shoe on his bare old toes, and letting out a defeated "E-e-e-k!"
that makes him feel his bruise with the wince. "Christ, she must a
hit me! . . . The old fool hit me—I remember! With a coal shovel!"
feeling his cheek gingerly. "God-a-mighty, is there no limit to
what she'll do! I swear," raising his fist too quickly, and letting
out a terrible groan, "O-h-h-h, my goddamn back! Feels like it's
finally sprung for good! . . . My Lord," rubbing himself painfully
in the general area of his liver, "they've taken to hitting a goddamn cripple, that's what. I wouldn't a *believed* it! I would have
argued with any man who said—" At that moment, his eye falls
on the galvanized tub, its placid leaf-strewn surface a-sparkle,
and he abandons his thought and creaks laboriously down on his
knees until he is squatting stiffly there on all fours, lean buttocks
awkwardly stuck out, swallowing dryly from the exertion, and
then he shoves his head resolutely down into it.

He comes up with a spluttering roar: "Goddamn son of a bitch, we ain't dead *yet!* Think they got me cornered 'cause it's Sunday, do they? Well, not me, not Will Molineaux, not this con-sarn year of the Republic!" and he plunges an arm right down into the tub, grimy sleeve of long-johns and all, exultant there on his bony old knees, and then he is wildly flourishing something above his head like a bladeless sword handle, something that glitters in the sun. "We ain't dead yet, Chief! Heh-heh-heh! Beat a cripple, eh? . . . An' there's *four* of them!" shaking the can of beer, and cackling with shrewd and crazy glee.

"And as Plato said to Socrates," I exclaim out of my venerable mood, " 'Don't mind if I *do*.' "

Then we are enthroned in the warm sun, the first relieving gulps from the dripping can have steadied my senses and stained my chin, and I watch Old Man Molineaux picking his corns. "Suppose the goddamn feet are gonna go along with the back— Look at that! Ain't they horrible, heh-heh?" and then he sips his beer, and sighs, and surveys his marshy kingdom with a narrowed eye, too contented for complaint. "This is one of them *last* days, see. Tomorrow, or next week, the wind'll swing around into the northwest, and blow stiff and get colder—right down out of Canada, clear from Saskatchewan in a rush—and it'll be so blue and sharp your eyes'll hurt for three days. And the river's choppy, black and white, and you bless your coffee them days, see. And then—uh, wh-a-a-a-p! 'Scuse me—then it'll gloom over, and the wind'll drop till them woods over acrost there are dark and quiet and full of Indians, you know—heh-heh-heh, like you used to think when you're a kid. And then, whoom, all of a sudden just whoosh! quiet though, see—*snow!* Dark and quiet falling in the river—*snow!* . . . You always know it, when it's *sweet* like this—"

He stares across that bland morning with winter in his eyes. "God*damn* it!" he exclaims all of a sudden, banging his can on the rocker arm. "Let's go get us one of Sally's Jack's con-sarn leaky skiffs, and a coupla six-packs, and go hang off Foxe's Island, put out a kedge anchor—*fish!*"

"You're kidding!" I groan in genuine astonishment. "You mean *row?* Get in a boat and *row* all the way down there? Just to fish? Could you *do* that, the way you feel?"

"Why, sure. You think you're pretty fair with a glass, don't you, son? But you got a few things to learn, eh? I done it for years—rowed the booze out of me. . . . Well, we ain't got any tackle anyway—though I know the spots, see, I know places these summer people ain't *ever* gonna find with their goddamn thermos jugs, and silly goggles, and dinky lures from Hamburger Slimmer, heh-heh— But all right, all right, what I mean is, *drink*, just lie around, but *away*, in the sun!" He finishes off his can with a huge swallow, and sends it flying in a wobbly arc over the bank where it clatters hollowly onto the pile. "Always could throw, used to throw a line a good forty feet and hit the spile every time. . . . But come on, Chief—don't want to waste these last days. 'Sides," peering nervously down into the bushes toward the bungalow, "the old lady's gonna be after me any time now, and," a frown, a rub of lips, a sniff, "I can't just clearly remember *some* of last night—" And he reaches for another beer at the very thought, muttering: "Well, maybe I'll shave, get myself cleaned up— Goddamned son-in-law probably wouldn't lend me one of his goddamned skiffs anyway. . . . *On* the river before he could hold his water, *off* it before he knew there was anything *else* you could do with it. And Sal," breaking off with sudden apprehension. "Yah, I'll just have me a shave before anyone else gets after me," getting up with a wheeze and shambling into the shack. . . .

At which precise moment, as I later learned from my mother, young Doctor Menaker, phoned by an outraged Sally, was saying in Bertha's parlor: "Now, there's nothing really wrong with your ma's arm, Sally. I don't think we *need* an X-ray. Just try not to use it for a couple of days, Bertha, go easy—you could stand a rest anyway. You probably wrenched it when you fell. . . . *Now*, as far as the other thing," studying Sally's implacable mouth, and Bertha snuffling into a handkerchief in her embarrassment. "I think maybe it's time to send Will off for a while. He's having his troubles—"

Bertha looked at him in teary alarm, dabbing at her nose. "Oh, Doc, I don't know. He's not gonna like that. He really don't want to go to that place, you know."

Doctor Menaker was reasonable. "Well, I don't blame him at all. But it's a good hospital, they'll give him fine care, and—well, he's not as young as he was, Bertha. You know that. And you can't go on the way Will is without eventually hurting *yourself*."

Sally swept the long, shiny hair away from her throat with a furious brush of her hand. "He's a menace, he's dangerous. I don't care if he is my own father. Why, if Jack ever laid his dirty hands on me that way, I'd—"

Bertha suddenly sobbed in her confusion, fiddling with the doily on the sofa arm: "Oh, Sally, wait a sec, dear. Don't say that —your dad, he's—Doc, you know Will, he don't mean it. He's just . . . just *disappointed,* and he gets angry, and—no, now you wait a second, Sally—"

"It's for his own good," Doctor Menaker said crisply. "And he'll have a fine time once he gets there. . . . And, frankly, it's up to me to do what I think is best—for everyone."

"You think it might really help him, Doc? Last night he was bad, really I thought he was—"

"Absolutely. And I know Will. Oh, he'll grouse about it, but in a week he'll be arguing about the Democrats with anyone who'll listen to him."

Bertha laughed uncertainly, against her will. "I don't know. I guess you know best, Doc. . . . But I couldn't tell him, I just couldn't."

Doctor Menaker was on his feet. "Well, don't worry. I'll go up there later this afternoon. No use disturbing him now. He'd chew my head off, if I know Will's mornings."

"Oh, it's a dis*grace!*" Sally said bluntly, ignoring the doctor's irritated frown. "It's hu*mil*iating after all these years!" at which Bertha sobbed again, remembering them. . . .

And I hear Old Man Molineaux muttering as he goes: "Old

fool better put on his socks, too, before someone sees, heh-heh-heh—"

Following him inside a minute later to look for a match, I accidentally witness the heroic ordeal of his shaving, a series of images that I realize at the time I will probably never forget: Old Man Molineaux at the pump, fighting the handle with both hands, like a bucking tiller in a gale, producing nothing but throaty gurgles, to be suddenly rewarded with a thick gush of water that overshoots his pan, and so to pause to move the pan, and then resume his frenzied pumping, only to watch the gush diminish to a dribble, and pause again to move the pan back, just as the dribble fiendishly erupts into a gush again—a good five minutes of this until, gasping and a-sweat, he has a panful.

Or Old Man Molineaux lighting his stove—the groaning crouch, the awkward peek in under the burner, the flaring kitchen match, the lower lip steadied by the teeth, and the lighting hand steadied by the other hand over the brittle wick that will not catch, and held there grimly until the fingers do, the grunting "ouch!" the match flung away, the smarting fingers sucked—all this again and again until success.

Or Old Man Molineaux getting the steamy water from stove to basin in a lurching rush of scorched fingers, spilling great whaps of it, and hopping out of the way like an amateur fakir on real coals. Or Old Man Molineaux before a shard of mirror, lathering his face from a bar of laundry soap that slips out of its saucer like a fish floundering on a wet deck, only to be retrieved by a lucky catch on its last bound before the floor. Or Old Man Molineaux, his nose sporting a large sudsy dab, his underwear awash down the front, his forehead beaded with cold sweat, poised with his razor and staring at himself as if for the last time, waiting for his shudders to subside. Or Old Man Molineaux trying not to wince at the first rasping scrapes around his sideburns; and, gaining courage, executing a reckless, slashing stroke down one cheek; then, cautious again, scratching gingerly at a tough section under his chin; finally bringing blood on his upper lip when a belch suddenly shivers him; and so, seizing his nose, and lifting it, and flinging soap in all directions to get finished. Slowly, arduously, he carves his face out of the lather, like a sculptor with the ague; throws down the razor with an expiring sigh, eloquent with all that it has cost him; washes off with a quick slosh, and exclaims: "Good God Almighty, now where'd I put my goddamn beer!"

We go outside to find it, and Old Man Molineaux slumps down again to regain his strength, and I am encouraged to open another can, and do. The day grows bland with noon as our cans lighten; a churchbell rings the hour somewhere across the valley. I suddenly feel exhilarated by the keen sense of seeing everything for the first time. A perky, broad-beamed tug goes down the river towing barges, and Old Man Molineaux follows it narrowly, musing out of his thoughts.

"Or there's Crowley, see, he was all right till he swore *off*. Been drinking five-ten years, working the whole time, brought boats down the goddamn river so drunk you'd swear he couldn't see the end of his cigar. And then last New Year's he took the pledge—wife kept after him, he got scared—and what d'ya know! First goddamn *sober* trip, he piles seventy-five thousand dollars' worth of oil onto that shoal above Ochre Creek, heh-heh-heh—

"Or Gallagher, for instance, just as an example—he didn't get drunk soon *enough*. I mean, he come aboard one night, and he had the shakes, you know, didn't get in his nips on the pier. And he got the convulsions, and passed out down there around the green blinker, and the bastard didn't come *to* till he hit the railroad bridge—crumpled up the whole side of a two-thousand-ton Esso!

"So, listen, they *all* drink, you gotta drink, nothing wrong with a man drinking. What do these young fool doctors know! I just had me a night of easterly luck, that night—you probably heard about my night, eh, Chief? Well, that's all it was. Goddamn river *retired* me, that's all." He squints jealously at it across the autumn marsh, quietly embittered. "Just threw me off it, whap! and it was too late to run. It was *that* finished me. I wasn't such a horrible old man till then."

He snorts the thought away, but I see him snatching peeks down through the bushes toward the bungalow again, his freshly shaven cheeks giving him an unnatural, vaguely embalmed look. He is worried, but has no words for worry.

"Good Lord," he finally exclaims uneasily. "Don't tell me we finished off all them cans! God Almighty, we make us a pair, don't we? And you're all right, Dan, yes sir. You're a hell of a lot stronger than you look." And he is on his feet, talking his way into the shack again to put on his shirt and shoes, cursing obdurate buttons and overturning piles of magazines, groaning over his corns, but, all in all, feeling somewhat better to be on that day's business—even though Sunday is a day of special difficulties, which only the wily and the prudent can survive, Saturday night having been the most imprudent night of all.

Then we are off in an unsteady jaunt down the hill, at the foot of which I intend to leave him, realizing that if I don't phone my mother, she will be in a panic in an hour. He is grandly hinting at sylvan bottles cached away against just such occasions, and apocryphal cronies less profligate than he, when, coming through the bushes, he spies two cars pulled up in Bertha's dooryard (a mud-splashed pickup truck, and a Ford hard-top kept finicky clean), and mutters: "Uh-uh, she called the family in, that ain't so good," but then stiffening again, and tilting his nose into the air, "Goddammit though, we'll just go in and *visit* for a minute. That's what we'll do. . . . 'Sides, the niece's wop husband almost always brings along some of that Dago Red on Sundays, heh-heh. . . ." And before I know it I am trailing after him through the rusted screen door into a parlor too small for all the Molineauxs it contains.

There is nineteen-year-old Wanda, with her baby-fat hips and bobby socks and pudgy ankles and pert jolly face; Wanda with her charm bracelets, and vermilion lipstick, and bra ridden high on her back from the weight of large soft breasts; Wanda, whom

I have seen wheeling a one-year-old girl-baby near the service stations, giggling with girl friends still in high school, passing the months while her young husband puts in his service time; Wanda with her movie magazines, her white even teeth with the traces of chocolate between them, her hair mostly in curlers under a skimpy bandanna; Wanda, always vaguely odorous of diapers, and Woolworth's 35¢ perfume, and TV dinners, and caramel sundaes; simple Wanda, trusting Wanda, whose face automatically lights up at the sight of her old man, and just as quickly dims when she notices his condition.

There are other Molineauxs too: nephews with wide ties, and faces flushed by overeating, and axle grease ground into their fingers beyond the reach of the most abrasive soap—volunteer firemen, Legionnaires, bowlers all; and their wives, who gossip in front of the Post Office in the mornings, and wash the ashtrays every afternoon, and are hypnotized through manless evenings by the Great Grey Eye that can be seen spectrally glowing through every picture window in Grafton; and their kids—the boys muddy, raucous, wily, armed to a man with plastic machine guns or chrome pistols; and the girls supercilious and bejeweled, with their dolls that have ten changes of wardrobe and hair that can be Tonied; and all the indeterminate infants, who alternately squall and gurgle and sneeze.

The room is thick with Molineaux Sunday life: the smell of roast potatoes and overdone beef and scalded coffee and cigarette smoke; women chattering, men arguing local politics, the howls of children hit in the mouth by other children; the scolding, the raillery, the clichés repeated like beads; the bathroom full of diapers, the dining room full of Sunday overcoats, the kitchen full of youngsters upending Cokes. It is the kind of rich family turmoil I first remember longing for when I was only seven, and visited a houseful of noisy and uncouth cousins, after which the thick stair carpets, the muffling portieres, and the hollowly ticking hall clocks of my muted world seemed funereal and dispiriting, as if they were an embodiment of a failure of feeling of which I was the unwitting heir.

Old Man Molineaux stands in the door, swaying slightly, and saying too loud: "Well, now, what'd'ya know? . . . 'Lo, Rufe . . . Bert, how's tricks? . . . You're gettin' fat there, Angie," all the time cagey little blue eyes darting around, looking for wine. Bertha starts to whimper at the sight of him.

The men are uneasy, trade covert looks, and then become stiffly jovial. The women look as if they want to cluck, and shake their heads, but remain impenetrable in an embarrassed righteousness, as this is impossible. Various children approach the funny old man, whom they associate with a lurching gait, a strong reek of breath, gnarled hands that smell thrilling and dangerous, and a flow of queer questions. . . . "That's our soupy old uncle, he's a pirate, and he ain't had a bath in maybe—oh, *never*, maybe!"

Old Man Molineaux musses hair, and pinches arms, and smothers squirming shoulders. "Jimmy, you're as funny-looking as a runny-nose rabbit. . . . God-a-mighty, who's *this?* Don't know you, you're some Indian girl stole out of a tent, that's what you are. . . . Get off my corns there, Horace, or I'll put you out to sea in a bottle. . . . Look at that petticoat, well I'll be damned, show me all that frisky lace now, well you're pretty fancy, aren't you, Arnelle?" ogling and winking and fumbling until the little girl is called away by a sharp command from her mother.

Old Man Molineaux steps forward into a dustpan full of smashed china, which he recognizes as the breakage of last night's ugliness, but resolutely ignores, fastening instead upon his thirty-three-year-old nephew, Rufe the Contractor, who has his father's lean cold nose, and ungiving mouth, and who, at the moment, is trying to hide a jelly glass of his brother-in-law's red wine behind his back.

"Well, Rufe, gonna snow any time soon, you think? Better get all them dinky little houses built before the first frost. Heard some of them up on King Phillip's that you put up two years ago already got cracks in the foundation, heh-heh-heh! . . . Good God, what are you blubbering about, Bertha!" his mouth strained with the costs of this conviviality.

Wanda's chubby face is not adequate to express her alarm, and she shifts her daughter to her other hip, and murmurs: "Oh, Pa, why'd you have to—?" breaking off so precipitously that I realize that my presence is making it difficult for everyone, except Old Man Molineaux. I peer closely at a calendar-landscape on the wall nearby, as if studying the brushwork in a late Van Gogh.

Rufe sniffs and says manfully: "I'm going to almost envy you this winter, Uncle Will, you know? You get all the headaches in the winter, in my business—uh, like you say," deciding against being surreptitious with his glass, and sipping openly. "Cheaper than a trip south anyway."

"Yah, that's right," Bert puts in. "Think they'd take *me*, Uncle?"

Old Man Molineaux's eyes narrow, Bertha is unable to stifle a gulping sob, and Wanda looks from me to her father and says helplessly: "Oh, and Eddie's learning radio, Pa. He got his transfer. . . . I—I got a letter yesterday," her eyes misting over in the nervous silence that comes down like snow, all of a sudden.

Little flirtatious Arnelle breaks loose from her mother in the midst of this, and minces up to Old Man Molineaux, turning her stiff skirt back to show him her petticoat. "And there's the blue pantries to match, too, and Tulip has the exact same," holding up a platinum-haired, long-lashed doll, its modest crotch exposed for the Old Man to see.

"Arnelle! Really!" her mother exclaims. "Come away from there now."

"That's all right, Angie," the Old Man says in a distracted rasp. "Never pass up a chance to peek under a girl's skirt, heh-heh-heh!" but he is plainly more interested in the wine. "What cha got there, Bert? That some of your *own* brew?" one hand nonchalant in his jacket pocket to disguise its shivers. "One thing the Italians can do, I always say, is make that goddamn *veeno*. Yes, sir! . . . Nothing like a glass of *veeno*, now is there, Rufe? Beats cider all to hell in my view," on the move now in the crowded room. "I mean, with cider you get yourself a jug, and you got a jug of plain old apple juice today—but day after tomorrow, what have you got?" swaying so close to a spindly end table with an imitation milk glass lamp on it that someone gasps aloud. "You got nothing but a jug of goddamn sour vinegar, that's what! You're *forced* to catch it on that day in between, see. You *got* to drink the whole con-sarn thing, or you don't get your value out of it. But with a bottle of *veeno*, well," frowning, and weary, and certain now no one will take the hint. "Goddammit, where's your manners anyway! Don't care for myself, but at least give my friend *Dan* a drink of your lousy con-sarn wine!" slumping down in a straight chair. "Never thought I'd see the day when someone went dry in *my* house," glaring at them all in a fury.

"Oh, you might as well, Aunt Bertha," Rufe says with a knowing pout. "Won't make much difference now—"

"What do you mean!" Old Man Molineaux snorts, giving up all pretense of civility. "Won't make much difference. . . . What d'ya mean? What in hell's going on around here anyway? Bunch of sour-mouthed loons—"

"But didn't Doc—?" Bertha exclaims, and then claps a fat hand over her mouth in horrified dismay. "Oh, Lordy!" and collapses into tears.

"What about Doc? Doc Menaker? I got nothing to do with Doc Menaker! Goddamn young fool! Gimme a *drink* in my own house, I tell you!"

Chaos. One of the women goes for wine; a baby starts to howl at the raised voices; Bert begins: "Now, wait a minute, Uncle"; the kids choose this moment to turn up the kitchen radio; Wanda fiddles nervously with the bawling infant's blanket, only increasing its outcries; and Bertha exclaims: "But it wasn't me, Will. Doc and Sally said it was for your own good! And I," sobbing again at the very thought of herself, "I'm just at the end of my rope. I don't know about these things. And I got to get to my jobs, stiff arm or no," raising the arm in my direction bewilderedly. "And if you're *sick*, Will—and that's what they say—well, up there they'll know what to *do!* I don't know what to do," blubbering hopelessly now, "and Doc says they'll feed you good, I asked him special about that—I'm just at the end of my rope, Angie, that's all," taking the offered handkerchief, and letting her niece pat her back in that most helpless and most comforting of gestures.

"They'll *feed* me! Why, you goddamn fool—you mean you let—!"

"Oh, Pa, can't you leave her *alone!*" Wanda suddenly cries, stamping her foot like a hurt child about to weep. "Making these terrible scenes in front of—just *anybody* this way! And everyone knows about it, the whole town! What do you think it's like for us kids?—Henry Molineaux, turn the radio down! Can't somebody make them turn it down in there?— And what do you think my girl friends say when they see you—oh, re*lieving* yourself right out in broad daylight, right on the Main Street of town. I could just die from *shame!*" She joins her mother in tears.

Old Man Molineaux is befuddled, and then unbelieving, and finally defiant. "Well, I'll be *screwed!* I'll be *buggered!* You telling me Sal and Doc Menaker—? Well, I'll be *damned!* Good God Almighty, Dan, they're running me off to that *Farm!* ... You mean the Doc's gonna sign them papers on me without my consent?"

"Now, Uncle Will," Rufe conciliates, "just look at it soberly. *You* know—"

"I know my own goddamn daughter is railroading me to a *home!*" Old Man Molineaux yells with a pound of the chair arm. "*That's* what I know! I know my own flesh and blood has turned on me! Just when I'm crippled, when my goddamn feet—"

"Now, listen, Uncle Will—"

"'Listen!'" grabbing the glass his niece has brought. "I ain't gonna listen to any of you! What d'ya know about a man's life! ... And you're just like your dad, Rufe, you always was a frowner just like him, a goddamn ninny, cutting down *trees!*" a certain haughtiness tinges his rasp. "Look at it, Chief. Bunch of grocery clerks and storekeepers, trying to cut me down like I was an old tree or some con-sarn thing!"

"But, Will, Sally said—"

"—whelps turning on the old bastard, like even creatures in the woods don't do!" in a sudden ecstasy. "Get rid of that tree! What's it doing there? What's it *good* for? . . . Wait'll the old wolf's got a sprung back, and his feet are going, and the winter's in his knees, and then—whap!—finish him off! Pen him up like a broken-down dog! It's unnatural! *Sally* says!" he roars, lurching to his feet. "I know what Sally says! 'It's just *mortify*ing, it's hu*mili*ating, it makes me want to *throw* up!'" in a sneering, evil parody. "'Get the lecherous old bastard to sit home, and drool in his oatmeal, and say I'm sorry when he wets his pants, or I'll *fix* him for good!' . . . That's what your daughter says. Well, ain't it? Ain't it? . . . But she ain't no daughter of *mine*, Bertha Kelly! She ain't no goddamn Molineaux!"

Further chaos during this, everyone uncomfortable and alarmed, a few faces peering in from the kitchen now where the radio is off, Rufe muttering to Bert: "Must have had something left up there," Wanda sniffling over her fingernails, Old Man Molineaux gesturing and gulping at his wine.

"And how do I know if she ever *was!* God-a-mighty, how does a man *ever* know for sure!" this such a palpable foolishness in light of Sally's Molineaux nose, and Molineaux quick temper, that Bertha's sob, and Rufe's exclamation, and the general outcry of protest, are little more than formalities. "—'cept how his kids love him in his miserable old age," the Old Man concludes. "You can always tell your own *flesh*."

"Now look, Uncle, it's been decided, and that's that. What's the use of going on this way?"

"What's the *use—!*"

"You can't control yourself, can't handle your liquor any more, and *you* know it as well as anyone."

"What in hell do *you* know about liquor? You never been drunk in your whole stupid life!"

"Well, now, Uncle, I know what I can *see*."

"Jesus-One-Eyed-Christ, they're *all* turning on me! The goddamn in-laws too. Ain't even my own *blood!*" raising his blotchy nose to the neutral ceiling in mute appeal. "I'll just crawl away and die! I swear I will! . . . My own no-good son turns away from me in the public street, my baby-girl here curses me 'cause I got to take a natural *piss* sometimes—and what in God's name is a man to *do* with it? Save it in a goddamn bottle of—of *veeno?*"

"Really, Will Molineaux, there're children here! Can't you—?"

"—tastes pretty much like that anyway," finishing off his glass with a completely insincere pucker of his lips. "Children? *Horse-piss!* I don't see any children. Where in hell are they?" looking under a pillow, in back of chairs, even lifting his feet one after the other. "I don't see any con-sarn children. Not *my* children! My children think I'm nothing but a horrible old loon, don't they? My children ain't even *ashamed*," peering malevolently at weeping Wanda, "to railroad their old dad to a goddamn farm! . . . Are you? Are you? And you was always my *baby*, too," the scorn in his voice like a whiplash. "Good God, I never would have believed it, Chief!" gesturing so rashly all of a sudden that he brushes the milk glass lamp, which teeters and starts to go over. "I would have *fought* any man," catching it miraculously as everyone stares in disbelief, "said my own kids would put their teeth into me! . . . You live sixty years with your eyes open, and you never see your own goddamn snotty nose!" He sets the lamp upright with a precise flourish, and peers at everyone disdainfully. "Drunk, am I? Not *this* goddamn year of the Republic!"

"Oh, Rufe," Bertha suddenly says, "maybe we been too hasty. See, Wanda, the way your dad caught that? Maybe we could talk to Sally, and—"

Old Man Molineaux is outraged. He is also finishing off my glass of wine. "Oh, no you don't! The day I beg to my own daughter'll be the last goddamn day of my life! She ain't gonna turn me on her silly bar-b-que pit! 'Cause I won't *cook!*" He stares at them all defiantly, his eyes fogged with drink and emotion. "I won't, Berth. I swear I won't. . . . I'd rather find me a culvert somewheres to live in, I'd rather collect huckleberries in my hat! I will, too, I'll do it!" clapping the greasy old cap on his head,

and turning away with a shiver toward the door, where he vows:
"I'll go off and hide in the woods, you darn fool idiots! See if I
don't. And I won't shave for no one either!" slamming the screen
door behind us, and muttering: "That's what you get for trying
to make up, Chief, that's just what you get—"

· 3 ·

My memory of that day fragments again at this point—the wine
on top of the beer on top of the night before. I can't recall why I
stayed with him, though it was undoubtedly that curiously filial
protectiveness that you feel for anyone whose mistakes have edu-
cated you; or where I thought we were going, though I suppose
I was on the lookout for a phone. I just tagged along in a fog, out
of which certain images and certain snatches of talk emerged like
lampposts, solid enough for me to remember to this day.

We are cutting through backyards among soot-caked incinera-
tors and abandoned flivvers that settle into the weeds on tire-less,
rusty rims. We are menaced by murderous washlines that Old
Man Molineaux never seems to gauge right, always ducking his
head while still four feet away, feinting and bobbing like a
rheumy boxer, or coming up smack into them with a strangled
curse, and almost beheading himself. The afternoon has worsened
over; an ominous shelf of grey moves hugely across the sky; birds
fleeing the North are lonely specks of black far up, tossed by Ca-
nadian winds. We stand in a run-down orchard among leafless,
twisted fruit trees that no longer bear, Old Man Molineaux hiding

behind a wholly inadequate trunk, in plain sight of red-checked café curtains, to relieve himself in a great gush.

"—goddamn bladder's gone, everything just runs right through me now. . . . Used to steal pears here, whole sacks of pears, fifty years ago. . . . None of them houses then, only Sootby's barnful of squeaky bats. . . . All wild woods right back there where they trapped the last wolf in '14. . . . Weary old ugly customer, half starved out of his mind or they wouldn't have got him, not him! . . . Something in them wild eyes wouldn't forgive 'em either!"

Then we are stumbling around woodpiles, and skirting rubbish heaps, and Old Man Molineaux is smelling the wind like a blind and mangy stag, antlers ruined butting into trees, and cursing his family—baffled, comic old man's profanity as rhetorical as a daguerreotype, that deals exhaustively with Bertha, Rufe, Wanda, and others I do not know, rising to inarticulate heights of foaming rage when it comes to Sally, and then dying away as abruptly as it came.

"—and where was Billy? . . . Come home to bolt his food and then run off to his cars, and them other young punks. . . . Don't even care when he hears the news, can't wait, his own pa, too. . . . Tell you the world's getting to be a cold place, ain't *my* world any more. . . . All this darn TV, look at 'em, like a lot of darn skeletons on the roofs!" standing there in a withered little meadow near an ancient stone fence, motionless as a soggy scarecrow, doomed eyes flashing contempt on distant antennas. I want to say something to him about Billy; I would be Billy's spokesman to him, and his to Billy; I hate the certainty I feel that this hurt, this misunderstanding, is the ordained process by which life gets on; I hate it, unreasonably, in the name of my own past lonesomeness.

"Don't care about nothing, rather be inside. . . . If he was smart he'd be off pulling his whistle in the damn woods somewheres, like I was at his age, heh-heh-heh!" cheered for a moment by this fanciful wickedness. "Good healthy *screw* outside, that's the best, woman sort of lets loose, gets the derndest ideas. . . . But next to that just spillin' it out on the ground, *away* somewheres, letting your mind go, see, just wham-wham-wham. . . . Used to think of some dark Indian gal, black tits, oil in her hair, don't *know* enough to give a damn, take a leak in front of a man and who cares! Heh-heh-heh . . . Ever have any ideas like that? Told you I was wild, Chief! Wanted to screw the *world* when I was your age—"

"I know that feeling," I murmur. "But listen, about your son—"

"Oh, I know about him all right. Christ, he's just like me, ain't he? Why in hell do you think I get so *mad?*"

At which moment, we become involved with dogs, for whom we represent the only diversion that somnolent Sunday has to offer. A big scruffy black and white bitch yaps gaily at us, tail aloft, hurling herself at the end of her chain as we pass, pride in her alertness changing into thwarted passion to join our jaunt. Others take it up. I fancy soft ears being cocked a quarter of a mile away. I imagine a townful of bored dogs perking up, coming out from under porches and autos and brittle forsythia bushes, sniffing self-importantly, raising a trial bark to let everyone know they are on the job, and taking off to scent out the situation. A young calico mongrel sports around us in a frenzy of ecstatic barking, knowing Old Man Molineaux perfectly well, but pretending he is a burglar. I do a skittering dance. He rushes toward us, sprawls down on his front feet, rump and tail stuck stylishly up in the air, at the ready, and barks furiously at our feet.

"Oh, stop it, you darn fool!" the Old Man yells with a snigger, and the dog is up and circling around us, raising the alarm. A beady-eyed little dachshund sticks a snout out from behind a garage not ten feet from us, and yaps-yaps-yaps ferociously, as if to make up in sheer noise for her size. Old Man Molineaux freezes, stares pop-eyed with mock terror, and then yells: "Boom! Whap! Whoosh!" at which the dachshund gives a last panicked yap, and vanishes in a pell-mell thresh of midget legs. A big regal collie stares at us with gentle seriousness two houses away, and allows herself a single, throaty bark.

Old Man Molineaux laughs and laughs. "Goddamn dogs're the

only things that have any fun in this town any more. Sometimes I got five-six follow me home at night, making so much racket you'd think the Old Leather Man'd come back from wherever he went. . . . They get fed up just like us."

He blinks, staggers over a hidden root, and straightens up, panting. "Think I can talk Sally out of it though? . . . But that's right, you don't know her, I guess. . . . Well, sure I can. If I could get me one little drink, I could talk her out of it," and I seem to have known all along that we are heading for Sally's, though somehow it hasn't registered, and I start to say: "Well, look, I ought to be getting home—"

But Old Man Molineaux won't hear of it. "Not on your life! Listen, I'll come up with 'least a can of beer or something. Or afterward we'll go out to Ben's—I'll bet he's got a little reserve bottle stuck away someplace. . . . No, you just hold on, Chief. . . . 'Sides, I'd appreciate some—oh," clearing his throat with embarrassment, "some company, you know? . . . No, and say, tell me about your trip again. If it was me, I'd head for Alaska or someplace. Someplace that's still *natural*," trying to intrigue me with his vision of Alaska, a vision mostly compounded of the dog teams, and snowbound cabins, and roaring saloons of Gold Rush days. I listen dutifully, knowing that no winsome Chaplins eat their shoes there any more, but not wanting to point this out to him.

A similar thought occurs to him. "But back here—I don't know. No one even goes out in the wind any more. The goddamn dogs bark at you if you walk alone in the woods—can't imagine a man *doing* such a thing, unless he's up to no good! But it's the pride I can't stand—they're all proud of bein' just like everyone else, and never doing anything risky, or wild, or just plain quick-witted! They're *proud* of it, my own goddam kin, too—"

"Children are scared of the woods, they say," I mumble. "And there are all kinds of woods—"

He is not listening. "Won't nobody around here sail after dark any more, even with their damn auxiliaries, and charts, and foolproof compasses . . . don't want to be caught out there in the dark, only the scary stars, once the sun's gone. I just don't understand it."

"But you *do*, Mr. Molineaux. That's the trouble."

He looks at me sharply, and laughs. "Yah, I guess I do. Damn stars put you in your place, don't they? . . . But where in hell's *wild* America any more, that's what I want to know? Where've all them Indians gone to, and the sailors, and bums, and crazy damn fools with funny notions in their heads?" He shakes his old head gloomily. " 'Swear, in twenty years we'll all be city people, won't we, hidin' in closets, lookin' at the TV— Thank God, I'll be done-for by then!"

"Me, too," I murmur. "Or different enough anyway to make it somehow."

We are passing a line where a capacious pair of pink rayon drawers flirts in the breeze, and a fetching white cotton brassière trails like a forlorn streamer, and Old Man Molineaux pauses to sniff: "Say one thing for Manzini though. Got a real classy wife belongs to those." He ponders for a moment, and then concludes: "Nope, wouldn't give us a drink though, no matter what lying story I told. The wife's built for fun, like you see, but old Gus—he figures a woman should only have herself a drink when she's on her knees down there in the Roman church—though he don't go himself, the hypocritical bastard!"

We blunder through a hedge, and come out on Route One near an ugly stucco house with a peeling "Live Bait" sign in its front yard, at the sight of which Old Man Molineaux straightens up, licking parched lips, and assuming (as best he can in his winded condition) a casual stroll.

"She can see us from the windows, see, and they might've phoned her up. Goddamn old woman never had the nerve to take the blame on herself. But you can't tell me Sal's gonna let them run her old man off to a *home*." He swaggers up his confidence. "Oh, Sally's all right, she gets huffy and mean, but—no, she's all right, you'll see. And I'm sober as a cod."

But there is no one home. "Stilty," I mutter blearily to myself.
"Here's two queer fish come to find you—"

The prim living room of blond maple furniture, with its Sears-
Roebuck modern lamps, an empty magazine stand, a console TV,
and a paint-it-yourself-by-the-numbers seascape, looks as if no
one had ever been there. A clock ticks complacently in the silence.
I follow Old Man Molineaux into the kitchen, looking for some
palpable sign of Sally. There is nothing but an empty coffeecup
with cigarette ash in the saucer, a paper edition of a love novel
with its back broken, and a Kleenex on which a wide, finely
shaped mouth has been blotted. Old Man Molineaux is banging
cupboard doors, looking for whisky, and comes up with half a
pint of rye from among the canned goods. "There now, Chief, told
you I'd fix us up," he says. "They won't miss a shot apiece. Take a
chair. . . . They're down to the marina, I guess."

We sit at the formica table, and he sloshes whisky into a
couple of jelly glasses, and accepts a cigarette, the ashes from
which he carefully collects in his trouser cuff. "She ran Jack so
hard about *his* goddamn ashes last year, he up and quit," he ex-
plains ruefully. "So watch it. . . . Oh, she's hard-minded. God-a-
mighty! But no fool Irishman's any match for her, heh-heh-heh,"
staring at his glass, and then raising it to closed eyes, to wince
with the drunkard's classic response to the first burning gulp of
no-nonsense booze. A cough, a grimace, watered eyes, and a new
edge to his rasp when he says: "Don't care what you—w-h-a-a-a-p!
—say, it's better than that con-sarn liniment for a sprung back.
Tried drinking both, too, so I can *tell* you."

I take this opportunity to use the phone in the living room. My
mother's voice expertly conveys the concern I have caused her,
but she hopes to evoke my remorse by bravely not mentioning it.

"No, dear, I assumed you were all right. And after one-thirty I
decided you weren't coming home. But then I was so worried that
you'd think you'd kept me up that I tossed for an hour. Still, I
don't really *need* sleep any more, so I hope you didn't think twice

about it. . . . But *are* you all right, dear? You—you don't sound like yourself."

"Yes, I'm fine. I didn't get much sleep either, but . . . No, I'm all right, I'm just a little plastered, that's all."

"Oh, Danny! I knew it. . . . In the middle of the afternoon? And on *Sunday?*"

"Oh, Christ, Mom, what's that got to do with it? . . . But anyway, look, I'm with Mr. Molineaux, he's off on a toot, and I think I'll stick with him for a while."

"You're going to catch cold, Danny. You're going to have your trouble again. Why don't you just come *home*, dear?"

"Because I want to stick it out with Mr. Molineaux. I can't explain now."

"Well, of course I've never wanted you to feel that you owed an explanation to *me*. You know that I trust you, no matter what you do. . . . But—but you'll be careful? I mean, he's—well, he drinks so *much*, dear. He can be dangerous, and—"

"Okay, okay, I'll be careful. And, really, I'm drunk *half* the time in New York, you know," regretting this detail as it comes out of my mouth.

"Don't exaggerate now. The Vergers always exaggerated everything. I'm sure you're just exaggerating—"

"All right, yes, but don't worry about me."

"Well, you young people are so troubled these days, it just makes my heart ache. And of course the *examples* you've had have only made it—"

"Look, I've got to hang up. Just don't worry. I didn't *mean* to worry you, you know. I'll get home when I can."

"All right, dear. If you *have* to. I'll probably still be up. . . . But don't be concerned about me. I don't want you to even *think* about me now. Not once. Mothers just have to be foolish sometimes. I know what a trial it can be for their children, but it's only because we love you, and can't help wishing—"

I go back to my drink with a will, and Old Man Molineaux grows talkative, his fears and angers lulled by the third shot I hear him sneaking out of the bottle while I am at the sink watering my second. He talks about Sally: the brightest of his children; always had a mind of her own; used to go fishing with him; better with a sailing dink than he ever was; all the boys sniffing around in high school; captain of girls' basketball her senior year, what with those long legs; got to be assistant supervisor in the telephone company in just fourteen months; never should have married Jack Doughty but you couldn't talk her out of it; knew what she wanted and got it—a washer-dryer combination, and a rotisserie, and a vacuum cleaner as light as an overnight bag, and a Rambler station wagon, and the TV, and a clock-radio up in the bedroom, and an electric blanket with dual controls; Sally'd always do all right, and he guessed she was a good girl when you made allowances; oh, he knew that; she'd named her son William, hadn't she? Sure. Four years old and looked just like his granddad; a Molineaux, every bit of him, except for that damn fool last name that sounded like a pain you got in your legs. . . .

"Oh, me and Sal argue, always did—she'd stand right up to me, face'd get so red you'd think she was going to bust you one, heh-heh-heh. . . . But I like a kid with fire, gumption, not like most of them today you talk to, and they listen but they *ain't* listening somehow—never can figure out what the darn fools are thinking about—what're they *thinking* about, Dan? You're a smart boy. . . . But like Billy there, last night, goddamn young punk. Or Wanda, blubbers if you just look at her—sometimes I don't understand my own *kids*. . . . But Sal was never like that. Maybe 'cause me and Bertha that first time—well," winking at me sagely. "I don't understand a lot of things any more, maybe it's the drink, like they say. . . . But, anyway, I'm sixty goddamn years old, a grandfather twice over, and I never been to New York and them places, but I've *lived*, I ain't wasted it, and," suddenly giggling, "and I'm still a goddamn old fool!" happily, insistently drunk now.

"But come on though. Let's just walk us out there while I get this damn business cleared up, and we'll do some real drinking afterward," leaving his glass and the nearly empty pint bottle in

plain sight on the table, so self-confident now that his earlier
caution seems idiotic. "Should only take a couple a minutes, and
they usually keep them some cold beer out there, too— Lord,
look at that! Might just get us some rain before sundown, wind's
gone around into the east—"

He no longer cares who may be watching from the curtained
windows we pass, or the front seats of cars that pass us, but
plods on in a haze of talk, while I try to keep up. It is chilly now,
that bleak chill of an October overcast afternoon when houses
and fences and trees are all bathed in the same shadowless grey
gloom of oncoming winter; and we are in the poorer part of
Grafton now, out where the town proliferated in the early Twenties into dreary one-floor shingle houses, with lean-to garages and
weedy driveways, some clustered around an occasional run-down
Colonial farmhouse that somehow survived the parceling off of
its land, and now stands empty, shuttered, in a tangle of honey-
suckle gone wild.

We cut down a side road making for the river. An uneven strip
of cracked sidewalk stretches ahead dismally. A cinder-block
chimney lets out a curl of blue smoke. Wicker chairs are cushion-
less on woeful porches. A little boy, with a harelip, hiding in a
rowboat up on sawhorses in a side yard, stares at us expression-
lessly over the sights of his chromium six-gun. I remember the
lonely winter twilights of youth in half a dozen ugly New England
towns; I remember aching for New York, for the anonymous
warmth of the thrilling cities where my father usually was. I remember hungering for life to begin, and a tinge of depression
edges over me.

The road swings to the left, running parallel with the river,
and ahead the great span of the bridge looms, cold and high on
its concrete piers. The riverside is a glut of boatyards, grubby
little twine factories, fish shacks, and marinas right here; a maze
of ailanthus trees, trashcans, and hand-lettered signs, one of which
says, "Doughty's: Boats—Tackle—Bait." We turn into a rutted
yard where barnacled lobster pots are stacked and empty oil

drums rust in grim weeds and hauled-out motor cruisers, up on blocking, sit huge and blind in canvas shrouds. There is another car there beside the Rambler.

We pause to catch our breath against a tar-splashed spile and Old Man Molineaux glances at the office-shack out on the end of the pier. The sound of a radio drifts back to us across the brackish water slapping around pilings, and the Old Man shivers involuntarily.

"Good Lord, that giggler Midgie Zander's out there, too. Ain't I ever going to get a rest? This girl's so *silly*, Chief, I swear you'd think she wasn't but fifteen. . . . I don't know what Sal *sees* in the darn fool, 'cept she can boss her. God-a-mighty!"

We venture out on the creaking pier, and I make the mistake of keeping too close to Old Man Molineaux so I can catch him if he lurches too far. Of course, he notices this, and a haughty wildness comes up in his eyes. "Goddamn it, don't *crowd* me there, son! You're stepping on my heels! If you're too damn drunk to walk straight, go on back there and wait for me."

Before the door of the shack, he hesitates for a moment, adjusting his cap to a more rakish angle, and actually brushing off his wrinkled old jacket. "Young self-righteous fools," he mutters. "Look at a man's shirt collar before they look at his face! . . . But I'm pretty sober anyway."

Meanwhile, I hear snatches of talk from inside: "—and you get this table lamp as a gift with it, Midgie, with that new imitation kind of parchment shade— Get your hands out of that, Willy! Jack, get your son away from that oil can!— And the whole set only costs forty-five dollars down. . . ."

Old Man Molineaux takes a fortifying sniff, and opens the door.

The shack is crowded with spools of fishing line, display cards of hooks and lures, a chugging Coca-Cola freezer, and a stack of yellowing linen fishing caps with green celluloid visors. It smells of marine oil, and salt water, and a faint trace of rose-based perfume. A radio blares dance music to which no one is listening,

but without which everyone there would have felt vaguely uncomfortable, not knowing why.

Jack Doughty and Midgie's laconic husband are in conference
over an outboard motor, dismantled all over the floor, with that
happy preoccupation of grown men with the intricacies of en-
gines—as egoless, for the moment, as enthralled boys, simply not
hearing the chatter, and not seeing the piqued looks, which the
women occasionally level at them, as at a source of elusive, irritating power.

"Look at them, Midgie," Sally is saying scornfully. "They're
never happy unless they're covered with grease! . . . Ye gods,
Jack, can't you at least be careful of those slacks? I'll never get
that disgusting *mess* off them!" The muttering and fiddling go on
uninterrupted, and Midgie's husband sucks his lower lip, and
says: "Nope, it's the fuel line, what'd I tell you?"

Sally balances carelessly on one lean flank atop the Coke machine, the sharp bones of her cheeks and shoulders and hips so
prominent they pick up the smoky light. She has small breasts,
hard as lemons in her purple cardigan, a flat belly, and a tensed
white neck. She keeps sweeping her long black hair back from
her face indifferently, to reveal a toothy, ironical mouth, and
black eyes squinted in cold appraisal. She is the sort of girl who
smokes like a man, and doesn't miss much, and says whatever she
thinks; and I say to myself instantly: an enemy of men.

She catches sight of Old Man Molineaux standing in the door,
frowns angrily, and warns: "Now, I know what you're going to
say, Pa, and I just want to tell you I won't listen to it. . . . What
are you doing down here anyway?"

Old Man Molineaux's confidence carries him over this, and
through the introductions, during which Sally accords me a
single, curious glance that makes me miss my necktie—the sort of
quick, downward swoop of eyes that makes a man feel instantly
disreputable; a female glance at once sardonic and yet coldly
sensual. "Oh, yes," she says. "I guess I've seen you around," looking from me to Old Man Molineaux, as if momentarily interested

that I, better born, more fortunate than she, all she desired and thereby all she detested, a source of the same kind of jealous resentment (because I have escaped to New York) that I used to feel with May because of Europe, should seek her reprobate father for a companioṇ on a dreary Sunday afternoon. Or did I only imagine all that?

"Get him a beer, Jack," she orders, slipping off the Coke machine.

Jack Doughty opens me a can, wiping his hands on his sports shirt with odd formality, and mumbles as an afterthought: "How about you, Will?" long since having given over trying to cope with the problems of that family.

"No, not me, Jack," Old Man Molineaux says primly, glad for the opportunity to turn one down, and peeking surreptitiously at Sally. "Little early for me, you know. . . . Always try to wait for the sunset gun, heh-heh. . . . But, well," as if this has earned him his dispensation, "well, all right, maybe just a can, don't mind if I do, just something to sip on, you know." Midgie Zander, a luminous ginger-haired girl in Sunday pumps and too much lipstick, giggles nervously.

"Well, *there* he is, there's my grandson," spying Sally's boy under the long bill of one of the fishing caps. "What're you doing there, Willy? Come here, want you to meet a sailor. . . . Dan here's off to the old countries, kids. . . . When're we going after whales, you and me?"

The boy looks up at him suspiciously from the floor. "Oh, you never caught no whale. And whales can't fly neither."

"But they can go deep *down*, Willy. Yes, sir!"

"Aw, who wants to go deep? I got a jet plane at home with a gun on it. I got a moon-book better'n that."

"Oh, you have, have you," taking a long serious choke on his can, and trying to remember that he is not there to argue with the boy. "Well, Sal," he begins manfully. "What's all this about the Farm, eh? You wouldn't believe what your ma, and Rufe, and even your little sis just put me through. You ask Dan here. I swear, they're all over there right now signin' them papers on me. . . . You know, I think your cousin Rufe's behind it—he never liked me, the darn fool—and then they had the goddamn gall to try and tell me it was all your idea—"

She stares at him with ominous impatience, seeing in his bleary face all the hand-me-down underwear from grown cousins, and the meager pork sandwiches taken to school in Manzini's paper bags, and the certain knowledge of the girls in gym class that she could not even afford Kotex when her periods began (because her father drank too much), and tore up pillow slips instead; everything that had humiliated her, and against which her proud nature (*his* nature) had wounded itself so long, and eventually grown hard. She stares at him, and waits like a portent.

"And did Wanda speak up for the old man? Did she take up for me? No, sir! Not *this* year! . . . You should have heard what she said, Jack. I wouldn't repeat in front of women some of the things that goddamn ungrateful child said about her own crippled-up father! Silly little bitch!"

"I suppose that's just what you'll call me, too, Pa, when I—"

"You? Oh, not you, Sal. Wanda just plain don't understand, she's still a kid. You recall what a cry-baby she always was? Sitting in a corner blubbering, scared if the *wind* even come up, I could never figure what made her like that. . . . But *you* know the way I am, you don't begrudge me my puny pleasures now I'm sick and old. They couldn't make me believe that. Just 'cause I got a little *drunk*. . . . I said it to Dan here, I said, 'Why, that goddamn sly bunch of *ninnies!* Tryin' to duck the blame that way! Sal knows a man takes a couple a drinks now and then—eh, Jack? Sure—and sometimes he gets horrible in his liquor, but he feels *sorry* the next day, real *sorry* about it—but you can't tell me she's gonna agree to run him off to some *Farm* up country just because—' "

"I *won't* have you touching my mother!" Sally explodes all of a sudden with a pound of her little fist on the freezer. "Do you understand? I *won't* have it. I won't put *up* with it a *week* longer!"

and something in her fury has nothing to do with Bertha. "Do you under*stand* that? . . . Well, it doesn't matter anyway," and she looks away for her purse, opens it, and coolly takes out a ciga- rette. "It doesn't matter what you say, Pa. It's been decided. . . . Willy, get away from there!"

"Decided! But what right have you or anybody else—?" But he breaks off, squelching the continually abused pride of the drunk- ard, who is judged by people who can't understand him (liquor being only a sinister mystery to them), and trying to keep his mind on the important thing.

"Who's got a better right?" Sally replies evenly. "It's my own mother, isn't it? Am I supposed to sit back until you burn the house down some night, and feel sorry later, *real* sorry! God!"

"Come on, Sal, don't make me mad," his face flushed, his eyes unnaturally bright, pleading. "'Cause I won't get mad. And what I mean is, about last night, I—"

"You almost broke Ma's arm. *That's* what you did last night. You smashed Aunt Martha Quartley's creamer, and two cups, that were coming to *me!* The kind they sell for over five dollars apiece in the antique shops! That's what you did," her face pale and righteous. "You're an old man, Pa, you're a drunken, danger- ous old man, and you simply won't admit it."

Old Man Molineaux is at a loss for a moment, during which Jack puts in uncomfortably: "Look, Will, I . . . I really agree with Sally. I mean about the hospital. If a person's *sick*, that's what they do—they go to a hospital. And everyone'll look at it that way."

"Oh, for God's sake, shut up, Jack," Sally snaps out with a dis- missing gesture. "Can't men ever act their age? I swear, Midgie, don't you just *hate* them!"

"All right, I admit it, I was drunk last night, but that don't mean—"

"You're drunk right *now!* Do you think I'm a fool! . . . Don't you treat me like a fool! I won't *stand* for it!"

"I'm *not* drunk now, goddamn it! How could I get drunk on Sunday, you con-sarn idiots, that's how much you know! . . .

They know so goddamn *much*, Chief, see, they know all about it, and they don't even know the goddamn bars are *closed!*" a last note of desperate triumph entering his voice, only to be quenched by the contemptuous flare in Sally's eyes. "But listen, honey, I'm not mad, I'm not going to get mad, see—and I admit it, I got horrible last night, I'm not trying to cover it up. But my con-sarn back was just *killing* me, I figure I must a pulled something for sure this time, stacking wood, or carrying groceries for your mother—"

"Carrying bottles from Manzini's, you mean—"

"Besides, they open about five, Mr. Molineaux. We know that."

"—and I been meaning to go down to Doc's and get him to X-ray the darn fool thing," he goes on stubbornly, ignoring Midgie's snickers behind her enameled fingertips, "and it ain't no *laughing* matter either," he finishes furiously, "'cause sometimes I think I *broke* it."

"Well, they can just check it for you at Norwich," Sally replies relentlessly, "while they're plugging up the hole in your leg."

"But Doc's got my file, Sal, he knows the case, and you know the way I am—takes me a while to get to trust these young docs. I'm an old horse that way, I know it—but I've seen some horrible goddamn things done in my life, and—"

"This time you're going to that hospital, Pa, and that's all there is to it."

"But you could talk Doc out of it, Sal, if you wanted to, if I swore it wouldn't happen again, and gave my checks to your ma . . . or maybe to *you*, honey, I could turn my checks over to you, and—"

"And sneak drinks from that colored man, and beg drinks from Phil because of the 'frost on your soul'—see, *I* know, too—and end up *stealing* them if I know anything about you—getting arrested, sent to jail—"

"That's right, Will. You don't want that to—"

"Jack, in God's name, go back to your stupid motor! . . . And I don't intend to sit here arguing about it, Pa."

"Come on," I say to Old Man Molineaux, draining off my can. "No one's talking about the same things."

Sally's quick eyes narrow, she takes my measure in an instant, and there is something darkly admirable about her direct response. "Well, what other reason could I have? Do you think I *like* this? What other reason could I have?"

"You never liked me, Sal," the Old Man murmurs surprisingly, swaying a little now, as if there is no longer anything to be gained by pretending. "She always was ashamed of me, Midgie—her own father."

Sally reddens. "This is ridiculous! And I said I don't intend to *talk* about it!"

"But it's the truth. Ever since that time in Junior High— But a man gets drunk sometimes, and everything seems tame, and he gets these wild ideas—he just don't care any more. I don't know why it happens, Sal, but how long do I have to *pay* for it, god-damn it! . . . But listen, I used to be all right, I was a good pilot once—ask Jack!—and I wanted the best for all of you, no matter how I acted. . . . *You* know that, honey, sure, sure . . . and I never blamed *you*, Sal, not once. . . ."

Sally's eyes brighten suddenly with furious tears. "I won't *stand* for this any longer! Blame *me*! . . . Look at you! Filthy, smelling like a brewery, that horrible *hat*! Can't you even wash it!"

"Come on," I say to Old Man Molineaux, and then turning to Sally: "Look, I'll wash the goddamn hat if that's all that's—"

"No, but listen, every time, as long as I can remember, every single time it was important, he was *drunk*, and acting like he was still on the river, and *better* than everyone else! And all the time he was nothing but a pensioned switch-tender, hanging around the bar! A drunk, that's all! A *bum*!"

"I *won't* get mad, goddamn it, so it's no good your tryin'—"

"Well, it's true, isn't it? You threw up at my wedding, didn't you? You sang too loud the *one* and only time you ever came to a game, didn't you? All the boys were making cracks—I could have died! What do you think that was like! Years, and years, and years! . . . Your *friends* don't know about that! Oh, no! . . . Sally Molineaux? Oh, her father's the town *drunk!* They carry him home from the alley every night, they pick him up along with the *garbage!* It's funny, it's quaint, it's a *joke* they tell in the drug-store! And they laugh—don't you know they laugh at you, like you were simple-minded! And even now, right this minute, you're drunk *again!* On *Sunday!*"

Old Man Molineaux has no cigar to work with, his can is empty, his hands are shaking, and the look in his seamed, needlessly shaved old face is unfathomable. But I fancy he is the only one there who is not shifting with embarrassment. "I know it," he rasps out. "I know that. . . . But you won't talk to Doc, Sal? Will you talk to him for me?"

"No! It was *my* idea, *I* called him, *I* convinced Ma. Don't you understand that? It was *me!*"

Old Man Molineaux licks his dried lips with a discolored tongue. "I know, honey. But you could change your mind, couldn't you? For your old man? You could say you had a talk with me, see, and I was sorry, and—and *scared* of myself—yes, that's the way to put it! And I *swore* it'd be different, and I'd keep out of Phil's, and you think I ought to have another chance. Really, Sal, you could do it, you know? Please. 'Cause I don't know—my back, and these con-sarn corns. Please, hon, please—"

She is staring at his weary, babbling face with a nightmare look, the blood has drained out of her cheeks, and her lips quiver in-voluntarily as if she is about to be sick. "Oh, Pa," she gasps with horror, "don't *beg* that way! Stop it!" But she cannot control the spasm that has seized her, and crushes it with a curse. "But I don't care! I just don't care any more! Can't you get that through your head? . . . And look at you! Crawling, sniveling, *begging!* From *me!* . . . Well, I've had enough of it in my life! Do you hear? So go ahead, go ahead, you goddamn old fool! Beg, *beg!*"

"Beg!" he roars, unable to contain it longer. "Beg!" actually shaking his fist at her. "I'll be axed down like a— What was I thinking about? You should have tied me up, Chief! . . . But you'd like that though, wouldn't you? You always wanted to humble me, and make a goddamn silly checker player out of me! Well, I'll fool you. You think I'm one of *his* day-sailors, scared to go out at night? You wouldn't know a man if you saw one—'cause I'll do things—I don't know *what* I'll do, I haven't had a chance to think yet—but I'll do things that'll make you sit up, scandalize this whole goddamn town—oh, you'll have something to *care* about then, don't you worry! . . . Talkin' like that to your own father! Shame on you! . . . Old *fool*, am I? We'll see who's the fool!" He claps his forehead with a choked cry. "Ye gods, did I live my life for this! Did I give it up for this! To be cursed by my own daughter! . . . Good God Almighty, I'll go mad, Chief! I'll die of it! . . ." He lurches around, stumbling over part of the outboard, and yanks the door open so violently that the whole building shakes. "You goddamn idiots!" he shouts rashly. "Told you you should have used the twelve-inch piling! River'll come up some spring and just wash all this away! Like it was never here! Don't you even know that? I may be an old fool, but I know *that* much!" and he slams the door with a crash.

"Well, *really*," Midgie says in the silence. "I never heard so much swearing in my life!"

"Oh, they can swear all right," Jack mutters fatalistically.

"What's that supposed to mean?" Sally challenges, still pale. " 'They.' What does that mean?"

"Keep out of it, Midgie," her husband says.

"Well, I just don't approve of it in front of infants, that's all."

"No, all I meant was I agree with you, Sal. Next, he'll be stealing bottles or something."

I start to laugh to myself, thinking of the near-empty pint of rye that waits for them in their kitchen, and Sally glares at me sharply. "Well, what am I to do? And I don't see that it's *funny* at all. . . . Do you know that he used to try to make passes at my own girl friends in school?"

"Sally!" Midgie is thrilled and horrified. "I never knew that! You mean, *actually?*"

"You know those woods by the girls' softball field? Well, *I* knew he was there, trying to snatch peeks up our gym suits, and just waiting for someone to hit a long fly—that was one of his favorite spots," her eyes drifting to me again, banked and outraged, and yet somehow intimate as well. "All he thought about was sex in those days, sex, *sex*. Oh, I knew perfectly well what he was doing up there in that shack with all those disgusting nude magazines. I don't know why they allow them to sell such trash! They show *everything*—"

"You mean, men and women—together?"

"Of course," Sally replies airily, though it is not true, for I have seen the Old Man's woefully naughty pin-ups. "I had *quite* an education. Nobody has any idea."

"He should have been put away years ago," Jack says to no one in particular. "I've always thought so."

"Oh, *you* don't have any idea either, Jack! Oh, everyone agrees with me *now*, now it's been decided. But when I tried to do it before—oh, no, then I was being mean—"

"Not everyone agrees," I say before I can prevent myself, suddenly woozy from the heat of the place. "If I was your father, I'd probably be the same way. . . . And why go on punishing one another? Are you so content with yourself that you can afford to lose him altogether?" looking pointedly at her hard little breasts, openly fathoming with my eyes under her clothes, and then glancing back to her face to be certain she has seen, and finding her lips parted with startled anger, exactly as if I had touched her nipples without so much as a word of warning. "Anyway, thanks for the beer," I say, and duck out the door.

· **4** ·

I don't see the Old Man at first, and then I do—standing motionless on the end of the pier, staring into the river. Night has happened while we were inside, like a huge, murky umbrella opened
over the gloomy afternoon—starless, threatening, the wind gathering toward a squall. The pale bridge lights flicker, submerged
in the great rush of inky water; the immense piers are cold mono-
liths in the dark; the wooded farther shore is an impenetrable
black—as awesome and bear-haunted as the North of the imagination.

Old Man Molineaux is hunched in silhouette against all this,
swaying back and forth will-lessly, cap pulled low over his brows,
huge shoes not an inch from the edge. I hear the gurgle and
rickle of water as I pause next to him, and his muttered, "—and
I'll *laugh* when it goes, all this . . . damn freshet comes barreling
down some March, and just clear it all away—who-o-sh! And don't
think I won't have the laugh *then!*" so that, sobered for a moment
by the chilly night air, I think in a panic he's about to give up,
and just slip into the dark water right below, and be on his way at
last, and then I see his hands fumbling in front of him, and put
mine back in my pockets. For he is only taking another leak.

We leave, and from then on I simply try to keep up with him,
all thought of going home to food and bed gone, as if he has become my charge, a long-evaded responsibility to the continuity of
life that I have at last been able to accept. I am obedient, and
enduring, and deeply drunk. As we pass the Rambler, his fury

boils up in him. "Laugh, will you! We'll see about *that!*" and he swings out a wild, glancing kick at the mudguard, almost upsetting himself, and howls with an enraged, "O-u-u-c-h!" having forgotten his corns.

We stagger down the dismal blocks back toward town, frost-upended pavement snagging our clumsy toes, a beer can kicked before us with a reverberating clatter, alarmed chickens cah-*cah*-ucking somewhere in a roost, an occasional car's blinding headlights discovering us, disheveled and a-lurch. We stumble into a "Lot for Sale" sign between two bungalows, a little wasteland overgrown with sumac, heaped with furnace ashes, broken bottles, moldering car batteries; and Old Man Molineaux laughs with doomed glee, and yells: "Can't you fit another goddamn all-electric privy in there, you bastards! Maybe *two* if you squeeze? . . . Fools! Idiots! Level it, I tell you! Level everything!"

And then the highway, Route One, the hypnotized flow of traffic, the swoop of harsh lights coming around the curve and wincing our eyes, the desolation of all roads leading into and out of a town. "Ain't gonna find *me,* they gotta find me first, don't they? . . . Know places no one knows about . . . cook your beans in a can. . . ." Somewhere near Sally's house, dizzy in my numb shoes, I am sure I am going to vomit, and try to hold on till there are no cars to see, looking for a bush, wanting to lie in the cobwebby dark under a porch.

"Oh, the bitch!" he yells, thick-tongued and aggrieved. "You're dead as a cod below decks, you hear me! No *life* in you, nothing but meanness. . . . And even her goddamn night-crawlers are pretty near *dead* by the time she sells 'em, it's *all* a cheat . . . ," and somehow my stomach quiets, and somehow focus returns to my eyes, and somehow we are blinking in the cold light of the clustered service stations, like stunned DP's, like street comics who find themselves suddenly shoved out onto a great lighted stage—glare, hurry, exhaust, neons hawking "Gas" and "Restrooms," a few large drops of rain splattering down ominously. And beneath it all, just as we reach the traffic rotary, the austere wail of a freight off in the dark, lonesome, already late, reminding Old Man Molineaux of something in a flash, for he brandishes a defiant fist and yells: "Johnstone's, goddamn it! Clean forgot! . . . Pasture me out on a Farm, will you? Well, I ain't got to the end of my con-sarn rope *yet!* . . . Dumb silly bastards don't even know about Johnstone's, see, heh-heh-heh," winking with bleary slyness. " 'S gonna blow for three days anyway. You listen to a river-man—smell the wind, son, don't listen to them goddamn radios," oracular nose sniffing the night, eyes alight with a last hope.

We drift across the highway amid screeching brakes and curses (all of which Old Man Molineaux returns with interest), and plunge into the dark toward the tracks.

"—just run off, got a good year or two in me yet," the rain settled down to a steady drizzle now, blowing through cold black branches, the crunch of roadbed gravel, the empty wet light of the depot platform down the tracks, the dim glisten of the tracks themselves arrowing off into the rain, and filling my wheeling head with the lonesome pang of all sidings, and switches, and stations in the homeless nights of a traveler's life in this bitter time, and with my own father's last words there in the dusk of the depot years ago: "Of course you blame me. You *should* blame me, I guess, and take your mother's side. . . . But I have to do it anyway. Just for myself. It's like you tried to swim the river that time when you were nine. Remember? And it'll probably end up the same way, too, so don't think I'm getting off scot free. . . . But why weren't we ever friends though, son? You're old enough now, you can tell me. Don't you have anything you want to *say* to me? . . . Well, I understand. You'll come see me when I'm settled, and we'll go out on the town, just the two of us, and get drunk or something, and make up for it. You'll see."

We pause by a stack of ties, nestled in railroad weeds, where creosote fumes up into my head, for a stoop, a reach in under, a grope, and the muttered: "Don't hurt to try, left one in there in '39. . . ." And then on, stumbling over the tracks and down the other side of the shaley embankment, to blunder through wet bushes, and get impossibly snagged in an invisible trail of rusty barbed wire beyond. "Get me a tender's berth, or sweep out somewheres up the line—unhook me there, Chief, will you?—think I'm some goddamn old geezer with a leak in my boards, come back in a couple a years and laugh, that's what. . . . Whoops, watch your balls!" and, finally getting free, to come up to a huge, old, dark house not twenty feet from the tracks, looming over us in a ramble of dilapidated gables and sooty verandas. Johnstone's.

I have never noticed it before—that bleak frame house, something out of early Edward Hopper, in sight of which mad, intent women collect coal from between the iron rails; a dark Victorian house, unpainted in decades, that has shuddered every two hours on the schedule for forty-five years, where a clan of pale Negroes serves hot meals to trainmen. Its gloomy eaves, gutters rusted through, drip into ransacked rosebushes where dogs cache bones; disintegrating window screens hang on moldy frames and flap in the railroad rain; the grassless yards are a litter of potato peelings and smashed pickle jars; and the chassis of a 1931 Packard, stripped for parts, is returning to the earth near the door. No light shows, but for the pallid glow in a remote upper window, revealing a wallpapered ceiling stained by leaks, where an idiot son turns the spongy pages of twenty-five-year-old copies of *Peek*. A house of frayed comforters, and loamy cellar smells, and clogged drains—all that's left of the authentic taverns of New England in these waning days.

A reel of images is all I clearly remember, disembodied voices, strong odors; the damp sofa, heaped with oilskins, in the narrow shadowy hallway; pieces of orange crate spitting in a shallow fireplace, before which a huge-handed Mr. Johnstone sits in a rocker, denimed, all black jaw and yellowed teeth, thumbing a smudgy newspaper; a farther room of garish calendars and muddy carpets; a single naked bulb of low wattage hanging from a raveling wire; a console Atwater Kent (lamination baked off by decades of standing too close to the electric heater) that is a blur of static and violins; a room tangy with bacon grease, and steam, and cigarette smoke, where red-faced men, in billed hats and immense galoshes, sit over chipped plates of nameless meat and potatoes and peas and fried dough drowned in a great gluey gravy, and talk in querulous voices, broken by the ghastly wrack of a true tobacco cough deepened by soot and wind, their thick fingers grimed to the bone, and hooked in the handles of cheap coffee mugs from Thirties dime stores; the worn veneer of the long table, at which they sit, scarred by years of penknives and hot cups, and the spills of the clear, colorless home brew which you bring yourself, and drink without ice or water out of Pepsi-Cola bottles.

Large railroad watches are withdrawn from linty fob pockets and snapped open. "Did ya lay over in Worcester last night, Charlie? How's Drunky Edna?" Mrs. Johnstone, tireless and huge with childbearing, head swathed in a sweat-cloth, slurs orders to her gangly and expressionless daughters, who appear in the supermarkets during the last fifteen minutes before closing in their boy's basketball sneakers, and say nothing, and pay in wrinkled, soot-smudged bills, and whose shapely rumps are studied by all the eaters with the speculative consideration of aimless lust.

"—up this side of One-Twenny-Eight, there they was, layin' in the bushes, goin' at it like a couple a spring pups, right there where you slow down for the Red. Orville says he seen 'em there, too—just kids, sixteen-seventeen maybe—"

"—kids these days . . . can't *wait*, that's the thing—"

"Well, what good did waitin' ever do, I guess—"

"*Kids!*" I hear Old Man Molineaux bellow. "Let 'em do their worst, let 'em curse, let 'em even *beg*—I won't love 'em, I won't care, not again. . . . Charlie, what cha got there?"

Belches, greetings, the creak of chairs leaned back in. Cigar smoke wreathes in grey arabesques over the table; in the kitchen dough sizzles angrily in the bubbling grease; above me the dark house rises in drafty, secret rooms, in which I imagine misanthropic third cousins from Carolina staring at a blank wall, or casual two-dollar prostitutions involving no more intimacy than exists around this table, but no less either.

I find myself reaching for a leftover rusk of bread near a vacated plate, and Old Man Molineaux is announcing: "—ready to go, I tell you, can *still* outwork you old monkeys, and stand the drinks when I'm done, you listen," the bread thick and buttery in my mouth so that I gobble it down, suddenly ravenous with hunger, "hitch me a ride on that nine-fourteen to New London, and see Dispatcher—sleep in the *yards*, goddammit, I don't care," a toilet flushes with a muffled gulge somewhere upstairs, "anything, anything, I can sweep out the cans. An' they'll reinstate me, you wait."

I am moved aside by one of the large bony girls, bringing mugs of hot coffee, and I stare, blinking and amazed, at the dark smoothness of the back of her neck, not five inches from my eyes, so warm and mysterious, and yet somehow so invulnerable to the touch. "—don't know when you're well off, you old roarer. . . . Road's going busted, don't you know that? . . . I'd rather lie around, scratching myself, like you any day—" And so I do not touch her, drunk as I am, and am blearily sad. And then Old Man Molineaux is drinking applejack out of a cup, and choking on it, hazy and doubled-up in the smoke, holding his belly against the cramp, and then he comes up, watery-eyed and spluttering, into that gentle guffawing that is tolerant of men's voices.

"That'll dry out your goddamn socks. Good God Almighty! But listen, Charlie—" And I take my turn at the cup—there in that stuffy room in that echoing house shuttered against the rainy world and its glum inanities, among that last dark fraternity of aging railroad men, whose talk and mien are still wild and cantankerous, but whom time and the myopic decade that is coming will relentlessly render as archaic as the stage drivers they replaced—feeling the oily sting of strong alcohol spread its dizzying warmth over my exhaustion.

"Viola!" the Old Man shouts imperiously. "Take your dad in a drink, girl! Here! . . . Right, Charlie? . . . He's your *dad*, girl. You love your *dad*, don't you? Sure you do. You don't want to see your dad out'n the rain like a dog on a night like this, do you, Viola? What do you say there, girl?"

She is unfazed and faintly ironic with her busy hands. "He could step out in it for a load of wood, an' it wouldn't trouble me much," followed by appreciative laughter at the goad successfully deflected in the thrust and parry of convivial talk.

"—carried his wood, and cut it, too, I'll bet, and don't you forget it, girl. . . . But she's just *fooling*, ain't she?" a shred of bewildered laugh. "Sure, heh-heh . . . But you respect your old man now, Viola. . . . The old cuss earned his paper and his fire, a man don't live forever," staring at nothing all of a sudden, and then snapping back: "But listen, Charlie, I'm ready to come *back*, see . . . let bygones be bygones . . . just to keep busy," the room drowned in shifting smoke now in my eyes, through which I hear the radio's twittering warnings about body odor, because there is no other sound.

"—don't think they'll do it, Will, you know the rules. . . . 'Sides, ain't like it used to be. . . . Ask Norton, thirty years and they made him a switcher. . . . Lucky to be out of it, if you ask me. . . . Take another jolt, you old bastard, and go home and dry out—" The coughs, the gouging, sympathetic coughs to blot out something that is shameful to them, and a hand pouring generously into the motionless cup he holds, and further shards of talk: "—gonna be worse, too. . . . Sure, it's no fun any more, Will . . . cuttin' service five-six trains a day, I heard . . . clean shirt, and no cards. . . . Remember '37 in Milford, you old son-uv-a-bitch? . . . Ask Norton . . . yah, ask Norton—"

The Old Man gulps in confusion, distracted by the radio and the clatter of plates. "But listen—anything, I'll take *any* goddamn thing, you bastards . . . 'cause what else can I *do*? . . . Listen, Charlie, listen," swaying and starting to babble. He turns from one to the other, blinking in the smoke, his chin slimy with spilled booze. "Missus," he says to the squat, perspiring body filling the kitchen door. "What am I gonna *do*?"

Her dark hands are flecked grey with suds; she squints at him, knowing him. "Get yourself sumpin in your belly besides *that*, old man. ... I swear, the way you boys go on—Viola, get him a plate—don't never eat, walkin' around in the rain, how do you expect to wake up some mornin'? ... Put on some of that nice bread, too, you hear, child?" turning away with a sniff.

"Eat!" the Old Man yells at the empty doorway, roused as if by some last demeaning outrage. "I'll be goddamned if I'll eat! You think that's all a man's life is worth?" eyes wild and doomed. "Women! God-a-mighty, all my life that's all they ever said to me was eat, eat! ... Well, you see if I do, Missus! ... Can't *talk* to 'em, Chief, never *listen* to you when you got something hungering in you. No, it's have a *nice* piece of bread, have some *nice* eggs now. ... Well, I *won't,* you darn fools! I'll die before I'll eat your con-sarn colored food! ... Ye gods, I'll go *mad!*" he howls all of a sudden. "No, I won't go mad neither. Just see if I do! I won't go mad."

And then, somehow, we are reeling through the other room, Mr. Johnstone's unwavering eyes noting us alertly over the rim of his paper, to which Old Man Molineaux mutters: "You wait, they'll turn on *you,* too, goddammit!" and on down the darkened hallway, stumbling over preserve jars where the smell of old paraffin is very strong, and someone's pacing of the floor upstairs clumps hollowly down the murky stairwell, to fumble at the door, and find the handle, and lurch out into the murmurous night again.

Fragments, outcries, dark. Was there fog? I think a cold, wet fog had closed in from the Sound, shrouding everything, distorting distances, muffling sounds. I know I was alarmed, and woolly-headed, and we got lost. The fine drizzle touched my hot cheek like an invisible dead hand; I walked straight into a vine-snarled outhouse, clammy to the touch, that suddenly appeared in the mist; I heard the Old Man thrashing around in the bushes somewhere ahead of me, bellowing: "Wish it would *rain,* you hear! Wish it would blow up mean and black for three days! Wish the river would come up black, you goddamn bastards! Then we'd

see who's mad!" the scrabble of feet on shale, the heavy panting
of his old chest getting over the tracks, and then silence in which
a hoarse foghorn keened moronically, far off.

I know, too, that I would not let him go, but had to go through
it right to the end, until he gave up, until he let go—following
him with that fool selflessness, with which we only cling to something that we know will lose.

I get across the tracks, and slide down the cindery embankment, but can't find him in the fog, calling out: "Hey, hey, where'd
you go? Hey—" I try to get my bearings by the faint, diffused
glow of the platform lights, turn from them to the tracks again,
holding my breath to hear, and locate a switch five feet away
from me, beyond which an abandoned siding trails off into the
mist. Blinking against my drunkenness, I turn farther and see, all
of a sudden, a huge indistinct shape, looming over me as big
and fatal as an engine, which is just what I take it to be for one
scared moment. I fling myself down in the wet grass, like a
panicky criminal, only to discover that it is a water tower some
distance off, blurred by the drifting haze. And then, at the same
instant, I notice a muddy shoe not ten inches from my nose, and
hear someone muttering: "—run from here and catch hold just as
she pulls out. . . . Son-uv-a-bitch Norton, what does Norton
know? . . . But watch them goddamn ties, ya idiot." The Old
Man is down on all fours, like a comic hunter or his equally comic
dog, gimlet eyes peering up the track—hiding from the nine-
fourteen.

"Come on," I say, scrambling up, for I have one fixed idea now,
to get him home and safe. "What are you doing?" reaching down
to grab a shockingly thin shoulder that is nothing but an old,
brittle bone inside the sodden jacket.

"Leggo, goddammit! Lemme *go!*" he pipes, trying to ward me
off, snarling and yet curiously petulant as well. "I chased birds
faster'n that, you fool! Lemme *go!*" pulling away and actually
starting to crawl in a desperate scrabble toward the switch.

"But what in hell do you think you're going to do?"

"Get me to New *London*, ya dumb son-uv-a-bitch," he says in a mad, feverish undertone. "—find me that Turkish gal down on Bank Street, that's what, get me a ship—she ain't gonna be workin' on a night like this—"

"What!"

"You think she'll be workin'? Naw, it's gonna rain. Ain't it gonna rain?" voice rasping with momentary doubt. "—sink all their fool skiffs, too, and fill their goddamn basements, heh-heh, washing machines floating away, power out. . . . Foolish bastards don't even know how to make a *fire* on their own, I tell you! You wait, it's gonna blow up *mean* when the con-sarn fog clears off. . . . Leggo, I say!" for I've gotten hold of one cold ankle, as thin and tendoned as a deer's ankle in a trap, getting a grip just above the brute shoe.

"Oh, come on, for Christ's sake, I can't *carry* you," yanking at the leg. But he has gone stubbornly silent, breathing hard down there in the dark, clinging to some part of the switch that protrudes, and holding on with mad, utterly serious tenacity. For a moment we struggle like an awkward wheelbarrow team after too much time around a keg. "Now, what in hell am I going to do if he passes *out?*" I mutter crossly.

"I ain't gonna pass out," he says with surprising calm. "Don't you believe 'em, I don't pass out," at which the other boot thrashes out and catches me sharply on the back of the hand. I let go with a grunt, and he falls forward into the dripping weeds, thwacking on something, and letting out an anguished "O-u-u-ch!"

I am dizzy, my stomach is turning over, and his curses sound strange and thick to me, as if his mouth is full, and so I bend down there in the chilly drizzle, and see blood, thinned by rain, leaking out of his lips, blood against which he is spitting and gurgling in furious bewilderment. "*Jee*sus-One-Eyed-Christ, I busted my goddamn tooth out of my goddamn head!" a dirty finger probing thickly between bruised lips. "E-e-e-e! Good Lord, ain't it all never gonna stop? I broke it, Chief," moaning with astonished self-pity, and then adding as a flat statement: "—try to *do* too much, I swear. . . . And I'm horrible drunk, ain't I?"

I am going to get him home. Something defiant and involved in me won't settle for less, and I am as intent on it, in my own intoxication, as I have recently been on arranging my escape to Europe. He allows me to get him on his feet, hacking out the blood all the while, and we start off into the thinning fog, for the wind has risen and is blowing it away in ghostly swatches.

We stagger the long way home in the black squall that thrashes over the town, and something has broken in Old Man Molineaux, other than the tooth. He walks in an odd, jerky stumble now; curbs all seem an inch too high for his step; he splashes into every puddle; his breath comes in quick, short hisses; he spits. Under the dim street lights, I try to gauge his condition, but his face is expressionless, masked-over; he looks incalculably old. His arm is shivering under my hand; his whole body trembles inside his clothes as if from a fever. "I'm cold," he mumbles with a shudder. "I'm real cold. . . ."

Beneath the grim trees, past the lightless houses down Bertha's street, a dog growls angrily at us, as dogs growl at homeless men passing in the dark—that warning growl that seems the ultimate repudiation on a bitter night, and Old Man Molineaux chokes on a swallowed sob. I talk on and on to distract him, but feel him slipping away from me, and stop by a telephone pole, against which I stack him, to light cigarettes, hoping a smoke will bring him back. "See," he murmurs, "they bark at me, them foolish dogs." He grunts when the first puff stings his lacerated gum, a little involuntary grunt like a hurt animal, his eyes blinking the rain away, and somehow we go on. Our cigarettes come apart immediately; I hear him softly spluttering out the loose tobacco; that last block seems interminable. "Come on," I keep saying. "Come on now. Almost there. Come on."

A single dim light burns warmly in Bertha's kitchen window; the rain falls across it in relentless torrents, smashing the forsythia bushes, drowning the flowerbeds. The Old Man hesitates for a moment, staring at the blurred light with some impenetrable thought flickering across his mute face.

"Come on. Where's the path? Over here?"

He stares at the window, and then in a sudden gesture, either deferential or relinquishing, one of those special gestures that seem to illuminate a whole inner view, but happen too surprisingly to be understood at the time, he takes off his filthy old cap, baring his head to the rain, and wipes at his eyes with it, as if to focus them. He stands in the night outside that window, hat in hand, with his bad back and his corns, his bruised cheek and broken tooth, swallowing stubbornly at something in his throat. And then his splashed face goes mute again; he abandons the hat, and staggers away from me into the dark.

"Hey, wait," fumbling around for the cap, but missing it somehow in the wet grass. "Oh, Christ— Hey, wait up. . . ."

I flounder blindly among the shadbushes, and finally find the path, and start up it with my hands outstretched to ward off branches, and come upon him halfway up, sitting in the mud, old knees drawn up for warmth, eyes open but somehow doused, murmuring like an Indian holy man at his toneless prayers.

"Can't make it—can't make my own hill—can't make it—get me up, Chief. I can't make it."

"Come on now, here, you're almost home."

"She was right—Sally. . . . I can't make it," helpless to disguise the sudden choking sniffle. "I'm sixty years old, Chief. . . . Never meant them ugly things I said, they oughta known that—"

"Forget it. Here. They're just mad, they're just hung up. And worried about you, too. It just comes out that way sometimes."

"Can't make it. Don't think I can, I got the shakes," a shuddering hand groping at my arm to try. "What? Them? They never been hung over in their lives. . . ."

I push, I pull, I threaten and cajole, I unsnag him from bushes. Somehow I keep him off his knees, and somehow we reach the top where the offshore wind blows, shrill and unobstructed, all the way from the Sound, driving the rain before it. He is gasping like an engine about to quit, absolutely passive in my hands now, and I leave him to get his breath under the moaning elm, and stumble into the shack to light a lamp. Of course, my matches are wet, and my fingers are soon smeared with pasty sulfur, but at last I get one to flare, and succeed in coaxing a few sputters from the wick, and manage to replace the grimy chimney before it goes out, though there is only enough kerosene left for a little while.

He is standing before his soaked throne when I go back to get him, in the full black drench of that night, the rain lashing about his hunched shoulders, peering off right into the cold gusts to where the channel markers wink near the mouth of the river.

"Come on, let's get inside. I've got to get home."

But he does not seem to hear. Wisps of yellowed grey hair are plastered over his brow; he keeps wiping them out of his eyes, as if he is searching for some elusive light, some besieged buoy that was perhaps extinguished long ago. The rain is a splattering fusillade on the soggy tarpaper, and I find I am standing in the steady overflow from the galvanized tub. I pluck at his arm insistently. "Come on. You can't see anything in this weather; there's nothing there anyway—"

"Should a gone fishing instead," he mutters. "We could a gone around back of Foxe's Island, and landed when it blew up, and be under the skiff with our food right now, looking *back* at the lights—" A sudden shudder trembles up through him.

"Forget about it. And, really, I'm wet down into my drawers—"

"I would a gone West, you know, if there'd been any real West left in my time," he goes on querulously. "Wasn't just the sea. I *would* have, I don't care what they say. . . ."

"Look, I've got your lamp going, and—"

"I *guess* I would have. There was that time in '24," sniffing at a memory. "Then I could have told these farmers tales, and the kids, too. I would of *had* my life, 'stead of—"

"Oh, Christ, for*get* it!" I say imploringly. "Can't you just forget it? Why go on paying and paying? And look, what's the sense of getting pneumonia? You're soaked through. . . ."

"I don't know, though. I always been all kinds of a fool but the right kind. . . . Maybe I wouldn't have, maybe even if Ma hadn't died," peeled eyes trying to disown the huge, invisible presence of the river off there in the dark, and the huger reality of the sea beyond that, and the beckoning unknown farther still—all that, and the fever for it in himself; only to catch on something, his stubborn old mind supplying what he couldn't see. "But out there, goddammit, beyond them last lights, see, *way* out there," leaning to point with a weary finger, the irascible note entering his voice again, and leaning too far so that all of a sudden, unthinkably, he falls away from me, just falls away into the dark with a startled little moan, right off the embankment, right down into the pile of cans, which clatter as they receive him.

I can't believe it, but I am suddenly alone there in the rain. "Hey!" I call. "Good God. Hey, are you okay? Did you—? Hey, Old Man! Old Man!" not realizing in my alarm how foolish it must sound, like the plaintive cry of the threadbare child in a temperance melodrama.

I scramble blindly down into the dark toward him, catching my trouser cuffs on briers, and sinking over my shoes in the spongy loam. "Hey, hey where are you!" I crawl around on all fours, the rain running down the back of my neck in icy rivulets, fatalistically certain that I am about to slash my muddy hands on jagged bottles, but groping around among them anyway. "Hey, hey!"

And suddenly there is a strangled croak: "I slipped off, goddammit! I forgot to let go—"

I find him lying like a turtle on his back, hands and feet scrabbling feebly in the cans to right himself. The breath has been knocked out of him, the rain is filling his mouth, and he hates being down there in the dark, defenseless and ludicrous. "Get me up outa here, Chief— U-n-n-n-h, wait, my con-sarn back! I must a broke it, I broke my back. . . . O-h-h, Lord! *Wait* a minute, for God's sake! I think I busted my back, I tell you. . . ." Nevertheless, he is sitting up, groaning woefully but miraculously unhurt. "Better get Doc, better get a stretcher, o-h-h. . . ."

"Let me get you up to the house first."

"How in hell can I get up that hill with a broken back, you darn fool idiot! . . . Go get Bertha, I tell you. I can hold out," he adds theatrically, sniffing and feeling his crotch. "Good God-a-mighty, I wet myself, too, I leaked all over myself. . . . Goddamn bladder turns on you, like everything else, no one knows. . . . Oh, horsepiss!" He is whimpering in his fury. He is quite sober at last.

At which point, a flashlight suddenly probes through the rain from the direction of the bungalow, picking us up in its stark beam, like Lew Ayres and the dead Poilu at the bottom of their shellhole.

"He fell off," I call out. "Who is it anyway? . . . He slipped in the mud—"

"Take the goddamn light out a my *eyes!*" the Old Man yells maniacally.

The light bobs up and down, blinks out behind bushes, and grows larger, as someone stumbles through the undergrowth toward us. "What happened? Pa? What'd he do?" It is Billy, in soaked pajamas and hastily stepped-into motorcycle boots. "Like, we heard someone holler, and—"

The Old Man starts to groan as soon as he recognizes him. "O-h-h, Billy, listen, I busted my back, son—don't know how it happened, but—"

"What? Hey, Pa," kneeling down in the cans with youthful alarm. "Whatcha been doing, Pa? . . . Hey, he's bleeding on his face—"

"We ought to get him inside somewhere."

"Oh, Pa, what cha want to do that for? And where's your hat? . . . We better take him to my ma's—"

"Yah, 'cause I'll never make the hill. . . . E-e-e-e! Take it easy!" he yells as we get him under the arms and hoist him up. "Oh, good Lord, I done it this time. . . ."

"Hold on, Pa— Here, watch that branch."

Somehow we get him back to the bungalow through the down-pour. He can stand up perfectly well, but he won't. He hangs limply between us, groaning and complaining, and he gets limper the closer we get.

"Jus' dump me someplace where I can lay out flat," he says pitifully when we get him onto the porch. "Don't scare your ma—she don't want to see me— O-h-h-h, if I could jus' stop this shiverin' though. . . . No, I'll stay out here, that's all right—"

We ease him through the door, despite his protests, and he is a disheveled ruin, dripping all over the rug, when Bertha, girdle-less and carpet-slippered, comes in from the kitchen where she has been sniffling to her radio.

"I tol' 'em not to bring me in," he starts.

"O-h-h-h!" she wails at the sight of him, as if she has been ex-pecting this very thing for years, and hoarding up her emotions in advance. "Oh, Will, Will, Willy! . . . He broke his jaw! Did someone hit you, Willy? . . . He tried to kill himself! I knew it. . . . Did *you* hit him!"

We get him onto the sofa. "I'm hurt, Berth," he whimpers. "Oh, I'm cold, and I—I ain't eaten all day." His teeth are clenched bravely against exaggerated agonies. He lets Bertha wipe his dirty face with one of her good towels. He lets her croon and weep. He lets Billy take off his muddy shoes, forgetting to wince over his corns. He sniffles a little, and begins to flower under their con-cern. He talks and talks.

"—and knocked my goddamn tooth out, too, Bertha . . . see, right there, see that . . . feels like the whole con-sarn jaw's splin-tered or somethin'. And I wasn't nowheres *near* the edge neither —it's all shearing off up there, falling away, the goddamn shack's gonna go next, you'll see. They keep cuttin' down all the trees, how do they expect the ground to hold? . . . But, Lordy, I guess I finally sprung it this time, Berth—"

Bertha wrings her hands, and weeps, and fusses with his shirt buttons and his matted hair. "Call your sister, Billy! Call Doc Menaker! Hold onto my hand, Will. We'll get Doc, and—"

"Yah, phone up Sally," the Old Man interrupts. "She'll know what to do. Tell her I busted my back. Be sure an' tell her now. You're sure I *busted* it, see. . . . 'Cause I got spots in front of my eyes—that's what that means, don't it?"

"Phone Doc first, Billy," Bertha says. "He can give you a shot for the pain, Will. . . . Take his socks off. Should we put a board under him? Oh, oh," clutching his jacket and sobbing.

"He can't do nothin' for this," the Old Man gets out with a grimace of spurious courage. "These small-town docs are okay for sprained ankles and runny nose, but I *broke* the goddamn thing, I tell you. Nope," swallowing bravely, "nope, there's no gettin' around it, I can tell when I'm busted, have to go to the *hospital* this time. Need X-rays, nurses, them hot baths . . . probably be laid up on my darn fool ass for a month, worse luck. You just don't mend at my age, I know that—"

Bertha peers at him, full of concern, and weeps happily.

"Can't help it, Bertha. You'll just have to make out by yourself for a while. We just got to accept it, that's all. Nothing you can do about *accidents*, no use cryin' over them. . . . And, Billy, you got to grab hold now, son, you hear me, no more nonsense. . . . Think I could have another pillow for my shoulders? . . . W-h-a-a-p!" he belches loudly as they lift him up. "Watch out there, you darn fools. . . . Ten-twenty years ago I'd mend up all by myself, Chief, wouldn't catch me in some goddamn hospital. . . . Ain't that right, Bertha? . . . But I'm pretty damn near sixty-one, you know. . . ."

He feigns to be breathing more easily. "I don't know. Probably never would have made another winter anyway. Earned me a rest—o-h-h," swallowing a moan that is just loud enough to bring a comforting sob from Bertha. "That's all right, old girl. I won't pass out till Doc comes. . . . But maybe something *hot*, a cup a tea or something? 'Cause I may of caught me a bug, too, out there in the rain. . . . And, Billy, get your old man a blanket, will you, son? No sense in catching the pneumonia. . . ."

They rush around at his orders, relieved by the very tone of his voice. "Sure hate being a bother this way, you know, Chief? I always took care of myself. But I got to be sensible now, I guess. . . . And what's an old fool to do? That's what you got your family for, for when you're old. . . . Billy, give your dad a cigarette, son. . . . E-e-e-e! Forgot my goddamn jaw! . . . Well, that's all right, don't matter. . . . Berth, listen, Berth—"

I felt suddenly superfluous there. The whole long day of drink accumulated and swept over me in a dizzying wave of exhaustion. I felt relieved, and vaguely sad, and yet somehow out of place. I was relieved, for myself, because I had managed to get him home, discharging thereby a duty of insight that I had owed my own ghosts too long; and I was relieved, for him, because he had found a safe way back into the life from which he had never been able to get free. But I was saddened, too, because I had had some obscure stake in his getting free, a stake I could now see had nothing to do with him, but with those ghosts and their legacy in me, no part of which could he take on. But most of all, I felt abruptly isolated from him by the realization that, though we had wallowed side by side in the worsening chop of that long day, he had been making for port all along, and I had been outward bound.

Sometimes, I suppose, an excuse to rest is all a proud man really wants, a reason for quitting the unequal struggle that does not involve a loss of self-esteem, and maybe this had always been the secret object of the Old Man's quest. Certainly he was a loser in his idea of life, but you can't lose without having dared, and if you dare you don't lose everything. Maybe the reach is all.

In any case, I know I left him in the bosom of his family then, sipping broth and enduring his aches and pains loquaciously. I know I slipped out into the rain without a further word, and must have looked back up into the night toward his shack, for I am certain I saw no light there. I remember noting that for some reason. And I remember as well (all these bad twelve years later) understanding why they honor old men in Haiti. For the best and simplest of reasons. Because they have survived. And honoring him for that—a young fool honoring an old fool. The way it mostly is.

NEW YORK: THE MIDDLE

"Look, I'm sorry, I know I woke you up, but I just got in, I'm at Grand Central, and—"

"What? . . . Oh, Danny . . . No, that's all right. . . . What time is it?"

"Six-fifteen. But listen, I need to pick up those clothes, like I wrote you, so—"

"What? . . . But what time do you sail?"

"Twelve-thirty, but I've got to be there by ten or so, or I wouldn't have called you so early."

"You mean *now*? You mean twelve-thirty *today*? I thought it was tonight."

"No, it's noon. But look, if you're busy, just put them outside the door. . . ."

"All right, but . . . No, listen, honey, you come in and I'll fix you coffee."

"Well . . . You must be beat, I don't want to disturb you."

"Oh, Danny, don't be silly, for God's sake! I'm alone, you're not disturbing me. And I'm awake now anyway."

"Okay. If you're sure."

New York at dawn seemed very fine to him. Bundles of news-

papers stacked by shuttered stands, street lights changing automatically at empty corners, the fleeting aroma of fresh coffee
from a steamy doorway: he realized that it had been months
since he had seen the first white-gold glisten of the sun on wet
pavements deserted all the way to the river, except through eyes
distorted by drink or its aftermath. A yawning janitor, a dog
straining the leash of his sleepy-eyed walker, cabs going in after
the long shift: for a moment he had a sense of the urgent beauty
of New York that he hadn't felt in years, a sense of its island nature, its sheer physical audacity, and all the invisible millions
slumbering fitfully behind the windows that caught the early
light of that fresh day. It seemed to him that life was actually
simple and thrilling; midnight and its confusions were a needless
complexity; and a poignant joy came up in his throat, a joy in-
tensified by the imminence of his going away from it all. He
breathed up the damp smells of morning in the city, famished by
awareness; his cigarette tasted rare and delicious; he was off on
a great adventure.

She was tousled and sleepy in her flowered kimono, with that
look of somnolent distraction that only the third cup of coffee
would dissipate, a look which instantly brought back their time
together in every graphic detail. But she had managed lipstick,
the pot was a-drip, and his things were in two neat piles on the
couch, folded up carefully.

"I'm really sorry about this. When I wrote you, I didn't know I
had to be there so early," peeking around for clues to her life,
expecting signs of Streik. But there was nothing. Not a shirt cardboard, not a shoelace.

"No, it's all right," clattering the cups. "And I hope you intended to at least *phone* to say good-by," she added pettishly, as
she checked the pot for the third time. "Will you switch on the
radio, honey, while I—?" and then she looked at him with a bleak
little smile that acknowledged a dispute of months before. "No, in
fact, don't."

"Yes, let's have some music."

"Not this morning. I don't care."

"But I'd like it. I probably won't be hearing any American music for a long time."

"Don't be idiotic. That's *all* you'll hear."

"But I'd *like* to have it on."

She brought the cups and the pot. "Suit yourself. God, don't let's get foolish about the damn radio."

He looked at her, unaccountably moved by the sense of her distinctness, her aliveness, with which their separation suddenly filled him. She was thinner, it seemed to him, more indrawn. Her hair was longer, and shone dimly from a recent shampoo; the meticulous polish on her toenails somehow suggested idle nights with nothing better to do. His copy of *Love in the Western World* lay open on the couch, its cover stained with midnight coffee, and she was saying:

"Well, how was Grafton? . . . How's your mother? . . . It's been raining a lot here lately, one of the wettest autumns on record. . . ."

They talked uncomfortably for a while, drinking hot black coffee to the moody pianos and moronic jingles on the radio, and the sun rose high enough to touch the walls a little with the first briny light of morning near the river. He got down on his haunches to pack his things, aware of her eyes on him as he did it, and her words droned on, carefully skirting something.

"And how about all the rest of your stuff, what do you want me to do with it? I don't intend to move or anything, but—"

"Oh, just hang onto it. Or get rid of it, if it's in the way. I don't care. . . . I'm through with accumulating *things* that way," still so unused to these new certainties that he almost flushed, repeating them. "I mean, that whole way of *thinking*—you get so many possessions, so many involvements, that you can't *move*. And when it's time to get away, you don't do it because of some damn box of *books*, or a *cow*, or something."

Her steady quizzical gaze evidenced an interest in the changes time had made in him, but all she said was: "Well, I'll hang onto everything till you get back then. . . . And don't worry, you already got rid of your cow, didn't you?" she added, and then grimaced. "Lord, I should never try to be bright and sardonic in the morning."

She seemed unusually nervous for that hour, and kept getting up to fetch ashtrays or find a better station on the radio. She lit cigarettes one from the other, and drank several cups of coffee, meanwhile talking in abrupt little bursts, and then lapsing into petulant silences. Outside the windows, the first trucks braked and shifted gutturally, and morning lights went on in kitchenettes across the street which the sun had not yet reached.

"Look, are you hung over?" he said finally.

"No, of course not!" she flared back. "Don't *assume* things that way, just because—"

"I didn't assume it. It's just—well, you're acting sort of strange, and we were usually under the weather on Saturday mornings."

"Well, I'm not," she stated. "I'm just not awake yet. And talk about acting strange," with a little pout of irritation. "Here you are going off to Europe like you've always wanted to, and probably if it hadn't been for your damn clothes you would have just slunk through town without even calling anybody up. Why are you such an idiot about some things?"

"I don't know. I always was, I guess. . . . Wasn't I?"

She sucked her mouth into a pucker of red lips, and dismissed this with a little flip of her hand. "Oh, well, don't listen to me, honey. I'm just envious. I'd rather be off for Europe, too, than going home, and— But I didn't tell you, did I? I'm going home to Louisiana for a few weeks."

"Why? What's happened?" he asked in alarm, because she had always resisted (by an elaborate series of deceits and evasions) any attempt on the part of her family to lure her South again.

"Oh, nothing," she replied so offhandedly that he became even more alarmed. "I'm just overdue for a visit. It's been almost four years. Ever since my mother died—and—"

"Things are going badly," he stated fatalistically. "Have things been going badly? ... And, wait, where's Jefferson? I *knew* something was missing."

"Oh ... I gave him away," taking another gulp of coffee. "In fact, I gave him to Tersh. ... But, no, things are all right, it's just— Well, *you're* going away, so you must understand. Sometimes it's just time to leave fo. a while."

"What happened with Streik, May? And why did you give Jeffy to *him*, for God's sake? I thought—" But he suddenly didn't know how to explain what he thought because, though *his* relationship with her was finished, and he knew that she had looked for a way out of it as long as he, still he had secretly hoped that Streik would not prove to be the way.

"It didn't work out," she replied simply, and he realized in a flash that she wanted to tell him about it, perhaps had been waiting for the opportunity since his arrival, and was grateful to him for cutting through the pretenses.

It all came out in flat, unemotional statements: the parties, most of them midtown with Streik's friends; the brawls, most of them pointless arguments in newspapermen's bars along Third Avenue that started with politics and ended with broken glasses; the embraces, most of them leading no farther than drunken oblivion on her bed or on his; the Bloody Marys, the stéak sandwiches, the restless cabbing up and downtown; and, eventually, Sally Spade in restaurants with them, Sally Spade throwing off Scotches in Streik's apartment like a man, Sally Spade staring indifferently down her nose as Streik tried to unzip May's dress, Sally Spade always around somehow.

"He—well, I guess he wanted the three of us to make it. I mean, it had to be weird or he wasn't much interested really. And—" She shrugged as if a thought had sent a chill through her shoulders. "Well, you know how some people are. Like nasty kids. I don't mean scary, or anything like that. Just unpleasant inside. He got very mean to me."

"The son of a bitch," Verger muttered, shaking his head. "Really, you ought to keep away from creeps like that."

"He wasn't so bad actually. I mean, I know how it must sound, but he was really just bored, I think, and sick from drinking most of the time," brightening a little, Verger's anger somehow lessening her own. "And, you know, I think he really wanted me to make it with *her*, if you want the truth," she added with a little laugh. "Isn't that pretty, though? I bring out the best in people every time. . . . Anyway, I stopped the whole stupid business ten days ago. And then he came around, terribly drunk one night, and sad, and I—well, I felt sorry for him, I guess. And I had nothing else to give him. He was awfully cute with Jeffy, too—I mean, it turned out that he really *liked* dogs. Isn't that strange? . . . So you see, I got rid of my cow, too."

"God . . ." There was nothing more he could say, except I-told-you-so, and that would have been justified only if there was still some binding emotion between them. "So you're going home," he went on. "That's probably a good idea."

"Yes, I suppose so. I'll do some of that corny thinking-things-over. I'll be sweet and dutiful with my grandmother, and probably get my accent back again," glancing at him all at once with a guarded, winning smile. "And I guess the only way you find out that you can't go home again is to just up and go, isn't it?"

"That's right. You have to come to terms with it. The hateful past. Otherwise you just fight it blindly half your life. Otherwise people just take out their disappointments on one another. Like we did, like my mother and father did, like most parents and children, I suppose. The Old Man showed me that, even though—"

"*Who?*" she broke in. "You mean your father?"

"No," he replied. "Well, not exactly. Just an old man I got to know up there. Actually, he *could* have been my father. Or even *me* in thirty years, if I hadn't met him now. . . . But anyway, sweetheart, maybe you'll be lucky, too—going home, I mean."

She touched his hand suddenly, on an impulse so warm and spontaneous and noncommittal that they were both embarrassed in an instant. "It's—it's just so *good* to see you, honey," she blurted out. " 'Cause we *are* still friends, aren't we? I'm so glad for once."

"I hope we are, sweetheart," he said, and the stir of a new, simple emotion, an emotion unclouded by love and its demands, made them both talkative and very gay all at once, as if the morning had taken on a special luster.

She asked him a stream of questions about his trip, teased him because he wanted to go to Vienna more than Paris, wondered if he had included warm enough underwear, and insisted that he pack the small purse-flask he had once given her. "Lord, we should have a drink together, but wouldn't you know it? I haven't got a *thing* around, damn it."

"Never thought I'd see the day when I couldn't get a drink in *this* house," he chided her.

"Well, you're seeing the day now, you silly. . . . But I wish we *did* have something, though. It's not a real sailing if you're stone cold sober."

Which made him look at his watch for the first time in half an hour. "Anyway, I should be getting out of here. It's almost nine."

He got up, and the moment of parting suddenly stood there between them. He did not know how long he would be gone, time in their lives had always been tinged with finality, and they both realized all at once that they would be different when they met again, no matter what. The particular poignance of steamships, and leave-takings on a crisp autumn morning, and verging destinies, filled them with a disturbing excitement. She hesitated for a second, and then said: "Look, I'll come over with you. It'll only take me a minute," and then: "Or is someone seeing you off?"

"No. Nobody."

"Would you like me to, Danny? I'd like to."

He laughed all of a sudden. "Only if you don't take longer than twenty minutes deciding what to wear."

"Oh, poof! I'm the fastest female you know."

She bustled around getting out clothes, talking gaily all the time, really trying to hurry, and then started to take off the kimono as a matter of course. She hesitated with it half-open down her nakedness, shot him a strange, uneasy glance, then

scooped up her things, murmuring: "I'll be right out," and fled
into the bathroom.

She put on a mauve woolen dress a little too tight over her
breasts, brown leather heels a little too high, a short cloth coat that
gave her a pert and efficient air, and a dark brown tam that was
typical of the headstrong, eccentric kind of style with which he always associated her. They stood on a windy street corner, bright
with chilly sunlight, trying to flag down a cab, very happy.

"God, it's beautiful!" he exclaimed as they paused for crosstown
lights. For everyone walks faster in late fall in New York, there
is a snap in every stride, car tops glisten lucidly, the air is alive
and has a taste to it, summer's tempers have cooled and even cab
drivers laugh philosophically at the snarls of traffic. Verger felt
it all in his throat, the old thrill New Yorkers never really re-
experience till they go away, and come back. And here he was
going away again.

May suddenly hugged his arm there in the cab, and said ecstat-
ically: "Oh, Danny, you're really leaving! I can't believe it. . . .
It's going to be so strange and wonderful. I'm as happy as if it
was me."

At which it came home to him that he would be at sea by that
night, out on the dark Atlantic that he had lived near all his life
but never crossed; hawsers loosed, no chance for reconsideration,
on his way at last; all *this* behind him, and the unknown, ceaselessly imagined experience of Europe (and all the very word stirs
up in Americans) ahead. May's face was aglow with excitement,
her eyes flashed, her lips were moist and parted, and it seemed to
him that she had never been so lovely, and so lost to him. For a
moment, the reasons for their separation, and for his going away,
got all mixed together in his mind, and he couldn't remember
why he was in that cab, or why he had ever left her. The panic of
change went through him with a sick tremor, and he took her
hand suddenly, urgently.

"Look, sweetheart," he began, just as she exclaimed: "There's
your ship! . . . And, Christ, you were so right. It's the only way to

go the first time. And like a damn fool idiot, I flew. I've always regretted it. . . ."

And all at once they were at the pier, and he was struggling his bags out of the cab, and paying the driver, and she was saying: "You know, honey, frankly I never really thought you'd do it—isn't that an awful thing to say though? But you fooled me," and he was replying: "Well, maybe for once I'm the *right* kind of a fool anyway," and the panic was over. "Come on," he said. "There's time. Let's go over there and have that drink."

They went to a tiny saloon (across from his pier) that was narrow and smoke-blackened and much too warm with steam heat. Porters and cab drivers snatched quick beers in there, it smelled of cigar and disinfectant, there was a jukebox with a yellowing "Out of Order" sign taped on it, and out the smudged windows the cobbled street lay under the cold roar and shadow of the West Side Highway with nothing beyond it but the orange rinds and oil slicks of the grimy river. Somehow it was perfect in its dimness, in its ugliness, in its comforting warmth, and Verger brought Scotches to their booth.

"You know, in the cab for a minute," he began. "It's ridiculous, but I almost—"

"I know. I thought you were going to crush my hand, you poor silly." She smiled at him, accepting a cigarette. "But listen, that's the way it is. I threw up in the little girl's room at La Guardia just before we took off. Don't you go and think you're special."

He laughed. He felt like laughing, and he gulped off half his drink thirstily, and stared at her with the feeling that he might not see her again for years, but without a pang. He felt very close to her.

"What queer people we all are though," he marveled. "Americans. We don't ever really feel we belong anywhere, and we can't seem to cope with unknowns any longer, and, you know, I'm suddenly so *glad* I'm going away."

"Well, that's not so special either, honey. And you'll find out where we belong soon enough when you get over there. . . . Anyway," she interrupted herself, "let's not have one of our famous disagreements about why we're all so crazy. Let me buy us another drink instead. Let's drink to something."

He got more drinks, feeling light on the soles of his feet, feeling warm toward the bored bartender, and the rickety stools, and the faded beer posters; full of the keen knowledge that this was to be an important day in his years, the end of something, the beginning of something else, amazed at life's mysterious shifts, ready for anything.

May chattered away, and he sat and listened, admiring her all of a sudden for her ease in bars, for her offhand way with a cigarette, for the dash with which she dressed, for her ability to meet life unarmed and yet uncomplaining; liking her enormously in a way he never had before. He watched her mouth that was saying: "I love departures, though. I always have. You feel something good might happen after all. So let's drink to the future for a change," and then she raised her glass to her lips, and he saw the soft pinkness of her tongue touching the rim, and felt a sudden twinge because of the chance for intimacy that they had lost, and then she said with odd abruptness: "You'll write me though, won't you? You know how I love to get mail. . . . Won't you, Danny?"

"Of course I'll write you. I'll send you postcards from places with funny names. But listen—"

"Promise. You promise now."

"I promise, sweetheart. But listen, are you going to be all right? I mean, this trip home and everything. I know how you must feel, but, really, I'm sure it's the right thing, and—"

"Oh, of course. I know. Don't you get silly now. 'Cause you'll get me all silly, too. . . . No, you go off to your funny old Europe, and I'll go back to America. . . . But don't you miss anything, you hear."

The time had come. A snarl of taxis honked and quarreled across the street, porters fought for luggage, the sun was high and brilliant now, flags whipped in the river wind. Verger wished the moment was over and he was alone. Or that she was coming with him. He didn't know what he wished.

"Well," he said.

Then she was talking all of a sudden, a gay, depthless stream of talk as he paid up. "And you be sure to go to Saint Chapelle now, don't listen to anybody, it's the most beautiful. And have pastis every afternoon, ask for Ricard, it's just as good as Pernod, and francs and francs cheaper," and then they were outside, and the day had become cold and burnished.

A furl of steam was rising from the forward stack of his ship, the cabs were thinning out, gulls shrieked noisily, the smells of tar, and truck-exhaust, and city-river blew through the late morning. Their breaths hazed up into their faces, and she was saying: "And find yourself a cute girl, honey, and write to me, and don't worry, things'll go better now. And don't you dare become one of those corny old expatriates who's always saying 'merde' instead of our perfectly good—" And suddenly he took her by the shoulders there on the curb opposite the pier, and said: "Don't come across with me, it's a mess over there, and I'll have to hurry. But listen—"

She took his hand, looking up at him warmly, and she said: "I swear I'm going to cry like some horrible syrupy girl from Georgia," making a woebegone, teary face, though her eyes belied it. "I'm going to blubber, and you'll be ashamed of me."

They laughed together as they embraced, and she kissed him simply, quickly, her lips as soft and wet as he had remembered them, so that for a moment he felt a yearn for the commingling that had always remained unachieved between them.

"Thanks for coming over," he said. "Really. It made it for me."

She squeezed his hand. "Oh, I hope it's everything you want it to be, honey—aside from all our silly talk," and she was looking at him with that brief, leveled glance that anticipates memories. "And there's something good ahead for you, Danny. I just know it."

"You, too," he muttered, and then she was looking beyond him, and exclaiming: "Oops, there's my cab," and, waving a frantic hand, she suddenly reached up and kissed his cold cheek fleetingly, murmuring: "You be well now, honey. And keep warm," and was gone all in a flash, leaving him a faint aroma of cologne, as a reminder.

HOBBES AND LITTLE ORKIE

May • South • Night   • 1 •

It was one night when I had gone home to Louisiana, that bad autumn when so many things came to an end for me, and I couldn't think of what to do next, and so, going South being no conceivable answer to anything, that is what I did. It was one of those evenings when the pecan groves down there are hazy with blurred yellows and pale greens, and the last October flowers have so recently gone that you fancy you can smell them still, and people get out the ice cubes half an hour earlier. Two weeks before, I'd been sitting with Dan V. over last Scotches, staring at the raveled end of an emotional rope I had been winding into a ball for months; and this was the first night since I had gotten off the plane in Alexandria that I felt really free of the exhaustion of spirit that had gotten me on it in New York.

It was one of those twilights that seem full of the thrilling discontents of the night to come—when you want people, chatter, drinks, and a place to wear that special dress you bought for that special party, and have not worn since. It was an evening when, in fact, I took that very dress out of its plastic sleeve (a billowing chiffon of electric coral, cut emphatically low across the breasts, and as unsubstantial, with its yards and yards of soft froth, as cotton candy), wondering where in hell I could go to flaunt it, and then remembered Maggie O'Fee's cocktail and buffet invitation, which I had lied my way out of two days before, and followed my whim, giggling wickedly to myself as I got into the dress, anticipating the startled disapproval of my old girl friends, who would think it too summery, too blatant, too New Yorkish, but who would be secretly envious, too, simply because I had had the nerve to wear it. "Isn't that just like May Delano, though! Really!"

But nerve was all I'd brought home with me that time, nerve and a kind of bitchy defiance; and after two weeks in my grandmother's prim old house, which, sadly, wasn't a home for me any more, I was fed up with the South all over again—the South that had changed so much less than I had since leaving it, but would be changing more than I ever would again once I went away this time.

I remember, too, that it was too warm for November, and the red-bud trees by the veranda seemed poised in the yellow hush waiting for rain, as everything in the South seems eternally waiting for the rain whenever it isn't actually falling; and Church Plouchet came by to pick me up in his stylish off-white Corvette with the silver flask in the glove compartment—Church, who had once been what we still stubbornly call down there "an old beau," which means that, as teen-agers, we had sweated genteel-ly against one another in dancing school in June, and later solemnly shared sticky julep-straws, and later still roused each other in a parked car near Pierson Lake, and drawn back as much out of lack of real passion as excess of phony scruple.

My grandmother stood in the doorway, as tiny and pert and fine-boned as a gay wren, eighty-two years old and the mainstay of two bridge clubs, the Historical Society, the Catholic Women of Rapides Parish, and the local chapter of the U.D.C.'s, gesturing briskly with her lacquered cigarette holder, and chirping: "Lovely, just fetching, dear. But you take a wrap now—do you have a wrap? Because I suppose that's what they're wearing up yonder, but it isn't going to keep the night air off your chest, that seems certain," my sweet, chic grandmother, with her just-so permanent and her perky hats (both in the style of the Twenties), who will always represent the best quality of the South to me, the one quality worth preserving out of the Old South and its languid illusions, and the very quality that would perish first in the New South reality would bring—its vain, unsurrendering women.

I remember everything so clearly: the evening that seemed bathed in dead roses and no-longer-important secrets; the frivolous dress that was just outrageous enough to heighten my mood; Grandmother's cautionary words that had always irritated me as a girl, but which now seemed rather like a valentine you are glad to receive despite its mawkish sentiments; the stately live-oaks, still heavily leafed, among which suburban two-bedroom houses had grown up like clusters of ugly toadstools.

It might have happened yesterday. I might be still only twenty-five, and resilient with youth despite a caustic tongue, and a skeptical eye, and a very real thirst. For it is my last, least poignant, most graphic memory of the funny Old South of my girlhood, whose borrowed time was running out then, and it has superseded all the other memories of my going home since—that long, long night a dozen years ago.

Maggie O'Fee had married Birmingham money, and divorced it two years later, and all she had to show for those two years, aside from alimony, was a perfect replica of Tara, copied from Selznick's set-designs down to the last brick in the gallery floor, and the last lofty white column—except that it was only one-room deep and built on a two-acre lot in one of the newer residential sections. Most of the money had gone into the facade and the landscaping, and Maggie liked to say that she was the only person she knew who *lived* in "a conversation piece."

She was a big girl, awkward and loud, with red hair and an overdeveloped bosom she had always been sensitive about, and just then her primary interest was heavy drinking—that is, most of her talk concerned booze, hangovers, and getting plowed; all of which was a harmless enough romanticism for anyone as resolutely extroverted as Maggie. You always caught her in jodhpurs, or pedal-pushers, or Bermudas (tailored by Neiman-Marcus to minimize her heavy thighs); you had always come too early, or she was running late, and so, at most of her parties, she neatly avoided having to compete with her female friends, and ambled around among the decolletage and bouffant, a hefty Scotch highball in her hand—faintly odorous of the stables, the golf links, or her flowerbeds.

They were all there, gathered on the gallery: bright clumps of taffeta and faille, blooming like late flowers on the white iron garden furniture; knots of tweed and gabardine hovering around them with a gallant nonchalance that was as spuriously antebellum as the house. Flora Lee Baines, who'd gotten fat; T. P. Reeves, who'd gotten handsome; Nancianne Bayliss and Lawtell Ducomb; "Turtle" Cheney, with her shiny carapace of lacquered blonde hair; Peony something-or-other of the coy squint; Phaeton (Fate) Davis from over in Pineville; Emily Lynn and Betty Ann and Ann Marie—and others whom I didn't know by face or name, but whose education and attitudes and follies I could have described simply by describing myself as I had been before I went away.

For a moment, I was as idiotically glad to see them all as they were to see me—so much giddy fun, so many girlish crises were associated with their faces and their drawls—and I felt the first and only twinge of homesickness I had felt in four years. Church beamed possessively, and I suppose I gushed, and I know Maggie's careless laugh signaled each fresh round of drinks. I had gin-on-the-rocks to go with my dress, and automatically flirted with the tanned, well-groomed faces that leaned toward me, slipping back into such harmless social hypocrisies as: "I just *love* those luscious shoes, Emmy, where did you *ever* get them?" and: "Now, Lawtell Ducomb, you mean to tell me you're an *actual* lawyer! You!" Until, as one gin followed another, Church continu-

ally in transit replacing them, I heard the sardonic asides creeping
into my voice: "—those shoes—well, I suppose they're wonder-
fully *comfortable*. Anyway, they *look* comfortable, honey," and:
"—because lawyers are the soldiers of the South, don't you think?
Now the war's entered another stage?" I got exhilarated, and
mean, and I didn't mind.

Patches of talk without connectives, like the moronic babble a
party becomes when you play it back on a tape recorder, reached
me as I sat near the screen door. "Ah really think the state may
go R*epub* next time because of Ahke— Well, just everybody saw
him up in Bossier with that trashy dancer— She wore that unbe-
lievable hat to Mass last week, honey, and I tell you— Tidelands
is *the* issue, sport, it's gonna split the legislature— Mama just
insists I keep attendin', and I keep telling her *we* don't care as
much about all that as her generation, but I go 'cause she can't
understand that, you know?— L.S.U.'s gonna take them by two
touchdowns— Don't know how I'd ever get out of the house,
'cept for Billie Dew— 'Scotch!' I said, 'Scotch ain't a *yankee*
whisky, Aunt Moore,' I said. 'Scotch is an *English* whisky—'"
Politics, religion, football, fashion, time: just what everyone talks
about, the reasonably pleasant chitchat that seems to go down
easily enough with a little alcohol to help; yet I had been away
from it too long, and did not realize at that time that New York
chitchat (books, theater, sex, and cynicism) was equally foolish.
And besides, some kinds of boredom make me vicious.

I wanted to rough them up, and open the darker cellars in
their consciousness. I wanted them to acknowledge what they
were like under their nice clothes, and I played the game I sometimes play with myself to this day—I tried to imagine them naked,
I tried to imagine each of them in all the grotesque, utterly solemn attitudes of lust, I tried to pair them off in the most unlikely
combinations—all with somewhat ludicrous results.

At one point, I went into the powder room to redo my hair,
and found Turtle Cheney adjusting a garter, her prominent upper
teeth holding her narrow lower lip.

"We should have lunch downtown one day next week," she said.

"I guess I'll be home by then."

"Heavens, you haven't changed at all, darling! You must be expecting a big night," she chortled into the mirror of her compact. "Well, I'll call you on, say, Tuesday then—"

"No, I mean New York, honey," I said, missing the city all of a sudden with an odd twinge. "And you haven't changed either. No one has very much."

"But why so short a visit? . . . May Delano, they've gone and made a yankee out of you! You're *bored* with all us country folks," slipping into a parody of what her mother might have said, like all the sad young white people of the South, behind whose ironies lies a nostalgia for a role they cannot play.

"Don't be silly," I said. "I only came down to get *over* something, and now I've gotten over it, so—"

She seemed uncertain for a moment, and decided on levity. "Sounds to me like there's a philandering *man* mixed up in it someplace."

"Not a philanderer," I stated. "It's the *faithful* men you have to get over, honey. . . . But, Christ, this panty girdle's strangling me!" and, to Turtle's amazement, I flounced up my skirt, unfastened my stockings, and wriggled out of the girdle altogether. "There!" I exhaled, catching just a glimpse of myself in the mirror, pleased by the gloating half-smile that was fixed on my lips. "And don't you go and tell the gentlemen now."

Gales of uneasy laughter from Turtle. "Heaven's sakes, May, you'd think—you'd think it was *August!*" unable to look at me srtipping off the stockings, folding everything up, and stuffing it in my handbag. "I'm just *parching* for a martini!" she said all of a sudden. "And they'll think we're conspiring in here!" at which she grabbed her purse, laughed pointlessly, and ran away to find someone she could tell.

I stared for a moment at my own face, and practiced an empty, brilliant smile. I pushed the hair on my neck back up into its pins in that automatic gesture we girls always employ to gain time. "I do de*clare*," I said mincingly, "what's going to keep the night air off your—" and laughed into my frown, unhappy to be making fun of my grandmother that way, and already a little tipsy.

In her consternation, Turtle had left her compact—an oval of gold no thicker than a cigarette lighter, with a delicate cameo affixed to the lid, nearly full of good powder, with a soft, hardly used puff. There was an aura of fragile femininity about it. It suggested porcelained eighteenth-century cheeks that blushed easily, and delicate fingers that had never touched anything capable of sweat. It must have cost fifteen dollars, and I shoved it into my purse, along with everything else—for nothing, just because I've always thieved a little: junk earrings, cards of bobbie pins, dickies or scarves, a book or two from the apartments of strangers, oddments. It makes you feel better; it's a way of getting your *own* back.

Everyone had moved indoors by now, and were clustered noisily around the buffet in the dining room where, like greedy shoppers, they attempted to balance glasses, napkins, and silverware while filling their plates with cold chicken, creamed onions, cheese and chive dip, biscuits, and potato salad. Church, by utilizing his pockets for the utensils, had prepared a plate for me as well.

"Here you are, honey," he said. "Turtle-girl said you were just fiddling with yourself, and would be right out, so I went ahead."

"Is *that* what she said? Shame on Turtle-girl." I let him take me to a huge leather armchair. "What? No collards? My God, that's all I came home for!"

Church, lounging at my feet with napkin carefully spread over one thigh, laughed eagerly—the way you laugh when your evening has turned into a surprise.

"Geez, I haven't had any collards in years. . . . Remember how we used to sneak into your grandmother's kitchen—that summer out at Fishville—to have collards that—you know, your cook—

fixed for herself? What was her name? Always wore a striped
head-rag. . . ."

"Lillian . . . You know, I think my main reason for coming home
was to see Lillian, but seems she died last June. And Granner
said she was bald all the time under the rag when they took it off
to lay her out. In fifty years, she'd never seen her without it,"
gruff ageless Lillian, whose muttered complaints and furious
banging of pots in the kitchen had wakened me, secure, every
morning of my life until I left home; Lillian, whom my grandmother had airily lectured for half a century on the condition
of the piano top, and to whom she had run, choking at her grief,
when my grandfather suddenly dropped dead in the street of a
stroke when I was seven, bypassing the crowd of priests, and
relatives, and bridge-companions without a thought; Lillian, who
had looked up at my frightened face in the doorway as she stood
over my tiny grandmother (sobbing in a kitchen chair), the black
seamed palm stroking the wet, white cheek assuringly, her own
angry tears dropping in my grandmother's hair, to say sternly:
"Now, you go on, chile. Go on now. Go find yourself a flower.
I'll fix you up some collards for your supper"; Lillian, from whom
(after a girlhood of watching) I had learned something of love.
And other difficulties.

"Oh, yes—Lillian. That's right. She was sure an angry old
woman, remember? I'm real sorry to hear it."

Church chewed his chicken wing reflectively, lean good-looking
face full of his own thoughts, and I remembered how he had
smelled of bay rum, and fresh catfish, and "boy" that summer we
were sixteen, and how I had bossed him, and how he had grumbled but been obedient; and how he had strutted with Lillian,
using grown-up cuss words, and then accepted her scolding
meekly. Looking down at him, I felt warm toward him, and his
good ineffectual heart, and wanted to touch the evenly combed
curve of his narrow head, just for the feel of it, and for the old
friendship—that had never been anything more than that, though
sometimes we had pretended. "Be a sweetheart, honey, and run

get me another gin," I asked instead, and watched him go off for it through the gay, talkative group around the coffee table, from which I felt unaccountably separated at that moment, as if more than a few years and some geography had come between.

I sipped my gin, and picked at my food, while Church sat at my feet happily, and before long half a dozen of the others had drawn around us.

"Oh, you know," T. P. Reeves said. "I meant to tell you. I tried to look you up in Rome September before last. Your grandmother told me you were there, and I asked around, but we must have just missed one another."

"I missed a whole lot of things in Rome," studying the grey-blue eyes and long patrician nose that were so expressive of the peculiar theatricality of some Southern men, who are idle and self-centered and constantly watching themselves be men—like actors who sometimes seem so lonely inside their good-looks. "Besides, by then I'd gone to Capri to see some fags."

"I would have thought you'd seen enough of *those* up in New York," someone said. "My Lord, when I was up there last fall—"

"No, but these were friends of mine," I interrupted crisply. "Francis and Vivian. I was teaching them how to walk, in exchange for their teaching me how to—well, it's a controversial story."

A few of them laughed—Maggie because she didn't understand, and some of the men because they did. "But where does everyone *go* now—for fun?" I went on. "I heard Beaujacques' was shut down."

"Oh, that was years and years ago," Turtle Cheney said, unable to keep her eyes off my knees, or off of Church's face that was on a level with them. "Now, most everybody goes to the Planter's Club out on Masonic Drive."

"Say, why don't we go on over there later?" Church said to no one in particular.

"Good God, was that where I had lunch with Granner last Thursday?" remembering the composition leather, the menus in four colors, the souvenir matchbooks printed in Chicago. "It might be White Plains. Or Bismarck, North Dakota—"

"Oh, everything's changed since you went up yonder, May," a girl said, waiting for some man to light her cigarette. "Aleck's right up with the times now—"

"Nancianne, honey," I replied, "that's just what *I* was thinking," for the grave changes that were coming were already foreshadowed by new highways cutting through the old plantation acreage, and that flash-growth of ranch houses, service stations, and supermarkets that appeared as soon as the bulldozers went away, giving everything the same brand-new, freshly painted, resolutely shallow veneer that was the latest mode of the Great American Ugliness just then; and what I'd come South for—high-ceilinged, odorous stores with four-bladed fans moving unhurriedly over bolts of yard goods, and red dust roads out of town where black snakes sluggishly sunned themselves like coils of cheap garden hose, and shaded streets of screen porches and brick walks—was clearly in the process of vanishing. And there is no bitterness quite so attractive as that which has its source in nostalgia.

"Come on, though, Church," I said all of a sudden. "Take me someplace dirty, and sentimental, and *backward*," finishing up my gin in a gulp. "Let's go out to that colored place on the Lecompte Road. Remember? Is it still there?"

Everyone laughed uneasily. "You mean Fats'?"

"You *have* been gone a long time, honey," Church said. "You don't just drop in to Fats' any more like you used to could. Besides, it's Fats' Wife's now. Fats died a couple of years ago."

"My God, have the women taken over even among the Negroes!" I said, eying the girls, impregnable in their femininity, who, like me, knew how much could be accomplished by a headache and the helpless flattery of ingenuous eyes, when you were dealing with men schooled to an ideal of gallantry that was outmoded.

"I haven't been out there for three years," Lawtell Ducomb said. " 'Cause it just makes *them* nervous, you know."

"And isn't that where they had that stabbing six months ago?" someone asked. One of the frilly girls. "You'd be surprised how uppity everyone's gotten—"

"Oh, I don't care about all *that*," I said. "I want to go out to Fats' like I used to."

"Well, I don't know. . . . What do you think, sport? I heard there are still *some* whites go out there."

It wasn't Fats' particularly. It was that I felt them drifting in indecision toward the breakup of the evening, and I wanted to avoid the inevitable, cloying moments in the car with Church until I was gayer and more tolerant. I wanted more drinks, and a new place, and half thought of suggesting that we drive to New Orleans or East Texas (just because I knew I could get them to consider it), but settled on what was at hand instead. "No, I want to go to Fats'. So is one of you *gentlemen* gonna take me out there?"

Church hesitated for a second, a second during which I faintly pitied him. "I suppose we *could*," he hazarded to Lawtell. "It's still early, and Fats' wife'll remember me. You got a bottle? . . . And you're right—isn't there some white-trash plays piano there sometimes?"

Maggie couldn't come, but almost everyone else tried to get into the right spirit, milling around saying good-by, laughing too loud in the driveway, and then squeezing into two cars, as if caught up for a moment by the memory of "The Old Days" (which none of them had ever really experienced) when their kind had been the last handsome, reckless, land-and-blood gentry of the last feudal aristocracy in America, and no place in that parish was off-limits to their whim.

As we drove off, I heard Turtle complaining in the other car: "But I seem to have lost my compact, T.P. I just don't know *where* I could have left it. . . ."

"Do you know where she left it, honey?" Church asked me.

"Search me," I replied, fingering the cameo inside my purse, and passing him my cigarette. He tasted my lipstick as he drove, absurdly happy.

· 2 ·

Fats' was a Negro bar on the shabby edges of town, in an old board building that had probably been a crossroads store in Reconstruction times, and certainly hadn't been painted since, though there was a stop light at the crossroads now, around which a cluster of tumble-down bungalows and a Gulf station had grown up. During the full heat of afternoon, it was a desolate emptiness of squashed beer cans, sun-yellowed cardboard signs, oil-slicks bubbling on the asphalt, and the refuse of car ashtrays. The highway south toward Bunkie shimmered with mirages, and gawky Negro children, in feed-sack shifts, stood scrinching their toes in the dust under the live-oaks, waving at you as you flashed by in your huge, fortunate car.

But at night it was a glimmer of mysterious lights through peeling shutters, and the muffled stomp of tireless hot music, and the acrid exhaust of muddied flivvers. Something dark and thrilling and untrammeled always hung about the stoop (that creaked as you stepped up) and the rotting cheesecloth curtains that blew idly in the dark of upstairs windows and the mingled odors of cape jasmine and fried meat; and in my last years in high school, when we were just starting to drink more or less seriously and hell around as a matter of course, we used to drop in to Fats' sometimes, keeping to ourselves, bringing our own pints, and only staying an hour or so. Indeed, it had been something of a cachet, among the boys, to be known by Fats, and to be able to say: "Come on then, you guys. I know where we can get us setups. *I* know a place that's open." Fats had looked the other way at our juvenile dissipations, because the cops looked the other way at the piano and guitar players that sometimes performed there, despite the fact that he was licenseless. In the old days, Fats knew just how far to let us go, and we knew just how long to stay, as a result of that curious and unspoken understanding across the abyss of race, which cannot be explained to Northerners, white or black. But now, as I was led to believe by Church, the traditional circuit of perception had been broken, and I could feel his unease as we rushed through the odorous night.

"Oh, don't fret," I said somewhat crossly as we pulled up in front of the place. "What's everyone so nervous about anyway?"

He glanced at me with a strange, apprehensive flick of his eyes. "Well, now, listen, you've been gone, honey, and things aren't," his glance snagging on the shadow between my breasts, which the dress was designed to accentuate, "well, just like they used to be," so that I realized that it wasn't me he was apprehensive about —what I might say or do—but my dress, which would compel him to bluster, and dare anyone to look at me cross-eyed. And poor Church wasn't much as a blusterer.

"All right, sweetie," I said brightly. "Give me your raincoat then, and we won't tempt the big, black natives with the apples."

"Oh, for Pete's sake, May!" he replied, reddening. "I didn't think anything like that," but he helped me into his big, soft trench coat nevertheless. It hung down around my calves, shapeless as an unpegged tent, and I rolled the sleeves back in wide, ludicrous folds, buttoned the top button, and put up the collar under my chin. "There. Am I *decent* enough for you?" I said, as the other car drove up. "I'm as decent as a cloistered nun, 'cept I'm not wearing any drawers." But before he could decide whether this was only another goad, the others were milling around us, and we were clambering through the door toward music, the men (who had obviously used the bottle in the other car) leading the way.

Fats' hadn't changed much. It was still the same long, homely cave with a dark bar down one side, a line of rickety booths as uncomfortable as church pews down the other, and a scatter of unsteady tables and cheap chairs in between. It was just as dim with dusty yellow lights, and as much a haze of smoke and heat, and still too narrow a room for the number of people and the amount of noise that filled it. Perhaps it had been painted, probably the calendars and beer posters had been changed, and certainly there was an ugly new jukebox toward the back where the frontless upright piano stood (surrounded, as always, by dark, hunched figures), but nonetheless it gave me the same feeling of expectancy and recklessness as it had when I was eighteen.

There was a sudden catch in the drawling laughter and the talk, beginning with the group of big, levied men near the door, and spreading back through the place like a wave of silence, isolating individual voices, and then dousing them, too, until I could clearly hear someone near the piano saying: "An' then the gal says, 'I'll roll over, you monster, only leggo my wig!' . . . What? Oh . . ." Lawtell and Church were conferring with the aproned bartender, and gesturing toward one of the booths. No one was looking at us, but no one pointedly looked away from us either, and gradually the talk ebbed back, oddly quenched and formal—the sort of talk *meant* to be overheard. Glasses were brought to the booth, and bottles of seltzer and Doctor Pepper, along with a bowl of ice obviously chipped off a large cake, and the men made us drinks out of their own whisky.

"Um-m-m, smell it," I said—the musk of cheap soap, pomade, Camel cigarettes, bacon fat, and frank sweat—the whole rich smell of the Southern Negro night that brought back my silly, lost girlhood in a flash; the fragrant, sensual South one knew through one's servants and the streets, and accepted naturally, and didn't think about till later, and didn't miss till much later.

"Yes," murmured Emily Lynn in a whisper. "Isn't it awful, though?"

But for a while I was too open to everything to be sarcastic about what Emmy said, or even to remember the last time I had felt as she did—which was the first time a Negro man sat next to me on a trolley in St. Louis when I was nineteen, and I had an instantaneous feeling of shock similar to the shock of seeing a wet-mouthed old bum expose himself on a midnight subway platform, and an equally instantaneous fear of some nameless contagion, moral as well as physical—I, whom Lillian had bathed, and dressed, and kissed, and confessed; who had known Negroes all my life in a casual intimacy few Northerners ever achieve, but who had never once sat next to one on a public vehicle. Nor did I remember, at that moment, the slow confusion that settled down over me when nothing happened as a result of the Negro's sitting there—no word, no insult, no taint, society did not collapse, no barriers came down—and after ten blocks he got off at his stop, leaving me precisely the same as when he got on, and yet utterly different—the way you are when you have lost an illusion.

I peered back toward the piano, and said to Church: "One of those boys back there was playing, wasn't he? I heard it from outside. Get them to play something."

"Now, look, honey," he said. "Let's just let 'em alone. Here, have another drink."

"But I want some music. Besides, they want to play. They were playing when we came in. Why do you think they *stopped?*"

"Well, I'm sure it's different up in New York, darlin'," Turtle began, "but really—"

"Oh, it's no different anywhere," I said. "God, you'd think this was Occupied France."

"Well, when in Rome—" someone put in gaily.

"Look, *I'll* go back and ask them then. And fix me a man-size drink this time, will you?" fumbling for money among the girdle, stockings, and Turtle's compact.

"Sure, let's have us some music," Church said manfully. "Why not?" And he sent a dollar back to the piano, and laughed a lot, intent on making a joke out of it.

"You're sure still a heller," he enthused with a boyish smile. "But, seriously, it *is* different now, honey. You can't just go anywhere and do anything you want to. Not since some of the trouble we've had here in Aleck in the last year or two. I'm not saying it's *better*, you understand, but it's different."

"Oh, things haven't changed that much. *They're* still over there, and *we're* still over here, aren't we?"

"Well, what arrangement are you suggesting?" a girl began archly.

"No, but we say: 'Can't go out to Fats', it'll embarrass them,' and they say: 'Man, here come the ofays, cool it,' and as a result the South's full of long faces. . . . But anyway I don't really care about all that any more, it's enough of a hideous bore in New York—and if the snub has replaced the lynching bee, I suppose it's progress, but all I want to do is have some *fun*."

"Well, I don't know what you call fun," Turtle sniffed, "but—"

"*That's* part of it," I snapped back. For someone had started to lay down chords on the piano.

The night really began with the music that took shape then, piece by piece, tentatively searching for itself, a guitar joining the piano in a heavy strum, and both buoyed suddenly by a young man da-da-da-dooming on a dented cymbal with a single scarred stick. When I think about that night these days, I think of the crude, four-chord blues they discovered after a while, and only then go back and remember Maggie O'Fee's, and all the silly, disputatious talk. For that music was as naturally a part of the background of our table of white Southerners, suspicious and on the alert, as it was of the other tables of black Southerners (ditto and ditto), and we shared it with them in the same way that we shared our drawls. And, for me, it was the music of the huge, urban night up yonder as well—the homeless, half-bitter music in which all rebels against the day hear the stubborn beating of their own blood.

But even more than the music, for me, was the boy who got up
to sing to it all of a sudden, simply coming out of the shadows by
the piano into a wedge of smoky light—tall, almost gangly, and
no more than nineteen, with huge, blind glasses dominating his
face, 60¢ dime-store spectacles painted over with black enamel;
coming forward uncertainly, to be stopped on the right spot by
the pale hand of the pianist, to stand there poised around the
tight bulge of his loins in the faded jeans, lean meatless flanks
held in in readiness; his small piquant head, with the thin crinkle
of tight kinks over the well-formed skull, turned to one side and
slightly up as if listening for a wild, faint call in the wind; the
soft flattened brown planes of his nose shimmering moistly with
simple sweat, his wide expressive mouth, pink inside the full lips
(that intimate pink of the inner body), suddenly coming wetly
open to let a husky, insinuating song come out.

"L-o-o-v-e my gal in Jeanerette, that soft brown," he began to
wail.

"Booze with Lake Charles Bessie when I'm down," hips swaying a little on the off-beat.

"Chick in Ponchatoula feeds me when I'm there—

"But that Houma woman's drawin' to my pair—

"Yes, oh ye-e-e-s, and *now* you know!"

Hands started to clap in the dark near the door, coming in half
a beat off—an oddly exciting discordance that only seemed to
intensify the rhythm. The yellow light in which the boy stood was
jaggedly edged by the black pump and lift of shoulders in between, and, at each break, the floorboards vibrated right up
through my shoes from the pound of a hundred feet drumming in
a relentless stomp, through which at one point I clearly heard
Turtle's nervous little snicker—the sort of snicker people always
accord any kind of nakedness when others are present, being
afraid of what they actually feel.

"When you find me by the sweet-gum tree—

"Come on, babe, and seal my plea," broad palm laid out in a
caress on the taut column of his thigh.

"I know. . . . Yes, yes, I know now—

"It's all all right now, oh y-e-s-s, I know—" The voice blurred
with little wicked grunts on certain beats; coy sighs expired
toward a whisper, only to erupt at the bottom of it into a sudden
joyful howl; the tranced face, dripping with the sweat of total
concentration, upturned to reveal an almost defiant exultation, so
that all at once I fancied I knew the amount of ecstasy that was
bottled in the dark of his life, and how much we wasted, muddled
by all our senses.

Everyone in the darkness around us laughed at his uncon-
sciously contorted gestures, the sweetly trusting ugliness of his
mouth trying to frame an impossible tremolo on the end of a
phrase, as if they knew he depended on their natural response to
the sight of him for any idea he might ever have of the world he
would never see. And, in astonishment, I realized that men, blind
from birth in my polite world, were deprived of some inmost clue
to visual reality by the very tact of those with corrupted eyes.

"Now, now, I got a no-good—" the boy began again, all teeth
and saliva, groin slammed into the chord.

"Yes, now, I got *me* one no-good—

"I got a no-good woman loves me when she wants," the fun in
the voice suddenly changing into pique, and the pique into
anxiety.

"I got a no-where, no-good woman—

"Burns the crease right off my pants—" the anxiety abruptly
producing a swallowed moan of helplessness, at which Church
laughed irrelevantly, as at the unwitting *double-entendre* of a
child.

"But listen here, I say it's all all right now," veering up again, a
certain hardness stiffening the voice, a certain incalculable opti-
mism brightening it.

"Listen to me, I say it's all all right now—yah!

"It's gonna be all right now—

"She blew town anyhow—no good, oh *yes*—" the voice itself
seeming to make its own peace with life's betrayals, the voice

speaking for the body out of which it came, and for its humors and agitations and bafflements, a little mournful with the subsiding sob that lingers for a while in a cheered child's first hesitant laugh; somehow suggestive, too, of the grief that purges as usually only art can purge; a voice without an emotional flaw, with no failure of feeling, and, as a result, almost unearthly to hear, because we are so unused to hearing anything so utterly earthly exposed to the disbelief of strangers.

"Is it gonna be all *right* now?" the wavering, drawn-out challenge of the revivalist preacher, followed (as the last chord banged down as tuneless as doom) by a yelled "Y-a-*a-a-h!*" from the excited crowd.

"Christ! Who the fuck is *that?*" I exclaimed out of a bad New York habit. "Does anyone know?" The ugly, graphic word lay there among the girls like an offense for which their upbringing had fashioned no way to comment, and the men started talking all at once, and very loud.

"Oh, yes," T.P. said. "I remember now. He must be the one I heard about. Son of my Uncle Willis's yard-nigger ten years ago, old 'Big' Small. . . . And you probably heard about *this* one, Church," with a jerk of his thumb. "Hangs around out at the old Prenderman place where Bett and that—"

"What's that?" I broke in. "You mean Betty Prenderman? Is she *living* out at the old house?" For I'd gone to school with her— a pale, thin-lipped girl, fleshless then, her mouth usually open in a look of gawky surmise, her brown pupils enlarged behind enormous glasses. We'd never been close, and I hadn't thought of her in years, but I remembered the old Prenderman house itself, ramshackle and unlived-in since the Nineties, out on a dusty country road that had been bypassed by a new blacktop; where crape myrtle ran riot over the smashed windows, and spider lilies grew in the washrooms; the house which, sometimes, we had all explored on puberty's last innocent picnics.

"Darlin', you just wouldn't believe it," Emmy said. "She was never much to look at, I'll admit, and she was always a little odd, but when she *married* that person from Georgia—"

"Didn't you hear about it?" Church said. "Bett's aunt finally died two years ago, and it seems there wasn't only but a little money left when they settled everything up—just the old house is about all, and then Bett came home from Philadelphia or St. Louis or someplace where she'd been at college, with this *cracker* from Macon, some Irish red-neck, and they had a child already, and—"

"And, May, they moved *in* out there, in that horrible old leaky house. Remember the *odor* in those cellars—*well*," and Turtle wrinkled her nose at the memory of the bad smell, glancing flirtatiously at Lawtell, for we had all traded mayonnaise-tasting kisses in those cellars years ago.

"Well, and this Georgia boy—what's his name, Church? . . . O'Hara? O'Meara? O'Flynn? . . . I don't know, but he works right here in Aleck at the T&P *freight* depot, nights—"

"So just *no*body sees Bett any more, honey," Turtle went on confidentially. "I don't know anyone who's seen her for a *year* or more. Really. I mean—well, they say they have *niggers* out there sometimes, I mean in the *house!*" her tone suggesting that even *I* wouldn't believe this, girdle or no.

"Oh, I never put much stock in all that," Church stated. "Oh, I heard the *stories* all right. But I'll bet they've simply got some living in the cabins out back, maybe renting or something. I don't care how plain she was, Bett would never—"

"You mean, she wasn't *that* plain?" I laughed.

"Well, all I know, sport, is that the State Police got their eyes on that place, and I heard some boys down around the City Hall bragging they were gonna burn it out some night—"

"Oh, shut up, T.P.," Church snapped back. "Don't pass on that kind of story."

"Well, *anyway*," Emmy put in with a grave frown, "I never thought Betty Prenderman would end up living like a—well, like an *Okie* that way. Why, they used to be the fanciest family in Aleck, my mother told me—"

"Yah?" T.P. replied with knowing scorn. "Well, *there's* someone *lives* with them," gesturing toward the hazy pool of light where the blind boy stood. "Should of figured he'd be here, too. . . . The white-trash you mentioned, Church. Playing the piano . . . Say, I hear he's a yankee, May. Maybe *you* know him," lips curled back provokingly.

I looked, and damned if I didn't. He sat over the all-but-ivory-less keyboard in a fatalistic crouch, as if struggling with his hands. The khaki work shirt was plastered black with sweat on his drooping shoulders; one sockless foot, in a filthy sneaker that was so worn through at the big toe that a yellowish nail protruded, pounded out the relentless beat, and the blond hair on his thighs, naked where the suntans had been hacked off raggedly at about the length of Bermuda shorts, glistened with the splash from his pumping forehead. He looked over his hunched shoulder to check the singer, and I recognized him—the fogged horn rims that masked blue eyes that were quizzical and enervated, the snub-button nose that should have been comic but somehow never had been, the dirty-blond hair fallen in long wet wisps over the seamed forehead. But he had changed: the face had incalculably thickened, blurred; the temples were flecked with a faint grey now; the three-day growth of stubble had come out shockingly white and uneven; his mouth, out of which brittle asides had most usually come just eight months ago, was loose and open around the Camel he had smoked down until it was streaked brown with wet.

"Well, I'll be goddamned," I exclaimed. "Of all places in the world—!"

It was Paul Hobbes. He had been one of our dissolute crowd in New York, and his apartment on Lexington in the '50's (along with Verger's old place in Spanish Harlem, and Agatson's in Chelsea) had been the scene of some of our most disorderly parties. He was trying to write a novel in those days, and there had been a wife around somewhere, who worked midtown and had to be treated gingerly—the sort of small, willful girl who has failed to snag her husband's deepest attention. I'd never known Hobbes well—that is, though we had been drunk in the same bars, and hung over in the same lofts, and though most of the guys with whom I was involved were his friends, we had never shared a word or an experience that meant anything important to either of us. He was just someone who was usually there, who opened bottles, and changed records, and was good for carfare if you were low; who said pointless things like: "Well, what's new?" and willingly put down his volume of Berdyaev or D. H. Lawrence when you rang his bell at midnight. I never remember him initiating anything, *or* failing to go along with anything that was initiated, and, discovering him at the piano in Fats', half a continent away from his copies of *Partisan Review*, and his Brandenburgs sandwiched in among the Bird LP's, was rather like finding Hawthorne in a nudist colony. I immediately thought that there must be more to him than had ever met my eye.

Now, he looked like a gone-bad white man in the tropics—just like the brawling Gauguins, without socks, who always seem to be waiting for Maugham to turn up, or the Ambrose Bierces with a strong smell that you find in the most outlandish Midwest towns—all of whom were once admen, or kid movie stars, or communist intellectuals. The smoke curled up into his slitted eyes from the cigarettes that a pretty Negro girl, leaning her small breasts over the piano to do it, kept replacing between his stained lips, and he carelessly banged out those few rudimentary chords while the boy made a song out of them that evoked paintless honky-tonks, sagging lonesome shacks, bailing chants, and wild Baptist revivals up in the pineys, all at the same time. Work-wrinkled palms clapped the sweat together, beer bottles thumped on splashed tables, gaudy print dresses rode up on dusky thighs, and someone's laughter wailed in right on pitch.

"They'll be getting out the ju-jus next," Lawtell yelled over the uproar. "You sure he's white? He sure plays like a nigger."

"When I knew him, he couldn't play at all," I yelled back, "so it's a clear win."

"You really *know* him?" Turtle's wonder unable to hide her automatic distaste. "From New York, I suppose. But I declare, honey, I know people go to Harlem and all that, but—"

"He's a novelist, *honey*, so don't worry. He's a graduate of Columbia, and one of the brightest people I know," which wasn't true for a minute, but she had so easily ticketed him as bum, renegade, and weirdo that I felt defensive.

"Well, I must say it's all awfully," snickering knowingly to the other girls, "oh, *basic* . . . just look at that girl. I swear she hasn't a *stitch* on under that dress," a quick glance at me, "and, of course, she's already got two pickaninnies at home," plainly aware that Lawtell's tanned palm lay noncommittally on her thigh just over the gartersnap, and flushing complacently, which told me in an instant that they were an item. For a moment, I wondered if they had made serious love together—the pin-neat hairdo and the knife-pressed slacks. Full-naked, lights on, masks off. I tried to imagine them gasping the obscene, importunate words, which pass for tenderness or passion in our day, and failed with a sniff, and turned back to watch Hobbes, as if he were my oldest friend.

The number was over, and he was standing up, so tall his bony shoulders sloped forward, thinner in the bare legs and harder around the elbows and wrists than I remembered. He upended a bottle of beer every now and then, drinking thirstily, and wiping the spill off his chin with the flat of a dirty hand. The pretty Negro girl had crooked two fingers possessively into his belt, and was talking to someone else. Then he turned and shuffled toward the bar for a fresh bottle, and noticed us for the first time. Something in his face (its natural expression at that moment, its spark) doused immediately at the sight of us, exactly as it had with the —I was about to say the *other* Negroes—except that it was replaced on his face with a look of beetling disdain.

"Hobbes!" I called.

He recognized me, and smiled with genuine surprise. But the

smile faded almost immediately as he approached. "Hey," he said hoarsely, "how're you doing? Christ, the Underground Railway must be operating in reverse tonight. There's a guy over there from Detroit, too," eying the others at the table, who were all at a loss in their various ways, and then looking back at me. "Say, has it started to rain or something?"

"No, no, I'm in drag— But what are you *doing* here, for Christ's sake?"

"Just having some beers," he said solemnly, paying no attention to Turtle's efforts to keep her eyes away from the dark sweat stains around the crotch of his makeshift shorts. "Oh, you mean *here*. Oh, I'm living with some people a couple of miles out of town. About three months now . . . You heading for the Coast or something?" pulling up a spindly chair and folding his length into it.

"No, I'm *from* Aleck. I mean, originally. I'm visiting back."

"Oh, yes," he said without much interest. "I guess I remember. . . . Hey, man, pass me another one, will you? . . . Well, Jesus, let's see—what's new in New York?" more curious than he was letting on.

"Well, Dan's gone to Vienna, two weeks ago, and Stofsky's gone to work—how about *that?*—and, oh yes, Gene Pasternak just vanished, Mexico City or someplace, but—" I had noticed the straggle of hairs where his shirt was open down his chest—wiry, sparse, most of them grey, somehow sobering to me. "But where's your cute little wife? What happened to—was it Kathryn?"

"Yes. Just what happens to wives. We split. I heard she got married and happy. Can I bum a cigarette?"

I took the opportunity to move Lawtell's pack over in front of me to smoke out of, and, frankly, it never even occurred to me to introduce Hobbes to any of them. In any case, they were adroitly acting as if he wasn't there, and chatting about their allergies. All except Church, who was keeping an ear in both conversations.

"But how come Alexandria?" I said. "And since when do *you*

play piano? I remember you and Gene making a hideous racket on saucepans, but—"

He laughed all of a sudden, a weary little laugh, almost a chuckle, as if he'd recalled something pleasant that he hàdn't thought of for years, and with it a whole lost life. "No, I just mess around. I guess I know about ten or twelve chords now. It's not as hard as I always thought. . . . No, but I picked it up to back Orkie —he's the blind kid who was singing—and we come over here some weekends, because there's no piano at Bett's."

I explained to him that I knew her, and Church tried to join in. "Yes, how is she? I haven't seen Bett in two years." Hobbes studied him, as he might have studied a policeman who was try-ing to be friendly, and finally said: "Yah? Is that right?" I asked him again how he happened to be in the South.

He thought for a minute, eyes fluttering shut as if he was un-used to gathering his thoughts. "Well, you know, let's see— After it was finally over with me and Kathryn—I mean, after we'd held onto it past any sense, the way you do, and ruined it far enough so we could finally call it quits—everything seemed to go sour for me. I was absolutely broke, and then I still cared when my shirts were a day old, and—oh, Korea, McCarthy, Dylan Thomas—I mean, the news was *always* bad, and I got to drinking in the morning—I drank a whole lot," oddly proud of this, it seemed to me, "and had panic-attacks from, you know, just seeing cripples on the street. . . . So I lay around reading *Time* magazine, hitting the 42nd Street movies before noon, and I seriously thought of going into publishing or advertising—I mean, I actually started making phone calls and all that." He shook his head with amaze-ment. "Well, anyway, one day I realized that I hadn't been out of town in five years—except a few weekends, and drunken flights to Hoboken or Provincetown. So I just took off. I didn't want to be in New York when it happens—"

"What?"

He blinked wearily. "What's going to."

"You mean," with a deprecating laugh, "the *Bomb?* The Last

War?" capitalizing them the way we all did then, as others once capitalized Judgment Day or The Revolution. "Oh, come *on*, Hobbes."

"No, no, no," stiffening at being taken lightly. "No, what the *anxiety* about all that's going to do to everything," he replied with perfect seriousness. "People are going to get *sick* of that anxiety. They're going to get *tired* of it, you wait and see. They're going to want to *forget* it. And I just don't want to be there when that happens."

"Well, that sounds sensible to me," Church put in with some puzzlement. "But maybe I didn't understand you."

"No, but everything's going to get *Ugh*," Hobbes said to me impatiently. "*You* know. Everyone's going to be well off, and scared, and yet *tired* of being scared, and so we're going to get *The General*. You wait and see. Babbitt Strikes Back."

"I never heard you talk politics before." I laughed. "Do you really *care* about all that? . . . Lord!"

"This isn't politics. It's psychology. *Child* psychology . . . I mean, what do you do when you're an adolescent, and sick of the burdens of your brand-new individuality, and worried about liking sex too much, and not liking football enough—what do you do? You become like everyone else, a reasonable facsimile of the bore next door, a pally little extrovert with somebody else's head —and you take to idolizing your teachers, or your father, or something. . . . You try to lose your acne in the crowd," a detail in which I saw his whole youth. "Well, I just decided I'd *miss* it this time if I could." He was studying me distantly, hardly listening to himself.

"Hobbes, you've changed," I pronounced. "You've gotten interesting. . . . But I honestly didn't think you'd ever leave New York. You of *all* people. I used to joke with Dan about it. Fairly mean jokes."

"I know. I know that," looking at me with expressionless candor. "But the time that's coming," shaking his head. "Well, it's a time a man should be *out* of step with, *bypassed* by, *exiled* from—that's

what I think anyway. So I decided I'd just vanish. . . . I suppose
I'll go back once it's over."

"So you live at Betty's? But how come? You *still* haven't told
me."

"Oh, that. Well, Jack was at Columbia for a semester after the
war—Jack O'Meara, her husband—and I was vaguely heading for
Mexico, and bumped into him at the bus station, and, through
him, Orkie and—well, I never got any farther."

"You're crazy," I said with a laugh I hope was warm. "But don't
you ever miss New York? Every time I go into Brentano's I expect to see you hiding among the textbooks."

"Sometimes. When it rains . . . But—" He was staring at Turtle's
glistening blonde page-boy, and the carefully folded, mono-
grammed handkerchief with which T.P. was surreptitiously wiping the perspiration from his forehead; and at Lawtell's college
ring, and Emmy's charm bracelet. "—but then Orkie," at which
he snapped back with the old, rather naïve, almost schoolboy
eagerness in his eyes that had once made all of us unkindly call
him The Cheerleader. "But, say, what do you think of him though?
Isn't he great? He's just nineteen—Orchid Small, that's his given
name, you see—Orchid! Yes, *actually* . . . So everyone calls him
Little Orkie—and he's got a strange touch with flowers too—I
mean, they seem to *understand* him—he tends someone's garden
for money—you probably know them, I can't remember—but I
stick with him, that's what I'm saying," growing confused, and
pausing to gulp at his new bottle. "But what he was singing there,
'It's all all right'—remember?—he says that all the time, when you
ask him, when you *talk* about things. . . . 'No need to shake,
Hobbesy,' he says, and he means don't worry, don't get nervous,
don't *shiver* that way," laughing in the middle of it to hear how
silly it sounded. "But that's what he believes, I mean about
*every*thing. . . . So I just go along, waiting for him to show me—
this nineteen-year-old nigra," the word sounding curiously ugly
because he had no drawl. "No, but really I'm just *studying* with
him in a way—like I used to study with Irwin Edman." He wiped

his palm over his grizzled cheeks, blinked, sniffed, and stared at me with a trace of his old embarrassment. "Well, I get to the end of my mind these days, and there's nothing else to do but sleep. . . . So you and Dan didn't make it, eh?" so pointed a change of subject that I felt called upon to explain in a few sentences.

"Well, you know Dan. All those New England preoccupations. He can't swing loose from them. He can't stop *caring*. I mean, you'll be drunk and happy, and then he'll say, 'But can all this lead to a new morality?' It just got pointless."

To all of which Church listened with infuriating attentiveness, as if it was a hint on my part, an opening. I started considering how I was going to cope with the pass that was obviously ahead, and heard myself saying to Hobbes in a quick undertone: "Listen, don't leave. I'm hung up here. . . . You going back to Betty's?"

He didn't flicker an eyelid, only nudged the ash off his cigarette on the table edge, noting Church with a blank shift of his eyes, and murmured: "Pretty soon. But don't bring all of *them* along, you know—"

"Okay. But wait here. I'll be right back."

"Where are you going, honey?" Church said.

"Where little girls go to go."

"In *here!*" he exclaimed before he could stop himself, and before he could stop *me*, I'd walked off in his raincoat to the john, moving among shadowy arms and shoulders that carefully never touched me.

It was empty, dreary, stark—yellowed toilet paper, a greasy mirror, slippery floors—that men's-room ugliness that women rarely see. I felt a twinge of revulsion that sobered me, and I started to take down my hair. I reached into Church's coat, hoping to find a comb, and came up with a packet of rubbers—neat, antiseptic, meant for me. I could just hear him telling himself with uncertain bravado in the drugstore: "Well, just in *case*—"and scorned the ritualized corniness of it, even though, not four hours before, I had scooped my diaphragm into my handbag, along with lipstick, change purse, powder, and key ring, just as usual.

The inconsistency of this reaction told me in a moment that I didn't intend to sleep with him, even to be nice, even to be polite.

Church? I thought, considering him one last time. His fastidious hands were certain to be gentle, urging, his mouth and eyes were certain to express his speechless gratitude for the gift, his words— But at the thought of his whispered "You're beautiful," or "I've wanted this so long, honey," and the inevitable "I love you," which his sort of perfectly decent, perfectly conventional man felt was required of him in the bottom of an embrace, I knew that I couldn't go through with it, even to see if I could feel something with him. I didn't want any more love; I wanted the wordless, overriding flood that comes before it.

Unpinning my hair, I decided to ditch Church and go out to Betty's with Hobbes. It was only a question of how. I was reckless with drink and boredom, and I suppose I was angry and hurt to find the South so alien to what I had become. I wanted "reality" (that magic word to my generation, our last resort, our last hope, our last value), even the reality of that ugly toilet, anything but the unreal chatter of my friends, so brittle with self-approval. I went back to the table intent on getting loose from the people there, and all they represented. More than a little stoned.

The sight of my hair, let down on my shoulders in heavy, uncombed, taffee-colored coils, alarmed Church in a flash, and by now he had the cross and baffled look of a man whose partner in a foolish game keeps willfully raising the stakes on him.

"I couldn't find a comb," I said meanly, "and I thought *all* you gallants carried a comb in your pockets—along with the *other* toilet articles," taking a long, rash swallow out of his glass.

I think he was actually speechless with embarrassment, not daring even to make a flippant comment for fear I'd say something so pointed that he'd have to take a stand. Hobbes smoked and drank in his incurious dishevelment, looking at the white girls as men look at nuns, eyes devoid of even the consideration of passion.

"Is he going to sing again?" I enthused, nodding toward Orkie, who lounged against the piano, shoulders sloped forward like those of a boy not yet used to the sudden growth of the past year. "What a crazy face he has, though! Like a small, canny animal. And why in God's name do the blind always look less anxious than the rest of us? I suppose it's something they don't know—"

"Probably something they *do*," Hobbes said. "The simpler, the clearer, after all . . . But he hasn't eaten yet, so I imagine we'll be cutting out home in a minute," giving me the cue to do with what I wanted. "We only woke up three hours ago," again that curious, muted pride in the admission.

He got up suddenly, as if he was uncomfortable; muttered, "I'll just go back and get everyone together"; paused at a thought; forced himself to take two more cigarettes from Lawtell's pack, one for his mouth, one for behind his ear; said sheepishly: "I think there's a machine somewhere, if you run out"; and went away before I could say a word.

"You sure know some oddballs, honey, I *must* say," Church commented sternly. "I suppose he's hiding out down here, isn't he?"

"That's just what he's doing."

"I figured that the minute I saw him. I once knew a guy who'd embezzled two thousand dollars from an office supply firm, and was hiding out in Phoenix when I was there in the Air Force. A very unhappy guy." He was vaguely fatherly as he touched my arm. "Oh, I believe everyone should have their fling all right. Why, I loafed around New Orleans for damn near a whole summer after college, and I swear I was *drunk* almost every night, hanging out with the wildest people—I could tell you stories. My daddy almost gave me up for lost! . . . But then, what the hell, you pull yourself together. You get sick of it." He looked at me sagely, ignoring the cleavage which the unbuttoned raincoat revealed. "You ought to get yourself married, honey, that's what you ought to do. I can tell."

I stared back at him in cold, defiant pique—at his mouth pursed with secret vanity, and his tolerant brown eyes leveled with con-

cern, and his infuriating, twenty-dollar silk tie. "Horsefeathers,"
I said amiably. "Bullshit."

His smile dissolved into a sadly persevering pout. He was a
mild person, who was always being put down, and his moments
of self-assurance were short. "Well, I don't see that *that's* an
answer to anything," he murmured without conviction.

"But who asked anything, for God's sake! And who are you to
tell me I ought to get married?"

"Well, I *thought* I was an old friend of yours, honey, and besides—"

"Besides, you figure I've had my 'fling,' as you call it, and it's
time for me to snap out of it, grow up, settle down, be mediocre
because, at least, it's a *mature* adjustment to the norm? . . .
Right?" quoting something my mother had read somewhere,
which had become over the years her single contribution to any
conversation about the various black-sheep drunkard uncles and
eccentric poetry-writing aunts who abound like gaudy weeds
around the edges of any shabby-genteel Southern family.

"Now, you know I never said anything like that," he put in,
somewhat aggrieved. "Don't be unfair."

Which, of course, aroused a twinge of sympathy in me that only
increased my fury. After all, I was trying to get away from him,
wasn't I?

"But, really, it's deliciously hypocritical, *honey*, in light of the
contents of your pockets. Ashley Wilkes during the day, Rhett
Butler at night, and all so Southern and hokey I could just break
down and *cry!* Ah could, Ah swear Ah could! . . ."

The others were listening now, sobered and on their guards,
for we are sensitive about our drawls down South, they can so
easily be parodied, and many's the time up North that I had gone
into a blind rage when someone, meaning no offense, fell into an
imitation of mine. But, now, I went on and on, hurting myself as
much as I was hurting them, which, I suppose, somehow paid for
it in my eyes—such ambiguities seeming natural in a region where

guilt and pride are so often only masks for one another, change and change-about.

"But as far as I'm concerned," I finished up nastily, "there aren't many experiences left that haven't become so stereotyped, and dry-cleaned, that they're meaningless, and the kind of cornflake marriage you're talking about isn't the result of growing *out* of silliness, but giving *in* to it, if you ask me. . . . And, honey, I'd rather go to hell in a hurry," giving him the dazzling challenge of a contemptuous smile.

"Well, we can just go on talking and talking about all of this if you've got your mind set on it, but why don't we get out of *here* to do it? . . . What do you say, T.P.?"

"I don't want to leave," I said flatly. "I want another drink, and some more music," taking the coat off my shoulders, and exposing all that orange, and all that white, to anyone who cared to look. "But you all go ahead."

Church stared at me with grim lips, as men stare at women who are drunk and willful, and flaunt themselves for no purpose, calculating how to cope with my bitchiness. I could see the alternatives presenting themselves behind his besieged eyes—conciliate or get tough—and, being weak, he made the wrong choice.

"Now, listen, I brought you down here against my better judgment, and we've taken a look, and had some drinks, and bought you some of that jungle music to make you happy, and that's all right. But if you think I'm going to leave you in a *nigger* saloon, dressed like that, just because you're feeling unreasonable, I reckon you're even drunker than I figure—and don't worry, *I* like my booze like anyone," finishing off his drink to prove it, and also to forestall *my* finishing it. "Now, I don't know what kind of no-'count man you've gotten used to up North, or how you been treated—I ain't saying they're *all* like your beat-up friend there— but no Southerner'd let you stay here alone no matter what kind of fool yankee point you're tryin' to prove—not even if you were some trash from Arkansas. So just you button back up, honey, and let's get going," and he started to rise, his forehead beaded with fine sweat.

At sight of which, I did an unpardonable thing. I laughed at him. He seemed so ludicrous and simperingly grave, like a small, Sunday-suited boy taking his mother's arm across an intersection, and I suppose I laughed specifically to hurt him, because, of course, I knew he was right. I couldn't stay there alone. The fear that breeds hatred, and the hatred that breeds violence, and the violence that breeds guilt—none of it had changed, no matter how I tried to ignore it, and the despair of the South flowed over me in a great dark wave for the first time since coming home.

No one can know that despair—the despair of being a relatively decent Southerner—but someone who has lived there: the inherited shame that must find cynicism or platitude as a mask, the intimate knowledge of the irrational side of man, which no other American lives with in quite the same way. No wonder we are given to fatalism, bourbon, quirk. I'd tried not caring, I'd tried convictions, anger, argument, escape, bravado. I'd hated the South with that hate that can only come from unrequited love, and defended it out of a perversity born of helplessness, and longed for it as a child longs for a lost parent—having known (from the summer of childhood) that beneath the languid air of gentility and order lurked red violence that could ravage the cabin night, dark doings with a rope a parish away, abstract passions that could convulse a sun-lulled town, some enigmatic taint in the very jasmine itself (like the smell of a bruise) that was the last thing in my life that could still make me blush. But how can you hate yourself without hurting yourself as well? So I laughed at poor Church, because he was right, and everything was just the same, and that left me nothing to feel but despair at being forever wedded to it.

"Well," he said, struggling against his mouth for composure, "I'm not just *about* to take any more of your—your *innuendoes!* I'm not just about to, you hear! I'm *not!*" He turned to stomp away, but then turned back to say in a strange, spiteful voice: "I don't know why you can't just be *nice*, for Pete's sake!" the sound of which, now that it was out, chagrined him even more, and he lurched off into the crowd.

"But I never have been," I murmured to no one in particular. "What in the world was he so huffy about?"

Everyone was embarrassed, and trying to occupy their hands. Turtle searched distractedly for her compact, Lawtell frowned, and then said: "Oh, he'll cool off when he gets to the car. He'll be back."

No one seemed to know what to do. They lit cigarettes and stubbed them out; they sipped their drinks; they tried to talk. But I knew. I knew I had to get out of there, away from them, and my understanding of them, right or wrong, and so I simply got up without a word, pulling the coat over my shoulders again, and walked away, back toward the piano, just catching a glimpse of Hobbes' stained shorts vanishing through a tin-sheeted door I hadn't noticed before. I caught it as it whooshed shut, shoved against it with my shoulder, and found myself outside in the red neon-dim of ashcans and broken bottles in back of Fats'.

• 3 •

"You feel like driving?" Hobbes said. "I'm pissed."

It was an old Thirties roadster, complete with rumble seat, wire wheels, and the shift in the floor. Once, long ago, it had been yellow, with black mudguards and red trim, but now it was covered with that ocher patina that accumulates from barreling into

someone else's dust on wild jaunts down the bone-dry dirt roads
of a long, rainless summer.

Now that I was put to it, I was not so sure I wanted whatever
lay ahead. Hobbes was deflated, wan with exhaustion, and I
found that I knew him hardly at all. There were three Negroes in
the rumble seat: one in an Hawaiian shirt, with a pencil-thin,
rather sinister mustache drooping over a vain mouth; the other,
huge-shouldered, bulging with superfluous muscle in his denim,
with a questioning, somehow bewildered tilt to his eyebrows; and,
between them, a sullen, pudgy girl named Ohla, all flesh and
gingham, with three chrome dime-store barrettes in her stiff hair.
None of them said a word.

I had trouble with the gearshift, and lost the other car almost
immediately—the one that I was supposed to follow, the one with
Orkie, and Hobbes' girl, and who knows who else.

"It cost me twelve dollars," Hobbes yawned, "and a dollar and
a half for the mule to pull it out of the field where it had been
parked for, Christ, about twenty years, I guess. Plus a set of re-
treads Orkie came up with— Take a right up here," slumping
lower until the back of his head rested against the gashed uphol-
stery. "But did you ever wonder how in hell cars get out into the
middle of bean fields, or pecan groves, or wherever, like that?
Lord . . . Think of all the forlorn, abandoned machinery of America— Is there anything more funereal than an automobile grave-
yard, for instance? I always feel like crossing myself when I pass
one—there's something we've lost buried there, some ideal.
Left at that picket fence— And do you ever wonder where all the
old refrigerators go, and the old console radios of 1931—remember? And those baby buggies with the brakes that always jammed?
And the office fans of Scott Fitzgerald. Or those old dented tin
bathtubs, for instance, and the zinc meat grinders you were afraid
would chop up your fingers, and those mysterious old Victrolas
with the cranks, and all the needles out of reach down in the
sound box! All that ugly old junk—where is it? Where did it get
to?—no, not here, the next one—I mean, the *snows* of yesteryear!

I always wonder, where are the *ice*boxes?" chuckling to himself, and talking on as the night air revived him.

We were beyond lights now, off on lonely back roads; it was starless and humid; something real impended in the fragrant dark. Cabin lights winked through heavy trees off to the left—the dim yellow of smoky kerosene lamps. A few somnolent peepers whistled eerily; the night smelled of dust, and flowers falling to rot; and there was a high-pitched rattle in the rear end of the car where the tailpipe was working loose.

"—because you can reconstruct a whole civilization from a few potsherds, you know. *Things* last longer than cities, or even ideas. . . . And so just think of all the cans, millions and millions of empty pork and bean cans, and beer cans, and oily sardine tins— I suppose there's a huge dump somewhere, like the elephants' burying ground, miles and miles of rusty cans, mountains of them, maybe in Utah someplace— Now, left again—"

We kept making turns into narrower, more obscure roads over which huge live-oaks leaned motionlessly, and I was having too much trouble keeping out of the thickets to have any idea where we were. A rusted tin sign, advertising spark plugs, hung crazily upside down in our dim headlights; there was a fleeting smell of pigs, and pig wallow, rich and homely and strong, as we flashed by a lightless frame house; my dress slithered up my bare thighs as I tried to keep my smooth-soled pump on the brake pedal. I began to sober up, and someone in the back—the one with the mustache—said gloomily: "I still ain't seen my cousin down in Lebeau, though. And, man, that's what I came *down* here for—"

"He's from Detroit," Hobbes mumbled. "William Jesus Glover —only he's a Mohammedan, so he calls himself Amil Ibn Sachib, don't you, man? . . . Willie Gee is what we call him, though, because who can remember all that Arabic?"

"It don't matter to me what *you* call me," the gruff voice said. "I figure down here, around a lot of country people and renegades —well, I got my own convictions. But, man, I *still* got to get down there to Lebeau, if only you white Christians'll stop tryin' to get me high every night like that," producing a bitter laugh, which he seemed to begrudge.

I kept listening for chickens in the breathless night, and looking for houses, or crossroads, or peculiar trees I might remember. We bumped on at about forty over those crazy roads, and I was just imagining Church's incredulous alarm at finding me gone, when Hobbes said all at once: "Oh, wait, I almost forgot. Pull in here."

I pulled over in a panic, seeing no turn, and slammed on the brakes just before running up onto the sagging gallery of what must have been a sort of general store. "Can't you give me a little warning? It's like driving a truck—"

"Be right back," he said, and jumped out.

A dim light from inside glowed through the rusty screen door, against which moronic flies thumped tirelessly, and the smell of an incinerator was acrid in the airless dark.

"You ever drive a truck?" Willie Gee said suspiciously. "You never drove no truck."

I turned and found his gloomy mouth right behind me, the whites of his narrowed eyes surprisingly close. Ohla stared at me, gape-mouthed, shrinking back between the men; and the unease of being alone with them there swept over me like a chill. "No," I stammered. "But I can imagine. And I'm just not used to this kind of shift—"

He looked at me, wary, lidded, curious, angry, and I suddenly realized what he saw—a tipsy, reckless white girl in a sexy dress and a man's large raincoat, who had stepped across a line no one stepped across in his experience, except for certain dark and dangerous reasons. And how could he know my motives? Or fail to wonder about them? I was panicked by what he might be thinking. He's from Detroit, I don't know Detroit, maybe Detroit Negroes are different—that approximates my thoughts. "I'd better get some cigarettes," I murmured, and fled after Hobbes.

He was slouched against a nail keg near the single kerosene lamp, which feebly limned horse collars, and lengths of harness trace, and cross-cut saws hanging from the board ceiling of the cavernous building. He was munching out of a cracker tin, and a fine fall of crumbs drifted down his shirt.

"I thought— Can I get a pack of cigarettes?" noticing, as I said it, that behind the counter (worn to a dull gloss by decades of small transactions), just out of the light, an old Negro man sat in a rocker, shrunken, beady-eyed, in huge overalls I could smell the way one smells the life in clothes in which people have lived for a long time; expressionless as a mangy old bird, with the tiny demented eyes of the incalculably old. He sucked on a charred corncob pipe, making horrible toothless gurgles, and suddenly chirped furiously: "Skidaddle on it, woman! Move yo' bones! They's a white missy come along out here, too—"

I heard someone shuffling in the darkness beyond him—the unmistakable soft slap and flop of loose carpet slippers, the clank of thick glass against thick glass, the sweetish aroma of raw alcohol.

"She's with me, Henry," Hobbes said. "She doesn't want anything. And we got Ohla-from-down-in-the-Bottoms out in the car, too— How's your boils?"

"Yessuh," the old man said, rocking in quick, maniacal creaks, a dribble of tobacco juice showing up in a glistening rivulet on his chin. "Gonna rain and crack, gonna boom big. Them bugs know it," eyes aglow with the aggrieved fury of an old man no one listens to. "Get yo'sef a dry place for yo' fiddlin'. Yessuh. Gonna rain down yo' back jes' when you gets warm, he-he-he—"

"Hush up," someone gruffed out, "shet yo' silly mouth," and an immensely fat, bandanna-ed woman, all persevering waddle and shiver, breathless and very black, appeared carrying a jar of clear, oily liquid with a piece of wax paper held over its lid by a rubber band. She studied me with a single appraising squint—my eyes, my mouth, my bosom—that neutral, old woman's look, a witch's look, a midwife's look, that takes your measure in a moment, having seen everything, and accepted everything, and given over everything but memory. "Evenin', m'am," she said. "That'll be a dollah, Mistah Hob. And mind you bring back the jar now. You already got three of mine out there already."

We left them in the huge, shadowy store there in the middle of the country dark, with the glow of that smelly lamp paling their sleepless, wily faces, and the old man called out over the idiot-banging of the June bugs: "Do it good, yo'all—'fore the plow breaks down, you listen to me!" his voice rising with a lewd and jealous glee.

Out in the murk of the gallery, which gave under our weight, Hobbes stopped me. "Wait up," the wax paper crickling in his impatient fingers. "Here, have some of this first," and, before I could protest, his arm was across my shoulders, supporting my neck, the sudden close smell of his shirt, and the body under it, came up into my nostrils, strong and individual, and I tilted my head back automatically (expecting his lips, I suppose), only to feel his hand raise the jar to my mouth exactly as if he was helping medicine into a child, as he muttered: "There now. Take a good pull. And swallow, don't taste," which I did, drinking too deeply of that liquor I knew, from its very colorless look, its very dizzying odor, was potent and treacherous to the senses, and which burned my tongue, going down my throat like acid, to spread hot, dulling tendrils through my flesh that radiated upwards until my eyes watered. Hobbes held me while I gagged, and kept it down. "That's right," he said. "In a second you'll know." But he didn't drink.

Back in the car, Hobbes driving now, I suddenly felt better, my vision had an edge on it, and once we pulled back onto the road again, I passed the jar into the rumble seat, where Ohla took one look, and said sheepishly: "I don't want none of that wild fire. Little Horace Jefferson—over Tioga?—got hisself belly-cramp fo' three days from that old—" breaking off all at once (perhaps my breath had wafted back to her), unable to swallow her embarrassed giggle. But the other man, the big-muscled, wistful one, pshawed her: "Oh, I had old Henry's bootleg before. I got up and danced till I fell down, whomp! Gimme some of that joy, man—"

Hobbes drove fast, knowing the roads. His bare thighs lifted and lowered as he worked the pedals; his rumpled hair blew back off his bony forehead; his forearms banded as he swerved the wheel to make the sharper corners. Huge bugs splatted against the windshield; the coursing night air was dense with that day's heat; I tingled all over, and opened the raincoat to it.

Then we turned into a straight stretch of road, wider than the others, and lined with massive old live-oaks at such regular intervals that they suggested the vision of a landscape architect long ago, despite the wild growth of japonica and myrtle that snarled the meticulous rows now; a road that would have been canopied with Gulf-stars glimmering in the soft night had it been clear, but over which now only the faint haze of settling dust hung—for we had almost caught up with the other car; and suddenly I knew that over to the right, across a field and into some woods, would be the marshy branch of Bayou Placide full of cottonmouths and cypress-knees and scum, and over to the left, and down half a mile, were the cold, ghostly chimneys and roofless cellars of Mannering (the old Reeve plantation burned by Banks in '63), its slave cabins, intact but untenanted, in a straggle out back, and, just beyond that, and across the road, the driveways of the Prenderman place so nearly obscured with wild mock-orange that you didn't see the house (three-storied, vaguely Norman, with a graceful double stairway of rusty grillwork arching up to the long, shattered windows of the parlor floor) until you were almost in front of it.

"It's right down here now, isn't it?" I said, quickening. "Do you realize that some of my weirdest dreams are associated with this house?" for my fear of snakes, unreasonable and unrationalized to this day, had its beginning in one childhood noontime I had found a cottonmouth's depthless, unblinking eye, like a dread bead, staring straight at me, not six inches from my mouth, as I bent toward the chipped Italian fountain out in the obliterated gardens to have a sip of the rain water that had collected there.

"Wait till you see it now," Hobbes said eagerly. "It's the perfect place."

"Lord, it's even wilder and more overgrown than it used to be!" I exclaimed, taking another swallow out of the jar to stiffen myself, just as we swerved into the tangled bushes, bumping over ruts between which the grass was so long that I could hear it brushing the exhaust pipe, and then plunged on through the blackness of branches that intertwined just over us, to come to a sudden, squeaking halt in back of the other car. I heard drawled voices, soft laughter, the scuffle of feet on stone steps. Dark silhouettes moved across the red eye of the taillight, and vanished as it winked off. A faint, diffused light, as of shaded lamps on the far side of a long dim room, glowed in two of the windows. The night was full of cicadas, and suddenly very warm.

The house—how can I describe that house? The carpetless parquet that creaked eerily under every step; the water stains on the expensive French wallpaper that had come away from the walls in brittle strips; the tracery of cracks that had opened in the damp plaster of lofty ceilings; the huge, almost furnitureless rooms, drafty and echoing, where a junk Grand Rapids easy chair stood cheek by jowl with an Empire end table delicate and spindly enough for a doll's house; where floor-length mirrors in wide gilt frames (out of which you expected the flushed faces of Victorian girls to peer, primping for a ball) reflected instead the swollen-breasted, vacant-faced nudes from Milwaukee that grace most feed-store calendars; the scratched banisters that gave treacherously when you leaned on them; the French windows with soggy shirt-cardboards in place of missing panes; the damp, caked ashes of old fires on the hearths; the dusty beer bottles like abandoned duckpins in the empty bays; the stacks of paperback novels in the cobwebby corners, out of which a child had tried to build a castle; the portable phonograph on the floor of the drawing room, connected to the single wall plug by a series of extension cords—jacketless LP's and greying 78's strewn around it, like flung plates in a slapstick comedy; the 40-watt bulb naked and dim in the antique brass sconce; the muddy overalls draped stiffly over the mahogany newel post; the lumpy mattresses with their discolored ticking that served as couches; the whole air of a run-down château being camped in by gypsies—the kitchens full of the steamy reek of garlicky soups; jockey shorts drying in the butler's pantry; the enormous ornate bathtubs a stew of diapers; tricycles and crayons littering the sun porch; a swamp-smelly dog snoring and scratching in the coat closet.

How could I describe it? Or the incalculable aura of careless anarchy, and underground freedom of whim, which pervaded it? It was as if you had gotten beyond all eyes at last, all restraints, all codes, all dreary necessities, and reached that oasis of overripe green and sensuous shadow that exists somewhere in every desert —even a desert as limitless as our lock-step age—and had nothing but yourself, and whatever was inside you (all that rich mystery of individuality that the penitentiary of modern society is bent on narcotizing) to rely on. A strange excitement, tinged with unease, roused in me. No mere wisecrack would arm me here.

Shambling figures were retreating through doors off the shadowy entry hall; a child was yelling to itself somewhere in a remote upstairs room; Dexter Gordon's tenor yawped over the surface scratch of an old 78 turned up loud; and Orkie was making for the drawing-room door and the sound, the tips of the fingers of one slender hand running along the wallpaper toward the jamb. Then he must have felt me standing there alone, because he paused and turned all of a sudden, his beardless cheeks eager and questioning below the blind glasses. "Baby?" coming nearer carefully. "Here you go, here we are, baby— Who's that?"

"Me," I said idiotically. "I'm—I'm May. I came along with you all from Fats'."

There was an almost indiscernible hesitation, the moist full lips arresting for a second, then broadening into a hospitable grin. But how can one really tell anything without eyes to fathom?

"Well, have yourself a swallow, baby," lifting an opened bottle of beer toward me, his other hand coming up suddenly to find my shoulder, and touch it, hot and impersonal, and stay there as I took the bottle in confusion, feeling the warmth around the neck of it where his hand had been. I held it for a moment, not really wanting beer on top of the rest, and then his hand was feeling the strap of my bra through the gauzy material of the dress, one finger idly running up and down the edge of the strap where it pressed into my flesh. I don't think I was troubled by this. I think I knew it was simply the way another man might have studied my face alertly in the beginning, learning me. "Go ahead," he urged hoarsely, liquidly. "Go 'head. We got us plenty more."

I put the bottle to my lips, tasting it where it was wet from his mouth, giddy with the intimacy of that as I swallowed, and staring into his dark face right there in front of mine, the burnished skin young and taut over the bones, the soft lips parted with traces of the laughing ecstasy that had loosened them when he sang—but with no eyes for me to see. I noticed he had a small, whitish scar, jagged as a lightning bolt, on his left temple.

"There you go," he was saying happily. "How you like this house though, baby? *Every*body goes crazy for our old house here. I'll show you around upstairs later, but we gotta eat now, see, and—"

The flat of his hand was resting in the slope between my shoulder and my breast, and I thought for a panicky moment it was about to slide down, and simply cup my whole breast in its dangerous warmth.

"I'm—I'm white," I said all of a sudden. "I mean, I—I don't care, I'm from up North now, but—" so flushing with horror at my own ineptitude that I was certain he would feel it right through the dress, and frowning angrily at the thought. "I'm white," I repeated brutally.

His hand had come away immediately, and he was looking *at* me, and *through* me, as blind people do. There was no expression on his face, no alarm, no hurt, just a simple waiting look of consideration.

"I—I know it," he said with a strange catch of embarrassment. "I could tell, see. Oh, sure . . . Only I was *born* blind—I mean, so it don't *matter* to me. And I don't mean to cause no trouble. . . . And I know how to *be*, if it matter to you . . . ," about to go on, but then simply closing his mouth.

I stood there in the candor of these words, utterly at a loss before this tall, hovering boy, still lanky with recent adolescence, his face dimmed and waiting, his hand closing in the air before me, slow as a rose in the first cool of dusk, the fingers retreating together, but the hand still held before him and toward me just as it was when he sang, as if when he sang he was reaching out to touch, too, to re-establish some broken contact, to reconnect a circuit that had been shorted. I took that hand in mine on a sudden impulse, in both of mine, pressing it foolishly, as if wanting to catch something that was falling away from me. I tried to say a word; I sniffed with the same huff of embarrassment that had marred his voice; and I suppose I would have kissed his cheek, gruff as a young, worldly aunt with an infatuated nephew, if he had only been white, or I had been blind, too.

"I—what you sang—well, you're really great, you know."

He laughed with sudden guilelessness, pleased and willing, accepting what I had said as the truth of what I meant. "Well, then, that's all right. Yes, sir, it's a-l-l all right—right? . . . But come on in and see everybody, and you let Hobbesy take care of you, see, 'cause we gonna have us a *night* tonight! I mean, 'cause I feel—" The face tranced again with those unimpeded emotions that came up in him so simply, so strong. "Well," laughing like a charming youth, "jus' watch I don't get tangled up with them radio wires in there, that's all."

At which moment, Betty Prenderman came through one of the doors in a flurry. "I just didn't believe it when Paul *told* me, honey. Imagine meeting up that way at Fats'! And don't you look good though! My, my," just as if no time had passed, none of those disordered years that had put bitchy dresses on my back, and sardonic thoughts in my head, but had changed her hardly at all; just as if I'd dropped over after a party to which she, as usual—plain Jane, nice but drippy—had not been invited.

She looked precisely the same, her abundant brown hair still high-school long, her eyes large and ingenuous behind the unbecoming glasses, her girlish mouth still palely paintless. And yet the mouth was somehow fuller, too, delicately sensual, and the eyes seemed clearer and less frightened, and her figure had blossomed modestly at bosom and hip, making the short cotton dress (exactly the same cheap print dress, faded by weekly washings in strong soap, that cleaning girls wear to their jobs all over the South, and undoubtedly purchased for $1.89 from the same colored store) look even more as if it was just about to be passed on to a younger sister. Her hands were covered with flour, some of which had sifted down the dress; she had the harassed mother's spare safety pins in a row along her neckline; and she was sandaled, and stockingless, and faintly damp with too many things to do.

"I'm just fixing supper—biscuits, as I guess you can plainly see, I *still* keep spilling things. But Jack's due home any sec, honey, and—my, isn't that a fabulous dress! Wait'll he sees *that!* . . . Are those what they call spaghetti straps? No, those are the *very* thin ones, I guess, aren't they?" cocking her head as she absent-mindedly wiped her hands down her thighs. "Is that Fern? I can't hear over the bop— Orkie, do you hear Fernie upstairs?"

Orkie grinned a dreamy grin. "That's her all right. Calling them cows home. She sounds 'bout as hungry as I am."

"Oh, Lord . . . Well, she'll just have to wait, that's all. It's not her feeding time anyway," dismissing it with a shake of her head, and touching my arm on a sudden impulse. "Honey, you've gotten heavier, it's real *nice* on you, too. Jack's always swearing he's gonna keep me pregnant, 'cause that's the only time I've got much chest," with a delighted giggle. "I just can't seem to keep weight on, though. Remember how gawky I always was? . . . But I suppose you've been seeing all the old bunch. How is everybody?" her hand going to her hair to primp at it in an odd little reversion to nervous habit that seemed out of place with her now.

"I just ran out on a whole cocktail party full of them. Lawtell,

Church, Maggie O'Fee—ugh! They're all just about the same. But I thought I'd die if another person said to me: 'Why, darlin', you just haven't changed an *inch!*' You know how they are."

She laughed and laughed, generously, without even a hint of malice—which, oddly enough, made me realize how much we all must have hurt her once by excluding her from our follies without even a second thought.

"So when I heard you were living out here now," I hastened to say, "I thought: 'Christ, Betty won't mind if I barge in. Anything to get away from Young Suburbia.' . . . How come we've never kept in touch all this time, honey?"

The fatuousness of which did not even make her blink, and there was a shaming simplicity to her reply. "Now, we never *really* knew the same kids, May. I was awfully square and withdrawn in those days. . . . Remember that time out here when you all went swimming in your underwear, and I wouldn't do it? And Lawtell said to that Simmons boy—what was his name? Oh, yes, Bartly, Bartly Simmons—'Goodnight, we got the Pill along, I clean forgot about the Pill—'" laughing again as if even the thought had become harmless. "Course, he didn't know I overheard him. But you remember that time?"

Which I didn't. There had been a dozen daring swims like that, all very innocent, all very fourteen-year-old sophisticated—the girls haughtily not looking at the boys, the boys snatching surreptitious peeks at the girls. But the time when Betty had been with us, probably the only time, had been so uneventful that it had left no trace in any memory but hers.

"And you know the reason why I wouldn't was because I didn't have any drawers on!" She laughed uproariously. "They were all in the wash that morning, 'cause Aunt was drinking again that week. Isn't that a scream? I was so mortified I seriously thought of just hiding in the cellar somewhere, and then *walking* home!"

I liked her all of a sudden; I could talk to her more or less as I talked to the rootless, life-shrewd girls I knew in New York; I felt vaguely guilty of a myopic snobbishness all those years ago.

"Oh, Lord!" she exclaimed all at once. "My biscuits— Ohla? Billie honey?"

At which exact moment, a little red-haired boy of three, stark naked and sleepily rubbing his genitals, appeared at the top of the stairs, and a tall red-haired man, stumbling under the weight of a peanut-vending machine, rushed through the front door.

It was Jack O'Meara—all angles and shoulders, all lank flung legs and big run-down railroad shoes; hipless, bony-faced, with stiff red hair as wiry as the stuffing in an old horsehair sofa, and powerful forearms spattered with small freckles and easy sweat— all active bones that you expected to hear clatter when he moved; with a funny W. C. Fields drawl, and pale blue electric eyes at once wily, and curious, and impatient with most things they saw.

"Lookit what I copped, sugar, right out from under the bas- tards' noses—Ork, boy, I got us *pea*nuts, man! We're gonna eat *pea*nuts, and drink us some brews, and play records, and swing all *night*, man, if I can only get the damn thing open," eyes suddenly stark with suppressed rage. "But, my God, sugar, them goddamn pious porkchops—I want to tell you, I almost—" the rage erupting into a derisive laugh. "Well, I copped it on 'em anyway. I got so doggone *mad*, I went right over to their goddamn idiot passen- ger station, see, and loosened the screws on this here with my little old all-purpose knife, you're hip, and this porkchop, waitin' for the ten-forty, is there and watching me—I mean, you know, he's bored, he's one of them porkchops gets to the station twenty minutes early just to be on the safe side—you know, all *that!* So he watches me, and *he* don't know, so he pegs me as the cat who services the goddamn things—and so I just worked it loose, no hurry—if you go real slow, and look down your nose, and kinda sneer that *business* sneer, you can cop their watches on them—if you *want* their goddamn time of day. . . . Well, I got it loose, and just picked it up, and just walked outa there like I was *public*, see," shaking the vending machine, "and, man, there must be a coupla bucks in pennies in there— But, Jee-*suss*, if I gotta eat their bullshit, I'm sure as hell gonna eat their goddamn peanuts, too!"

He set the glass globe, smeary with old butter and old salt, down on the floor at his feet, whipped out a large checkered handkerchief to swab his streaming face, shot a quick appraising squint at me when Bett introduced us, eyes lidded with interest, mouth breaking into a lax grin, as he said: "Hiya there, May. What cha say?" and then suddenly noticed the little boy coming down the creaking stairs—one huge yawn under a pillow-rumpled shock of hair, feeling himself sleepily.

"Stop fiddling with your peanut there, kiddo. Look at him— just like your old man, eh?" wacky, gasping laughter as he swept his son up in his arms. "Look at the pretty lady, Jocko. Ain't she fancy, though? All orange that way ... You little jack rabbit! Eh? Eh? Little old fat porker, aren't you? An' what cha been doin' there, boy? Look what I brought you. . . . How come he ain't asleep anyway?" mussing the giggling child's hair, pinching his round pink little buttocks, tickling him in the tender armpits, and then setting him down all of a sudden.

"God*damn*, man, gimme some of that brew, though. I'm so *mad* I could spit, I could wreck something," shaking his head, all chagrin at his own feelings, and taking a long glubbing choke out of Orkie's bottle. "Whew! ... *Now*," eyes bright again with impatience. "Sugarbabe, I ain't eaten all day—where's Paul? But, say, get the gal a drink, Orkie, can't you, boy?" smacking a big blunt fist all at once into the flat of his hand. "Oh, man, but I'm going to make you wail tonight, you blind bastard!"

At which Orkie broke into a soft, acknowledging laugh that told me in a minute how he valued Jack O'Meara. "You surely do get mad—you like your old car on a cold morning."

We drifted through the other rooms toward the kitchen, and Jack was all hands on Bett; down her back as he bent to fiddle with the phonograph needle with which Willie Glover was having trouble; up her meager hip as he came out of his stoop, saying: "Yah, man, but I gotta eat first. But where in hell is Paul?"

For her part, Bett gossiped with me, scolded Jocko, called out to Ohla in the kitchen—quietly alive to his touch the whole time.

I had another choke from the mason jar. The dim loungers on the mattresses were drinking beer, Jack wouldn't join me in the bootleg, and I realized that Hobbes had bought it just for me—a curious thoughtfulness. In the big, dark kitchen, damp with washing and stacks of dirty plates, smelling of singed biscuits and vinegar, Ohla and Hobbes' girl were frying eggplant. Slices of tomato and cucumber marinated in a shallow, flowered plate. A huge chuck-wagon coffeepot steamed on the iron range. I felt foolish in my East 50's dress, and took off my shoes for Jocko to teeter around in. The girls kept snatching peeks, whispering and giggling.

"Now, where *is* Paul anyway?" Bett said. "We're just about ready, aren't we?"

Hobbes' girl, whose name was Billie—a slender, fine-boned creature, with long legs, small wrists, and wide eyes—shot a glance at me, and then murmured: "Upstairs. He be down in a minute."

"I'll go get him," I said, because the heat and the smells were making me giddy, and the bootleg had taken a firm grip all of a sudden.

"First door on the left at the top of the stairs," Bett sang out.

The upstairs hall was high-ceilinged, full of shadows, and molding that was coming loose, and piles of soggy newspaper. The fretful child had gone back to sleep. The dim glow of a candle shown wanly through the first door on the left, and I entered a large, carpetless chamber, empty except for an enormous Victorian bed (sway-back from love between its tall head and footboards), and an almost rungless kitchen chair over which a fraying black slip hung. There was a cheap enameled bureau against the farther wall, with ill-fitting drawers and ugly tin pulls, and a card table, littered with dusty papers, set up in front of the bamboo blinds that had been let down over the floor-length windows. There was no one there.

Then I heard a soft, distracted little hum, the fragment of melody people only sing to themselves when they are utterly unaware and engrossed, and I recognized a stately phrase from one of Handel's Concerti Grossi, interrupted by: "Let's see—then tie up with the other hand, dum de-de, dum dah-dah," and noticed a door a little ajar, and a wedge of faint light.

I opened it, and there was Hobbes, stripped of his shirt, his chest sepulchrally ribbed, the hacked-off shorts sagged low on his hips, gingerly holding a spoon over the stub of candle that sat on the edge of an ancient porcelain sink, and counting out the measures of the song with unconscious little flaunts of his other hand. A pocket syringe, a greasy striped necktie, and a carefully unfolded packet of white powder were arranged in a finicky still-life on the toilet seat.

"They said to call you down to supper."

He turned on me, startled, somehow fatalistic, and yet careful with the spoon. "Oh—yes," embarrassed now in the way he used to be, the way of a man with secrets of which he is ashamed only because they are trivial, actually licking his dry lips. Then he adopted a somehow theatrical air of casualness: "I—I just chip a little now and then, just to be sociable—oh, sure. And when guys like Willie come through, I score for a few fixes. . . ." His eyes were drawn and weary behind the smudged glasses, and he seemed shy because of his sparrowy half-nakedness. "It relaxes you, you know. You want to turn on? I've got enough. . . . Anyway, I'll only be a minute—"

I poked around his room, waiting. A brand-new pair of tie shoes, oxblood colored and still uncreased on the uppers, sat disembodied in the middle of the floor. There was a crudely lettered sign tacked up over the bureau, obviously done with a child's water-color brush during a profound hangover, which announced sternly: "No More Words." Matchbooks, stiff cigarette butts, a wad of Kleenex in which something wet had dried hard, a glass with asphyxiated flies in the bottom, and a collapsing copy of Amiel's *Journal* strewed the top of the orange crate beside the bed. In the middle of a cracked section of wall, a badly focused and disintegrating newspaper photograph was tacked, and I had to lean close to make it out. It pictured an old woman, awkward in her everyday shoes, running in a half-stoop down a gutted street through the drifting pall of a burning city, her face an indistinct blur of animal bewilderment. She was carrying a radio.

"Where's this?" I called out. "The news picture over here?"

"What? . . . Oh, Madrid, Berlin, Manila, Rostov, maybe Nagasaki—I don't know. I've forgotten. Maybe somewhere in Heaven, eh?" and he sighed all of a sudden, an involuntary exhalation having nothing to do with what he had said.

I wandered over to the card table, and struck a match to inspect the scatter of papers there, all ash-smudged, spilled-on, in a hopeless chaos. There was a carefully typed-out quote from Lawrence's *Letter from Germany;* manuscript copies of someone's poems sent on from Yucatán, of which the only one I read began: "Unreachable islands of sentience—oh, the drag—"; a scribbled list of tentative titles for unwritten works, which included: "The White Collar Peril," "Holy Fruitcake Illusion," and "The Passion of Ilse Koch"; and a penny postcard from Pasternak, which said merely: "Get on a bus, you sad bastard. Wisdom is a heartless occupation."

"Are you working?" I hazarded. "Whatever happened to the writing?"

He came out of the bathroom, shirt back on but unbuttoned, an indefinable languor to the soft pad of his sneakers, though he looked sick to his stomach, and his hands shook as he lit a cigarette. "Oh, well—pah-pah, let's see. . . . No, not working. . . . Why? It was surfeit, I suppose. . . . I got surfeited."

He glanced at the sign over the bureau—his self-conscious motto, his reminder of something he easily forgot: " 'Do I know nature yet?' " he murmured by rote. " 'Do I know myself?—No More Words. I bury the dead in my belly,' " staring at the sign reflectively. "And my arm," he added with a little wince, and then looked at me with a gloomy smile. "Rimbaud. I was always

taught to identify sources. It's the hardest habit of all to break,
the sign of a ghoulish civilization. . . . I mean, Ephesus and Rot-
terdam—separated by twenty-five centuries, and yet they're both
just unpiled *stones,* when you think about it. . . .

"No, but surfeit," he repeated, brushing the tangle of hair off
his forehead. "That's the word. I got surfeited with literature, and
surfeited with politics, and surfeited with—well, just *words.* . . .
You know, for six years I read four newspapers a day. I kept *up,*
I cared, I squandered my nerves," shaking his head and sniffing
the way you do when you remember the obsessive emotions of
an old love affair. "It's funny to think about it now. I used to be
positively melancholic because of the Czechs, or the Bantus, or
someone. Honestly. I mean it," as if he were confessing to a folly
of which even he could not quite believe he had ever been
capable. "But you want to know something? Sometimes, when I'm
alone, or very hung over, or prescient from weariness—the way
you get sometimes—I think we're all going to wear ourselves out
here in America, just burn ourselves right up. I have this vision
of the *nerves* of America, all the butchered ganglia, the flayed
tissue, the teeth ground to powder in the night, the cindery
brains that are starting to run amok from the tensions of life here
now. . . . And I find myself thinking that we'll never make it in
this century, because we've lost touch with something—something
wild and natural, call it bliss or reality, a capacity for spontaneous love, whatever—but it's the only thing that can renew the
consciousness when it's exhausted by anxiety . . . and I get scared,
real flesh-fear, my body telling me to stop something before I go
too far," rubbing his forearm painfully. "So I suppose what I'm
really doing is searching for the natives, for the lost America. But
like a Schweitzer-in-reverse, you see, because I want *them* to
help *me.* Because, really, only rebels, and oddballs, and outcasts
can still feel freshly any more—the ones The General and his
crowd, who are the Deacons of the Last American Church Social,
don't care about—who represent no power or influence, and have
no public interests, and don't really give a damn about abstrac-

tions—the ones who are still free enough to perceive the wonder in what's left of the Flower," blinking self-consciously at his own rhetoric, and sniffing. "Well—'a very drunken sleep on the beach, that's best,'" followed by a sheepish little smile. "See, I never did get over quoting other men's truths. I quote Orkie the same way these days."

"Hobbes, you're crazy," I said. Because introspection—what was the good of it? And all the men I knew talked that same dark way now. So I changed the subject. "That girl's pretty—Billie. Are you making it with her?"

He gave me a cigarette, trying to disguise his nausea. "Oh—oh, sure. That's Orkie's sister. Billie Dew. Wouldn't you know it? 'No More Words,' and I pick someone with a name like that. It's typical," and I found myself agreeing, and suddenly knew that it had had to be a dusky girl for Hobbes, for his whole life had been a series of symbolic actions.

"She can't decide about me," I warned him. "I caught her looks. She doesn't know whether I'm just an old friend, or a *good* one. You'd better watch it."

He laughed wanly, and took my hand. "Well, who knows? Jack always says you don't know anyone you haven't balled, so perhaps later when I feel better," automatically squeezing my hand to go with the compliment; and, all the while, I knew he was only being nice. For there was no charge between us. "But, come on," he said, drawing me toward the door. "I ought to keep moving or I'll throw up, damn it. I'm not good at it yet. . . . Are you high?"

I was—the deep, surprising disequilibrium that occurs when you are suddenly taken drunk. The soles of my bare feet were dark grey from the dusty floors. My hair was damp on my neck. I felt the tingle in my thighs where they pressed together. I sat on one of the mattresses, cradling my mason jar possessively, while everyone else ate, and Willie Jesus Glover stared with lidded aggravation at the bottom of my feet, his chin slick with butter. Billie filled plates for Hobbes and Orkie. Another candle had been brought in, and it shaped her forehead, and her cheekbones, and her grave young mouth with a mysterious bronze light. Hobbes blinked, and chewed a little, enduring the quease stoically, his thin hairy legs folded under him, and she watched him with proprietary glances as he picked dutifully at his food. Jack sprawled, and talked with his mouth full of eggplant, and scratched himself, and belched with huge pleasure, slapping Jocko's hand away from the biscuits. "Christ, give him some beer there, sugar. . . . Here, have a brew, you goddamn hungry chipmunk— No, now you can't have Daddy's supper, that's all, kiddo." I sipped out of the jar without a thought, and wouldn't eat anything, and Bett stopped insisting after the second time, just as if she actually believed what I said.

Records were put on—diligent weary saxes and uncomplicated drums. Little Jocko yawned and danced in the dimness like a drowsy wood sprite, and Hobbes began to talk directly out of his thoughts, as if someone had to say something: "Once in Cleveland though—in Cleveland once—but, listen, does God smile on Cleveland, do you think?" Ohla wiped her plate clean with a last half of biscuit, going over it, and over it, again and again, unaware I watched. "But do you realize this day is perishing over some dreary gas station in Kansas, too, and—think of it—who's there? What do they know? Can they be reached by phone?" The peepers queerilled eerily on and on in the huge lush dark outside; I spilled warm liquor, all sticky and pungent, into the crevice between my breasts; Jack's flushed face grinned down at me, eyes banked, wiping, wiping helpfully with his body-hot checked handkerchief. Orkie sat, as motionless and at his soul's ease as a lean ebony Buddha, a calm smile, attentive and innocent, playing about his lips, as he listened to Hobbes: "But somewhere a man goes down, you see, all the way down where you have to go to make despair fruitful," the smile changing when Willie Gee snapped back impatiently: "Man, I mean it, you just talk and talk, and what in hell do you know? You ain't never *had* to be in Kansas, you don't have to be *here*. What do *any* of you people really know? . . . Ork, man, don't listen to all that existential crap!"

Dizziness turned my stomach treacherous, the faint lights bobbed and swam, shapes melted one into another in a giddy wash, and then I heard Jack snap out: "Roll a joint there, Abu Amir— Here, baby, lay off that till you take a couple of pokes," taking the jar away from me. I snickered foolishly, and managed to sit up, and everyone was suddenly moving, supper over, but for Willie, who was morosely pouring greenish tobacco out of a plastic prescription pill-container, his big flat thumbs deftly rolling the cigarette tight, muttering: "Just throwin' it away, just to sober up some hincty blonde," and I heard myself saying: "Well, don't be so superior, honey, I'm sure I couldn't care less," challengingly, and too loud.

· 4 ·

The pot sobered me in three minutes. Bird's tumbling kinks of raw song uncoiled until I could hear how stunning and precise they actually were—phrases of such comprehension that (as always when high) I seriously wondered if he didn't have a different sort of nerves than the rest of us. I experienced the fluid presence of my own body as if I was bathing in a new element, something between cotton and ether, and watched myself lighting a straight (between turns on the marijuana) with a benign and absolutely clear perception of how idiotically nervous and abrupt, how deliberately tough and even masculine, so many of my gestures usually were.

I became outward, amused, whole. The piston-like proddings of Jack's glistening forearms, as he tried to jimmy open the peanut machine with a screwdriver, struck me as very boyish. I felt warm toward him, but wiser. When he took a hammer to it—there between his flopped-back thighs, the sweat standing out in clear beads on his busy brow—then flung that down after a few angry whacks and started working on the catch with a hacksaw, I laughed and laughed, and heard my chiding voice drawl: "If it was me, I'd just break the stupid glass," but took it as no rebuke when he pouted, and replied irritably: "Listen, I don't care about the pennies, sugarbabe. I'm after them goddamn *peanuts!*"

Everything seemed singular and interesting: Billie's cotton dress unbuttoned a little off her chest to reveal a silk slip of pale blue lace, so frivolous and inviting that I suddenly knew something of her meager hopes, her delicate, guarded femininity; Hobbes swallowing and blinking among the legs that forested around him, intent on enduring the revulsions of his body in the name of a sensation he desired only abstractly—how brave and foolish he was, there on the floor! The music seemed to express Ohla's sinuous movements, as she stooped and balanced and walked away with dishes, as if it was an improvised accompaniment to her actions. There was a sudden waft of alfalfa through the open windows from a field somewhere, sweet as childhood, full of the simple hunger of the uncorrupted senses. I swooned with drowsy languor, pleasantly aware of my eyelids, and the way my little toes turned under demurely. I felt unconcerned, tolerant, beautiful for sure. Even Willie Gee's gloomy pout, as he rolled more joints and warned people about walking by him too quickly lest he lose a few flakes, seemed only an armor to me, a bitter mask behind which the loneliness of hate, and poverty, and knowledge hid itself in shame at its own nakedness. I fastened on him, impishly certain he could be made to smile the way Orkie did, and for the same reason: just because it was truer to reality. Jack was talking to me, glancing up from his saw at every word or two, and I knew he knew I knew he was watching me get high. But I only smiled mysteriously, and concentrated on Willie's doomed frown.

"—cat in East Texas brings it over, see," Jack drawled, "the pot—in an attaché case. He's the *big* head in Palasteen, see, the big, lonely swinger in that town, no one to turn on with, so he lights up over his paperwork at night, you're hip. Sells drilling mud for the oil wells up around Shreveport and the Arklatex, but he used to work spade timbering gangs twenty years ago, and his foreman turned him on, his *colored* foreman. . . . See? Secret, hip America!" laughing shrewdly at my wild giggles, fascinated by any person's particular reactions when they got high—right in the middle of everything, I knew that for a certainty. "You know, an old funny lonely old *fart*," he went on, playing to me, "wife and kids, bunions, gas bills, but he's always staring at his suit jacket in some dreary hotel room on the road, see, twiddling his thumbs, and wondering who he can scare out a bed at two in the morning, and so we're sort of the fire house to him, place to unlax. . . . But, *you* know, the kinda old bastard who talks about poon-tang and all that, but don't mean it dirty—they's just the only words he knows. Yes, *man*, but he gets so high sometimes he just *cries*—' 'cause everything's suh neat!' . . . Ain't that what old Nelson says, sugar? Man, man—"

"Whyn't we dance?" I heard myself pronouncing carefully. "I feel like dancing," saying it (I realized with faint surprise) to Willie Glover, still intent on breaking him down. He glanced at me, the contempt in his frown barely disguised, and looked away, and said nothing.

I passed the joint on to Bett, who casually took her turn while struggling Jocko into a pair of underpants, and became aware that I was swaying dreamily back and forth to the jazz, and humming a tuneless solo to myself. Hobbes smiled at me uncomfortably with his sad, encouraging eyes, holding Billie's hand the way an out-of-town youth might take his younger sister's damp palm amid the wicked splendors of Times Square.

Then someone had put on a scratchy blues—one of those urban

blues that always suggest to me cheesy recording studios in dark-town Houston or Memphis, and hot summer afternoons of exuberance, and bottles of warm beer, and cold chili in a paper container; a blues sung by Wynonie Harris or Jimmie Wither-spoon, as simple as a foot planted down smack on a floor, yet somehow wistful in its very zest—and I was dancing with myself, aware that an ironic smile was fixed on my mouth over the snaking of my hips. No one seemed to pay much attention. I was only another shadow in that shadowy room. Jocko stared at me sleepily, and the girls were cleaning up. "Come on," I dared Willie Gee. "Is everyone so cool they won't dance any more?"

"Go on and dance with her, man," he muttered scornfully to Hobbes. "You always *talkin'* about swingin'—or don't you swing with your own kind of chicks?"

I had turned away in a liquid little turn, fascinated by the obedience of my knees to the promptings of the sax, and pivoted back at this without breaking the step, to find Hobbes' hurt and baffled eyes glowing faintly in the candlelight, and beyond him Orkie just rising off his hams, out of darkness into darkness, his long gawky legs moving from rest into dance in a single, effortless flow that seemed to me, high as I was, baldly expressive of his intention to distract everyone from this.

"Over here," I called, falling in with him, and holding out my arms. "Over here, honey. There's nothing in your way."

The boyish grin came over him, loose-lipped and unconscious, and he danced trustingly toward me, jerking his hips in fey little contortions, slamming his groin forward on every beat, unaware how shamelessly apt it was, his thighs banding tautly as he circled his pelvis.

I took the dark, spread fingers that were held out to me, and, having that much pivot, he started to dance to me, all sweat and concentration and joy, alive to me as I came close or danced away, intuiting all my movements through my fingers. The others were watching now, and I was giddy and certain, and gave myself up to it. Drops of his perspiration fell on my bare shoulders, our knees touched impersonally, and I let him whirl me in a blind, perfect turn, close enough to his moist lips when he gasped, "Tha's right," to see his hard pink gums, and his soft pink tongue. We went into the final chorus, rousing toward the guitar, and he suddenly whipped off his glasses, which were running with sweat, and threw them aside, his face naked with exultation, the eyes rolling and ugly and shocking to me, seeing them for the first time that way, and his mouth indescribably loose and yet intent—as a man's mouth sometimes is at the instant of orgasm, if (as I have) one has looked up in the midst of the spasm, and seen the lips parted with that ingathered thrall of disbelief caught at the exact moment of its change to certainty. I let him lead me, I let him take my waist and move me, the dance in me answering to the dance in him, as if I had suddenly understood how separate we all are, or how close—something silly like that about the simplicity of reality. I experienced an instant of womanly tenderness and acquiescence that flooded through my limbs without forewarning, and wanted to take that dreaming, ecstatic face between my hands, or bend beneath it at his behest, knowing in my intoxication the inmost leaf of female feeling (that warm willingness, that simple surrender), having little to do with him. But there are no words for moments of illumination, though his are as good as any, I suppose:

"Yes, yes!" he exclaimed as we stood, panting and wet at the end. "'Cause I thought we was gonna *fly* there he says: 'Open them windows, open the doors—!' You see that, Hobbesy, the way we did that?"

"Man, you blind to a lot more than daylight," Willie Gee grumbled darkly, dragging on a joint with an ugly hiss, and holding it in; then sucking another gulp of air in on top of it, like a chaser. "What you want to play Tom to her for? 'Dance, Sambo! Come on an' *dance* there, you big gorilla!'"

Jack O'Meara cackled wildly at this, sawing away with maniacal impatience, and Ohla's wide, frightened eyes watched, like a banished child's, from the doorway.

"I mean, someone say 'dance,' and you get right up like that," Willie went on in an ominous whine. "You don't have to dance with *no* one, man. Listen, up in Detroit they don't *dare* come into our part of town," falling into an enraged sneer all at once. " 'Le's go see them happy darkies laugh and sing, le's go down and get us some *dark* meat, day of Jubilo, yah, yah—' S-h-e-i-t! Man, ain't you got no *pride*?"

"Oh, for Christ's sake," Hobbes began wearily.

"Well, *that* don't mean nothin' to me either, so don't bring Him into it," eyes blazing up with pedantic anger. " 'Sides, don't you even know they finding out Jesus Christ was *black!* Man, he was an African all the time! You supposed to *know* so damn much, but—"

"Oh, come on there, *You*sef," Jack said. "You take the ass out of everything. Let yourself get high, man!"

"But it don't take the ass out of it for *me*," Willie shot back with a clench of teeth. "Man, it *makes* it for me— But, see there, that's just what I mean. I don't care what you people say, or how you act, or play it cool—you *thinkin'* the same old lily-white bullshit all the time! You see that, Orkie? You *see* that?" failing to notice how ludicrous this sounded in his untiring obsession. "Man, you got to learn. I got a book on all this you oughta read, that *proves* the whole Christian religion started in Egypt, and where in hell do you think *Egypt* is, you dumb bastard! Egypt is in *Africa!* You gotta read these things, and find out—"

"Well—well, see, I *can't* read," Orkie mumbled with chagrin, "but maybe I can get Hobbesy to read it *to* me—"

Which only produced further helpless fury, and further wearying argumentation, to which everyone paid less and less attention. I sifted through the records, and was just putting on Monk's "Round About Midnight" when the catch on the peanut machine gave way all at once, and the bottom dropped off, sending a dry scatter of peanuts all over the floor, among which Jocko crawled in a scramble of dirty knees, stuffing his mouth.

The raw, shorn chords (which would always describe for me

the debris of feverish parties, and the ruins of emotions that had flared too high, and the premonition of beat dawns that would inexorably come, no matter what) echoed under that lofty ceiling, shimmering with pale candle flame, and I was very high, and felt an incommunicable and simple wisdom, intent on harmony.

"Oh, come on," I goaded Willie Gee's grudging scowl. "Maybe you're right—I don't know—you're probably right," taking the joint he offered me out of the automatically generous protocol of all pot smokers. "Let's dance this one anyway, this one's so great, and it won't compromise you. . . . I won't tell anybody," wheedling and winking, and, to my own amazement, I took his hand, and swayed before him, urging him up, confident and uncomplicated.

We danced stiffly. I could feel him trying to fuel up his contempt, I could feel it in the ungiving grip of his hand at my waist. I let him dance out his anger, going pliant whenever he got rigid, and mostly trying to keep my bare toes from under his hard-soled, cruel black shoes.

"Well, anyway," he murmured crossly, "it ain't *you* any more than any of you ofays, you understand. I been schooled, I was *born* up there, you know—but with these country people you got to put things simple, you got to *reduce* everything so they can dig . . . Though, listen, it's true what I say. I studied. . . ."

We wheeled in slow arabesques, our feet hardly moving, our shoulders swaying together as if to the invisible currents that sway the shoulders of drowned slaves chained together in the woolly silence of five fathoms down, and his petulant voice droned on in my ear through the somnolent largo of the sax, over which the jangle of Monk's piano played like a multi-faceted reflector sprinkling darts of light around an empty ballroom: "But I got my religion, I got my *own* convictions—about drinkin', for instance. I don't booze like you, or all these sorry colored down here, they just druggin' their faculties with all that juice. And you don't know what it's like to be *ahead* of your own people that way—you don't know how it wear you out all the time, and leave you mean—"

At which I got piqued, despite my intentions. "Listen, honey, some streets run *both* ways, there are all kinds of ways to be ahead like that," like lonely Monk (I thought), a dire Alice in a dreadful wonderland, our day's monk, no less Gothic than *theirs*, but a monk of smashed cathedrals, emptied of faith. The soles of Willie's shoes crunched on the peanuts, and all of a sudden he snickered reluctantly: "Jesus, it's like on roller skates the first time when you're a kid," his arm somehow lighter across my shoulders, yet more ingathering, so that, muffled almost into his armpit, I knew the exact moment when he gave something up, and became alive to me, "and, listen, there's nothin' in Moslem against pot, or jazz, or chicks. . . . Man, you people don't realize, but Mohammed—" eyes lidded, breath hazing down into my face from under the arrogant mustache that now seemed more than ever a wishful emblem of some bitter image of himself that was woefully false. "And *I* saw Monk in the Deuces in 1947. Yah, I got *all* these records," and then he didn't talk any more, but shuffled against me, the sweet cheap reek of his pomade dizzying my senses, and his hands *on* me in a different way, that way all women instinctively recognize, though there is really nothing different in it but the warning pressure of each fingertip stiff with the abrupt awareness of desire. "Bitch!" he breathed at nothing. "Yah, yah," head ducking to the sink in the beat, his palm suddenly very hot and tense on my bare back, his lips nibbling my neck behind the ear, lips and tongue tasting my damp flesh as he said in a muffled whisper: "Bitch, you a cute little freak, ain't you?"

"Oh, come on, now stop it," I said, pulling away, only to see the banked half-rage in his eyes, and hear his insinuative murmur: "Huh, yah, you like that, don't you? Oh, I dug you in the car, baby, I know *how* you want it—and don't worry, I don't care *who* you tell," his big hand firm on my neck all the while, his face doomed with want, so that I got confused, and reached around and harshly pulled it away.

"*Stop* it. It's—it's too hot for wrestling," baffled by his laughing

breath, and the sly drawled words I heard next: "You dumb
freaks, all you think a man is, is to ball. . . . Well, all right, I
don't care, I don't mind, I been two weeks since even gettin' my
fingers—"

I freed myself from his hands, wiping at the back of my neck,
furious. "Now, lay off, for Christ's sake! Keep your hands *off* me!"

His mouth understood the tone in my voice in an instant, and
twisted into a snarl: "Listen, baby, you don't fool me, *you* don't
care. I'm black, ain't I? An' you only dig spade joint, don't you
now? I know your kind of twat," grabbing my shoulder roughly,
but in such a way that I knew one sort of passion had replaced
the other. "You think we some kind of big black animal don't
never get tired, don't you? . . . Shit, I knew you when I wasn't
but sixteen, comin' around lookin' to have it *dirty!* Can't be dirty
enough for you, can it?" His eyelids beaded with that cruel sweat
which the neurotic subservience of rebellious white girls had de-
manded of him before, and that his rage had made easy all those
times he had gotten his own back for all the things continual
indignity could do to a human being, and the tossing hours of
trying to fantasy it away each night. "Man, you white freaks
really somethin'!" he spat out with curious revulsion. "You think
I want some white chick feelin' my wig just to see how it feels?
Well, I ain't *no*body's stud, you hear?" shaking me as you shake
an hysterical child. "I got my own *personal* convictions, you hear
me!"

"Lay off her," I heard someone say, and looked where Willie
looked, expecting to find Jack O'Meara, but found Hobbes instead, rocking a little on his sneakers, his lean face still punished
with nausea, the hand that brought the cigarette to his pale lips
actually quivering. "God, can't you *ever*, even for a minute, just
for a second, forget your *skin?*" the despairing whine in the voice
(as if some rock-bottom hopelessness had come home to him in a
flash) incensing Willie further.

"Can you all forget it? Man, even when you forget your own,

you never forget mine! Or hers neither," gesturing crudely at Billie's alarmed eyes and caught breath.

"Yes. Yes, I do," Hobbes said, sobered, saddened, his mouth shamed. "I do, too. . . . Really, you can believe me, man—"

Willie's laugh was wild and ugly. "Man, the minute I believe you, the *next* minute I get myself lynched," grabbing my elbow all of a sudden and pulling me forward into the candlelight like an exhibit. " 'Cause does *she* forget it? . . . Go on, tell the man, baby! Hip the man how it is! . . . But no, no, *I* got to forget it! That's the way it goes! . . . If she forget it so much, though, why don't she want my black hands on her lily-white then! Or if she did, man, don't you even know it's *'cause* they're black!" He released me with that same revulsion, eyes burning at Hobbes. "Besides, man, you dis*gust* me—"

"Hey," I heard someone murmur to someone else. "Le's get out of here." One of the Negroes.

"But—but couldn't it be a *human* thing?" Hobbes stammered out manfully. "Her not wanting it? . . . Because what in God's name are we going to *do*, if you can't put up with us a little while longer? What are we going to do if it goes on mattering, and mattering, and *mattering!*" For a single second, I thought he was going to sob.

"The white man say put up with it, baby. He say you oughta be *proud*, he doing you a big favor, see," Willie said with harsh authority to Billie. "But look at him, look at him! Jesus, don't it make you *sick?*"

Billie had drawn back from Hobbes, as if commanded, staring at him fearfully, and the huge darkened room was dotted with watchful eyes.

"Well, it *doesn't* matter," Hobbes said, swallowing insistently. "That's—that's nonsense. . . . It was *you*, honey, it's always just been you, I mean what you *are*," embarrassed by the clichés.

"There. You see? 'Cause what is she to you? She just a little gal you met in—in a *nigger* saloon!" using Church's exact phrase, and so like him at that moment in his refusal to let his fatal idea go that I blinked to see him. "And she should be so *honored* you want to use her. But, man, if it goes the *other* way," pointing at me without even deigning to look. "But, oh no, no, I'm hip," eyes suddenly slitted with unhappy triumph. "But, man, all that's gonna change, you know—all this white domination, all over the *world*—you all finished, buddy. You all had your goddamn day—"

"Oh, I know *that!*" Hobbes exploded, flipping his hand with almost feminine impatience. "My Lord, *white* domination, indeed!"

"Listen, come on," Jack broke in, eating peanuts calmly, and licking the salt off his fingers. "Let's all get stoned or something. You guys're losing me with all this silly porkchop racism. . . . Man, all that's for the *day*, ain't it? the public? . . . Say, ain't we got no more brew there, sugar? Give them two idiots somethin' real to belch about—"

Everyone suddenly began moving around. Tall shadows stalked, slantingly, across the ceiling. A nameless tenor sax wailed hoarsely of back streets, and sweltering nights, and rotgut, and the best euphoria of all, the euphoria without cause. I found my mason jar, and drank blindly out of it, listening to Jack as he said: "No, sir, I don't care what they say—you don't know anyone you haven't balled. Man, what in hell is there to know you don't know already from lookin', or can't make up out of your own goddamn mind, but for that? Isn't that right, sugardoll?" speaking (I realized abruptly) to me, his bony red face glistening there in the dimness as he popped nuts into his slackly chewing mouth. "I mean, I figure you're alive all right, see, everyone's alive, but the point is you gotta know it, you gotta *feel* it—and that means getting out of your head, getting *beyond* your evaluating mind," smothering a sleepy Jocko against one wiry thigh, and slipping peanuts between the boy's lips one by one, "and that leaves nothin' but *ballin'*. So I say everyone should ball everyone, every which way, all together, any old time, all the times they can—you dig? . . . You think they'll arrest me for sedition?" so that I blinked at him as the bootleg struck the back of my neck with the first dull throb, only gradually noticing his sardonic smirk and gay eyes, and laughing back at him. "I agree. Right. Yes. And 'course they'll arrest you."

"Let joy remain confined," mumbled Hobbes' pedantic, throaty voice from somewhere I couldn't see. "That's what The General would say—if he could only *speak*. 'Cause joy smells of body odor, and irresponsibility, it stinks of the unreconstructed individual, who won't play bingo, and *that* could wreck the Republic, it could level Topeka!" giggling to hear himself.

Willie's dark furious eyes on Hobbes were the last thing I saw as I wandered into the kitchen. I got dizzy in the pantry, which was too dark for me to keep my bearings, and swayed back, clutching for something to steady me, and grabbed onto a small hand, cold and smooth, which turned out to belong to an almost life-size marble shepherdess—a piece of Victorian garden statuary —that stood incongruously in a dusty corner. I lit a match and inspected her blind eyes, and shy smile, and the cavity where her nose had been broken off. Someone, probably Jocko, had carefully applied lipstick to her mouth, and the finely detailed nails on her slender white hand were meticulously polished. My fingers traced over the maidenly curve of her breast, and I felt a funny, wicked thrill of curiosity which, at the time, I attributed to the pot. "Watch out, girl, you're so high you don't even know it," I warned myself, aware of the fine sweat that beaded my forehead, and going on into the kitchen, suddenly very thirsty.

There was a low murmur of voices there among the dirty dishes and the ghostly laundry. The kerosene lamp had guttered down, bathing the room in weird, undersea flickers, which unfocused all surfaces, all shapes. I stood in the door, trying to remember where the sink was.

"No, le's cut out, 'cause them cats from up yonder," someone was saying. "Man, that's *trouble* talk, and don't you know it—that talk o'ny go one place. 'Sides, honey, we go down there into the grove, and—" and I saw a thick, powerful black wrist limned in the light at the table, no hand visible, and studied it, and realized that the hand had disappeared inside an unbuttoned dress front, "find us that same place, you know, cause I *feel* like it," the tendons in that wrist banding as the hand worked.

"No, now, I don't want to," an answering voice said, Ohla's voice. "I—I got my time on—"

I spied the sink, and mumbled: " 'Scuse *me*," and they looked up, a-start, the hand pulling out of the dress instinctively. "I just want a drink of water. It's—it's gotten so *hot* all of a sudden."

Ohla clutched the dress together, and they stared at me without a word—those blank, alert eyes, public eyes behind which the private mind works on, out of reach. I drew a glass of water, wetting my fingers, too, and cooled my forehead as I drank. My back was to them, and the silence seemed ominously prolonged.

"I completely forgot it still gets this warm this late in the fall," turning around, entranced by how casual I was being, and promptly spilling half the glass down my dress. "Christ, look at that . . . butter fingers . . . the glass's slippery," wiping at myself with the flat of my hand, and laughing too much. "I should have kept the raincoat on, shouldn't I? But you all go right ahead, don't mind me—"

They stared at me as I wiped myself and jabbered witlessly, but they said not a word. I was soaked through to the skin, and saw Ohla's eyes suddenly narrow, looking beyond me, and noticed the voices from the other room, raised hoarsely over the music, that she had heard a full minute before I did. "Well, it sounds like it's getting to be quite a party in there, doesn't it? I'd better be getting back," on which foolish line, I fled their patient, ungiving faces.

Three tall shapes were silhouetted against the candles in a menacing triangle, taut with violence, and Jack's voice was rasping and low: "Now, listen, I'm telling you, I got to put up with that all day—I don't want none of it in this house at night. I'm tellin' you both now."

Willie's eyes flashed ominously white, and that fury that is peculiar to some kinds of despair gave him the look of an outpointed boxer, tasting defeat in his mouth at the very first punch. "I get sick of *listenin'* to him, I get sick of having to *hear* him all the time—"

But it was Hobbes who was sick, the sweat running off him in streams, his hair plastered in wet bunches on his forehead, shirt and shorts soaked. One sneaker had come untied, and, all unawares, he was standing on the lace with the other one, his face valiantly contorted by his efforts to swallow his nausea. "But what did I say? I don't even know what I said—"

The record had come to an end, but the changer hadn't worked, and the loud scratches of the needle in the run-off grooves filled the room with wavering static. "Man, just keep him away from me," Willie warned, "that's all. Keep him *off* me. I don't have to listen to that."

"But I just said maybe we could learn something from the uncomplicated ability to accept reality, the basic joy that you people—"

"Tell him to shut up!" Willie yelled. "I'm *askin'* you to please not say anythin' more about us happy, philosophic *darkies*, you son of a bitch! I won't listen to it, man," he shot at Jack. "He can kiss my shoes if I do—"

"Willie says he's not so uncomplicated and joyful right now, Paul," Jack said with a mildly rebuking purse of lips. "But you listen, too, man, he's sick from his fix, so take it easy—"

"He can kiss my shoes is what he can do," Willie spat out. "You got it all day—well, I had it from you people all my goddamn life," facing them both now with hunched belligerence, through which I knew the pot was making him feel a little ridiculous. "Listen, I had me a white man say to me once: 'Boy, you know I *envy* you somethin', 'cause you colored people sure do have more *fun* than we do.' I told him what he could kiss, and to just see if it was fun!"

Jack laughed, a wild hungry laugh I recognized, a laugh I've laughed when hearing things like: "They're working out a bomb now that'll kill just as many people as ever, but won't damage real estate," or any of the other perfectly solemn, perfectly insane moral contradictions which characterize our murky time, a laugh which says: Yes. That's right. The greater the confusion, the clearer it gets.

"Yes, that's right," Jack chortled. "Like they say to me: 'If you play your cards right, and try for dispatcher, you could probably get into the country club, bein' married to Bett and all,' and I say: 'You really think so? And get to go to them dances? And be able to talk to the JayCee's about politics and scatology? You really think I got a *chance?*'"

"And Jocko could be a Cub Scout like *real* kids are," Betty snickered. "I could have my very own analyst."

"That's right. We could *enter* the community, we could be a *family* who pray together, we could have us a fallout shelter don't have to take second-place to *no* one's!"

"You could walk through the streets with your head held high," I sallied.

"—knowin' I never had me one dirty thought since I went straight, and Bett and me only balled on Saturday nights, like the rest of the crowd—"

"—with the lights off," I laughed, "full of martinis—"

"But," Betty said with a devilish smile at Jack, "always in positions one and two—"

"Like *folks*," Jack exulted. "Like members of *society*, like *adults!*" turning his sharp profile on Willie. "See, man, the porkchops are all alike. No use gettin' hot with them. Man, they just don't *know* nothin' else—"

"And I didn't mean anything," Hobbes interrupted in a queer, strained voice, as if his time was short. "I've just forgotten how to *talk* on that level," gripping his shirt front against cramp. "I mean, it was a kind of compliment—"

"Well, buddy, you can just kiss my shoes with your goddamn compliments!" Willie snarled, turning away from him, and so not seeing the wince around those stained lips, the gulping shuttle of the adam's apple in that lean throat, or the helpless, obstinate glow in the blue eyes. Hobbes must have been higher than any of us realized, for all of a sudden he muttered: "I don't mind, that's all right, too—and anyway I think I'm gonna throw up in a minute"—any of us but possibly Orkie, that is, who must have sensed it from the odd timbre of the voice, or heard something else inaudible to the rest of us, but who, in any case, said sharply: "No, Hobbesy, don't you do nothin' like that, man, 'cause *he* that way from havin' to do that—" just as Hobbes stepped toward Willie in a lurch, actually starting to bend down toward the cruel, black shoes, only to be tripped by the untied lace, and pitch over in a heap onto his glasses.

· 5 ·

"Would you get me something to wash out my mouth with?" he said weakly to Billie, and, sitting beside him there on the bed, I watched the faint rise and fall of his bare chest as if looking for the life in a spent bird, and saw the weariness of the bone that was reflected in his spectacleless face, like a shadow off his soul; that altered face that looked younger all of a sudden, or incalculably older—the way the faces of the dying sometimes seem to escape time altogether a moment before time dies out of them. Billie had taken off the dress down which he had been sick as we got him up the dark stairs, and glanced at me, and then back at Hobbes, and went off in nothing but her slip to get him a drink from downstairs.

"They broke, I guess, didn't they?" eyes focusing myopically.

"One lens. And one of the ear-things cracked off. . . . What in the world were you trying to do? I thought—"

But he had sniffed to himself, a dry little sniff as if he was trying to clear dust from his nose, and I wondered if he was trying to keep tears back, and frowned. But he was laughing instead. "*Thus* I give up my wand—or, no, that's wrong—my *spear*. Whatever you fight life with, you have to be willing to relinquish it. Prospero or Ahab—huh," the musing sniff again, a finger automatically raised to touch the nose-bridge of the glasses that were no longer there. "But I'm just like Orkie now," rousing a little, confused. "But what do you think of him, though? Do you see it? I mean, why he's important to me? Did you hear what he said?"

I looked down, lighting a cigarette, and tried to feel tender toward his search. "Go home, Paul," I said more harshly than I'd intended. "You ought to go home. Really."

But he was coughing and didn't hear. "You have to say 'no' before you can say 'yes,' though," he mumbled, moving his head sharply back and forth on the pillow, quelling dizziness. "In our day, you have to keep looking for new boundaries to cross, new taboos to rifle for experiences nothing has prepared you for. . . . Isn't that strange and sad though?" the sudden earnestness of this giving me a stir for him. "Perhaps we're the last moralists, after all, all of us, our generation—but, no, that's wrong, too, because Ork doesn't care, or even *know* about all that—"

The hush of that long night, the heat of that room, the weary unflagging voice in its baffled speculations—I was suddenly terrified by the lonesomeness of life, everyone isolated in their hopes and disappointments, everyone going on. I felt myself sitting in that house, with no way home. Another voice began somewhere below, rising out of the opened windows down there and coming up through the bamboo blinds to us, clear and unaccompanied and urgent, the way the first voices must have sounded among savage, inhospitable rocks.

Later on, wait an' see, when the somedays come—
It's gonna be over, all over and done—
You gonna want me true, an' I won't come—
When it's finally over, and I up and run—

A thin, punctured forearm lay motionless and fish-belly white
under my eyes, its humble veins so relentlessly probed-for by
that tireless mind, the besieged blood pumping on obediently,
nevertheless. I stared at it with the seriousness all wounds evoke
in those still whole. Then it lifted, and he touched my arm with
his all-but-fleshless fingers, staring at me with those steel-blue,
wondering eyes that looked out on everything from such a pathetic distance.

"Look at you," he murmured strangely, the hand gliding up
into my armpit to pull me forward a little so he could see. "So
pale, all white—I used to wonder what was behind all your eyes,
all of you, and I knew I was never a part of it," those fingers
tightening infinitesimally, urging me closer until I could smell his
sour breath, and see the strained intensity of his large pupils.
"But I always meant to tell you—you know what's beyond sex?
All of it? our kind? I don't care how far you go, what you do—
with Kathryn I went down and down, tableau, costume, pornog-
raphy, you have no idea, anything to flay the mind. But you
know what lies beyond the wildest, weirdest thing that you can
dare? Listen, listen," he whispered with the breathless urgency
of an awful secret that is only revealed in an ultimate moment.
"Despair, May, just despair. Because we've only ourselves, after
all. It's nothing but despair, like everything else."

I was sickened by his breath, and uncomfortably aware that I
was sweating into his hand. Also, I suppose, I was irritated by
his assumption that his secret would have meaning to me, irritated because he was so close to the mark, and I would have
pulled away, but his feverish eyes held me there in the dimness
as Orkie's voice rose in stabbing, mournful laments against the

inevitable end of the chorus: "They just won't—they just won't—they just *won't* ever let me b-e-e-e-e-el"

"Despair," Hobbes gabbled, his lips flecked with saliva. "Despair. Despair. A funny kind of down-sinking in the belly. Because you can't ever get the quick in your mouth. You know what I mean? I know you know. . . . Because we're either trying to die ourselves, don't you see, or to annihilate the other, never to fuse —I always meant to tell you. I mean, I thought of you a couple of times in the last year, and I wanted to tell you, because, listen," he went on (as I remembered his little wife in a clear flash of understanding—her grieved eyes on him, his guilty eyes on her, and all the abysses in between they'd tried to cross with words, with mere knowledge—like all of us). "Because touch is all," he sighed flatly, releasing me as if some last strength had drained down out of his fingers toward his heart, the body saving itself no matter what. "Just touch. *Touch.* Turn the lights out again. Even Jack doesn't know that yet," dry eyelids fluttering shut and releasing me more completely than the fingers had done. "You know, I'm still sick, and I've got nothing more to throw up," letting out an amazed little giggle, just as I noticed Billie standing in the door with a glass.

She was watching me with a jealous, deferential gaze, as I poised over Hobbes as if in recoil from a kiss, and I wondered how long she had been there. The child somewhere down the hall mewled forlornly, and then began to cry for food. A sudden gust of warm wind rustled the blinds, filling the room with the odor of wax and mock-orange, and wavering the candle so that, above my head, the old woman ran on and on through ruins that were lurid with the light of worse conflagrations ahead.

Billie helped Hobbes drink, her unsmiling face, with its startling gentility of feature, impassive under my eyes. I watched her hold his head against the tawny sheen of her shoulder bones— that lean, burned-out face in which nothing but the mind smoldered at that moment, mouth gulping, eyes fluttering, resting against her soft, substantial flesh, his lips brushing the firm curve of her breast as she shifted his weight; and I knew he went to her for what such uncomplicated movements against her could renew in his withered heart. And envied him all of a sudden, incapable of that solution.

"Billie," I began, wanting to tell her something no mere candor could express.

"He gonna sleep now," she said almost crossly. "Aren't you? You go on to sleep now."

He looked up at her, blinking and swallowing, and the bootleg (I could smell its sweetish aroma) had revived him a little. She let him rub his wondering hand across her belly, kneading the young flesh. "Not yet," he murmured hoarsely. "Not yet, please," fingers drifting down over the blue silk toward her thighs. "Don't you want to sin with me, honey? Let's do our sin," in such a tired, private whisper that I realized he had forgotten I was there. "You didn't think I wanted her, did you? You don't believe Willie, that's all nonsense," his hand working at the spark that flickered up unwillingly in her embarrassed eyes. "Yes, yes, feel it, how does it feel?" stirring arduously in anticipation of her responding touch, and saying softly: "Sin with me, honey, 'cause I think I can make it if—"

I started to get up, and he noticed me, and let out a little ironical: "Goodness me," and then said: "But see about words? There aren't any adequate words for the deepest things—love me, screw me, lay me, *sin* me. . . . It's as good as any, and she doesn't care about words. It's only me who cares about them, and loathes them. . . . Give me a cigarette, will you?" he added with the theatricality of an actor dying before the cameras. I lit one with some impatience, and he puffed on it drowsily. "When I came down here, they made me sick—did I tell you that? I mean queasy, I wanted to vomit the minute anyone started to *explain* anything —my stomach went back on me somewhere—but, anyway, now I can listen to them without getting sick, and even use them too sometimes," Billie frowning now as she stroked his forehead worriedly.

"He oughta sleep now," she said to me. "Maybe you can get him to go on and sleep. . . . You want me to rub your back that way, baby? You want *her* to do it?"

He laughed at her solemn concern, with the tender amusement that only comes out of the deepest kinds of communion, and his weary eyes were wet. "Listen, now," he gruffed out, unaccountably moved by the sight of her lips. "*I* owe *you*. I'm three behind."

"No, jus' last night and yesterday morning is all," peeking at me with some trepidation because of these intimacies.

"No, there was Monday night, too. You're cheating on me," touching her cheek all of a sudden with an impetuous gesture. "Billie *Dew*, Billie *Dew*," he repeated in a little singsong, and then: "She cheats on me that way, you see, and then I scold her. But she likes to be scolded, it's our sweet-nothings. . . . It's all very queer and simple."

"I'd better go," I said. "I want a drink anyway. . . . And you rest, like she says."

His eyelids had suddenly closed over again, leaving his face masked, empty of life, as if oblivion was slowly edging across the exacerbated consciousness that toiled on behind it. I got up gingerly, with a quick nod at Billie, and then he said in a clear dreamy voice: "But you stay—sleep with us—all together," a soft hum of Handel throbbing deep in his throat, a wan ingathered half-smile touching his lips. " 'Children afraid of the night, who have never been happy or good.' . . . See, I c'n still 'member. . . . And in the morning, maybe in the morning we'll all have simple love without thought. . . . No, you sleep here with us, it's best . . . ," the words trailing off into the tranced little hum again, as Billie dislodged the cigarette from between his will-less fingers, and came with me to the door.

"Listen, Billie," I began, fishing in my handbag. "He'll be all right, won't he? And—"

"He got himself sick enough, I think," she said. "It's when he don't huck up, he hurts himself," looking at my shoulders, my dress, my chin, anywhere but my eyes—that reflex of subservience that is so shaming to the Southern white, when seen for what it is. "An' if you want to stay, if that'll quiet him— Someone got to get my brother home anyway. . . ."

"Hush up," I interrupted. "He was never my man," knowing suddenly that I wanted no scraps of enervated sensation, no part of the corrosive mental heats that had ravaged his worn, inquisitive face; knowing, too, that it was only another politeness on his part, like the bootleg, a last shred of ingrained hospitality; for there was no flesh-reality between us.

I was still fumbling among my stockings when he murmured with soft remonstrance out of his sleep: "Quiet—quiet there—th' holy fruitcake's in th' holy oven—raisins, big nuts, blessed oranges—it'll fall if you jus' go on *talking* that way, you sad bastards—on'y perfect emp'iness anyway, yes—"

You cannot really desire what you pity.

But he was safely asleep in Billie's eyes, the words left no troubling mark there, they were only words to her, and I wanted to say something more, but only said: "You clean for the Cheneys, don't you?" and at her puzzled glance and nod, added: "Then here," and slipped Turtle's compact into her small, rough hand. "It's gold-plated and—and you can see yourself," at which I turned sharply, and left her with it, wanting either a lot more drinks, or none at all, but nothing in between.

The squalls of the hungry child reverberated down the murky hallway, and I hesitated for a minute, and then went looking for it. A door stood ajar at the end, and beyond it was another large room, starkly illuminated by a naked bulb in a teetering wrought-iron standing lamp. Bett stood near a rickety, cream-colored crib, pulling her dress off over her head, and cooing: "All right, all right now, Fernie. . . . Mama's getting ready. . . . Wait a sec—"

"Oh, you heard it. I didn't know whether you could hear it over the music."

She glanced around, arms full of dress, her breastbone thin and pale in the faded pink slip, one of the fraying straps of which was fastened with a safety pin. Her glasses had ridden down her nose, giving her the owlish, absent-minded look I associated with her from years back, and a badly rolled joint sent up a delicate spiral of blue smoke from the seat of a straight chair nearby.

"Oh, come on in, honey. . . . Did you all get Paul to bed? I saw his mess on the stairs," leaning over into the crib so far that the slip lifted up to her thighs. "Pardon the condition of the room. I never seem to have any time what with *this* one," pursing her mouth comically down into the red face of the furious infant. "Do I? Do I, Little Angry? Well, just hold on," sitting down in the chair, one arm around the small, thrashing limbs of the baby, the other bringing the joint to her moist lips for a last, deep hiss. "Here, honey, have a drag—and stay and talk with me."

The room was like Hobbes' room, but for the light: sparsely furnished, clothes discarded everywhere, bottle caps and "roaches" on the bureau, a smelly diaper pail under the crib, a dusty radio that was a mosaic of crayon smears, the moldy remains of a shared-sandwich stained with lipstick, a makeshift clothesline strung in a corner, on which a baby's cotton shirt and a douche bag hung, dripping onto an unfolded newspaper.

Bett talked on as she elbowed out of the slip strap, and bared her drooping breast to little Fern's searching mouth. "That one— Willie," she clucked. "How hung up he gets sometimes! But then I suppose we forget how it is for spades once they go North, and find out— Anyway, I hope he didn't bug you too much," holding her breast in her hand, and looking at me with the distracted, lulled expression of inner listening which all nursing mothers exhibit.

I relit the joint, taking too deep a pull on it (though I managed to keep it down somehow), and found myself trying to focus my eyes on a heap of snapshots that lay on the dresser under one of those lead souvenir Statues of Liberty which every garish Times Square novelty shop offers to the traditionless throngs who gape through its stickered windows. "Oh, family pictures," I drawled. "I love to snoop through pictures," feeling the cottony wooze of the marijuana heavying my head all of a sudden.

"Those—oh, those are just silly," she said. "Jack took those three years ago—for when I was away. When we were up in Chicago. The lighting's perfectly awful—"

I leafed through them. Obviously taken by a cheap camera in a small cluttered room with the help of a couple of unshaded lamps, and just as obviously developed in a bathtub by an amateur following oversimplified instructions, they were all pictures of Bett, except one. All nudes. A few were art shots—the thin little body woodenly posed in positions approximating cool grace. The rest were sex shots—meager thighs awkwardly open; fingers helping to spread; knees and breasts flat on a couch; rump half-mooned by drawn-down pants; nipples enlarged with lipstick; the repetitive dark triangle and soft tongue; blurred close-ups of sad immodesty, over all of which Bett's small intent face, willing and nearsighted, hovered with the limpid, disembodied innocence of a spring moon. There was one of Jack, too, naked but for striped socks, snapped by mistake in the middle of some explanation about the camera—incongruously erect. I lingered over them as you linger over the snapshots of someone's children you've never seen, simply because it would have been impolite to hurry. Fern's contented, sucking noises gurgled in the silence.

"Aren't they silly though?" Bett said. "Men are so silly. And he just leaves them around that way, no matter how many times I tell him. . . . But you can see the kind of place we lived in then—a real horror down on the South Side—the john in the hall—I can still smell the boiled cabbage. . . . Lord!"

"You're happy with Jack, aren't you?" I said, leaning back against the bureau and looking at her. "You can feel the charge between the two of you immediately."

"Oh, yes," she said. "We have fun. He tells me what to do, and he needs me almost every day. And," a glance at me, at my dress and let-down hair and bare feet, "I was always too simple for the *other* kind of life. I mean, I could never com*pete* like that, and I wanted children, and Jack came along and said to me: 'I'll bet you don't know anything much, but you don't give a damn about it either, so you're all set to go.' . . . That's actually what he said, the very first night, and it was true, you know. I could admit it by then."

"You love one another," I said to no point, for isn't that how we are taught to sum up what she was saying?

"What?" she asked, wiping Fern's mouth with the cup of her slip. "Oh, yes. Yes, I suppose so. Something like that."

I took another drag, holding it down until my lungs ached, and watched her gingerly lift her drowsing child back into the crib, to fiddle with the sheet, and then rise from her bend back into the harsh, hot light, turning into it, her small breast shivering as she awkwardly pulled the slip over it again. "Well, *she's* done till eight o'clock," a curious note of tension behind the relieved sigh, as if she was embarrassed, one hand primping at her long hair again. "Is there another poke in that one?" and, when I held the "roach" out to her, she came over, and leaned toward my hand to take a deep pull on it as I held it, her thin, pursed lips touching my fingers.

"Are you high?" she said in an oddly conversational tone. "I'm just *flying*. And, you know, I'm so glad you came over, honey. I mean, I never see anyone in Aleck any more, and—"

"Lucky you," I replied with a reckless laugh, holding the joint up to her mouth again, and shivering all of a sudden. "Lord, I forgot I'm soaked through. I spilled a drink down my front in the kitchen, and—"

"You are," she said, "aren't you?" and she was feeling my dress solicitously. "Why, you're sopping wet. Will it stain? You want to change?" pinching the material between thumb and forefinger. "Isn't it lovely, though? Just like fine tissue paper. I used to daydream of dresses just like this—you know, just yards and yards and yards."

"Well, it's really impractical, 'cause you can't iron it yourself because of the satin lining here," turning back the bodice a little to show her.

"But how soft against your skin," leaning down to see like an enthralled child. "I never knew how to dress, it never mattered enough to me, I guess—and, anyway, I never really had the nerve. But I used to daydream about the *feel* of nice things. You know?"

Her mouth was tremulous with a párticular memory, one particular day, a particular mood, a sudden yearning once; and the earnest, unenvious, plain little face of years before came back to me. I was perilously high, and the feeling of life's isolation, that feeling of baffling perspective which had come to me with Hobbes (as close to a real emotion as only the recognition of the absence of emotion can be) melted through me again.

"... and Jack digs you," she was saying in the middle of this. "I can tell. He never digs anyone who doesn't *know*, so that's all right. You know what I mean?" and for one suspended second there was something clear between us—I could feel it, and knew what it was, and yet wouldn't know what it was, wanting to believe I had missed something.

"And, really, we don't mind," she breathed. "I mean, if you like someone, well," and then she suddenly leaned forward awkwardly and kissed me—that kiss we substitute in a kind of rash frustration for the words that somehow are never adequate to the simplest of feelings.

"Whew," she said with an odd, choked laugh. "It's *that* sweltering, isn't it?" still holding onto my arm with strange giddiness. "Have you ever, before? I mean—" and I knew what she meant beyond a doubt.

"No. Have you?"

"Once or twice. It's," the eyes behind the glasses shy, gauging, banked, "it's all right. It's not the same—it's sort of *funny*, and pleasant, like—well, the way tickling is sometimes—"

We each had another drag, helping one another, standing face to face there in the embarrassed nonchalance of the utterly wild moment that had opened between us. "I'm so *high*," she giggled, touching me with impersonal, urging motions. "Have you ever made it with Paul, though? He's not much good for a woman any more, but—"

The pot seemed to have blanked out that thing in my mind that
interceded with reality. "No. I never thought of it. Have you?"
chiefly aware of the nerves that vibrated drowsily in my body,
and the hazy light from the far side of the room that was too raw
for my eyes.

"Oh, sure. Once. The three of us. We were just kidding
around," her voice remote, almost indifferent, her eyelashes,
which were surprisingly long, fluttering down with distracted
languor. I became aware of her nipples, stiffening inside the slip,
and realized that I was feeling them harden against my palms,
which had reciprocated her gestures automatically; and all of a
sudden I felt faint and sickish in the pit of my stomach, as if
something unsettling was about to rouse up in me.

"Not too hard," she murmured, "I'm sore—" at which I remember thinking how awkward and idiotic it was for us to be caress-
ing each other that way, and yet how absolutely real it was at the
same time. For one prolonged moment, during which her hands
explored lower out of reflex, I think I tried to jog some stir out of
myself by imagining the details—the feints, the removals, the
acceptance of roles (only to discover how little I actually knew
about those details), but willing enough for that moment to
consider the act, and let the neutrality, the physical reticence
between us, change into something else if it would. But all I
could really think of was the pantieless little girl of all those
summers before, mortified and lonely and proud, at which I knew
for a certainty that at best it would have been mechanical, almost
comic, a mere sally into deviation for the relief of certain nerve
centers—something I could have done, with fewer embarrass-
ments, for myself.

"This is pretty silly," I said, breaking it off abruptly, and feeling somewhat abashed. "And you can ask whether I'm *high* or
not!" moving away to get a cigarette from the bureau, which I
lit with nervous fidgets of the match. "What time is it anyway?"

She glanced at her watch. "Quarter after five about," a curious
note of pique in her voice, as if she had miscalculated me, and I

had made something seem important that wasn't. We were both
sobered and chagrined.

"I—maybe I'm *too* high," I made myself say. "You know what I
mean? I mean—well, the moment wasn't—"

"Oh, Lord, honey." She laughed woodenly. "Don't be foolish.
Don't be so *serious!* Jack says, keep the mind out of these things,"
already over by the chair, folding and refolding her dress, her
long brown hair mussed on her shoulders where my hands had
been. "It's all just a way of being glad, the sex-thing—and *forgetting* what time it is," her back to me as she said this, without a
hint of rebuff, almost wearily, flatly. And then she turned around,
one slip strap sliding off her narrow little shoulder, and smiled
at me impatiently, the smile dissolving into a yawn, over which
she put a hand with a tired chuckle. "Pot always makes me so
sleepy this way. Isn't it awful? And that Jocko gets up at seven
o'clock, no matter what. Just as mad as a jay every morning. . . ."

• 5 •

Anyway, dawn inevitably quenches what flares so high at night,
and the sky had lightened a little through the long windows of
the shambled room downstairs where Jack sat amid a litter of
peanuts, cigarette ends, records, and stale glasses, crooning a
hillbilly song to himself as he rolled a last joint. Willie sprawled
impassively, like a man in shock, in a deep chair nearby. The
candles had burned down into mounds of wax, and then burned
out, and the acrid smell of singed wicks and dampness reminded
me of the bombed cathedral of Beauvais, where I had gone one

winter Sunday once, exhilarated in a yellow haze of pastis, to light an ironical candle to a frowning Virgin before driving on, in a car full of revelers, to Le Touquet. Orkie had disappeared, and I had a headache that promised much.

"Hey, sugardoll," Jack slurred, "sit your ass down here," patting a pillow at his side. "We're talkin' about the Mountain Men—back in the 1840's, you know? . . . Well," noting Willie's glassy stare at the broken peanut machine, "*I'm* talkin' about 'em anyway. . . . But them bastards jus' wanted to take a *look*, see, that's what I'm sayin'. I mean, they wanted to see themselves some birds, and skunk cabbage, and moose-droppings, old Chippeway fires, and bear trails, and the way a Colorado fern grows like maiden hair— I mean, all *that*," pausing to lift, lick, roll, and shape with absolute self-absorption. "I mean, they didn't want to *think*, see—that's my point. They wanted to get lost in the world, the *real* world— that big old simple skunk cabbage, I mean—"

There was a hush in which you could almost hear the dew falling; only the flaring hiss of Jack's match marred it. Birds twirkled somewhere in a wet hedge; a sudden chill-to-the-marrow made the room seem huger, emptier. I stared at my dirty feet out of an exhaustion too profound even to suggest sleep.

"But I figure these days," Jack drawled on in a mad preoccupied struggle to keep the joint alive. "I mean, there ain't no more mountains, see, nor any of them red-nose whisky towns for when you gotta blow—or chicks who want it weird—I mean, want all that hoarded wildness, you're hip, all that big thick fatal *juice*, baby, poured—whoosh!—right on into them, *so*," sucking and smacking his lips and raising lidded eyes to me that did not even notice my dead stare, "you gotta con, that's all—you gotta make it *with* the porkchop world, I mean *in* it, see, and still keep your old skunk-cabbage eyes—"

I understood nothing he was saying; my body felt weightless and heavy beyond lifting. The chirps of those hidden birds, throaty and contented, broke my heart with their sweet indifference to our unceasing fret, and Willie murmured a kind of antiphonal to this: "—ain't gonna show 'em—can't learn a bunch of fiel' hands—can't—" which only seemed a further evidence of something I was too beat to name.

". . . jobs—well, I mean, holy fruitcake, it's just money, ain't it? I say give as little for that there money as you can—you don't get no *truth* for it anyway. So take you some idiot-job, you dig, like they on'y figure idiots would take, and, man, *have* your life. . . . There's something fine and strange in everyone, that's what I say."

He passed me the joint, and only seemed to become really aware of me when I shook my head. He peered at me, swaying a little on his bony flanks, so high the expressions rippled across his face like the widening rings in a pool that has just swallowed a stone.

The new sun, still out of sight in the tangled oaks outside, started to turn the sky beyond them that wan, empty blue that only milkers and dissipates really know. Willie Gee snored fitfully, one hand spread on his crotch with sad protectiveness, a look of impenetrable isolation about his bitter lips, vanquished into sleep.

"—guess I gotta finish up myself then, eh?" Jack was muttering with sniffs, and peeks at me, and wry simpers. "Las' cock to crow's the las' cock in bed—they used to say that up my daddy's way in Georgia," grumphing to himself with bleary nostalgia. "Them dumb crackers, break their balls on some hard-scrabble field, and then get ugly drunk, and maybe ball their daughters," swallowing dryly and looking for a glass. "But, man, they knew how to *see*, anyway, the bastards—man, man. . . . They died *angry*. I mean, when them kind die they look so *mad*—not just tired and disappointed like the rest of us," peering woozily before himself. "An' I'm jus' a damn old cracker m'self, you know. Oh, sure—mud in my soul, and lead in my pencil, an' I sure do like my grits!" suddenly snickering in little, goofy whinnies to himself. "Sugarbabe, I'm so damn high I'm flapdoodled! Whe-ew! . . . But that's what I was sayin' about them Mountain Men, see, that they—"

I wanted to get away. A bottomless weariness, beyond despair, had come down on me; that lonesomeness of life, and time, and all dawns, in which I could think of no one I wanted to see, no place where it would be any different, no song that would purge the feeling by expressing it. I longed unreasonably to believe in God or any other fortuitousness. My very flesh seemed sad and somehow violated to no purpose. I had come to the end of my imagination. I sat, disheveled and girdleless, in that dazzling dress turned merely silly by the dawn, and, for one graphic moment, I longed for any oblivion in which I might rest; a longing to give up filled me—and then, as Jack said, ". . . that game, remember though, baby? . . . kick the can or something? . . . How they yelled: 'Allee allee out infree' when someone had really booted it a long way off, and you had a chance to get home safe, and you were so *glad* hunched up down there in the slimy rain barrel, you felt it ache right down in your bladder?" When he said this, something from childhood scared up in me, and I wanted only to sit by a chill Cape sea in autumn, and stare at the gun-metal swells that heaved shorewards at no behest—toes, thighs, defenseless groin itself let down on impulse into the cold salt surge, breaking grey over stark rocks in a sullen November, muttering with squall. The nerves of cities seemed tendriled through my body like avaricious roots seeking blood; the lees of all the nights of search were as sour as bad wine in my mouth; I thought back on my fruitless twenty-five years with a sink of loss down in my stomach, and wanted a man to follow (just like a foolish, over-solemn girl), to wash for and watch, to do for without asking why; I wanted to be told to be quiet, to open a can and heat whatever was in it, to keep my eyes on the ground; I wanted a distracted companion to live silently beside through days and days and days of nothing at all. I longed for it the way we (who never knew it) sometimes long for the tranquil summerworld before 1914—distantly, calmly, and without hope.

"—home free," Jack said, holding my ankle, one rough thumb massaging the bones inquisitively, "that's all you want—to get

home free—to go as far out as you can, but get home *free*. . . .
And, sugar, here's home," his hand sliding up my thigh, "right
up in here, that's home. . . ."

"Come on," I said. "Come on now," frowning and pushing him
away, thinking: Christ, it'll be Jocko next. "Really, I don't want
to."

"You ain't high enough. Here—"

"No. *Really*."

He shrugged his shoulders with a yawning smile. "Well, sure
then, okay," taking the drag he had offered me. "Sure, sure," and
leaning back all of a sudden as he held his breath in, the first true
light of that day revealing a faint scatter of smallpox scars on his
sunken cheeks—something sad and ugly about his boyhood coming quietly home to me. Those cold blue eyes were closed now,
and nothing came out of his harsh lips when he exhaled at last.
"Jus' rest anywhere you can find when you're ready. . . . I gotta
think about Jim Bridger and them awhile. . . ."

I went into the kitchen, leaving everyone asleep.

The screen door was full of milky light, and through it I could
see the morning come. Faint wraiths of ground mist rose, delicate
as spirits, through the heavy trees; glints of sun winked white-
gold among the laden branches, and I smelled the freshened air—
cool, farm-dewy, fragrant with loam. I went out and sat down
among milk bottles on the wooden back steps, feeling lonesome
to myself.

The yard was trampled flat by furious little feet; a length of
knotted rope hung damply from a quince tree in a forlorn swing;
the ruined gardens beyond (hedges, borders, symmetry obscured
in undergrowth) seemed smaller and less haunted than I remembered them; mad jays screamed "Cat!" half a field away; and
somewhere breakfast meat fried, and strong coffee boiled. That
morning was rising over Oklahoma and New Hampshire, too, over
places I had been and people I knew, and yet inexplicably there
I was in my rumpled finery, miles out of town, addled by stimu-
lants, with no idea what I was really doing there, or how I'd ever

get home, or what it was I'd wanted in the first place, and melan-
choly at having to endure the ebbing of my high alone that way.
I felt resentful and teary, and didn't want any more cigarettes,
but had one anyway.

"And how can he be someone's *gardener* if he's blind?" I complained aloud, thinking of Orkie, and then heard a rustle, and
saw a movement, and there he was at the foot of the steps, having
been slouched there all the time behind the railing post, just out
of sight.

"Good*night*, you scared me! What are you doing out here?"

"I jus' come out to smell," he said with a confused smile, and I
must have interrupted him in some private communion with the
smells of dawn, because his nostrils were actually quivering when
I moved down to the bottom step, bringing with me the scents of
cigarettes, and booze, and hours-old perfume. But he hid his distaste, if he felt any, and only said: "Is there a rabbit out there
though? Them finches are clucking like they do for a rabbit—"

I looked, and there, indeed, just out from the japonica bush
some thirty feet away, a small motionless rabbit crouched on its
haunches in the long grass, absolutely still but for the whickering
of its pink nose and the turnings of its ears toward the gossipy
birds.

"Yes," I whispered with a sudden lift of joy, "yes, just over
there. He's listening, but he doesn't see us yet—all soft brown, and
white under his tail. And the inside of his ears are like some shells
you see up North sometimes, that tender light-coral—"

"And I like their teeth," he said, his full lips parting expectantly
at my words. "I mean, the way they do with their mouth when
they eat," laughing shyly as he imitated them by drawing his
upper lip back, and nibbling at the air. "My sister told me rab-
bits when I was a kid—and all the different looks of birds, too.
Them icy jays, for instance, and them finches that are like a
buttery handful of yam, ain't they?" eager and perhaps a little
embarrassed. "Billie always told it *good* to me, so I'd know—I
mean, I think she left out the bad parts. Like she used to scream

at spiders, and she'd never tell me them—'cept I felt one once runnin' up my pants leg, and I guess I know," facing out to the yard, and so alive to everything there that, though I saw his blinkless eyes staring at the painted-over lenses half an inch away, I couldn't believe he saw nothing, and never once had.

"Ma told me, first thing almost that I remember, that if I could hear summer and smell love that's all I need. . . . But you know—from the way she huffed, and held onto me like she was mad, I knew what it'd be like—if I had my eyes, I mean. I guess I ain't missing much but the bad," turning that pellucid face (through which his whole life seemed to shine) toward me a little. "I mean, like they say some blind folks *fret* about it all the time, but I think it's probably *all* all right somehow, you know. . . . I mean, it's the way it is, and there's no *use* gettin' mad. . . . Hey, listen to him go," his ear cocked in tranced attention to the lonely saws of that autumn's last field cricket. "He's real blue, and he's almost played himself out. . . ."

I looked at everything he heard and smelled, all the myriad, thronging life to which he seemed so attuned, and found I was translucently open to it—the gnats, like a fine cloud of golden specks, swarming in a ray of early sunshine; the wild asters meek and fragile in the glistening grasses; the cock that crew with lazy conceit somewhere over near the bayou; all the verdure, and the growth, and the awakening—tiny hidden worlds from which we are mostly excluded by our formulating intelligence—all there in the dewy sanity of morning. And I suddenly thought: best to sleep, and wake to it, yes. Because there's balm in that rabbit—the day's just little green shoots and caution around fences and the silliness of birds to him. There's balm in that flower, and those gnats, and balm, too, in the spider wherever he is, and the snake curled up in a dank shadow waiting for the warmth of noon—intent mites of sentience, a little mysterious, a little maddening—but there's rest in them for us, because they're *there* no matter how we wound, or are wounded. And he knows that, all that: he's still part of it, he's never lost the wonder. I looked back at his black, thralled face, and I was *full* all of a sudden, and was telling him the snakes before I knew it, my snake.

"But, anyway," I finished up, hating the reflex of self-consciousness that came over me. "How *can* you work as a gardener, though?"

"Oh, I ain't—I mean, I work in Mis' Reeve's greenhouse where I can feel my way all right—just mornings," but something was troubling him. "But you was scared of him 'cause he could *bite?* He was probably only havin' himself a drink, too, though, wasn't he?" he said shyly, as if he hadn't understood.

"No, it was just—" not wanting to talk about it. "Oh, I guess it was just those little black eyes. They were so hateful. It was just the eyes, I suppose. I know it sounds silly—"

"No," he murmured gravely, and with such politeness that I realized how much of what was said out of the visible world was probably incomprehensible to him.

He seemed a lonely, solemn boy at that moment, and something in me melted toward him, something gave way a little in my breast, as it had when I danced with him. But I wasn't friends with the emotion, and didn't know what to do with it, so I asked him about girls. He seemed chagrined, and we chatted pointlessly for a moment, and then he lapsed off with: ". . . an' they want to be *seen*, I guess—you know? Told. Most of them anyway. Hobbesy's learning me some things to say. But he tol' me I *dance* real good now—" with a hesitant, almost flirtatious little smile.

"You do, you certainly do," I said. "But everybody doesn't want to be told. Don't listen to that. You can get sick of hearing," knowing that whatever he felt, he would feel without doubt, and had probably never once asked himself: "Is this the way I'm *supposed* to feel?"—a question that seemed the sum of my inner life just then.

The black skin inside his work shirt gleamed like old copper. The pink of his palms, with the etch of darker lines across it, was somehow as intimate to me as the first full nakedness before sex would have been. His small, piquant skull with the fine grizzle of kinks over it, the clarity of his forehead as yet unmarked by a single wrinkle of anxiety or perplex, his lips over which the moist tongue ran as I looked (knowing he didn't know I saw): all this seemed to intensify that startling awareness of another human creature, complete and isolated in a consciousness beyond our possessing, the pang of which sometimes drives us into love or violence. And Orkie couldn't see. I could have raised my dress over my thighs on a wanton impulse, or taken it off altogether to rouse something in him, the sight of which (*my* effect) might rouse it in turn in me, and he would never know. He was as blind to all the mechanical rituals of life as he was to black and white. Only if I touched him, as Hobbes— But he was listening beyond me, into the house, murmuring: ". . . didn't think I recognized *either* of them cars," and then I heard someone coming through the kitchen.

The screen door creaked, and it was a rumpled, irritated Jack. "Listen, Ork, you stay out here, man, okay? 'Cause it's that nosy old fart, Buford, from the State Police, and some cat—I think maybe you know him, sugar. His name Plouchet? . . . Anyway, they just drove up, and I can't get that goddamn A-rab to move."

I followed him inside, leaving Orkie to his morning there at the foot of the steps. A path of bright sunlight, pebbled with peanuts, led across the floor, and at the end of it Willie sprawled rigidly asleep in the huge chair—like a migrant sailor in a railway terminal in land-locked Nebraska.

With the opening of a door, Jack's voice drawled from the entry: "Well there, Bufe, what cha doin' out this way this time of the mornin'? Ah'm just goin' to bed—" And, as I shook Willie roughly, urgently, whispering: "Come on, come on," another voice, as twangy as a wagon spring in the run-down parishes of north Louisiana from which it obviously came, said: ". . . not too bad, Jack, caught me a drunk Pontiac from Noo York 'bout one o'clock, and some nigger got himself knifed up good around three. . . . But, listen, this feller here says—"

Willie's eyelids finally fluttered a little at my proddings, but he didn't really wake, and I took him under the arms, and pulled with all my strength. "Come on, now you stand up, honey, just into the kitchen," pulling until he started to raise himself with the obedience of the semi-comatose, eyeballs rolling, slack mouth trying to harden around words, and I had him on his feet, holding him up, and wondering if they could hear me as clearly as I heard Church saying: ". . . about four hours ago . . . some guy, that piano player who lives out here. . . . Now, but listen, O'Meara—"

I stumbled Willie into the kitchen, his arm draped inertly around my shoulders, and slumped him into a chair, and left him murmuring thickly: "—jus' havin' mah good dream, too," his dark, spent face (with the shrouded eyes) clouding over, and then he fell back into sleep again, like a drowner giving up

"Well, sure now, isn't that somethin', though," Jack was saying as I came back. "She gonna be real upset you got so worried," to find them there in the hall—Jack and the beefy officer just about as low-hipped, and slouchy, and night-weary as each other, and Church with the look of all alarmed citizens of the day, who have stayed up too late, and are out of step with everything. "Now, there she is, all safe in one piece," Jack said sardonically, his red-rimmed eyes noting my bare feet, "but for the heat maybe. Yes, sir!" with that odd, calm alertness of the very high when they are endeavoring to keep their funny perceptions to themselves. "I mean, man, it was *hot* las' night," he snickered, "so we jus' sat around, drinkin' us a bunch a Doctor Pepper like in August—"

"Are you all *right*, honey?" Church exclaimed resentfully. "God, I didn't know what— Why didn't you say something to someone? They told me you were just in the bathroom. . . ."

Officer Buford, a red-faced laconic man full of sweat, with the quick little eyes of those who move slowly, glanced into the drawing room just on the chance that Jack had been careless this one time, and said: "You got this feller here all lathered up, Miss. He says he been runnin' all over hell and gone, lookin' for you," the eyes checking me coolly, sarcastically.

"For Christ's sake, I just came out to see Betty," I said to Church. "You mean you've been driving around ever since?"

"Well, God—well, Jesus, *yes!*" he spluttered reproachfully. "I didn't know what else to do. You might have been—" with a quick look at Jack's dreamy sway. "Well, *anything* might have happened to you!"

He felt ridiculous, and I felt genuinely sorry for him. "That's awful, honey. I—I just didn't think, I guess," which hurt him even more. "But you look terrible. . . . I mean, you look worn out."

Buford was sucking a tooth with a comic pucker of his fat lips, and I had the sudden impression, known to anyone whose instincts are even faintly lawless, that he knew perfectly well that Jack was high, and that there were Negroes somewhere in the house, and probably drugs, too. An unpleasant mixture of curiosity and scorn oozed out of every pore of him like a bad smell. "So you got no complaints, Miss? I got to make me out a report anyway to justify my gas all the way out here, so—"

"No, of course not. What in the world should I complain about?"

Jack managed to smother his chuckle with a loud, snorting honk in his nose. "Goddamn hay fever," he explained. "Ain't it holdin' on awful late this year? I been really *sufferin'* here. . . . But you want to look around, Bufe? Or have yourself a cup a java?"

"No, if the lady says she's awright," fingering the tooth with a grotesque probe of one hairy hand. "But, hot damn, I thought I had me a real kidnap here, or at least a good case of nigger," eying me again with that wryly disapproving squint. "You been a big disappointment to me, Miss."

"If you want, I'll take you back now," Church frowned out, wanting to get away from there, and almost as furious with me as he was with himself. "That is, if you're *ready*. . . . And you can just forget about the raincoat."

I was ready, and I managed to find the coat, but my shoes had vanished, Jocko having probably teetered off in them upstairs somewhere. I was giddy with that incongruous second wind that comes up in you just before you collapse, and Jack winked at me with conspiratorial glee, and said: "Sure was good meetin' you, sugar. And you all come back and see us soon again," such a parody of Southern manners as it came out of his mouth that I pecked him a giggling good-by.

He leaned a hip against the door jamb as we sat waiting for Buford's Police Ford to pull out ahead of us, and I saw that he was lighting up his roach in plain sight of everyone, as if it were nothing more than a cigar stub, peering cross-eyed down his nose toward the match; and then he called something out to me in a lazy drawl, all of which was lost in the angry leap of the engine, except ". . . but get home free, sugardoll, just you remember that. . . ."

I remember it now, despite the years. It is still as clear as the drive back down the morning roads; as the clean country air, the sun not yet high enough to have turned it tepid; as the big trees that gave way to intersections, and the intersections that led to houses, and the houses to home.

I remember poor, angry, sheepish Church, whose relief at finding me unraped made him feel so foolish that he muttered: "I didn't know— And I thought— 'Cause the things they say about that place . . . and, well—oh I even phoned up your grandmother—" I remember mollifying him, and being grateful. And I remember that it was there in his car, letting the wind cleanse the night off my face, and seeing the world renewed once more a drop of dew at a time, that I first realized that you can't explain anything important to anyone. Some things, the inmost changes in the soul, must wait on time. The lens of consciousness remains a personal mystery in its particular scope. I remember wanting to thank him for his concern, no matter how silly it had been. But such thanks are pointless, so I held his hand instead—which is apter, after all.

But most of all I remember the sweet exhaustion that threw

everything into such poignant relief, and how I wanted bed, and sleep, and no dreams, but life back again anyway if I woke from them. What is it that we know so elusively at such times? I think we glimpse an end of something. I think we scent out the poor heaven that has been under our noses all the time.

I know I went up the walk, feeling the ants squiggling between my cold toes, and the wet surface of the worn bricks, and the sun's first promising heat on my bare shoulders. Willing to let the rest go for a while. A little scared, a little solemn. But not lonely. I remember that I wasn't lonely. I wasn't, though there was a tremble in me. I suppose it was just the poor South, and poor Orkie, and Paul, and Church, and everything—realizing how desperate and beautiful is the urge in all living things to survive life, and enter into reality at last; to reach that surpassing understanding that is held out, beyond the hangover and the orgasm, to all those who are exhausted by excess—the single understanding I know about, that need not be bitter simply because it is bleak.

NEW YORK: THE BEGINNING

She went along very carefully through the winter, as if walking across ice in high-heels. She worked hard and late, and the dark, slushy blocks in her neighborhood were often deserted by all but scavenger cats when she got home. She spent her weekends absorbed in redoing the loft from paint to pillows, until all signs of Agatson's years there were obliterated, and all signs of Verger (except his books) were buried in a closet. She read a lot, and paid her bills promptly, and managed an expensive winter coat out of her modest budget. She grew accustomed to being alone, and some of the panic passed, and eventually there were times when she didn't even answer the phone if she was busy with something else. She made some new friends, and saw some of the old ones, and went cautiously to a few parties, and got tipsy now and then, and even had a harmless affair with a man from her office, which she carefully limited to a few lunches, a play or two, and the anticlimax of awkward wrestling on his couch. She was lonesome most of the time, and yet calm, and she wrote chatty notes in answer to Verger's occasional letters.

One Saturday morning, which dawned a shimmer of glistening new snow, when shovels clanged and scraped on the pavements everywhere, and there was an air of holiday excitement in the frosty sunlight, she made an appointment on a whim, and had her hair cut off and shaped to her head, and came home, already regretting it, to stare at the strange face looking out at her from the mirror—no longer the face of a rash and pretty girl, but older and soberer, so that she had a cry, letting herself have it; and then decided through her sniffles that she liked the new face well enough, after all. She felt life take one of those mysterious turns in her, and dusted her new marble coffee table twice a week, and scoured her copper and brass every Sunday afternoon, and bought her lavender toilet soap three bars at a time. And then, after hearing nothing for over three weeks, one evening Verger phoned. He had been back for ten days, and had found himself an apartment midtown, and needed his things.

When he arrived half an hour later, she had coffee ready, but he wondered if she had a drink instead, and they settled down over Scotches to pack up his books.

"It really looks terrific," he enthused, nodding at everything. "I wouldn't have recognized it. . . . And you, too, by the way. But what is it that's different? . . . Oh, Lord, sweetheart, your *hair!* Well, I'll be damned. . . . But, you know, it suits you, I wouldn't have thought so, but it really does," glancing at her appraisingly, and then: "Hey, but look, you might as well keep this De Rougemont, I won't read it again. And how about the Faulkners? Do you want them? I can't remember *who* they belong to. . . ."

He seemed taller to her, and yet less lanky, as if he had somehow knitted together, and filled out his frame from the inside. They sat back over a second drink, and he lit her cigarette, studying her with level, curious eyes that had no trace of unease in them, and answering her questions about his trip in brief, almost indifferent statements.

"Oh, it was great, of course. . . . Paris—though everyone was tired and bitter somehow. . . . Vienna where I got sick. . . . I drank too much in Florence . . . a lot of sad, raucous Americans, myself included. . . . So I was glad to get home, even the taxi drivers seem tough and excited and awake. . . . But you know how it is, sweetheart. I'm looking for a job, I'm just about broke. . . . And you see everything differently. It turns out that travel is so easy, after all, so everything else seems easier than you thought it was, too. There are things I want to do now, I got a lot straight. . . . But listen, how about you? You look," pausing for the precise word to come to him, and then not waiting, "well, you look *good*, I guess. I couldn't really tell anything from your letters."

They talked on, and she found herself oddly irritated by his air of certainties arrived at, and decisions taken, long enough ago so that he felt no need to explain them, and gradually she realized that it was his friendly, yet vaguely impersonal manner that was irritating her. She was amazed to discover (now that he was different) how attuned to her he had always been in the past. She had never really noticed it before—his steady gaze, his attentive face; and for a moment she felt a keener sense of loneliness than any she had experienced while he was away.

Then, all of a sudden, he leaned over right in the middle of her ramble of gossip, and touched her breasts, his eyes narrowed and not-listening-to-her, his lips pursed intently.

"Quit that," she said. "What are you doing, silly?" his hand too explicit for her to have any doubts, his lips trying to catch hers, as she turned away from him. "Now, *stop* it, Danny!" she exclaimed angrily. And all at once he did. He simply let her go, smiling blandly with a funny little shrug that angered her even more.

"Okay," he said, taking up his cigarette again. "No harm in trying though. It's that goddamn new hair-do, I guess. I told you it suited you." And he laughed a light, indifferent little laugh.

"Well, listen," she went on, endeavoring to disguise her confused reactions to his touch. "That's all over. . . . I mean, it's *over* between us, isn't it? So why can't you be nice?"

He took a slow pull on his drink, and then stared at her with a warm, candid gaze. "Sure, sweetheart, it's over all right. But—

well, some things are never *finally* over, are they? Anyway, I'm sorry if it bothered you. Just forget it."

"You certainly have gotten sure of yourself," she snapped out unhappily.

She was somewhat irritated by this exchange after he left, as if he had spoiled their meeting on purpose. It was just like him to try to start something up again, and she decided that she'd do best to be busy when he called. But he didn't call, and after two days of trying to restrain her curiosity, she invented a pretext about a book of hers that must have gotten into his box, and called him, wondering if she could pick it up on her lunch hour.

"What? I don't think I've got it, sweetheart. . . . But, sure, drop by if you want to. I'll be here."

She found him in the midst of writing letters in a small, bleak, high-ceilinged room in the West 50's. The room was over a record store, and popular tunes, as shallow as saucers in which the butt ends of Love and Heartaches and Fun and Last Summer had been stubbed out, came up through the windows all day from the outside speaker. There was a lumpy studio couch, a strip of rug worn to the threads, paper shades yellowed by the blank glare of vanished summers, and Verger's bags lay open, but still packed, in a dusty corner. A leaky radiator hissed and gurgled, the toilet in the dim bathroom ran continually, and the cold roar of avenue traffic down the block made it difficult for her to concentrate. Verger, too, seemed distracted, and she waited on the studio couch, idling through an issue of *Time*, while he finished up his paragraph. He sat hunched over the pen in a white shirt, open at the neck, and corduroys so obviously from Paris that she had another flash-sense of his having actually gone to Europe, and had experiences there that were unknown to her, and come back changed. She was dying to know how and why, but didn't ask him while they searched for the nonexistent book, and then afterward, as they talked casually, she couldn't get over the impression that she had interrupted him in the middle of something (perhaps no more than a complex train of thought); and, though he was glad enough to see her, he was busy.

Before she knew it, she found herself telling him about her single love affair in deliberately exaggerated detail, lighting cigarettes one from the other, and looking at him now and then, expecting a response that never came. "And, of course, it didn't really *mean* anything," she concluded airily. "But he was fun, and—well, not too hung up, so it was pleasant enough. Until he got silly about it."

"That's good," Verger replied. "I don't think I remember you mentioning him. But I'm glad."

She took to walking up and down his rug, growing ever more irritable when she noticed that it was worn in precisely her path, as if she had somehow joined the army of lonely, transient pacers that had passed through that room before. She talked in a glib torrent, poking rudely into his papers, asking pointless questions, and then not pausing long enough for him to answer. He sat, and smoked, and watched her, and then all at once he reached out and took her hand as she went by.

"Come on," he said. "What's wrong?" pulling her toward the couch. "Stop getting so worked up. What's the trouble anyway?"

"What the hell do you mean?" letting him pull her down, and sitting beside him with a sullen pout. "And I'm *not* worked up. . . . I mean, but things have happened to me, *too*, you know, Danny."

"I know," he replied, giving her inert hand a light squeeze. "But why get so agitated with *me*? I'm on *your* side, remember?"

She glared at him, furious with him the way she had been in the old days, furious at his mild, observant eyes that betrayed only concern, and his thin, expressive mouth on which she could read nothing but puzzlement at that moment; so furious, in fact, that all of a sudden she took his face roughly between her hands and gave him an aggressive, tight-lipped kiss—the sort of kiss an angry mother bestows on her child when she is sorry for blowing up, but is still angry. He pulled her hands away with both of his, as if immobilizing an attacker, and snapped out: "Now, come on, don't *bitch* me that way!" But then, staring into each other's hostile eyes, so close their breaths mingled, a fuse seemed to go off in both of them simultaneously. Something broke open in her chest, and her mouth groped up for his, opening hungrily, wetly into it, and he pinned her hands above her head in the pillows. "Oh, Danny," she moaned, "oh, damn it all," sick to her stomach with desire.

All in a moment, they were trembling with wild haste, an urge toward one another that was so unexpected it allowed no time for undressing; and they clung together there on the narrow couch, all mouths and hands, without a word, without a thought; her dress simply fumbled back over her hips, his trousers merely unzipped, their excitement threatening to outrun any effort to accommodate it. But at the first deep touch, at the first spread and the first thrust, Verger pulled back, and left her, murmuring urgently: "Come on, down here," pulling her off the couch all of a sudden, and down onto the rug. She lay back, eyes closed, thighs flung, skirt bunched up in the small of her back, uncomfortable and uncaring; and when he came down upon her, and into her, in a single thrilling stroke, she gasped to realize how long it had been. He caught her gasp in his mouth, he was heavy and indissuadable on her breasts, and she felt her hips responding involuntarily to his pace, as if she was doing a dance step she had never learned. He took her all in a moment, and something in her seemed to dislodge a little.

They lay together there on the floor, catching their breaths, feeling disheveled and slightly foolish. "Whew!" Verger exclaimed with an amazed laugh, for he had not even removed his glasses. "Any luck, though? I was too busy to notice."

"No, not really, but it was—" not knowing how to put it, and still shaken by the sharp and unappeased throbs of pleasure, ebbing sadly away in her now. "But—well, I hope you don't think I *meant* this to happen. I mean, it's pretty silly after all this time, and I—"

"You what? . . . Does it matter why it happened? And it was *good* for me." He got up, hair tousled and boyish over his forehead, and gave her a hand. "But, hey, I didn't even stop to think," he said. "Did you take any precautions?"

"No, I— Of course not! I told you I didn't *plan* this, didn't I? You think I came up here all *prepared?*"

"Okay, okay. Don't get mad. But listen," lighting her a cigarette, "will it be all right?"

"Christ, Danny, do you think I'm a *complete* idiot? . . . Don't worry, I've just had my period," feeling exposed, and disturbed, and a little cheated, and so trying to make light of it. "I feel like a goddamn fool, though. You'd think we'd never done it before. . . . God."

"We never have," he said wryly. "Not on the floor at least."

"Well, anyway, it was stupid and silly," she stated, wanting to get up immediately and leave, but somehow unable to do it. "But look," she went on, just to be saying something. "You haven't *really* told me about Europe yet."

So he began, his mind freshened by their sex, and turning to other things with an ease she found impossible for herself, even incongruous, though changing the subject had been her idea. The day darkened, the room grew gloomy and poignant with a sense of life going on ceaselessly elsewhere, and Verger's absorbed voice evoked that life in images: Paris, confusing America's soul with its refrigerators . . . Vienna's done-for faces, sick with too much history . . . Berlin, smashed by politics, having no black market in ideals any more. . . . Sad armies of U.S. students, so many wistful Attilas, come to drink at a dry well. . . . The pimps of Milan, eyes full of scorn and lire, hating the Americans *because* they wanted to be loved. . . .

"So what can they really know about how sleepless, angry, disgruntled, hopeful, drunken, and foolish we are? Even I had to leave in disgust before I realized that the American these days is an exhausted, disappointed man, who's shamed in his soul because some other American always seems to be debauching *his* idea of America. . . . Because somehow America never lives up to our dream of it, and sometimes the only way to preserve the dream is to get away from the reality. So Europe beckons us, and rests us for a while. But then you find yourself missing something —the cruel beauty of New York, or an ugly intersection outside of Philly where half the signs point to Chicago—that creative turmoil that keeps us nervous, dissatisfied, improvising—that strain of violence that's always the best goad to aspiration. And ten minutes after you get off the boat back home, you realize what it is. We've lost our national innocence, I think, and we're bitter about it. But *if* we're bitter, it's because we haven't given up hope. Somehow there's still *room* for anger here. There's still *time* for joy," grave eyes peering speculatively into the shadows, and then looking back at her. "So, anyway, I don't hate it any more, not like I used to at least. . . . I don't, I'm not *going* to. You can't afford it. . . . And, anyway, there's always a second chance, you have to feel that, and here, when you can't believe it any more, you can always go out and take another name, or flee to the Wind River Mountains, or go get drunk until you *do* again. . . ."

She tried to listen, she really wanted to know what was in his mind, but she seemed to be doused in a dark, unsettling warmth, and her attention, though intense, had inexplicably narrowed. Her eyes kept drifting to his mouth, but she registered few of the words that came out of it, and somehow couldn't care about him, or herself as distinct from him, or anything else but the fact that she wanted him to touch her someplace, to rouse her body, and bring it back into the full quiver of life it had promised for a moment on the floor. Her mind pinwheeled around a single thought: "No, I don't love him—he's dear to me, and I trust him, and I know I can't shock or offend him—but I don't love him any more, and maybe I never did. . . . Have I ever *really* loved anyone? . . . And shouldn't I be sure of that before—?"

"Well, I'm boring you. God, what could be duller than someone's—"

"No," she faltered out, getting up for fear she would just reach out and touch him, and distractedly stooping to rehook a stocking. "No, I'm interested, Danny. I really am. It's just—"

"You know, you've lost some weight," he said all of a sudden, his gaze snagged on her thigh. "Been dieting or something?"

"No, just not drinking so much, I guess."

"Well, you'd better drop your skirt. 'Cause I don't care about the proprieties any more, I'll just *use* you—" looking at her with an admission in his eyes that was so unadorned it had the power of a bald immodesty.

"I don't care either," she got out. "I don't give a damn either, Danny. But we shouldn't. It's just going to make another mess, and—well, isn't it too *soon?*"

"Undress, this time," he said, and it all started up again—that keen, emotionless passion, closer to lust than to love, too specific and too selfish to have been assuaged by the first time; which made him, this time, pointedly watch her strip herself, and made her willfully prolong the stripping; which made each one, this time, kiss the deepest kisses of the body, the lidded gaze of the other looking down at the intimacy, not content with mere sensation, but having to have sight of it, too. She let him have her with an obedience of limb, a spreading at command, an acquiescence to the strange, the funny, or the playful, that stirred her deeply— the act of surrender itself. She was transfixed by his tongue, her breasts tingled in her own hands, her words came in a voice she barely recognized, she sank toward his thirst with the ambivalent ecstasy of the drowner. She knelt before him, holding him between trembling fingers, knowing it was in her power to give him pleasure, and that for a moment he was absolutely *hers* because of that, and slowly bent toward him with parted lips, her desire heated by his, until their two desires fused into that single cleaving need in which the mind is extinguished at last, and close is never close enough, and the astounded moan of pleasure comes abruptly of itself, abolishing something—some illusion of the isolated self. And this time she saw an end ahead, and, even though she didn't reach it, she felt a sharp thrill inside herself to experience his experience, his lips seeking in hers, his arms binding her to him, his flesh taxing itself to become complete. She felt his ejaculation blossom wetly inside her, and caught a brief glimpse, and for the first time, she was drowsy and spent once it was over.

"Ummmm," she murmured. "Now I know what you were doing in Europe. No matter what you say."

"Bullshit," he replied amiably. "But you were close that time, weren't you? You almost caught up."

She leaned over and pecked him on the cheek, and then sat up for a cigarette. She didn't want to talk about it, and yet somehow she was not piqued by his post-mortems, as she had always been before. She felt as lovely and self-centered as a sleek cat; she looked down at her nakedness with a neutral, uncritical eye; she was suddenly famished, and realized that she had skipped lunch and was an hour overdue at her office.

"But really," she said as she dressed. "You must have had yourself some wanton little girls over there. 'Cause your technique smacks of a graduate course at the Sorbonne."

"The hell it does. You've just gotten a little less hung up on technique. . . . Say, those are new, aren't they? Since when do you go in for black?"

"Oh, poof . . . *everything's* new. I've got drawers full of the wickedest underwear at home, just like some corny trousseau. . . . But come on, you had all the usual adventures, didn't you? The essential European experience'? *Tell* me."

" 'Usual adventures!' " he gruffed out. "Humph! Wouldn't you like to know, though."

"Come on, amaze me, see if you can shock me," she goaded delightedly. "What's an old girl friend for, if you can't brag with her?"

"I don't have to brag with *you* any more, honey chile," he said, standing up, fully naked, and tweaking her nose. "Anyway, maybe I'll tell you another time. . . ."

Then all of a sudden he was staring beyond her toward the

windows. "Hey, look," and he got up, and went to the dusty sill, to peer out at the desultory, early-March snow that had begun to fall in a cold grey hush into the streets. Seeing it, May felt a sharp stab of longing for the spring that it postponed, and then noticed that Verger's face had dimmed.

"Listen, though," he said with queer urgency. "Don't go back to the office. Can't you phone and say you got sick or something?" He touched her shoulder. "We could go have us a drink. Or take a walk . . . No complications, really . . . Come on, though, be a pal and take off the rest of the afternoon."

She wanted to do it, she was suddenly starved and very thirsty, she felt reckless and vaguely conspiratorial. She studied him for a moment, trying to decide whether it was wise or not, but all she saw was the engrossed pinch that had come into his eyes at first sight of the snow, and nothing more, nothing messy. All at once, the idea of thieving a few hours from that dark and chilly afternoon exhilarated her.

"Where'll we go?"

"I don't know. A bar. There's one down the street."

"I'll call from there then."

It was wet snow, big hurling flakes that melted as soon as they touched the pavements. People hurried along that street of afternoon-neons, shrouded in New York's peculiar isolation, coat collars up, eyes down. Cabs whished by in the slush with wipers working blindly. The abrupt, ineffectual blizzard whirled around lighted windows four stories up. There was that feeling of siege that a sudden eruption of bad weather always brings to narrow, side-street blocks near Times Square.

The bar was downstairs—an island of dim chrome, leather banquettes, low ceilings, the warm sparkle of bottles: a consoling emptiness. A waiter idly cleared away the stained tablecloths of hasty lunches. The bartender had gotten to the back pages of his *Daily News*. The jukebox strummed with sad South American guitars, and husky voices, incomprehensible with Portuguese, mooned against a light scatter of irrelevant bongos.

They sat at the bar, and had Scotch sours, and picked at a bowl of salted nuts. The snow swirled comfortingly against the hazy plate glass, they kept their coats on and their wet feet warmed, they talked quietly and not very much. Verger was oddly moody, leaning on his elbows and fiddling with the stem of his glass. "You know," he said all at once. "Sometimes I hate the Twentieth Century. Sometimes trying to keep yourself sane and alive in it seems such an unreasonable thing to expect of anyone. I felt it all the time in Europe—there was so much old death in everyone's eyes. . . . But then you get fed up, and morose, and you go out to a bar, and there's some music like this, and all of a sudden you find yourself loving it, too. Even the hopelessness becomes curiously moving. At least it clears the decks. And you look at other people, and you can't help admiring them, because they've survived, too, and suddenly there's a joy that pangs almost as much as the despair. You seem to *know* something that shames words, and for a while it doesn't matter a damn that you'll have to wake up tomorrow, hung over and edgy and disappointed. . . . Does all that sound idiotic?"

"No. I came to something like that when I was down South."

"And yet most people can't see it. I mean, like this girl I've been going out with. I met her a week ago, and something about her—I don't know what it is," pausing to sort out his thoughts. "But last night's an example. We were downtown. You know—the Village bars, shall we go to a movie, wandering the Square among the ghosts, where do you want to eat. And she was badly depressed about something, somehow she always is, and she kept saying: 'I'm not *winning* tonight, you might as well take me home, I won't be any fun for you.' And I kept denying it, because I always seem to be trying to cheer her up—but, Christ, it was *true*. And she wouldn't just forget it."

"You sound as if you really like her, honey."

"Yes," with a puzzled little frown. "I do. I guess I do. . . . But she had a bad marriage during the war, her husband was killed in an auto accident while *she* was driving, she was drunk, and, of

course, it was *snowing*, and so his family got the custody of their
child—that sort of thing. . . . But the point is, I want to be some
help to her, but she's so bitter and defeated all the time, and all
I can think to say to her is: 'Forget it, get drunk, take off your
clothes, anything, anything—because it's all more impossible than
you know.' . . . And other nuggets of wisdom along that line," he
finished up with a lame laugh, signaling for more drinks. "You
know me, sweetheart, I'm about as helpful as an aspirin when
you're hung over."

"But maybe that's what she wanted," May replied, "to take off
her clothes. Maybe that's why she wanted you to take her home.
Did you ever think of that?"

Verger looked at her, considering the idea. "You think so? . . .
No, I would have caught that. Wouldn't I?"

"You can be awfully obtuse sometimes, you poor silly." She
laughed gently. "Sometimes you get to thinking so hard about
what you think the *other* person's thinking about that she could
have stood up naked in front of you, and you probably wouldn't
even have noticed." She smiled a warm rebuke at him. "I seem
to remember doing that sort of thing in my time."

"Christ, is that the way I am?" he said with amazement, and all
of a sudden he laughed. "You know, I guess I am. I never realized
it before."

"Well, it's not such a terrible failing. You could be an icebox,
after all."

"I'd rather be *inside* an icebox," he replied with a wink. "Besides, sweetheart, we've both changed. You know that? . . . And
nothing lasts, not even the worst things. That's the mystery, I
guess. That's the hope," brightening as he took her hand.

They sat and talked like this for a while, feeling very open to
everything around them; and half an hour passed, and another
drink. Something moved in the afternoon, something hovered
very near their consciousness: a simple closeness to each other
that made them wait there, distracted by the clear premonition of
how keenly they would remember this day. A languid flute, bur-

bling over the strum of the guitars, roused, in both of them, that most piquant and perhaps illusory emotion modern people can experience: that everything is impossible, and yet somehow it doesn't matter; and we touch one another only briefly, but the brevity intensifies the touch; and so Time has a pang in our day that arms us against itself.

"But what will happen?" May kept thinking, unable to imagine feeling more for anyone than she felt at that moment for him. "Why can't I care about that any more?" knowing she wasn't in love with Verger, and didn't need him, and that now he would take care of himself, in any case. And all at once, she was able to admit that what she really cared about above everything else was the love-making just past. She thought of his body, she thought of what they had done together, and suddenly she was glad that nothing had to be said, and no more debts incurred. She felt complete, and uncomplicated, and pleasantly empty.

She touched his open palm with her forefinger, and said: "What would you say if I said that I'm—well, it's silly, but—"

"Interested?"

"Something like that."

His eyes narrowed unmistakably. "I'd say, drink up."